My Guardian Angels Jack™ & Fred™

By
Joseph St. Angelo

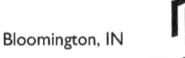

Bloomington, IN   Milton Keynes, UK
authorHOUSE®

AuthorHouse™
1663 Liberty Drive, Suite 200
Bloomington, IN 47403
www.authorhouse.com
Phone: 1-800-839-8640

AuthorHouse™ UK Ltd.
500 Avebury Boulevard
Central Milton Keynes, MK9 2BE
www.authorhouse.co.uk
Phone: 08001974150

This book is a work of fiction. People, places, events, and situations are the product of the author's imagination. Any resemblance to actual persons, living or dead, or historical events, is purely coincidental.

© 2006 Joseph St. Angelo. All rights reserved.

No part of this book may be reproduced, stored in a retrieval system, or transmitted by any means without the written permission of the author.

First published by AuthorHouse 6/26/2006

ISBN: 1-4259-4798-0 (sc)

ISBN: 1-4259-4797-2 (dj)

Printed in the United States of America
Bloomington, Indiana

This book is printed on acid-free paper.

For I know well the plans I have in mind for you, says the Lord,
plans for your welfare, not for woe! plans to give you a future full of hope.

When you call me, when you go to pray to me,
I will listen to you.

When you look for me, you will find me.
Yes, when you seek me with all your heart,
you will find me with you, says the Lord…

Jeremiah 29:11

Dedicated to a generation whose own guardian angel was somehow forgotten.

*For Mom and Dad,
and
Jack & Fred.*

"*I believe in you.*"

Static in the Air

A lone angel was flying down to Earth. The tinkling sound of bells and a trail of light were left in her wake as she soared through the upper atmosphere, a carefree joy in each and every stride. The frosted blast of cold winter air hit her head on as she slipped into the night sky somewhere above the city. A virtual cacophony of sound assailed her senses, forcing her to tumble uncontrollably. Her wings stretched out, slowing her descent. When she finally stopped and listened to the sound, she heard the echoes of a thousand voices, angelic and human overlapping one another. It was as if a great hand was adjusting a radio tuner of cosmic proportions. The chatter swirled about the sky, humming and reverberating from days and hours past, out into space. The voices all spoke of just one thing. It troubled them all equally so. A tear fell down the angel's cheek, her hands crushing down on the red velvet outfit that dressed her slight form. She futilely grasped to regain her composure and flew on.

"At approximately 1:36 Christmas morning, the boy you know as...your Henry will be admitted to the city hospital, running a fever of 105. They don't expect him to last the night."

"Just say 'Jack & Fred,' and even if you don't see us, we'll be right by your side."
"No matter what?"
"No matter what."

"What if we can't help him?"
"Then we'll take him home with us tonight."

"When you write our story someday, make sure you give us a happy ending."

"Will you be my guardian angels, Jack & Fred?"

"Goodbye, Henry."

"He's all I have in this world, Lord. Don't take him away from me."

"They don't expect him to last the night."

"Oh, God."

"I love Jack & Fred. I believe in them."

"They won't recover from this."

"I haven't felt that in such a long time."
"What?"
"Love."

"I pray that you hear me this night, Lord, and that you send his guardian angels to watch over him and bring him back to us."

"Is that where they go, Jack? Do they go to heaven?"

"They don't expect him to last the night."

"Mr. Artie, I think we're in a lot of trouble."

"Oh God. What did we do to this poor boy?"

The Beginning

So the angels were at their usual spot in heaven, a wall that separated paradise from everything else, looking up at the passing clouds, thinking about all sorts of things.

"Jack?"

"Yeah, Fred?"

"What are you thinking about?"

"(Sigh) Oh, not much. How 'bout you?"

"I was just thinking…Jack, do you think anyone would ever want us as, you know, guardian angels?"

"Maybe. I don't know. Why do you ask me that all the time? There's nothing wrong with being request angels."

"*Somebody* must want us. Maybe we'll find that person on our travels someday. You think?"

"Maybe Fred, but…but that person would have to be awfully special. I mean, it's not like we haven't looked before."

"I guess so Jack, but maybe, maybe we *will* find somebody someday. Maybe *today*."

"Today?! *Someday*. Yes, sure, someday, my friend. I hope so. But why do you think it's going to be today?"

Fred just shrugged, sighing happily with a certain glow in his eyes.

"It would be nice to be loved and believed in by one person, wouldn't it?" Jack asked.

Fred crossed his arms, leaning on them.

"Yeah. It really would be nice Jack."

"Yeah Fred, it would," Jack agreed, sighing.

He sat a moment, resting his face on his hand, noticing Fred looking upward at something.

"What is it?"

"Jack, is it me? Or do those two clouds up there—not there, over there. Is it me, or does that look like an orangutan and a wrinkled dog eating breakfast together?"

Jack sighed, giving his friend up eyes.

"Well doesn't it, Jack? Jack, are you giving me up eyes again?"

"Yes, Fred."

"Oh. Jack?"

"Yes, Fred, what is it now?"

"Jack, did you notice?"

"Notice what, Fred?"

"The gate. The gate didn't squeak when we came in today, did it?"

Jack thought for a moment.

"No, no it didn't, did it?"

Fred smiled.

"Nope. It usually sounds like Captain Hook with a rusty hinge. But not this time, it didn't. I'm *telling* you Jack, I think *something wonderful* is going to happen today."

"You always say that though, *every* day."

"But today is different. Something wonderful's going to happen today; I can feel it. Very soon."

"Yeah, well, we'll find out soon enough. Come on. We're late as it is. You ready to get back to down to Earth?"

"I'm ready. Let's go!" The little angel was excited about going downstairs. "But I'm *telling* you Jack…"

"Oh shut it, Fred! Let's just get back to work."

And they set off, flying downward, their wonderful day just beginning!

Or so they thought.

{ Chapter 1 }

When It All Started

What was this all about? They were separated! They *hated* being separated. They worked best as a team. Everyone knew that. It's all they had. This stunk. This was like being summoned for jury duty. But still, it had to be done. It wasn't the first time. This was almost to be expected though; this time of year was always the busiest for angels. Christmas Eve was three days away. Still, something about the whole thing seemed very strange. Things were not starting out right. This was not the plan.

They had two take-homes already and it was barely eight o'clock in the morning. The weather outside matched the mood. In was sad and gray in New York City; seemed like everyone was dying. Angels were being dispatched down to Earth left and right, Fred included. He was there in an apartment, cradling a little girl in his arms who was losing her battle with leukemia; as if she had a chance to begin with. He was whispering to her as she was passing on, telling her what heaven was like.

The whole family was there. They were put through so much, and now they were just devastated. This isn't what her family wanted; this wasn't the plan. It wasn't right, dying so young as she was. It wasn't supposed to be. Their hope spent, they could only pray that God would take their little girl into His arms, home. All those prayers over all those weeks by all these people, and no matter what they thought all that time, God did answer them. It just wasn't the way they would've liked. Sometimes prayers are answered differently from what we want. That's where faith comes in. Believing that even at the worst of times, an angel will appear and make your heart breathe a sigh of relief. For a moment, someone will appear out of nowhere and just make it all right. And an angel did appear, and he was getting ready to take the little girl home with him.

"I have her," the little angel whispered to the mother with red, tear-soaked cheeks. The little girl closed her eyes with a smile on her face. She was only eight, and now she wouldn't get to nine. When the moment came, Fred raised up her spirit. He touched the mother's face. *"I'm taking her home with me."*

The mother closed her eyes and nodded. She knew, and for just the tiniest of moments she smiled in spite of herself as morning sunlight broke through the gray umbrella above and came streaming into the room. The little girl was in heaven by the time most people got up to eat breakfast. Fred kept her company and had some breakfast with her, too.

Across town, Jack ran into a Mr. Exley on the subway. He was a man who apparently had bad luck in all that he did, except for today. A lotto ticket in his pocket was good for a $1500 win, and because of that he had booked a cruise with a travel agent just last night. He had found ten bucks in an old coat he hadn't worn in some time. He'd even caught the train on time this morning! A lovely lady across the way smiled at him. It wasn't the greatest of days for anyone else, but for Allen Exley it worked out just fine. He was hot today, and what a breath of fresh air that was!

As he came up the stairs of the subway station humming the Beatles' "Help," a bullet intended for a young woman at the hands of a jealous ex-lover pierced Mr. Exley. He fell backward and Jack caught him straight away. His angelic hand was clasped over the hole in Mr. Exley's throat. He held him, whispering in his ear as the man bled to death all over the sidewalk. Despite the rush-hour crowds, only one lady called for help.

Mr. Exley, half away, said to Jack, "But I was having such a good day."

Jack smiled. "You still are," he said. The angel took him to heaven shortly thereafter.

This is what they did—every day—for what seemed like an eternity.

This is who Jack & Fred were: request angels. They answered the smallest of mankind's requests. And they were doing this for decades without a break. They were tired. And it wasn't so much their arms and legs and wings that hurt; it was their souls that were aching.

There were so many people, so many requests. For these angels, the day didn't end at five. Their workload far exceeded mere strokes of the clock. This was a twenty-four-seven job, and when they were tired, well, they had to just suck it up and keep going. They didn't have time! Lives were at stake; that's why. They were much like their earthly counterparts, nurses, in that regard.

There was no great pay or days off or vacations to be had. People were depending on them—real people with real hopes and dreams and destinies to fulfill. Those sorts of things. Little things. The smallest requests.

Request angels though were different from the others, especially these two. They felt the plight of the human condition that we all go through every day because they dealt with it every day, just like us. Spending so much time down here, they'd sometimes forget they were angels. *They are just like us!*

The angels loved having wonton soup and egg rolls on a cold winter's night! Oh, and they hated the cold winters. Always with them was the relentless desire to sit with their feet in the sand at the beach and a drink in each hand, doing nothin' special all day. And when that would tire them, they would take a nap in a hammock letting it sway in the breezes. They'd wake up in the late evening hours, roll over, and do it all over again. They'd do it all, if only they had the time…

The only difference between us is they are so much more beautiful in spirit, and they can actually fly. But they're not at all as far away as you might think. They aren't complex, and you don't have to be rich to afford seeing them. Simple belief makes them real and it makes their jobs so much easier. The angels have always been here. It just happened that, at this point in time of human existence, people really needed to start believing in them. It got really messy out here in the world, and that's why all of this is so important. *That* is what this is all about.

So besides that, with that amount of stress always on their backs, you can understand why would-be accidents, near-misses and falls, slips on the ice, and tumbles down stairs—those kinds of things—became old hat to Jack &

Fred. They didn't sweat the little things; you could catch those, stop them. People could get up from those sorts of things and walk away. But some things you couldn't walk away from. That's what stuck with Jack & Fred the most. The other angels would sometimes mistake their cavalier attitude and blatant disregard for authority as signs that the two were too full of themselves.

"They're so rude!" the others would say.

It was easy for them to say when they didn't have Jack & Fred's worries. It was easy to be happy playing a harp, but when you held someone taking their last breath, that was something else entirely. Jack & Fred realized that particular sentiment was the same among angels as it was with people. Unless you experienced it yourself—unless you lived that pain—you had no right to comment. And so it was and still is.

There was one constant in Jack & Fred's lives. They had each other. Friends. Partners. A team. The best ever. And that's the way it's supposed to be.

But not everything lasts forever…so they found out.

{ Chapter 2 }

Home

The little one, Fred, watched as his partner Jack soared right through the express line of heaven, getting Mr. Exley acquainted with eternity. Good people didn't have to wait for long check-ins. This was one of the benefits of leading a good life: When you die they let you fly right into paradise without stopping.

Fred was surrounded by a host of angels who were, like always, asking him about his adventures like eager children with delighted eyes and excited agitation. The little one stepped through the crowd, ignoring the others, setting his gaze on Jack as he flew over.

Jack had black circles under his eyes; he was pale and drawn. Even his hair looked "sick." He looked *old*. It was strange. He never looked like this. Fred began wondering if he looked the same way. Angels always said that they were like the Corsican twins; pinch one, the other feels the pain. Hurt one, it shows on the other's face.

It was finally wearing on them. They knew it too. They'd been down here on Earth too long. They had a name for it upstairs: Long-term parking. It wasn't exactly complimentary, but it was true. After all these centuries helping people, it had finally caught up with them. It was upsetting to no end. Fred wondered if the others around him noticed. "Betcha they do notice. Betcha they talk about it when we fly away," he thought. Neither Jack nor Fred would settle for that, and made every effort never to speak of it aloud, lest it become their reality. As they always said, life is short enough as it is; there's no time to be miserable. They were going to be happy as much as they could, for as long as they were able, before closing time was called.

"Hey Fred!" Jack nodded as he landed in front of his partner.

It seemed like they hadn't seen each other in years. It was a *long* morning. They looked around for a moment at all of the others flying by, carefree, happy as anything. They didn't have these worries. Not like this. Weren't they just at their wall, talking, just a few hours ago? Where did that go?

The little one, Fred, looked at his comrade. "You having a good day?" he asked, smiling abundantly in front of the others.

"No!" Jack said matter-of-factly, shaking his head.

"Neither am I," said the little one.

Never let 'em see you sweat. And they didn't. They refused to give the other angels around them the satisfaction of seeing them that way.

Jack ran his hand through his tousled hair and smiled just as wide at the little one.

"You want some breakfast?"

"Already had some."

Jack sighed. "What about coffee?"

"Coffee?" Fred's eyes brightened. "And donuts?"

"I could do donuts!" Jack's eyes gleamed just as bright.

"I want jelly."

The flew out of heaven on their way back to Earth…back to us.

There wasn't time to sulk.

Jack pondered, "Powdered or sugared?"

"Powdered."

"I like the sugared, Fred."

"Then get the sugared. No one's stopping you."

"Powdered gets all over my hands and wings and—"

"Jack! Get the stinkin' sugared. Man alive!"

"How many?"

"Dozen?"

"If we get the two dozen, they give you free refills on the coffee."

"Like it's gonna cost us!"

"No, but still." Jack flapped his wings faster, gliding away, then soaring within earshot of his pal. "I got *such* a headache. A real kabanga."

"Me too."

Jack nodded downstairs.

"We goin' back to the Apple?"

"Of course. Let's go," the little one said, pressing to keep up.

And before you knew it, they were back down to New York. Sinatra could be heard as they broke through the cloudbank above. The music in the air was staticy and the crosswinds bordered on treacherous. The pair had to right themselves several times as they approached the heart of the city. It was still very weird looking out. And it wasn't because the first snow of the season had already dropped upon the city some days back. It wasn't that. Christmas Eve was three days away. That was the reason. Time just felt like it was moving too fast. But why should it matter to them? The angels didn't keep time like us. It bothered the pair to no end. They only knew one thing with absolute certainty: Something was up. The sky just looked…

"Strange, Fred."

"When you're a stranger," the little one sang as the Doors' lyrics sprung to mind.

"Thank you, Mr. Jukebox. Do you have a song for everything?"

"Yup."

Jack smiled. "Here we are. Look out now. The city that never sleeps. Just like us."

"Jack, why so many today?"

"People? The take-homes?"

"Yeah."

"Somethin'—"

"It *is* strange out here today. It's not just me."

"Fred, I've been seeing a lot of odd things happening lately. It's not just the people being sick…it's…the sky's just…"

"I'm not the only one whose noticed then Jack."

"Nah, it's not you."

"You know what? We just need a vacation, that's all."

The very idea made Jack warm all over. "The Brits call it a holiday. I like that!"

"Jack, you call it whatever you want. We need a cruise or something. No flying, just sitting on your butt in the sun, eating all-day buffet and drinking Coronas with lime."

The angels lit up. They needed this, their second wind.

Jack was excited. "And a boatload of *Hawaiian Tropic* models and their angels!"

"Oh yeah!"

"Hey, brother, I'm down!" They bumped fists together. Jack drifted in the dangerous airstreams. "Yo!"

"Almost bought the farm there, chief. What're you doing?" Fred frowned, as his partner was almost snapped up by the high breezes.

"What's with this, this crazy wind? All morning it's—" The little one hit the brakes suddenly, his eyes trained on something. "Fred, what is it?"

The little one spotted something. "Aw," he moaned, closing his eyes.

"What, Fred? What is it?"

"For the love of...*Don't do this!*"

{ Chapter 3 }

Praying for Time

Things were already set in motion. It was only a matter of time now. More than a few miles and time zones away in France, two neatly-pressed gentlemen walked about the Louvre, interested, it seemed, more in their conversation than the art they were surrounded by. The vaulted majesty of this breathtaking place did not go unnoticed by even two esteemed visitors such as these. One was a saint of legend, the other a barrister of some repute, to the angelic community leastways. When they walked the halls of this place, they were only Peter and Sidney on business. It was a shame that meeting here always precipitated some kind of impending disaster. It never seemed like they had the time to appreciate what was around them.

Sidney was the shorter of the two men, and he was still over six feet tall with broad shoulders. He spoke as if in a fit of hysterics, animated like a marionette during a stage show. He was exceedingly handsome with dark skin, tightly-cropped black hair and a pinstripe Armani suit that settled on his frame as perfectly as a GQ cover could ever capture. St. Peter was equally outfitted, despite his somewhat gargantuan proportions. Judging by the silver hair and the lines on his face, you could tell that he was somewhat older and carried a greater burden on his shoulders than anyone could possibly imagine.

Tourists and a thousand other souls moved about the rooms oblivious to their presence. Sidney couldn't help but envy their momentary lapse of obligation to the world as they moved about the museum. It was nice to be free. A small group moved past the two invisible divine spirits, led by a petite blonde tour guide. She spoke in short, eloquent bursts about the beauty on the walls that sung all about them.

"What you're asking is impossible, Sidney."

"You *must* get them to reconsider, Peter. You said it yourself. They haven't much time left."

"The decision is final. They won't reconsider."

The two men walked through another archway and Peter abruptly stopped. Sidney strayed a bit farther and realized his composure had lasted well beyond what he originally thought it would have at this point in the day.

"How many years have they been down here Peter, waiting, hoping, wishing for this very day, and just when it's within their grasp you're going to take that from them?! That's what you do? That's how you reward them—by *crushing* them? They won't recover from this."

Peter's expression became stone.

"Sidney—"

"No!" Sidney threw his arms down at his sides. "I've had enough! This is ridiculous! I—" As the barrister started to walk away, Peter grabbed him roughly, tossing him into the wall, oblivious at times to his own strength, even now.

"Now you listen to me. I know you're their barrister, and beyond that, I know what they mean to you. To all of us. But they've been down here too long. Far longer than the others. And now—"

"And now somebody up there suddenly realized that. 'Hey, we put too much on their backs, and they're finally exhausted!' That's it," Sidney said in a regretful whisper.

"It's time to bring them back home."

Sidney put his hand on St. Peter's sleeve, letting his calmer, rational side come back into play.

"Peter. We all know they're tired, and you know them. They won't admit it. They've raised generations and carried them home. And in all that time, the only thing that did not change—the only constant—was their resolve to make people remember that God loves them, trust that someone cares. And they never got that in return—*ever*. But they did their jobs anyway. They didn't expect anything. Do you know what that feels like, Peter? When people forget? When they always look through you?"

The saint looked off into the distance.

"Yes."

"You know I won't give up on them."

"We've been talking for an hour now, and you still haven't understood what I'm trying to tell you, Sidney."

"Make me understand, Peter."

"They aren't just bringing Jack & Fred back upstairs. It's a complete redefinition of their duties. (Sniff) What is that?"

"Meaning?"

"The smell. I've smelled that before."

"No, *meaning…*"

"Oh," the saint continued. "Meaning, things are accelerating too fast down here. With all the innovations, things are getting far more complicated." St. Peter paced. "People are busier. Nobody is home for these kids. Nonexistent parents. In twenty years it'll be worse. And before you know it, we're going to be busier than we've ever been. It's going to be chaos. Everyone will be on cell phones and computers all the time. They'll get lost in the technology. They won't believe in *anything*. Not us. Not anymore. They'll be a great disconnect. When that happens, we'll need all the help we can get. Someone's got to give these people hope back."

"What happens to Jack & Fred?"

"They'll be reassigned. They've got great experience that can be passed on, shared. They're teachers. They have been in the past. They'll train the new generation of angels for what's to going to happen. We've suffered through bad times, but it won't be anything like what's to come. Not on this scale. There are going to be wars and catastrophes the likes of which generations cannot compare."

Sidney closed his eyes, absolutely spent. Peter continued.

"Two won't be enough, Sidney. I need thousands of angels. People need hope. Fleets of angels could give them that. It's a blessing Sidney. Jack & Fred will be the leaders, part of something very special."

"How much time do they have left?"

"We've run out of time, Sidney. They wanted me to recall them over a month ago. I didn't. Now I'm out of time, too."

The barrister removed his glasses.

"What's the rest of it?"

"The rest of it," Peter said with a sigh. "The rest of it is Jack will come back upstairs. Fred will stay down here. Occasionally, they'll have to coordinate upstairs/downstairs things—they're going to be separated. Permanently."

"No! Not yet!" The barrister's brain was a flood. He was frantic. "No, no, no. Oh God. I've got to think. I've got to think…I've got to think." He paced. "Peter…I need a favor."

The saint looked at him with sorrowful eyes.

"Anything."

With a piercing gaze, Sidney said, "I don't care how you do it. Stall them upstairs. I need you to do this for me. Please. I just need…time."

Peter clapped him on the shoulder.

Sidney's prominent eyes fell upon what appeared to be a museum security guard. Catching his attention, the fellow angel in human form, walked over briskly. The always resourceful barrister pulled out a note card from his breast pocket and handed it to him. Sidney was tough in a pinch. He never gave up, never surrendered, even to what seemed like the most insurmountable odds. His piercing brown eyes burned a hole in the middle-aged looking courier.

"Go," he insisted with a nod. And the angel flew off. Unbeknownst to Sidney, someone else had been watching the entire time. Someone heard the whole thing. And there was no evidence of it, save the scent of jasmine that wafted past the barrister's nostrils at what was the most inopportune of moments.

A gentle French accent echoed in his ears, and the blonde tour guide brought her group around the bend. People looked upward at the infamous painting "The Sistine Madonna" by the artist Raphael, which featured Jack & Fred at the bottom rather prominently, if not unusually placed. The guide offhandedly mentioned the cherubs at the bottom of the painting, describing them as mere details. *Details.*

If they only knew.

{ Chapter 4 }

The Chase Begins

"Fred, don't!"

The little one reached out to grab hold of the speeding car's doorframe. The car broke right and shook Fred clean off. He went flying across the asphalt on his rump, like a stone skipping across creek water. Jack cringed as the little one slammed into storefront garbage pails, tumbling into the streetlamp with a pots and pans falling crash! When all was said and done, Fred laid in a twisted upside-down pile of himself, looking like a yoga technique gone horribly wrong.

"Yeah!" he barked as loosened snow from the light post plopped down upon his head with a dull thud.

Jack gave him up eyes, shaking his head. "Never listens to me."

The little one sat for the smallest of moments, like a smooshed cupcake, spitting snow out of the corner of his mouth.

"They're tryin' to kill me today. That's what it is!" he growled. His face scrunched up into a snarl, and Fred rocketed off, determination in his wings as they snapped into action with a bullwhip crack. "I'm not happy, Jack!"

"You're never happy! Keep up, Fred!"

"I *hate* runaways, Jack!"

"I know!"

"I hate runaways! And I've got a giant pain in the butt to boot!"

"So do I! I've been flying with *him* for years!"

"Yeah, ha-ha. Hysterical!"

"What's wrong with you, Fred?! This is exciting! Adrenaline rush times a thousand! Can't ya feel it? YEAH!"

"Yeah, great, good, whatevah." Fred frowned. "These things never go right. Someone always gets hurt. I haven't done a car chase in years. What do they think this is, CHiPs?!"

"I get to be Ponch."

"I'll be John. I always liked the yellow gloves better anyway."

"Hey Fred. It'd be cool if we got the show's synthesized drum-beat BOOM-BOOM-BOOM seventies music as we went chasing after the car wouldn't it Fred?" Jack called into his hand, "N.Y. SEVEN-JOEY-THREE in pursuit of a mustard yellow Pontiac goin' eastbound c'mon back. God I love this stuff!"

Fred frowned again. "You're getting into this entirely too much, Dr. Nostalgia." The little one was surprised when a voice actually answered Jack back.

"Ten-four, SEVEN-JOEY-THREE."

The car below took a turn for the worse, diving into the steel and concrete canyons of the city. "Geez. Hold on Mr. Wallace!" Fred called. "We're a comin'!"

Something suddenly pinged in Jack's ear. "Oh hey, Fred. You hear that? Somebody's lost! I can hear the parents praying!"

{ Chapter 5 }

Can You Tell Me How to Get to Sesame Street?

"We're not lost!" Joey insisted.

It started off as a trip to the Metropolitan Museum of Art in Manhattan. Somehow or the other, an offhanded comment became a spark of inspiration, like most things, and before you knew it the four kids broke away from the rest of their class trip and disappeared into the gigantic world around them. The snowy remnants of the season's first storm were dotting the features on the face of the metropolis everywhere. The children walked about, mesmerized by this great big world around them, one that was only glimpsed at in movies and on small trips here and there. The kids were as excited as if they were on a prison-break. They were all ten years old, except Henry, who was a mature nine; his birthday was in November.

Joey was determined to lead them to the alleged location of Sesame Street, which he guaranteed was just past the cross streets of 86th and Lexington, some distance away. It was like the blind leading the blind. Joey was the type of boy to follow the map on the side of a box of animal crackers, using it like it was word from on high, and then he would argue with you if you dared to think otherwise. Patty was the only sensible one who was able to keep him in check, as best as anyone could of course. It seemed like they had been walking forever, and at this point, she lost it.

"Oh my God! You are *so* going to get us killed."

The thin boy frowned, pushing aside his mop of black hair. "I am not, *not* going to get us killed."

"I can't believe this. I can't believe I let you take us here. How stupid am I?" Patty's face was blistering red beneath the freckles and dirty blonde hair.

Joey the Navigator was so sure of himself. "According to the *Christmas Eve on Sesame Street* special, they get off the subway at 86th and Lex. And walk."

"And..."

"And what?"

"And where do we go after that?"

The boy thought for a moment. "Oh. I don't know. They just walk."

Patty blew a gasket.

"You see, Henry!"

Henry laughed in spite of himself. They were an absolute trip. It was hysterical. When he looked at Joey and Patty arguing, it was like watching an old married couple who'd been a pair since time began. Everyone knew they'd always be together, except them of course. They were perfectly matched, like right and left shoes. Still, it took great effort to keep Patty's hands from wrapping around Joey's throat. This really was a class trip they'd never forget. If their folks ever did find them, they would surely kill them!

They were troublemakers, the both of them, as mischievous and disorderly as two mice could be. Henry knew better than to pull a stunt like this. He'd never done anything like this before; the worst that had happened to him in school is that he'd gotten scolded for talking incessantly. He thought of what his parents would say and his stomach went all aflutter. But when he looked into the hazel eyes of the girl in the red sweater walking next to him, he couldn't imagine any punishment taking away from this. She was the reason he couldn't help but go along on Joey's wild if not curious adventure. He wouldn't leave her alone out here like this. Kristie. His Kristie.

The little girl looked concerned for real this time. She had bitten her lip so many times along the way, but this took the cake. It was getting colder and colder, and her hazel eyes caught flickers of snow falling like cotton balls from heaven. She was really getting scared now. There were no familiar streets; this was so far away from home it wasn't even funny. They weren't even in the same borough. What if they got lost for good? No one was going to find them downtown like this. Maybe Patty was right. Maybe they *would* get killed. In her life, Kristie had enough grief. Someone had already died on her once upon a time.

Henry looked at her. "You okay?"

Kristie looked back at him. Her soft cheeks were turning pink but she made no sound. Tears welled up in her eyes and began to cascade down her porcelain-doll face. But she still made no sound.

"I'll get us home," Henry said, rubbing the tears off her cheeks, brushing her hair aside. "I promise."

He grabbed her hand, cool as a cucumber, reassuring her when he didn't even know her that well. She was new. Her family enrolled her in school past the normal deadline. From the moment they had met in the schoolyard, though, it always seemed like they knew each other. They joked that maybe they met before in a past life or something and they were becoming reacquainted once more. She squeezed his hand hard. She felt safe, as if nothing in the world would ever cause her harm when she was with him.

The angels were not far away, still dogging the car. It was a quick old thing, despite its age. For the faintest of moments a thought came to both Jack & Fred: that maybe it wasn't the car but they themselves who had gotten a little slower over time. The mere thought made the little one grimace to no end.

"Can you believe this thing, Jack?"

"Big son of a gun, ain't it, Fred?"

"Yeah!"

"Buick?"

"Pontiac."

"It's a tank! They don't make them like they used to!"

"Us or the car?"

Fred looked over at Jack. Jack glanced back at him.

Further ahead, Joey was still protesting all the way. It was like pulling teeth with him. "Come on Patty! What, what'd I do now?"

"You exist!" she barked and began walking in fast headlong strides ahead of the group. Joey ran to keep pace with her. She walked quickly, just like her father.

"Come on Patty! Tell me!"

"How should I know what we're eating tonight?! Like you're coming over anyway. Like we're going to *be* home tonight! Besides, my mom can't stand you," she scoffed.

"Your mom likes me!" the boy protested.

"She *tolerates* you. There's a difference!"

"Tolerates?!" You got some nerve! Come back here!"

Believe it or not, by sheer dumb luck, they were actually heading in the right direction to find 86th and Lexington. Henry and Kristie weren't far behind them. He looked around and realized where they were, as if someone snapped their fingers, awakening him from a hypnosis session.

"I know this place," Henry said aloud. "Kris, I know where we are. I've been down here before with my father. We're okay. Where is it?"

"What?" the little girl sniffled, rubbing her eyes.

"There used to be a place on the corner somewhere. It had these fruit drinks and hotdogs, smelled so good. It was called…"

Some distance away…

"Papaya King!" Fred screamed. "That's it!"

Jack's face scrunched up in thought. "That place on 86th and 3rd, the one with the hotdogs and the fruit drinks."

"That's it!" the little one shrieked.

"Are we near that?"

"It…it should be like three blocks away. Can you say lunch?"

"Let's hurry up and stop this thing, I've got the growls but good," Jack said, rubbing his stomach.

"Let's try this again. Here we go!" Fred screeched.

The car struck past like a lightning bolt on wheels and round fenders, and they nearly missed it, again. It was almost like the old thing didn't want to be caught. Or the wind didn't want them to. They did all they could to snag the door handles and hang on for all the marbles as it went diving down the wide, icy streets before them.

"Ow!" the little one went, bending his fingers backward as he threw himself into the car, holding onto the window frame for dear life. Inside, Fred found a worn old man named Mr. Wallace who was flopping all over the place in a stupor. He had a pudgy face and a great, round, cherry nose with cheeks to match. Jack slingshot himself in through the passenger side window, landing with a loud smack.

"Finally!" he bellowed.

The rush of wind blew Fred's hair from his face as he perched next to the man's ear, holding onto the seatbelt strap so tightly his fingers swelled. There may well have been a tyrannosaurus in the front seat. Mr. Wallace had no idea the angels were there; they were completely invisible to him, except for some small sixth sense that picked up on there being a gentle goodness about him. Goodness was the one thing that he had little need of. He just wanted to die. This was taking too long for him.

The little one put on his most decadent smile. "Well hello there, sir! Woo. Out of breath here. Some day, huh? Kinda breezy!" he squinted. "Think I got a bug in my teeth to be honest with you."

"Fred!" Jack admonished.

"Yo, buddy! Mister? Sir? Heyyy, Tubby!"

The man stirred. "Hmm?"

"Sorry 'bout the whole tubby thing. Gotta lose a few pounds here myself."

"No kidding," Jack mumbled.

"My name's Fred. This is Jack."

"Hullo," he said drolly, closing his eyes, still somewhat mad they caught Mr. Wallace's car and didn't have to chase it in the frosty winter air and high wind any longer. Jack loved a good chase; something that had a challenge. At some point Jack missed his calling as a would-be Olympian—in his opinion anyway.

Fred continued. "So mister, we're gonna be your angels today."

The old man belched.

"Thanks for that. Bring it up again. We can vote on it. Jack, this guy's drunk!"

"Nooo. Whatever gave you that idea, genius?"

"Aw, man. What's this guy's name again, Jack?"

Jack pulled out a note card he and Fred had been given by an angelic courier shortly after Fred spotted the car and the chase began. "Wallace," he said.

"Say Wal—can I call ya Wal? Anybody ever tell you, you look like a shorter, dumpier W.C. Fields?"

The man groaned.

Jack pointed. "LaFong," he said, thinking of the classic Fields' sketch. "Carl LaFong. Capital *L*, small *A*, capital *F*, small *O*, small *N*, small *G*."

"That's it!" the little one pointed back with a chuckle, adjusting an imaginary tie knot. *"Ahem…"*

The man's eyebrows raised, a slight grin creased the corners of his mouth. His senses recognized the angels' unending joyousness in his front seat. Their happiness in some small way seeped through the perpetual bleakness in his heart. He was at least halfway there.

Fred clapped him on the shoulder. "So, Mr. Wallace, Jack and I are starving here, and I'm sure you're bored to tears with this whole thing. So let's go on and hit the brakes before we have a disaster here!"

"Aw crap!" Jack barked, spotting a woman moving into the street as the car all but aimed for her. It wasn't so unusual a sight for Manhattanites, as most pedestrians could attest to. That's what crosswalks seemed like they were for, lining up people to hit them!

Fred's eyes bulged. "Oh, look at this. Don't cross now, lady!"

The old lady took one step off the corner with her shopping cart, then darted back onto the sidewalk as the rush of excitement screamed past her at breakneck speeds. The Pontiac went whipping round the corner. It amazed Jack how the old bucket cornered for a vehicle of such advanced years.

"I say, hot damn!" the old woman squawked.

"You said it, honey!" Fred called as they rocketed past. She didn't see the angels. No one did. But that old complaint wasn't going to stop them.

The man yawned and started stretching.

Horns bellowed everywhere as they bounced through an intersection.

Fred grabbed Mr. Wallace, shaking him. "C'mon, don't bust my chops here, Wal." The old man began to pass out as the storefronts rolled past his side window. The little one bit his lip. "No, don't do this!" he said breathlessly, pulling the car out of the rush of oncoming traffic.

Jack sunk down into the front seat, reclining with his fingers laced behind his head, crossing his leg over the other as he relaxed upon the leather upholstery. He was smirking in spite of himself. The little one threw him a glance. He was getting very angry.

"What is with you today, Jack?" he asked with palms out, looking at his partner. "You having too much fun or what here?!"

"I'm not having fun. I'm just tired. Besides, I didn't even expect to *be* here," Jack said with a sly grin.

"Where'd you expect to be?"

"I have no idea. Turn."

"What?"

"Turn!"

"Shoot!"

The man hoped that he would just crash—hard—and be done with it. The bull-nosed car crossed lines and started going head to head with a giant green garbage truck, fitted with a snowplow that bobbed up and down with each convulsion the truck made. Jack was suddenly concerned—for the man.

"Uh, Fred!"

"Oh geez, he's playing chicken." Fred grabbed the man's shoulder, physically shaking him like crazy. "Mister...uh, sir? Garbage truck. *Big* garbage truck. Super-humungo-sized garbage truck with a big-ass snow plow!" Fred stared at the speeding metal leviathan. The plow blade came down with guillotine chops, chipping away the frozen blacktop beneath it.

"He ain't stoppin', Fred."

Fred again yanked the steering wheel from Mr. Wallace's hands, turning the car away, within a split hair of disaster. The rolling black wheels growled past the angel's face, bellowing a sound of resentment as it sped by.

"Go back to Jersey, ya creep!" Fred yelled, waving a fist. "Are we getting no help here or what?"

"Maybe the other angels just got stacked over Kennedy airport. Flight path is always jammed."

"Figures."

A strange noise like a wounded cow echoed in their ears.

Jack yelled. "Cat!"

Fred reached over and turned the wheel at the last moment, skidding the wayward runaway box away from the rotund feline.

"Whoof!" Jack went.

The large black-and-white cat stared at them, unmoving, with bright yellow human eyes, if that were possible—but it did look that way.

Jack recoiled, looking over at Fred.

Fred shook his head. "This is just one of them days, isn't it?"

"Did you see that? Didn't that—"

"Look like a mutant person cat thing?"

"Yeah!" Jack exclaimed. "Just like one. But it kinda resembled a cow."

"A cow cat?!"

Jack snapped his fingers and pointed at his partner-in-crime. They both shuddered at the thought of the creature.

"Just wrong seeing a thing like that!" he said.

A few blocks away...

"Buy you lunch?" Henry smiled, walking backward in front of Kristie, trying to keep her smiling. And she was…the face just lit up like sunshine.

"C'mon dimples. Five bucks." He nodded over toward Papaya King. "We can dine al fresco!"

She choked on her stifled laughter. "You're crazy, you know that?"

The boy smiled. "Just a little."

"So this is our first date then?" she sniffled, with a devious grin only someone so cute could get away with.

Henry went nose to nose with her. "And if it is, you got a problem with that?"

She looked at him for moment. "No. I just wanted to make sure I always remember it. That's all."

They walked, hand in hand, and there on the corner, in all its glory, was the Papaya King, decked out in its sun-drenched oranges and yellows, shining amid the humdrum blah of the city in winter. Kris smiled. Even though they were both so young, she knew then that she liked that he took care of her. From her very first day in the schoolyard, she knew he always would, too.

Jack began having a nervous breakdown, watching in the passenger seat. This should've ended several blocks back.

"Watch the bus! Watch the bus!"

Fred yanked the car out of the incoming behemoth's path.

"How bad?"

"Fender bender!" Jack yelled. "Not bad."

The noise stirred Mr. Wallace conscious, and he rubbed his eyes with his smooth, chubby fingers. "Oh, Father...please *help me*."

Fred's cheery facade fell away. "He's tryin', fella. He's tryin'! What if you—Whoa!"

Jack swallowed. "Fred, hit the brakes, Fred."

"I'm trying!"

"Fred."

"Wasn't meant to be going this fast. Car is ancient." The little one slid down to the floor, smashing down on the brakes. Jack was reaching over to grab the steering wheel. "I got it, Jack."

"No, ya don't!" The car was weaving through cars at a speed it shouldn't have been able to reach. "This is suddenly not fun anymore!"

"Okay, Mister. Whaa-ooo. Geez!"

The wind whipped through the tassels of silver hair, flowing off the sides of Mr. Wallace's balding head. The old one grunted as he began passing out again. His head became top-heavy and flopped onto Fred's shoulder. Fred nudged it in the other direction and it fell over toward Jack. Jack elbowed the man's noggin back the other way; it looked like the angels were playing Ping-Pong with his cranium.

Jack was angry. "Would you stop shoving this melon at me! He reeks of Jack Daniels!" The angels hated seeing people self-destruct like this.

Fred's fingers peeled open the man's eyes.

"Look into my eye," he said, mesmerizing him. Wallace's hands grabbed the wheel, and he instinctively turned as cars around him went flying out of the way, crashing into each other.

"Watch the bike, Fred! Ugh, Lord. Fred, this is not working, Fred."

"I KNOW ALREADY!"

"Man, I'm hungry."

They were sailing toward a traffic pileup ahead of them. Fred fought with the man for control of the wheel as the dodgy car skipped from side to side on the slick streets. The cars ahead were at a total standstill.

"Um, Fred?"

"Damn."

A few blocks away...

"Patty, I'm starving!"

"Good! That's because you're skinny and nasty Joey!"

"Hey, come back! Why do you have to be like that?"

Patty looked for their two friends and spotted them at the place on the corner. "Look at these two. They're stopping for lunch! Puhlease. Give us a break here. Dating nonsense. Sickening."

Joey's eyes darted back and forth between Patty and his friends. "Yeah, like...the hell with them!" He waved a fist.

Patty leered. "Yeah. The hell with them."

"Uh-huh. So Pats, are *you* hungry? 'Cause...Patty. Patty wait up! Ugh, man!"

Not too far away now...

As if on command, Mr. Wallace pulled the car over to the right, driving up unto the sidewalk, dodging the stalled cars before him. Jack shook his head.

"Didn't think we were gonna make that one!"

The car slammed into a traffic sign, and the little one hollered, "No Parking Anytime? Try never again!"

Jack was disgusted. "Ya know, you're being too gentle with him."

"Am not."

"Am too. This is *not* that difficult."

"Why aren't you helping then?"

"I'm just watching the master at work." Jack put a hand over his eyes.

The car drove over the sidewalk; people were screaming and diving into store fronts, dogs were barking madly, and a bike messenger went flying head over tea kettle. The Pontiac continued its onslaught, plowing into a fruit stand's shelves, a public trash barrel, and a stubby red fire plug. Water spouted out like Old Faithful, saturating already-freezing pedestrians from head to foot in frigid ice water.

The stalled drivers out in the street stared dumbfounded as Mr. Wallace coasted over the sidewalk, slamming into parking meters, knocking them overlike dominoes. The metal poles totally destroyed the front end, but the old tank kept going. One of the clicky, turning things—you know, where you put the money in the meter—well, that thing got detached and smacked into the windshield. Jack, Fred, and Wal ducked as the glass cracked and fractured. The Pontiac rocketed past a traffic cop doling out tickets. She leaped aside, nearly getting flattened. In the mirror, Jack could see her get up on one knee, looking at the time-expired parking meters (now expired themselves) flattened to the ground, and she threw her ticket book down in disgust.

"Ha, ha!" Jack laughed at her. He steadied himself as he hovered above the seat. "Whoa."

"Sorry. So sorry. So *tired*," the old one moaned, wiping the sweat from his brow. Mr. Wallace shifted in his seat, fidgeting all over the place, thinking that his long-lost wife was speaking to him from beyond. "Deirdre, honey, is that you? You callin' me from heaven, baby? Deirdre?"

"Great, just great!" Fred grumbled.

"I miss you," he said.

Jack shook his head. "Don't miss her too much. You'll be joining her momentarily."

The angels thought it was all about this man, and this car, this stupid car. But in the midst of getting caught up in the hubbub and ridiculousness of human stupidity, for once Jack & Fred didn't realize that maybe it was meant to be like this. Maybe the car wasn't meant to be stopped, right away. Maybe it was drawing them away from everything else. Maybe it was taking them someplace on purpose where, maybe, just maybe, they'd find *something wonderful*.

Down the avenue, Joey and Patty were still arguing.

Patty, in a lover's spat mood, walked briskly away from her unknowing beau. "Why do I have to account to you for everything that happens in my life?!"

"What, you think that eighth-grade guy likes you? Please Pats! Like he hasn't dated every other girl in his class."

Patty cocked her head to the side as she sauntered off the corner and stopped.

"Jealous?"

Joey recoiled.

"Of what? He has no neck! He looks like a giant chest with eyes."

"You're just an idiot, you know?" she sighed, growing tired of walking and arguing for miles.

"You ever see where he sits? They have a Don't Feed the Animals sign posted over him. Uh, hello?"

Joey looked at the rush of cars passing by as the Don't Walk sign flashed on, *again*. He threw his hands up in the air.

"Today! Why don't you wait a little longer, stupid. Maybe 400 *more* cars will pass by."

"Excuse me!" Patty squawked. "I don't want to be made into someone's hood ornament."

"No," Joey continued, "Let's stay here on the corner like the old people. Maybe we'll get across sometime next week. Go ahead, hit the crosswalk button ten more times. They never work!"

"Go to hell!" she cried as they crossed over.

The car screeched in pain as it turned the corner.

Fred screamed aloud, "I don't have time for this. Lord, give me strength. This man's not listening to me!"

Jack pushed Fred aside. "I told you you're being too gentle with him, Fred. We don't have time for this bull—"

"Jack!"

Jack popped Mr. Wallace across the jaw.

"You hit him?!"

Then tossed him in the backseat.

Fred's eyes bulged. "I can't believe you!"

"We don't have time for this crap! He's gonna be guacamole if he hits the intersection! We're saving him!"

"By hitting him?!"

"Fred, if life down here has taught us anything it's that being nice is great, but every once in a while we all need a good smash to see things right."

Fred stared at him, his mouth wide open.

Jack shrugged. "Better he gets smashed than killed."

"You're unbelievable, Jack."

"I know," he said flashing his pearly whites. "Are we doing brakes? Hello? Yeah? Huh?? You gonna hit the brakes or what here?"

"Would you stop yelling at me! I told you I hate runaways!"

"I'm not yelling at you, twerp! But we're on short time here! Are you—"

"I hit the brakes already, you damn pelican!"

Jack leaped at Fred and the two began smacking the ever-loving crap out of one another in a flurry of feathers and fists.

Henry and Kris dipped in and out of the food stand in a proverbial New York minute, realizing they were short two people as they sipped drinks.

"Kris, where are they?"

Ahead, Joey proudly announced, "Patty, look. 86th and Lex. Told you we weren't lost!" He tugged at his black locks in the excitement.

Patty flailed her arms exaggeratedly. "When was this?! Was I gone when you said this?"

"Patty, where's Hen and Kris?"

Henry frowned. "C'mon munchkin!" he said to the little girl as he pulled her along. "Hurry!" They tossed their drinks in a trash barrel with a wet smack.

"What is it? Is that them? How'd they get all the way over there? Geez, Henry slow—"

"Can't. Hurry!"

The angels' hands were pressed against one another's faces when Jack suddenly shouted, "Okay, Fred. Stop, stop, stop! We—"

A light spilled down upon Jack's head. He shuddered and stopped—frozen in place, listening to something. He looked back and forth frantically, trying to determine where the sound was calling from.

"Jack. Jack, what is it?"

Jack spotted something. He squinted, and then his eyes opened wide in terror.

"Oh, Lord, Fred! It's too late. The children. You stupid old man! We gotta stop this thing. It's going to hit the children!"

Fred scrunched his face up as he pounded down on the pedal in earnest. The car made an unearthly scream but it just didn't stop.

"There they are!" Jack whispered.

Kristie spotted their friends immediately as she and the boy came upon the avenues whose location they had sought all day.

"There they are!" she whispered.

Realizing they had gone out too far, Joey and Patty turned and started to march back to them. The skinny boy whispered, *"Henry…"*

The car dropped its muffler, running over a pothole. Metal screamed as it ran along the ground like tin fingers on a stone blackboard. Orange sparks leaped up like a jumping jack light storm. The car's brakes burned done to their pads, smoking, then let go. Henry and Kristie heard the sound a second before they saw the fireball headed for their friends.

Patty instinctively took hold of Joey's hand as they started off the curb without a care; they looked at Henry with blank expressions as he and Kristie's screams were drowned out by the sounds of the city. Henry's feet were rushing toward them in headlong molasses strides, but he knew he'd never reach them. *"Joey, Patty!"* He pointed at the car, but he just couldn't get to them.

As it always happens in these situations, the car just appeared out of nowhere. The kids found themselves in the middle of the street when the realization hit them. They were even walking with the light, but there was the car barreling down upon them. Without thought, Joey yanked Patty backward.

"Watch it."

"No!" Kristie screamed.

Henry reached out in vain.

The children stood in the street, one supreme moment frozen in time, paralyzed.

"Look out!" Henry screeched.

"Go for it, Jack," Fred whispered with a smile.

Jack rocketed out of the car, grabbing the children by the scruffs of their necks, hauling them back up onto the sidewalk.

"Woo-hoo! Gotcha!" he hooted.

Kristie froze in mid step, an expression of unspeakable amazement across her face. Her heart did not know whether to cheer or cry; her mind was unable to comprehend what her eyes had just seen before her. Henry, however, saw something *very* different. He saw the majesty behind the miracle, and they had smiling faces and bright eyes. They could fly! The boy watched as they brought the chase to an end.

Fred joined Jack outside the car, and they pushed against it with all their might, digging into the asphalt—hard. Throwing their weight against the speeding tank, their feet lit up like cherry tomatoes; smoke billowed from their toes, screeching, grinding, and incinerating their arches to all heaven. Realizing they had no time for finesse, as the intersection beyond quickly approached, the pair somersaulted to the back of the car in one grand synchronous flip. Grappling onto the bumper, they popped their wings apart wide, creating a funny car parachute. The Pontiac groaned and pulled, sparking like mad; it finally ground to a deafening halt inches before the mad crisscross of speeding traffic. A red car zipped by, beeping into the distance, a breath away from the front fender. Only when awakening sometime later would Mr. Wallace realize how close he had come to ending his existence; God had given him a second lease on life.

Jack & Fred high-fived one another with congratulatory faces, then simultaneously looked down at their blackened, well-done feet, and started hopping about like crazy.

"Ow! Ow! Ow!" the little one went.

"Good God, man! Ahhh! Ahh!" Jack added.

"Geez…man! Sss…Ughhh!"

"Owwa…ahh…"

They both sighed, "huuhhh" and slumped to the ground in front of the motionless monster. Fred flopped his head on Jack's shoulder. Both were trying to catch their breath. Jack looked down at his partner, shaking his hand vigorously. The agitation made Fred's eyes bulge.

Jack's chest puffed out over and over. "Good job, par-ten-er. That wasn't so hard, now was it?"

"I feel like I'm going to pass out."

"Yeah, me too."

"Jack…"

"I know. You hate runaways."

"Uh-huh."

Joey and Patty were gathering themselves up from the pavement. Joey took her hands in his own, shaking them, just to see if they were both alive. Kristie ran over to them, screaming madly.

"Oh my God! Joey, Patty, are you alright?"

Still in shock, Patty looked at her for a moment in silence and then began falling apart crying. Kristie wrapped the taller girl up in her tiny arms. Patty squeezed her tightly, her usually rough facade a thing of memory. People on the street were already stopping and pointing to the scene. Joey just stared in silence at the smoking car. His concave chest was heaving. *No way.* It couldn't have stopped in time. *It couldn't have.* He watched the car and saw Henry walking toward it.

"Henry?" he called to the boy, as he drifted away.

Kristie looked up to see where he was, confused. Patty didn't want to let her go. The daughter of a boxer, Miss Toughy didn't want to pull away from the one they all called the munchkin. The very thought of that surprised even Patty. Kris was right. Where'd Henry go? She turned back to Patty, consoling her all the more.

The angels sat a moment in silence. The car crackled and popped, its engine expanding and contracting all at once. For a moment it sounded as if it would fall apart at the seams.

"Jack?"

"Yeah Fred, what is it now?"

"Why'd we do the feet thing again?"

Jack raised an eyebrow. "Always worked on *The Flintstones,* didn't it?"

"I guess. Only Fred Flintstone never got fried tootsies on the way to the quarry. Sssss...*Ouch,*" the angel said painfully, rubbing his burnt feet. "God, do I miss the old days when people just walked. Even horses weren't this bad. That was a tiptoe through the tulips compared to this. How long ago was that?"

"A few decades."

"Seems like just yesterday."

"How's Mr. Jack Daniels doing back there?"

"Um...He's throwing up!" Fred said like a headline. "Now he's moaning, retching, *rolfing*, making these *really* strange gurgling noises."

"Alright. *Alright already!* You don't have to make a nuisance of yourself!"

"Nuisance! Humph!"

The little one grimaced, folding his arms before him in a huff.

"Yeah, you *are* a nuisance. Still, aren't ya glad we're a double act?"

Fred closed his eyes, recapturing his breath, smiling.

"Yeah Jack, I am. Gimme a minute."

{ Chapter 6 }

An Old Song in the Breeze

Something delightful caught Jack's nostrils. "That..." Jack looked around. "That smells like rose petals," he said curiously, wondering where it was coming from. The scent of rose petals always meant that angels were nearby. But if someone else was there, they were hiding. "Fred do you see any...Fred. Fred?"

Fred went back to the car as the traffic started to jumble up the roadway, rubberneckers all around. Jack had seen a travel documentary once, showing some tropical island traffic cop bopping and flourishing in a neatly pressed suit of white—right there in the middle of the street, giving James Brown a run for his money. Since then, any chance he got, he would get his groove on in the middle of traffic. Jack was special like that, Fred would always say.

Though invisible to human eyes, Jack managed to entice the disgruntled blue traffic cop who was still moaning about the downed parking meters behind them. She put away her ticket book and joined him in the open street.

"Officer Emma Burrows, *come on dowwwn*!" the angel called with a smile. She immediately made for the children on the sidewalk.

"You alright?!" she called to them.

"They're fine," Jack whispered.

"But..." She spoke aloud, seemingly to herself.

Jack subliminally pulled her away. "Come with me," he urged. "I need you." The woman stood deliberately in the sea of cars that were rolling by at slower speeds, gawking at the Pontiac as smoke rose from the engine, which looked as though it was going to explode. Jack, like her shadow, spoke and moved as she did.

She waved at the cars, "Keep it moving, keep it moving people! Ease on down, ease on down the road, woo!" She mimicked the angel's choreography as he directed like an orchestral conductor. His hands were rolling one over the other. He was shaking his *thang*, trying to whistle through his fingers, somewhat unsuccessfully (her too!).

"That's it, honey!" he complimented. "Pedal to the metal people, one time, no gawkin'!" He leaned close, his breath tickling the inside of her ear.

"The ambulance is gonna need a clear shot, Emma," he whispered to the woman. "There's an old, sick man inside. I'm depending on you."

"Okay," the woman in blue said aloud, not knowing why. "Move it, people! Let's go! You doin' okay?" she called again to the kids. They nodded back at her. "Good! Come on people, m..."

"...ove it!" Jack went. "That's a girl," he subliminally winked.

"Get up!"

Feeling the flow, she just added, "Get on up!"

"Stay on the scene!" Jack added.

"Get on up!"

"Like a sex machine."

"Get on up!"

"Ow!" Jack and Emma twirled.

The woman grinned, as if someone had smiled at her and told her how beautiful she was. People in the passing cars stared. Officer Burrows just shrugged, cackling as she directed.

"I haven't felt like this in years," she said loudly, smacking her hands together. "Woo...Let's go, people. Head 'em up and move 'em out little doggies! C'mon now...woo!"

Someone giggled and Jack stopped in his tracks, looking around. He wasn't alone and it wasn't Fred. *Who could it be?*

"Uuugh," Mr. Wallace moaned as police and ambulance sirens wailed in

the near distance. The vehicles were speeding toward the minor accidents the Pontiac had left in its wake. Fred took the keys out of the ignition, tossing them away. For the briefest of moments, the smell of the car seats preoccupied his senses; the car must've been preserved in a garage for an untold number of years, Fred thought as he admired old Mr. Wallace, the frail little person inside the old metal box.

"Hey! Dopey!" Fred lightly smacked Mr. Wallace awake.

"I'm not happy," Mr. Wallace grumbled.

"What's wrong with you? There're so many ways to get hurt in this life, and you do this intentionally? What's up, man? Honestly."

"I'm sorry."

"You're sorry? Listen Wal, I know how rough it is for you, especially this time of year. But that doesn't give you a pass for what you did here today. If Jack didn't pull those kids out of the street, you would've killed them because you were selfish."

"I'm sorry."

"I know what's wrong. I understand. She died on Christmas Eve, didn't she? Your wife."

The old one pinched his eyes shut and nodded.

"I know what it feels like to be alone. But you can't change things. You are here now, and this isn't the way. Your Deirdre is safe and sound in heaven. She's happy."

"What about me?" the old man said, choking on his words with a mighty lump in his throat. "She's not here with me. Nobody's here with me. I'm all by myself."

"*We're* here with you."

"I miss her *so* much."

"That's because you love her."

Mr. Wallace sobbed quietly, his face in his hands.

"Look what you're doing. You're destroying yourself. She loves you. She wouldn't want you to hurt anybody or yourself, no matter how bad you've gotten without her."

"I'm just...*tired*."

Fred sat down in the backseat, putting the man's head and shoulders across his lap, holding his hand.

"I love her so much."

"I know, Mr. Wallace," the angel whispered to the man. "*I know.* I'm tired too. You can't do this anymore. Someone else's kids wouldn't have been home for Christmas this year, and someone *else* would've been lonely. You don't want that."

Mr. Wallace sighed with a nod. Fred looked down at the lost soul, stroking his cheek gently. Horns were beeping outside, and for a moment the little one swore he could hear the ocean for some reason.

"I know you don't believe in me. Shoot, you don't even *see* me. But you gotta believe that the Big Man upstairs loves you, and He *does* care, even when you're at your worst. Especially in those times. Like the old saying goes, *'when you don't see Him, it's because He's carrying you.'* He's given you a second chance, Mr. Wallace." Fred smiled. "Don't screw it up or I'll be back to kick your butt, alright?"

The man's rosy cheeks shone brightly, and he smiled, shaking his head with dearest conviction.

"They've got places that can help you. When you wake up, go find one for me."

The little one gently rested the old man's head on the soft leather seat and started to climb out the window. Fred tilted his head, looking down at the peaceful face that was red from crying for so long and so hard.

"*Stay,*" the man whispered.

Fred pinched his eyes shut.

"I can't."

"Please, for just a little while."

Fred swallowed, blinking away the tears that he couldn't afford to cry just now.

"Look, I am like *really* late," the little one said, looking at his bare arm, the place where a watch should be. "I have people that I got to take care of, like…like you! They need me. Lot of accidents to prevent, people who need smiling, and people who need a ride…*home.* Let me do the job that God has given me."

"Okay…"

"Fred. My name's Fred."

"Okay, *Fred*."

"And Jack, you met him. *He's* the one who gave you the shiner. Sorry 'bout that!" Fred cringed. "His fault!"

The man grinned.

"I'll be back to visit you, though, *I promise*. You get well for me, for Christmas, huh Mr. Wallace? Alright?"

The old one sighed, quieting his restless heart down; the man was smiling. Little miracles. There was joy for the man, but for the angel the moment was already passing. Fred's voice was already but a dream to him, but the meaning left an indelible impression on Mr. Wallace's heart.

The little one wanted to grab the man and shake him, saying, *"Look at me. I'm here. I'm real! See me! Just believe in me after I stop talking to you and my voice begins to fade from your thoughts like an old song in the breeze."*

But the man just couldn't. For the angel it was like trying to hold onto a joyous dream that you were being ripped away from by the tolling of an old alarm clock. The angel's greatest desire appeared before his eyes as he inhaled, only to have it drift away into nothingness the moment after his breath slipped away. Fred asked one thing before he said goodbye for the time being.

"Hey, Wal. Before you slip into unconsciousness. I wanna ask ya…just for flaps and giggles. What's your first name anyway?"

"Barcephelus," the man whispered.

The little one smiled, shaking his head to himself.

"Uh-huh. So long, *Mr. Wallace.*"

Mr. Wallace could still hear the angel's voice in his ears as he fell away. *"There's always hope if you just let it into your heart. Just have faith and you'll find it. And it takes time, but it does get better."*

The old one whispered a breathless *thank you*. He would have the best sleep in ages. The cop cars were all wailing away. No one was hurt. Mr. Wallace wouldn't get into too much trouble. The first day of his new life would begin when he woke up.

"I wish to God that you could have at least seen me in person, after all that," Fred remarked to himself as he popped out of the car. Jack was outside waiting for him. The little one was surprised but glad to know he was there, like always. It made him feel better. At least he had someone.

Jack looked at the little one. "What?"

"Know somethin', Jack? Our job—"

"Hurts sometimes?"

Fred swallowed and shook his head. "Yeah," the little one shrugged, shaking his head as they drifted away.

Henry ran over to the Pontiac, a heartbeat behind them, and then suddenly stopped short on his heels. For a moment he was scared. He didn't know what he'd find if he looked into that window. Was the man dead? But he looked anyway and smiled when he saw the old one fast asleep with a grin on his face. He whipped around, and dashed away. He wasn't letting them go—not until…

The little one and Jack flew over to the next avenue.

"So, Jack, you do your little James Brown traffic-cop *thang*?"

Jack spun in place and threw out his hand. "Of course!"

"God. And *I'm* the crazy one?"

Jack snapped him up by the wing.

"No, you're the short, snotty one."

"Ow!" Fred wailed, trying to slug the taller angel behind him.

"Hey. Question, Fred."

"What?"

"Did you smell anything before?"

Fred looked around with a disgruntled puss. "Oh I've smelt lotsa things down here."

"No. Like, like rose petals?"

"Rose petals?"

"You're gonna think I'm crazy."

"No Jack, I think you're a whacko."

"Fine, whatever. Say, you ready to go home, now that this little adventure is coming to an end?"

Revived and smiling, Fred looked into his friend's eyes.

"An end? Jack, I have a feeling this little adventure is just beginning!"

Jack turned away, visibly annoyed. "Oh, here we go again. Yeah, whatever,

Fred. Come on, let's just get out of here. Tell you one thing, though. We're never going to have another day like this. Something very special about today. And I'm not talking about the strange wind. Can't put my finger on it. But I do feel it."

Henry rushed around the corner, catching a slick patch of ground and wiping out on the pavement. The pant leg of his right knee was shredded down to the skin below. He was breathing so hard his chest ached. He swallowed what tasted like razor blades as the blood rushed to cheeks. Sweat was pouring down the back of his sweater and a chill ran up his back, shoulders, and arms, making him shudder. He just realized it was snowing.

"Where are you guys? Where? There!" The boy vaulted away.

{ Chapter 7 }

George

"Jack! Hey! Listen!"

"You hear that? It's—there it is! It's the Mister Softee ice-cream truck! You want to get some ice cream before we go back upstairs?" Jack asked.

Fred licked his lips. "Have you ever known me to say no? Hey wait. Look over there at that guy crossin' the street. He's not lookin.' He's gonna get hit!"

"Hey, stupid, watch out!"

BANG! Impact.

Jack, Fred, and Henry cringed as the man went sailing across the avenue, sliding and then stopping right before the angels' feet.

Fred cocked his head, looking at him. "I don't think he's goin' dancing after that one."

Jack gave him up eyes. "God, what is it today?! See if he's alright, Fred."

The little one checked for a pulse.

"Well…"

Fred looked up at his partner. "He's dead."

"What?!"

"He's dead. He's been killed by Mister Softee."

Jack & Fred looked at one another, then back down at the man.

"You klutz!" they said together.

"C'mon, Fred. Let's scoop him up and get out of here."

"Hey, Jack," he said slapping him on the back. "That ice-cream joke is not in *good humor!*"

"Look at him, *sprinkled* all over the place."

"Couldn't he have at least waited till *Sunday?*"

Fred peered over his shoulder.

"What?" Jack asked.

"Just looking for the big hook that's gonna yank us offstage is all."

"We're not in a play!"

"Not this time."

"Huh?"

Fred shrugged and they both lifted up the man's spirit, which reflected his expression at the time of impact. He was smiling for some reason; they took him up out of his body and were ready to carry him away. Jack had his arms; Fred had his feet.

Jack was beat at this point. "Come on, dopey, let's get you to heaven. Let's go, little one."

"Does he have a name, Jack?"

"I don't know. Check his tags," Jack suggested as they fumbled with George's lanky spiritual form. "Here, like…turn, yeah…turn him around. That's it. Ow! Ow! My hand, Fred! Okay, there," he nodded to George's spiritual pedigree, the identity tags around a person's neck only the gang upstairs can see. They contained the life and times and everything in between for the person you're handling, if you're an angel, that is.

The little one read. "Um, human…blah, blah, blah…uh…George Mor… Morano."

"Morano?" Jack grimaced.

"George the Moron," Fred said enthusiastically.

"Let me see that!" Jack pulled the spiritual identity tags from Fred's hands. "Blah…blah, um, George Mohr-ahn-oh " he sounded out, shaking his head and sighing loudly.

"Told you. This is the kind that gets out of the car with the seatbelt still on, Jack. I'm tellin' ya!"

"Lord…"

"And he gets hit by a slow-moving ice cream truck."

"In December."

"That spells Moron to me."

"Me too."

Jack looked at the man for a moment.

"C'mon George, let's get shakin'!"

"That's Jell-O humor, not…"

"Oh, would you shut-up Fred!"

Someone was giggling. The angels looked around for it, but the source ducked his head back around the building.

Jack asked, "I wonder if he had a family."

Fred flipped over the tags.

"Nope. He was an orphan."

"No family, friends, a home, nothin'?"

"He didn't have a home. Like us." Jack avoided Fred's eyes. "He had a landlady. And he used to have cat. That's it really."

"Was he sick?" Jack asked.

Fred looked up.

"Not a day in his life."

Jack shook his head, shrugging.

"Okay," he said.

"What?"

"Nothing. Just…yeah. Long day. Alright, let's go."

Jack & Fred took off into the sky. They inadvertently flew in two separate directions, making a wish with George's spirit, almost pulling him apart.

"Ugh!" he groaned.

Jack cringed. "Oh, geez. Sorry, fella. Oh hey, mail's in!"

A flying courier dropped out of the sky delivering a message to the pair. It detailed the whereabouts of their missing barrister.

"Jack, is it?"

"Yep. Houston, we have liftoff. Found him."

"Cool. Let's boogie."

"Aw crap in a hat! Wait, Fred!" He turned to the courier. "Can you…?"

The courier looked at the disembodied spirit in the angels' arms and vigorously shook his head *no*.

"Fine," Jack said. "Gimme a hand with this thing, Fred."

The little one frowned at the courier as he sped off into the sky. "Why can't *he* take George home?"

"He's a courier, like those Western Union guys. They don't *do* this stuff."

"Why not, Jack?"

"Union rules."

"What?"

"He only delivers messages. We handle the baggage. You know that," Jack said as he secured George for the trip.

"We've gotta lug this thing around with us?"

"This *thing*, Fred, is a person and… God, you're heavy man!"

"Ugh," George groaned again.

"I can't believe this," Fred grumbled. "I'm not exactly Joe Skinny."

"You can say that!"

"But," Fred looked at him sideways, "this is some serious beef to carry. This guy's spirit is chunky. Look at this! He was thin, too. He should be light as feather! We gotta fly all the way back up there. This is gonna be like carrying an elephant on your back the whole trip."

"Story of my life," Jack quipped.

"Shut up, Jack!"

"Sling him over. That's it! Don't…caught my hand last time. Okay! Here we go!"

"What would you do if you didn't direct for a living, Jack?"

"Live on a beach."

"Thinkin' about doin' that myself."

The angels hauled George away, drifting back over the avenue where Officer Burrows directed traffic and the paramedics were arriving to tend to Mr. Wallace. The children sat on the sidewalk, looking at the chaos around them as snow fell softly.

Patty stared at the car as the paramedics tended to the old man. "How did it swerve in time?"

Kristie looked up. "It didn't. You were right in its way. Look where it stopped."

"But...how'd it..."

"You would've been killed if it wasn't for..."

Patty pulled back and looked at her. "For what? Kris, what're you saying?"

The girl, visibly shaken, tried to explain herself.

"I saw something; something grabbed you two by the back of your necks, by...by the collars. It pulled the two of you out of the street...it...it..." She rubbed her mouth as tears streamed down her cheeks. "I saw it. *Something* saved you. The car was going to hit you. It had to be..."

In the sky behind them, Jack & Fred found themselves inadvertently listening to the children below. They were huffing and puffing, sinking to the ground as they struggled to handle the heavy form of the new spirit. Snowflakes were landing on Jack's eyelashes, blinding him. He shook his head like a mad, soaked puppy, brushing at his face and losing a grip on George. Fred moved to compensate and the weight nearly yanked his arms out of their sockets. The little one's wings flapped frantically and his feet paddled to keep them all aloft.

Below, words rushed out of Joey's excitedly confused mouth.

"Be what? What could it be? What was it, Kristie?"

Kristie trembled uncontrollably. "I don't believe in miracles and those kinds of things, but I don't really know *what* else it could have been. I think you guys were saved by angels."

Upon hearing the word *angels,* Jack & Fred wheeled around as if their names had been called out at an award ceremony. With their hands on their hips, they instinctively puffed out their chests in what was their *bestest* of super heroic poses. George's spirit slipped right out of their hands and dropped to the ground like an anchor. If it were a tangible thing, it would've sounded like a fallen cartoon piano dropped from a great height.

The angels shrunk away at the sound. Somewhat embarrassed of themselves, despite their invisibleness, they swooped down. One by one, they grabbed a leg, then an arm, and they were about to say something about needing a vacation, and there it was. At that moment the whole world stopped. And everything from this point forward would change their lives forever. Just one thing mattered now. And there he was—out of breath; bleeding from the knee, elbows, and arms. He was all ripped up; heart pounding, but still smiling.

Henry was staring at them. *He could see them!* Just like they were, as angels. Invisible to everyone else.

"Jack, he can see us!" the little one said in a whisper.

"I know." Jack was breathless. He didn't know what to do.

"*Gotcha,*" the boy said, panting.

Fred's eyes lit up. He raised his hand, holding it there for a moment before he realized he could move it again. Henry waved at him. The little one waved back.

"*Jack, Fred, come on!*" angelic voices called down from above, beckoning the pair back upstairs. But they didn't want to leave.

Henry had the biggest smile. And it was at that moment the angels realized that after all those years they had finally found their *something wonderful!* It was right there across the street, in front of their noses the whole time.

"*Come on, guys!*" the voices beckoned again.

The boy and the angels looked upward for whoever was calling them. And their eyes turned back upon each other at the same time. Henry's heart kept saying the same thing as the angels': *Yes, this is real.*

Henry felt his legs moving on their own, taking him to where they were.

"Henry, watch it!" Kristie called, taking his attention back to the street even though the traffic had stopped. Henry looked at her almost in a daze. She took his hands, looking at his banged-up form. "Are you alright? What happened to you? Where'd you go?" she asked.

When the boy turned back to the same spot in the sky, the angels were long gone. He stared at Kristie, speechless and lost all at once. For a moment he was almost angry that she had torn his attention away. They were real. And he saw them! Didn't she see them as well? She had to…didn't she?

Joey, more than a little humbled by the day, rolled up. He was holding onto Patty; he didn't want to let her go anywhere. The girl, for once, didn't disagree with him.

He smiled faintly. "Henry? Hen…How're we going to get home?" They all looked at Henry.

"Come on," the boy whispered as he took Kristie's hand. The children headed for the subway station by way of a payphone. The boy turned his eyes back to the sky. He thought he could still hear them.

{ Chapter 8 }

The Six Train

"Off the map. What's that mean, Sidney?"

"It's like...(sigh) not according to plan, Madison. You know? When an angel does his or her duty, then goes beyond that for whatever reason, dealing with things not assigned to them."

"Is that what Jack & Fred are doing now?"

"No. They're just doing their job. Yeah. That's right."

As dusk came around and night began settling in, one distinct sound buzzed in the air for all those who could listen; it was louder than all the rest. It was repeated over and over again as it had been for hours. *Voices.* It was the parents whose children were missing.

But two voices in particular resonated in Jack & Fred's ears. Who—the parents. The boy's parents. They were asking about their boy. So that's what the boy's name was! *Henry.* It was a wonderful name.

The boy's parents sent up their prayers, an Earthly message in a bottle, pleading with all their hearts that it would reach its divine destination. And it did.

A light shone about the cherubs and the human spirit they carried with them; a warmth filled them to the core. Jack & Fred closed their eyes, and in their minds they could see the faces of the parents whose words rang in their ears. The poor things were so scared.

Through the haze, they could see the face of the mother, then the father, overlapping as each prayed the gentlest of prayers, the smallest requests.

Mom pleaded. "Dear Father…"

As did Dad. "Father, we're at the end of our rope here. He's on that train without me. I'm supposed to be with him."

"Lord, after all we've gone through. I've taken this boy through every illness, ache and pain, and cut and scrape he's ever gotten, but this…this I cannot fix. I'm…"

"I'm worried about my boy, Lord. He thinks he can take on the world. That's why he said he was coming home no matter what. He didn't wait for me to pick him up. I told him I would be right down there…God…he's…"

"Lost. He wouldn't wait for us to pick him up. Now I have to…I can't wait, I need to get to him—and I can't!"

"I have to get to him Lord. My boy's gone through so much, with all the colds he's had. I won't let him down. I'm not going to lose him this way!"

"He's all I have in this world, Lord. Don't take him away from me. Not like this. I only have the one. Don't take away my baby."

"I don't ask you for much. I've always tried my best, given you whatever I have, Lord. Now this is all I ask you for…I beg you, Lord, please."

"Please help my little Henry, Lord. He's all I got!"

"His mom and I are heartsick over this. Please."

"When I am at work, I feel as though your angels are guiding me. I ask you to send them to watch over my boy now. Bring him home."

"I pray that you hear me this night, Lord, and that you send his guardian angels to watch over him and bring him back to us."

Their hearts seemed to be speaking at the same time.

"He's all I have in this world, Lord! Please bring him home." The words reverberated in the angels' ears over and over again. Mom and Dad made the sign of the cross and the light faded over both faces.

Jack opened his eyes. He looked at Fred and the little one looked back at him. The light that was around them grew thinner and thinner, until it became a narrow beam that pointed down to a house—a house with a yellow awning—on a street somewhere in the Bronx, a half hour or so outside of the city. The angels nodded to one another and flew right back down without words, carrying George's spirit all the way with them. At times they dragged it behind them like a wayward kite in the breeze. They knew they were off the map but didn't care. They had to get the boy back home safe. They'd worry about the rest later.

"Fred. The kid's taking the subway."

"It *is* the fastest way back."

"I know. But he should've waited for the parents to pick him up."

"He'll be alright. We won't let nothin' on this Earth hurt him."

"He's gonna give them a nervous breakdown. They're panicked!"

"Duh, Jack! Of course they are. He's on the subway."

"The kid was smart enough to call home, so someone'll meet them at the station. But he should've waited for them to grab him by car."

"They don't have cell phones yet, do they?"

"No Fred, not yet. Few years."

"Crap. I bet the school hasn't notified the parents they're missing, right?"

"Boys upstairs say no."

"Figures. Imagine what that conversation's going to be like? Someone's getting reamed!"

"They should be! I still smell rose petals. Do you?"

"You're not crazy, Jack. There's another one out here with us."

"Another angel? Who?"

"Maybe it belongs to one of the other kids."

"I heard bells before, too."

"Bells?"

"Sorry about this, George."

"He'll be alright, Jack."

"I know he'll be fine. Don't like to keep anyone waiting." Jack sighed. "Why's he got to be so heavy?!"

"Jack, he's not heavy. He's my moron."

"He's like a sack of potatoes."

"Like a sack of something!" Fred replied.

The rhythm of the six train and the long day lulled the children to sleep in the subway car. Joey and Patty sat silently across the way, nodding off every few seconds as they held onto one another. Henry stared at the ground, though he was aware of everything that happened around him. Proper train etiquette. He was taught by the best, his father, and he learned well. He had been with his father on this trip dozens of times before, but he never thought he'd find himself on the train without him. But there he was.

Kristie's head fell on his shoulder, and for a moment—just a moment—he stirred; he reached out for the railing next to him. For that moment he realized how alone they were, and if anything happened… After all, this wasn't his seat. This was his father's seat when they took the subway downtown together and back again. How'd this all come to pass? When was this ride going to end, and what was he going to do? The overhead intercom interrupted his momentary panic, announcing the consecutive train stops in a guttural life-worn voice, and he knew the six train wasn't far away from where he needed to be.

They would be waiting for them, his parents. It was always a comfort to know you always had a home filled with people who love you waiting at the other end of the ride. He supposed to himself that there was a time in everyone's life when they thought they were special—that they were different, that they stood out, unique and alone. It was a burden and a blessing, and even though he was only a boy still, Henry knew that feeling would follow him his entire life.

He always knew he was different. He just didn't realize how much. He knew the responsibilities he carried on his shoulders were greater than the others. And he knew someday he'd be called upon to do things that would test him and bring him to a newfound glory; it was something hard to register as a kid, but he felt it in his heart. It had to do with the angels. It was funny. He saw them for the first time that day, but he felt as though he'd known them his entire life—as if they'd always been there with him from the start. They were with him now, and he knew it. It was the calm that quelled his panicked heart. Defying subway convention, he looked up at the ceiling as the train charged up the tracks on his way home.

Jack & Fred sat atop the train car with George stretched out across their laps, resting his spirited self. They looked down into the train car, sensing the boy. George awakened occasionally as if drugged on heavy cold medication, mumbling things every now and again, still not realizing that he had passed away some time ago.

"Where we going?" he asked.

The little one looked down at him. Jack patted him on the head.

"Taking a ride, George," Fred said to him.

"We goin' home?"

The angel looked over at Jack. "Yeah, but," he whispered, "takin' our boy home first."

"Good. Get him home. Parents are waiting."

"You can hear them, George?" Fred wondered.

"Yep, sure can."

Jack leaned over. "Sorry for the wait, George."

"I don't mind. You have things you need to do. You don't have time. Storm's coming soon."

"I know," Fred told him. "Saw the flakes earlier."

"Nah, not that," George grumbled as his spirit turned on its side. "It's coming. Big. And the boy. Gonna start mmfhh..."

"What?" The little one nudged the spirit. "George? What?!"

"I hear the ocean," he whispered with a smile, closing his eyes.

"What'd he say, Jack?"

"He's out of it, Fred. Don't bother. Let him rest. Man...they're gonna go crazy when they find out we've dragged him along this far."

"We couldn't help it. You heard the parents. Who's going to watch after the kid...and the other kids? We had to make sure."

"Fred. Fred. I'm not arguing with you."

"I know. I'm just over-tired, Jack."

"Close your eyes. I'll wake you when we get there. Few more stops."

Jack didn't even get the last word out and Fred was asleep. The little one stretched himself out on the roof. The angel's ear was pressed flush against the metal, his head bouncing with every slight turn and motion of the coach. Beneath him, inside the train car, Henry stared up at the ceiling. Jack could hear the child's heart beating below, and the rhythm drew his thoughts away from the day and all its troubles. He looked off ahead, seeing the track unwind before them. The train began racing uphill, out of the darkness and the tunnels below, out into the light.

The sky was a dark menagerie of winter colors. George was right. It was coming, whatever it was. The train brakes screeched like a thousand fingernails on a chalkboard, and Jack was stirred back from wherever his mind had wondered. *How long was he away?* He looked down onto the platform and saw Henry running into the arms of his mother and father, who were waiting for him. They loved their boy. Jack was beginning to understand that feeling very quickly. The other children followed them as they went down the platform stairs to the street below. For a moment, Jack thought he saw Henry's eyes take a glance back, but Jack ducked away. He regretted that he did that almost immediately. Time seemed to drift away from him again. It was only when the train slowed to a crawl and opened all of its doors that Jack forced himself to shake the floating sensation from his head. He listened to the train's compressors hum and saw the motorman walk across the platform, as the downtown train waited on the other side.

Jack was so preoccupied with his thoughts he didn't realize the motorman was himself an angel disguised as a person. They did that sometimes. The man looked upward at his angelic brother, who was staring back at him. The look caught Jack off guard, and for a moment he thought another person was able to see him as he was, like Henry had. Jack nodded at him and the man reached into his breast pocket, pulling out a musical pocket watch, examining the time.

"We leave in twenty-eight minutes."

"Sorry?"

The man glanced at the train through his half-rimmed glasses.

"Twenty-eight. You have time to get situated. You *do* need a ride home?"

Jack clenched his fists, frowning with pure disdain in his eyes.

"Who do you think you are?" he asked horribly offended.

"I was merely—"

"Merely take a walk, chief. I'm not—no. No! I…absolutely not! Vulture! Go see where you have to go!" He shook his head, disgusted.

The gentleman shrugged and put away his watch as he strode across the platform.

Jack's heart was racing. *Why did he ask? Where did he get the gall to…* The train ride home for good was not something he ever conceived of being on—especially without Fred. Angels were leery of the station for that reason. It was a dead-end for human passengers, and also, it seemed, for the angels that watched over them. Jack had forgotten where they were and was angry more at himself than the motorman for informing him of it.

When angels were recalled to heaven for whatever reason, they were usually transported back upstairs by train, whether they wanted to go or not. Oftentimes this took place because request angels, like Jack & Fred, grew too attached to their temporary charge or station downstairs when they weren't supposed to be. To be recalled back, brought about a spring of unending sadness in them. The request angels' dedication and love was so great that, when all that they lived for was taken away, they had to be taken back home by some other means than their own wings. The agony suffered by the angels was like dousing butterfly wings with water. It rendered them unable to fly.

Fred yawned and stretched, feeling as though he hadn't slept in forever.

"Hey!" Jack shook him awake, happy to see him here. "Rip Van Winkle. Get flappin' kid. I'm out here all by myself. We got stuff to do."

"Oh man! Where are we?"

"End of the line."

"What?"

"The train, Fred. Last stop. Grab George. Let's get the hell out of here!"

"The kid!"

"He got off with the others a while ago. Henry's parents were waiting for them, just like we hoped."

"You saw his parents? Why didn't you wake me? What'd they look like?"

"Like Ward and June Cleaver. I dunno! They look like someone's parents."

"Shoulda woke me, Jack!"

"I—"

"You fell asleep too?"

"No. I don't know. Kinda nodded off. Just—"

"I'm *so* sorry I fell asleep on you."

"It's cool, Fred. It's fine."

"Yeah, but I wanted to see the kid again. Damn!"

"You needed the rest, little wing. We both do. C'mon. Grab George and let's go."

The little one shook his head, looking all dejected.

"Go *where*? Where are we going, Jack?"

"Don't start. We have to take George upstairs. It's really late now. We've got to get him checked in with St. Peter. He's way overdue."

"Then what's a few hours more?"

They stopped midway. The wind was whipping through them. Jack's hair was flying against his face.

"You're not serious…are you Fred?" The little one went silent. "Oh I get it. You're leaving this to me. This is going to be my fault, isn't it?" Jack sighed, looking off into the distance, holding an armful of George's spirit.

"Hey Jack," a voice called.

Jack wheeled around. Fred was using George's spirit like a ventriloquist's dummy, holding his spirit's droopy head and moving his limp jaw with his hand. George was completely unconscious the entire time.

"Let's go visit the kid again!" Fred said out of the corner of his mouth, looking completely unconvincing. *"Ain't that right Fred?"* Fred cocked George's head back and turned it toward Jack, then back at himself.

"Visit the kid, George? Really?" Fred went.

Jack stared at Fred playing with the unconscious spirit with big eyes.

"Yeah, Fred! Why not?" the little one pantomimed. *"What the hell else do we have to do tonight?"*

Fred continued to converse with himself. "But George, don't we have to take you upstairs?"

"Nah, it's alright. I'm dead anyway. All my appointments are cancelled." The little one started to break apart laughing, despite his best efforts to keep a straight face.

"Ya got a point there, George."

"*Know what else's cool, Fred?*"

Jack's eyes bulged.

"What, George?"

"*Besides being able to eat anything I want and not gain any pounds, I'm gonna be in paradise forever after, and I don't have to pay off any of my leftover credit card bills. Woo-hoo!*"

Jack's arms were crossed over his chest. He shook his head wildly.

"You're a crazy, sick, lunatic angel. You know that?"

Fred shrugged laughing. "*Whaaaat...*"

"No really, Fred. The Old Man was right. Our old pal Salierno was right on the money too. You have parts on order kid, seriously."

"Well?"

"Let's take George back upstairs."

"Ugh. C'mon, Jack! If—"

"If—if—they're crowded, Fred. If the line goes on forever, we'll just take him with us and check back to see the kid. Good enough?" Fred raised an eyebrow. "C'mon, little one!" Jack said with his hands on his hips.

"Oh...alright. Killjoy. Peter will probably be clearing the line person after person today. Then they'll reassign us to someone new and we won't be able to—"

"Let's just see, okay?"

"Yeah! Fine!"

"Lord. Alright, navigator. Point the way!" Jack mumbled, "Hello, unemployment check."

"What?"

"They're gonna fire us, Fred. You know that."

"They can't fire us. They'd *miss* us!"

"Ya know, Fred, I'm getting kind of used to George being here."

"Yeah, he's kinda like a favorite old duffle bag. Hello, Duffle," Fred said with a smack.

"*Whack-a-doo,*" Jack grumbled. He looked backward at the station, wondering why Fred hadn't said anything. He must've noticed. A shiver ran up his back as they flew away. They weren't going anywhere...*yet.*

{ Chapter 9 }

Determined Strides

Madison was waiting by the window again. Snow fell gently upon the campus. She watched as a lone figure made his way across the school's promenade. He walked in firm, determined strides as darkness fell and faint light set in the west. The tall, slender spirit moved deliberately to one of the outlying houses adjacent to the football field, which the school owned. It was a small broken-down wooden house that acted as the school's legal department; it stood in stark contrast to its angelic residents, not the least of which was Sidney, the barrister, and his assistant, who just plain hated the place.

Madison wrung her hands over and over; there was always some phantom pang about the weather she could never get over. Despite her angelic nature, her hands were always freezing. The executive assistant looked like a small China doll come to life. She was as precious now as she was so many years ago when she was human. She tossed the door aside, shivering as the cold air hit her head on.

"Get inside! It's freezing out!"

Snow blew through the front door in a rush as Sidney stepped inside.

"You're always freezing," he said. "Why're you still here, Maddie? I thought I told you to go home. You were supposed to be off an hour ago."

"I had some things to arrange. Give me that," she said, grabbing the barrister's hat, pulling his trench coat off his shoulders. "You're late."

"Hear anything?"

"Nothing yet."

"Damn."

"It's still early, Sidney. How'd everything go on your end?"

"They made contact with the boy."

"It's for real then?"

"Yes. It's for real, Mads."

"Coffee? Tea?"

Sidney unfurled his scarf. "Whatever," he said, making his way to his desk. "What is that perfume? *Obsession*?"

"I love that scent!" Madison shined.

"That's one of us."

"What do you know?"

"About perfumes? Obviously not much."

"You'd probably get along better with my twin, Gabby. She loves jasmine. So, Jack & Fred. Unbelievable."

"You never liked them."

Madison teetered on one foot, examining her nails. Her other hand was pressed precariously on her hip. "I like them just fine. I don't have a problem with them…other than…"

"Other than *what?*"

"Well, they're rude."

"Rude."

"Yes. And, and angels aren't supposed to act like that. They're supposed to be model beings. These two…they barge in and out of our offices like a heard of elephants making a giant racket. My papers usually go flying all over the place. Plus, hello, they're always in trouble with the upstairs. And the tall one calls me *toots*, and I swear he's hitting on me."

"He is. Didn't you two once—"

Madison turned up her nose and looked away. Sidney chuckled as he shifted a few items on his desk.

"And the little one once called me," Madison leaned close. Sidney feigned worry. "*Snootpuss*. I don't have a snootpuss, Sidney. I'm just very into my job. They just…don't like, *me*. I can't see why. I'm nice. I'm cute. I'm—"

"You're too stuffy. That my dear, is your problem."

Madison stamped her foot so hard she nearly broke through the floorboards.

"Easy there, Rumplestiltskin," Sidney barked. "I know this isn't the Ritz, but for now it's home."

"I am just *organized*. That's all, Mr. Barrister. And I'll have you know if I'm not needed—"

"Would you relax. Organized. Are you kidding?"

"No, I'm not kidding, and if your angels understood that—"

"That's just the thing, hon. Jack & Fred don't *do* organized. And neither do I. Not everything in this life or any other fits inside a neat little box. You'd do well to remember that."

"Well, someone has to be on top of things. Can't just do everything haphazardly. Nothing'll get done with slap-dash—"

"Okay, okay. You made your point. I need you, okay?"

"Well, yes."

"I feel like I'm still in court."

"*They* are something, aren't they?"

Sidney raised an eyebrow. "Yeah, they are."

"Did you eat?"

"No, I can't handle food now."

"Yeah, well I can, Sidney." Madison sat down across the way, wondering to herself aloud, "It's a curious thing. I've never heard of anything like that happening. Just doesn't make sense. What are you looking for?"

"I'm looking for…wait."

"Wha…"

"Shh, shh. Do you….listen. The teletype."

The two spirits moved with haste to the next room, seeing the pre-fax machine device churning out a paper communication with a loud, repetitive ratcheting sound that shook the very table it was sitting on. Madison shook her head.

"How out of date is that thing?"

Sidney grabbed the paper sheet, his eyes darting left to right, trying to read the communiqué.

"I like this *thing*."

"Typewriters, old clocks, that phone, even this loud thing. When are you going to remove these antiquated pieces of machinery?"

"I keep you around don't I?"

Madison frowned.

"Besides Maddie, these antiquated pieces of machinery keep me in touch."

"With the folks upstairs?"

Sidney ventured a glance toward her. "And my humanity. Among other things."

"What's it say?" she asked, nodding toward the sheet.

"Seems like they're on their way. They were spotted twenty minutes ago."

"They going to see Flo?"

"Yep. She and Ida have some kind of surprise party planned."

"Oh good Lord. They'll be raising the roof for days over there. Literally."

"I know," the barrister said with a sigh as he crushed the paper into a ball and lobbed it at the trash pail. It bounced off the rim and landed somewhere behind the furniture. "It's alright. We the need the time."

"What about the spirit they picked up?"

"George the Moron?"

"Sidney!" Madison smacked his arm. Sidney gave her a double-take; it was still his office.

"*George* is with them."

"Oh my goodness. Give me the phone. They'll be expecting him upstairs. He's overdue! They can't do this! He's languishing down here too."

The barrister smashed down on Madison's small hand, smacking the receiver back into the cradle. Madison's heart raced.

Sidney realized how rough he was. "Maddie, just leave it alone," he nodded. "Okay?"

Madison nodded, puling her hand away from the phone, crossing her arms before her with a shiver.

The barrister looked away. "Sorry. It's just...too much rain."

"What do you mean?"

"It's been said that into every life a little rain must fall. For them, there's been too much rain for one life. Even one as long as theirs."

Sidney shook his head, digging his fingers into his temple.

Madison crept around behind him, putting her hand on his shoulder, massaging his back. "I've never seen you this worried."

"You were right, Maddie. You said it earlier. We're going to lose this one. You know that. It's like shoveling crap against the tide."

"Then why bother?"

"You know the reason." Sidney inadvertently found himself glancing over at a picture of a young woman on his desk. "When I was human, they answered a prayer of mine, once upon a time," he said, admiring the picture. "Anyway, Peter said he's going to call. He'll call. He's never let me down."

"How about dinner, Sidney?"

"Why're you so nice today, Madison?" The angelic assistant gave him a look that would turn one pale, then fell away at Sidney's smile.

"I'll get things going," she said as she drifted into the kitchen.

Sidney called to her. "What would I do without you looking after this place?"

She peeked her head around the corner. "Go crazy."

"Too—"

"Late for that," Madison finished.

"Yeah. Dinner sounds good."

As the night drew on, it seemed as if the sky grew even darker than it should have been, and the snow kept falling in wet dollops upon the ground. Sidney was allowed a brief moment of peace and found himself looking out the window, his belly full, the dishes still sitting in the kitchen sink. The campus was covered in a carpet of frozen powder, but it wasn't cold enough for it to last more than a few hours, the barrister mused to himself. Madison was standing in the doorway. She had been for moments now, but Sidney's brain just registered what the corners of his eyes had been telling him.

He turned around and stared at her hypnotically. "What is it?"

"They're not coming," she said, holding up another communication.

Sidney regarded her in silence.

"Off the map. What's that mean, Sidney?"

"It's like…(sigh) not according to plan, Madison. You know? When an angel does his or her duty, then goes beyond that for whatever reason, dealing with things not assigned to them."

"Is that what Jack & Fred are doing now?"

"No. They're just doing their job…yeah. That's right."

The barrister got out of his seat and stretched. His spirit felt as tired and worn as his body in his past life. The grandfather clock in the living room tolled, and somehow not trusting it, he stared at the watch on his wrist. They were running out of time. He took a sip of the tepid coffee that had been placed before him an hour before and went back to his office, back to work. There had to be way to help them. There just had to be.

{ Chapter 10 }

Something Wonderful at Last

Jack & Fred flew across the Bronx on that dark and blustery winter's night. Fred knew that the *something wonderful* he and Jack felt earlier was but a heartbeat away. It was there, at the house with the yellow awning. As they hung over the avenue, a gentle hum resonated in the little one's ears.

"This is it. This is where we're supposed to be."

The angels perched themselves with George on one of the girders of the elevated rail station up the block from Henry's house for what seemed like forever and a day, and a half. The snow fell steadily as George snored, his head bobbing up and down, flanked on either side by the both of them. They had hardly spoken a word over the last several hours, which for them was quite unusual and probably a record to be taken down somewhere. Their hearts were racing in complete anticipation, so much so they could hardly breathe. After a while, it was the only sound.

Jack looked around. The ground was covered over with white, and for a moment all the dirt and filth of the city streets was buried. There were no cars moving, no people, no hustle and bustle. It was all quiet—nothing but the snowflakes, light as air, shaking down from heaven as if by a sugar sifter.

It was late. The boy had to be asleep by now. They had to check in on him. They just had to see. Fred grabbed George by the left arm, and Jack took the other, and without so much as a word they lifted off the el. Their wings flapped away the snow that had accumulated over the hours, and they set off into the muted glow of the streetlights. If you held your breath in that moment, the city became its own wonderland, a place that you could never see yourself leaving.

If only in that moment.

Jack stopped as they neared the house.

"That's…*impossible*."

The little one looked at him.

"We've been here before. Fred. We've been here *lots* of times before. Fred, this is *our* house. This is the house we've always flown to when we were here in the Bronx."

"What?" the little one looked around. "Are you sure?"

"Yes, I'm sure. They have the TV antennae on the roof that looks like a cross. This is it. I just never noticed the yellow awning before. This has always been our home away from home. I just never looked down."

The little one rubbed his mouth, admiring the roof from the height they were at.

"Jack, I remember when we used to watch over a little girl here. I remember when they moved this house from three blocks over, where it originally was. I remember a tree, right there in front, and it's gone. And the roof used to have a cover along its sides. You and I used that side of the roof, right over there, as our downstairs wall."

Jack had bright eyes. "Yes, I remember!"

"I betcha she still lives here, the little girl. I bet she's still here."

"Why would she be here?" Jack asked.

"One of the parent's voices, sounded familiar," Fred said, closing his eyes, feeling the impressions in the air about him, warm and whispering through his soul. "She's still here. She's his mother."

Jack was awestruck.

"But Fred, do you think—"

"Jack," he cut him off, "*I know it*," the little one said with those excited, glaring eyes.

"Hmm. I guess the Big Man—"

"Works in mysterious ways, my friend," the little one said, tapping Jack on the shoulder.

"Well," Jack sighed apprehensively, "Certainly blew my socks off."

"Sure did," George mumbled. "You guys should get some shoes. Something with good arch support."

Jack lit up. "Hey Fred, look who's awake? What's up buddy-boy?"

"I was in retail once upon a time. Trust me. Do *not* get yourselves anything that fits tight in the store. They never break in."

Fred spun George's groggy head around.

"George, what're you talking about?"

The man spoke with his eyes closed, looking like he was three shades to the wind.

"Shoes. When they fit in the store. When they feel like slippers, those are the ones to take home. 'Cause they're perfect. I used to work in retail. "

Fred looked at him as if he were nuts. "Uh…yeah, you said that."

"You guys make sure you get somethin' with a good arch, and make sure you have enough room in the toe box. Especially you," he said, pointing to Fred, eyes still shut like a newborn puppy. "You've got a wide foot, Fred. And it's okay, honestly. Don't be embarrassed. But do me a favor. Don't get anything that pinches or squooshes the toes. You're looking at an E or double E width. You get anything D width and your feet are gonna be a real train wreck. I mean they're gonna feel like they're in a vice all day. You also need somethin' with some serious tread. I mean Jack…where are you?"

George looked around with his eyes seemingly stapled shut.

"Yes…(cough) George?"

"Where are you?"

"Um…here," he waved to the confused and blinded man.

"Oh. You guys—Fred still there?"

"He…" Jack fell apart laughing. "He's still—*Erghhm…God help me*— he's still here with us, George."

"What the hell! You keep movin' around!"

Fred stared, open-mouthed, with his one free hand on his hip, visibly disgusted with the moron's tirade. But George wouldn't stop.

"Anyway…you guys go all over the place, nonstop. Your feet hurt that much and trust me, you're gonna be *pissed*, pardon my French. And don't get me started on blisters."

Jack was trying to stifle his laughter with his free hand, so much that he nearly dropped George several times because his entire body was convulsing.

The moron was nose to nose with the angel.

"Hey, don't feel bad, man. People never get the bigger width 'cause they think their friends are gonna see the size. Trust me, if your friends are that nosey, they ain't worth it. It's like underwears…"

Jack tossed George into Fred's arms, and let him hold the man for a bit. He couldn't float there any longer. He was choking with laughter.

George continued. "Who's gonna know you wear the bigger size? Meanwhile you're comfortable all day." He pointed with authority. "There's nothing worse then havin' tight, ill-fitting shorts. Your equipment's gonna be all…"

The little one squawked, "Alright George, enough! Enough! Sure, Jack! Go ahead and fly away! Leave me with this—this lunatic!"

Jack flew back over and grabbed his portion of the spirit.

"What? (cough) He's right!"

"I know he's right. That's all the heck I need, another director. Shoes and underwear. Are ya kiddin' me?"

George's twisted facial expressions copycatted Fred's verbal onslaught.

"Are you? You are! You're making fun of me. So help me, George, I'll put you through next week! I'll—"

Jack restrained the little one. "Slow down there, fireball!"

George butted in, shouting at Fred. "Yeah, don't blame me for them boats of yours!" he nodded at the self-conscious angel's feet.

"I'm gonna kill 'im Jack!"

Fred flailed at George while Jack played U.N. between them.

"George, go back to sleep! Jack rubbed away the tears of laughter in his eyes with his forearm. "And you…c'mon, little wing. Gimme a break here!"

"But—"

"Hey!" Jack pointed a threatening finger at him.

The little one backed down. "Yeah, fine."

George continued though. "Don't come cryin' to me when your feet are killin' ya and they look like rutabagas because you're too stupid to—"

Jack frowned. "Hey, George. Look. Ice cream!"

"Where?" George zipped around with shut eyes.

Jack's fist landed atop the spirit's head, knocking him out once more.

Fred was still insulted.

Jack said to him, shaking his head, "Oh sure, the old guy you mind. But you don't care when I smack the moron around."

"Well, he's annoying! And you shut up, Jack! Surrounded by crazy people my whole life. Can we go visit the kid now?"

Jack smiled that giant toothy smile of his.

The little one frowned. "Go ahead, keep laughing. You're gonna have a fit or something."

Jack sighed. "Ugh, God. *I needed that.*"

The angels flew over and landed with a running touchdown upon the boy's rooftop, like parachutists in an open field. They set George against the rim of the flat rooftop, the place they used to lean against like their wall in heaven, many, many years ago.

A pair of yellow feline eyes watched them from below in the backyard.

"This way," Fred beckoned as the angels dashed toward a small hatch people used to gain access to the rooftop. Jack stopped.

"Where are you going?"

"The kid. What're you—"

"Whoa, whoa, hold on there, chief."

"What?"

"Quietly. We're just gonna look in on him."

"What're you talking about?"

"No, what're *you* talking about, Fred? You didn't actually think we were going to…"

"Going to what?"

"Talk to him. Did you?"

"Maybe."

"Fred."

The little one was nearly jumping out of his skin.

"You worry too much, Jack. You always do. You'd make a cup of coffee nervous!"

"Fred! Come here, listen," Jack pulled him away, and Fred shrugged him off, hard. "Look at me! We don't know what this is all about. We could be making a really big mistake."

The little one's head dropped. "Mistake? Come on, Jack."

"Fred…"

"I'm not letting you do this to us. This is no mistake. Let me have this. I know you. I know you worry, but for God's sake let us have this. I'm all excited here. Don't burst the balloon, Jack."

"Okay."

"Don't—"

"I said okay! Now will you open the damn roof hatch! And quietly. Don't wake the whole house."

Fred smiled. He popped the hatch and the angels floated down a ladder and onto the top floor. It was dark, but that strange hum was in their ears again, beckoning them louder than perhaps it ever had. They felt the boy's presence down the hall. It felt as if they had known him forever. They glided down the hallway and moved through the door like a dream, and there he was, sitting up in bed nice as you please, waiting for them. And it scared the crap out of the both of them.

{ Chapter 11 }

Dinner for Three

Jack jolted backwards. "Jesus, Mary, and Joseph!" he exclaimed, scaring Fred half to death, more than himself. The little one clapped his hand over Jack's mouth, and they looked around to see if anyone else heard them—anyone besides the boy, who had smothered his own mouth because he was laughing so loudly.

"So, how're your feet?" Henry asked.

The little one's heart raced.

"What?"

"From the chase. That had to hurt."

"They're um...fine. We're okay."

The boy smiled at them.

"Good."

Jack peeled Fred's hand away as he and the little one hovered there, staring at Henry. They were so stunned they could barely breathe. He was so little too, just a kid. They didn't expect this to happen *twice!*

The little one grabbed Jack by the arm and yanked him closer.

"Uh, uh...err, humph, he, he..."

"I know."

"He can see us, Jack. He's awake and he can see us. Again! My goodness!" he said in a somewhat, audible whisper. They were so completely bowled over.

Henry looked into the little one's big round eyes. *"Fred."*

Fred blinked his delicate eyelashes. It was like the world slowed to a gentle crawl.

Henry looked at them. "So, Jack & Fred. Are you brothers?"

"No," Jack said to the boy. "We're a double act, a team!"

"Like Hope and Crosby," Fred suggested.

"That's right. Like Hope and Crosby," Jack agreed.

"Or Abbott and Costello."

"Yes. That's true. Them too."

"Or Bert and Ernie."

Jack began to look flustered.

"Batman and Robin. R2 and 3PO. Han Solo and Chewbac—"

"Okay, Fred!" Jack squawked, suddenly realizing how loud he was. "He gets-the-point."

"You're an idiot," the little one said with a swat. Fred waved his hand in front of the boy's face, still checking to see if this was real or not.

"You *really* can see us. And…and hear us, right now, right kid?"

The boy looked at the angels for a moment.

"Yes."

"Pinch my arm," the little one insisted with grim determination.

"Alright, but it's gonna hurt."

"Doesn't matter. Just do it, kid. I have to know," Fred insisted.

"Alright."

"Ow! I felt that! Jack, I felt that!"

Jack frowned. "Well, what'd you expect? What'd that prove?"

"I thought maybe *I* was dreaming here. I'm not, am I?" He leaned closer to Henry, touching his shoulder. "How is this possible?"

The boy shook his head, looking into the angel's eyes.

"I don't know." The boy turned to Jack, who had no answer; all he had was joy across his face. But the faintest touch of worry touched the edges of his soul.

The little one admired the child. "You waved at me today."

"Yeah, you waved back."

"I'm Fred."

"I know. I heard you guys talking…after you stopped the car. You saved him, the old man. You saved Joey and Patty, too. They're my friends. They were going to get killed by that car. I saw you pull them out of the street. I saw you do it."

The little one whispered with a nod, looking away. "Yeah."

"What if you didn't get there on time?" The angels looked at the boy; his brain couldn't register what was going on, but his heart told the whole story.

"I'm Henry by the way."

The little one reached out and shook the boy's hand.

"This…is Jack," Fred said exaggeratedly, slapping his partner on the back. "He's my road dog."

"Bark. Bark," Jack went as he reached for the boy's hand as well. The angel regarded him a moment. The boy had such a look about him; it was his eyes. They sparkled.

"I knew you two were angels. Couldn't be anything else. I never expected to see you. I mean, *really* see you."

Jack whispered, "Neither did we."

Fred wondered. "You've never seen any others like us, have you?"

"No. Not for real, I mean. I've seen pictures in books, but not *real*. Gonna be really disappointed if all this turns out to be a dream."

Fred sighed. "Same here, kid," he said, needing to sit on the bed.

"You're not a dream though, are you?"

Jack sat on the toy trunk across the way.

"No," he said. "We're as real as you are, Henry."

It was difficult for the nine-year-old's brain to make heads or tails of this.

"This isn't supposed to happen, is it?" he asked. " Us meeting like this. Us meeting at all. Is it?"

Jack closed his eyes, shaking his head somberly.

"No, kid. It's not."

"Ever happen before?"

"Nope," Jack added.

"Oh well," he said with a shrug. "You guys hungry?"

The angels looked at each other, then back at the boy as if it was their birthday, and maybe it was. *"Come on,"* he waved.

The boy walked them quietly down to the kitchen, whispering as they floated beside him. It was like standing next to the heater. You could just feel the warmth they brought along with them. As they moved, the boy noticed a scent about the angels; it wasn't rose petals, but it was something so pleasing to the nostrils that your nose almost couldn't keep up with it. It was literally like a breath of fresh air—something that had the qualities of baking cookies, pizza, and Chinese food; all at once recognizable, and overwhelmingly joyous to the senses. That's what they were. Pure joy. Just that.

The boy whispered, "I've been waiting up for you. I kinda figured you'd be coming here. I don't know why. But I didn't know what you guys liked to eat. I was going to do a whole cookies and milk thing." Fred's eyes lit up. "But I figured that's a Santa Claus snack and forget it. So I was thinking of nuking you some leftover baked ziti."

Jack's expression spoke volumes. This kid was smart, and someone in this household cooked. Jack & Fred were never going anywhere else again!

They tried their mightiest to restrain their need to talk aloud. *They were so happy!*

"You guys *do* eat, right?" the boy asked.

Jack grabbed a handful of Fred's belly.

"See this? One hundred percent pure chub!"

"Ow! Stop that!"

"You can pinch more than an inch! More like a foot and a half. Look at this!"

The little one wheeled around smacking him hard.

"Geez, Jack!"

Jack smiled at the boy. "P.S. We don't miss too many meals, kid."

Fred rubbed his bruised chubbies. "Dope. I'm going to be all black and blue now. Look at that! He does this to me all the time."

Jack grabbed him. "Didn't I tell you not to wake the whole house? Now shush!"

The little one frowned as the other two went into the kitchen. He floated there in the hall with his arms crossed over his chest. Jack reached around the corner and yanked him into the kitchen, much to Fred's chagrin.

Henry kept the lights off, so to not wake anyone. The street lamps from the neighboring avenue lit up the kitchen through the curtains. The room was a dull orange glow, but the angels themselves seemed to radiate from the inside. Funny thing was, they didn't look like any angels Henry had ever seen in books; you know, the ones with the white cotton wings and flowing gowns, playing musical instruments or something like that. These two would definitely *not* adorn a Christmas tree of any kind; that was for sure. They had a more rugged look to them; it was like the difference between something showcased in a store window and something that was actually used in real life.

It was obviously true. Raphael, the painter, was a genius, despite his massive ego and lack of belief in the holy imagery he painted. The angels resembled their painted images with a delicate perfection no photograph could have duplicated finer. Without consciously realizing they were doing it, the angels moved the chairs around the kitchen table, making sure they were side by side with one another. That's the way they sat. That's the way it always was.

Jack & Fred.

The boy busied himself with pulling out plates and utensils, insisting that they sit as he prepared everything for his guests. Occasionally he'd see them nodding to one another out of the corner of his eye, unable to comprehend how this was at all possible. They were angels, and knew things no human mind could ever conceive, but this simple act of kindness left them awestruck. It was more than that, though. They had to keep reminding themselves: He could see them!

They were handsome little angels, the both of them. They had very tanned skin, as if they lived on a tropical beach a long way away from the city they called home. They weren't wearing specific clothes, but they weren't naked either. It was just something a human eye, even one as blessed as Henry's, could not make out. They were just *there*.

Jack was right. They *did* have small chubby bodies, and adorable faces. There was no doubt they had bellies and weren't shy about it like people were.

It just made them look healthy (Fred a little more so than Jack). Jack was the taller one. And more than once when they argued or 'discussed' things, Jack referred to Fred as "the little one over here." Truthfully, though, they weren't much bigger than the boy, but their personalities made them larger than life.

The boy was piling ziti onto plates and noticed there was a haze and glow about them at all times, like starlight dashing through foggy air. It was a constant warmth and a feeling like your spirit could leave the confines of its failing mortal form and be free to be fly; forever happy someplace beyond.

Henry waited on the microwave and sat there talking with them. You felt safe with them—safer than you could ever possibly imagine, as if nothing bad existed back outside in the world around you. And you knew deep down, if something bad was out there, the two of them would smack the heck out of it double quick!

Henry knew this shouldn't have been. He kept telling himself he was living a story. In his mind, he was of no importance to anyone. He wasn't a saint or a pope or someone important that was supposed to have angels visiting him in person. But they were here, and they were eating. The kid was rattling around with the ice trays, getting cubes for the cups while Jack grabbed the two-liter of Coca-Cola from the fridge. *Look at them. There they are!* It was a very late dinner for them. They had been waiting to see Henry again all day.

Sitting there at the table, you couldn't help but notice that Fred liked to hum and swing his feet over and over when he ate, moving his head from side to side as if he was constantly listening to happy music playing somewhere.

Both would get quite animated when they'd talk, too. Neither could stay put or hover in place over their chairs for very long. As they'd move about, you could see that, despite the chubbiness around the sides, they had muscles like tightly-wound springs and could probably lift tons; something like the Russian weightlifters you always see in the Olympics, with the barrel arms and beer bellies.

When their wings fluttered or rustled, they made a sound you couldn't mistake for anything else. They moved their wings just as you would move your arms or legs, fingers or toes. Every now and again they'd unfold and refold

{ My Guardian Angels Jack & Fred }

their wings, which looked like eagle feathers, darkly colored in mahogany and auburn. They even had bits of lavender coloring the feathers around the back. As they got into their conversation, you'd see them regularly drift upward, floating for a moment, refolding their wings and sitting back down again. It was what a person would do with their legs if they were sitting on them for too long. Even in the hazy room, your eyes would catch dust flopping off their feathers like construction workers who never came home from a job to wash up. They were both a bit self-conscious about that. Jack's only excuse for it was that they flew over Jersey quite a bit.

It wouldn't stop them from nitpicking at their features all the time, though, especially Jack, who would regularly run his fingers through his hair to move it off his face. If you caught him, he'd smile at you because it was an old habit that he didn't realize he was doing until someone stared. But then again, not many people did that.

Fred was like a bouncing ball of joy that would not stop once he started talking, and Jack would have to try and corral him. He seemed like the big brother or the parent, and Henry and Fred were like the kids. Jack didn't mind. It was what he was supposed to do, and he knew that.

Jack & Fred explained that they were mostly city angels but they traveled often, so their wings got dirty, their hands and feet were calloused, and they had broad shoulders and strong backs that could pull ox carts, with exceedingly powerful legs and wings. They were *very* strong for their size, physically and mentally. They were not averse to playing a game of rugby with some of the big boys, like their friend St. Michael and the other Archangels. Fred explained that they loved football; but rugby was their favorite.

They played on a great wide open space called the Salisbury plain with the big boys when they actually had time to do such things and could rustle up enough guys for a whole team.

Jack described some of the other angels as far bigger and more imposing in size, but easy to take down once you hit them behind the knees, or *in the gut for good measure,* Fred added.

One of the larger angels actually described them in a memorable way, after he took a hit from the pair during one of the games. He said, "Lord, they may be small and cute to look at, but they'll really knock ya on your ass if you mess with them!" And I think that says it all.

Free time was few and far between. They never stopped flying. There was no home to go to, only stopovers and a wall in heaven that they leaned against when they needed to think; it was something of a resting place more than anything else, and a good cover for a well-stocked fridge full of food goodies. But no one knew about that except them—and now, Henry. For some reason they kept arguing over the number of jars of vinegar eggplant they had left.

For angels, even ones that looked the way they did, you could see that they both appeared tired, almost exhausted, like they never slept. Both of them had dark circles around their eyes, as if they were wearier than they should have been. Even if he'd asked them, Henry realized they'd never admit it to him, though. It was just the same with the other angels they knew.

They told Henry stories about their friend Flo and her sister Ida who ran an angelic café atop a building's rooftop somewhere in the suburbs. It was at a college no less. Jack said it drove them crazy when Flo would pinch the heck out of their chubby, squeezable cheeks or squash them in giant hugs. But they loved her anyway.

The angels then described how they'd follow crosses on buildings, what they'd call guideposts, to show them the way to get something to munch when they weren't visiting human restaurants on their adventures. It was just like the TV antennae on Henry's roof. That's one of the reasons it was so easy to find him.

Here you are in my kitchen, an arm's length away. You're real.

He couldn't think of any other way to describe it: They just belonged here with him. Even though it was the first time they were meeting, the angels seemed like old relatives come back to visit. Maybe they were just supposed to be here all along.

How? both the boy and angels wondered. Maybe it just didn't matter; it just was. Some things didn't have answers. This was one of them. How else could you describe such a thing? Jack & Fred, who knew the ecstasy of heaven, never believed they could find such happiness on Earth. It had eluded them for so many years, and now it was here before them, and though they were witness to many miracles, one had never happened to them so personally as this.

It was as if the boy seeing them made them real, made them alive—like they had not existed before and now they did, and they wanted to tell the world about it. And so did Henry. But the world was asleep. It had been for so long.

"Blueberry waffles. Jack loves them," Fred told Henry.

Jack rubbed his full belly. "If dinner is anything like breakfast kid, you can guarantee we'll be back. Woo!"

Fred dropped his fork, making it clang against the plate. He reclined and rolled his eyes, his wings smooshing against the back of the seat.

"Ughhhh. Foodgasm! This was *so* good. Who in this house cooks?"

"My mom."

"Oh my God was this good! And we're eaters, so we know. Right, Jack?"

"Deeelicious kid. Man! Props to the chef."

"Alright, alright," Fred grumbled, shaking his head.

"I'll tell my mom when she gets up."

Jack sipped his soda. "Think she'll believe you?"

"Yes," the boy said directly.

Jack smiled. "Cool."

"She and my dad were freaked out when I was lost, and she said I had angels lookin' out for me because there was no way I was going to find a way home by myself. We were *really* lost. But somehow I just remembered where we were because of my Dad…"

Jack asked, "What were you doing down there?"

"Looking for Sesame Street."

The little one smacked the plate.

"Sesame Street? You mean like 'Can you tell me how to get, how to get to Sesame Street' Sesame Street?" Fred asked.

"Yup. My friend Joey once said that in the *Christmas Eve on Sesame Street* special they show Gordon and Maria and all of them getting off at 86th street. He's right, but you can't see where they go."

"Um…" Fred looked around mock-seriously. "It's a show, people!"

"Duh!" the boy returned. "I know that. But I...well. It's not down there."

Jack chuckled.

Fred picked some extra ziti off Jack's plate after clearing his own.

"You coulda got killed, kid. What's wrong with you?" the little one said, trying to act parental.

"I knowww, but..."

Jack's eyes brightened and he pointed at the boy.

"It was the girl."

Fred stopped mid-bite.

"Wasn't it?" Jack asked with a grin.

Henry recoiled as if someone had read his mind.

"What?"

"I knew it. Get out of there!" Jack said, smacking Fred's drifting fork. "She's a cute one, that one. I saw her."

Fred dropped his fork on the plate again, much to his partner's chagrin.

"Noisy Mcgee, would you *not* wake the parents please?!"

"Fine crabby! Always with you and the wings, Jack. He sees a nice set of wings and he's gone."

"The kid knows what I'm talkin' about Fred. Girl with the dimples and the hazel eyes. Shoot. That'd make anyone crazy. Right, Hen?" he winked. Henry grinned, all of a sudden, shy. Grabbing a napkin, Jack asked him. "What's her name kid?"

"Kristie."

Jack nodded. *"Nice."*

The little one smacked Jack across the arm. "Will you not give him the third degree please? He serves you dinner and you question him. Henry didn't expect the Spanish Inquisition."

Jack and Henry shouted simultaneously, thinking of the Monty Python sketch, *"Nobody expects the Spanish Inquisition!"*

Jack laughed. "You're good, kid! You're young and you know that one! Ha!"

"Thanks. We got PBS."

"I guess Fred does too. That's why he's so cranky tonight."

Jack looked sideways at his partner, who leaned over to confront him.

"Jack, why you bustin' this kid's chops?"

Jack tossed his napkin at Fred's face.

"I'm gonna bust *your* chops in a second, little wing."

Fred puffed up and floated above the table.

"I'm here! What's up?"

Jack stepped up and they started going head to head. The boy looked up at them in their angelic standoff.

"You're from the Bronx like me, aren't you?" he asked. They stopped and looked down at him. "Anyone for dessert?"

The angels escorted the boy back to his room some time later. The hours had just melted away, and it came as no surprise when they saw it was ten minutes past four and Henry had to wake up in about two hours for school. The angels were almost embarrassed. Fred was sitting on the edge of the bed poking the boy in the belly over and over, making him giggle uncontrollably. Jack was perched atop the bedpost, leaning over to ruffle his hair, swatting him with his wings.

"So," the boy asked. "Where do you guys go now?"

Fred explained. "Well we have to make a stop upstairs—"

"Ahem," Jack interrupted, not wanting to broach the subject of dragging along the spirit of a recently moved-on dead guy with them, and storing him on the roof while they ate dinner.

"And," Fred continued. "Yeah. Some, stuff..."

"Then what?" the boy asked.

Jack jumped down on the bed, knocking Fred to the ground and making Henry bounce in place under the covers.

"Fred shh!" Jack went with a wily grin. The little one wasn't too happy on the floor. Jack continued. "We really don't have a set schedule, kid. We go wherever the work takes us. We have couriers that'll drop us a line, give us a heads-up as where to go."

"It's true," Fred explained. "We've been told where to go most of our lives."

Jack agreed. "Uh, yeah. We stay mostly in New York, but we pretty much fly all over the place on Earth."

The little boy looked at them. "And you've seen all of it?"

"You can never see all of something, but we know our way around," Jack said.

Fred nodded. "These wings got a lotta mileage on 'em!"

Jack grabbed the little one by the neck and pulled him up off the floor where he'd been sitting.

"Ow, ow, ow! What is wrong with you, Jack?"

"What're you doing under the bed?"

"Trying to see something. What's under here?" the little one asked.

"Leave it, Fred. Fred!"

"What?"

"Leave-it-alone. He doesn't need you messing things up."

"But I just wanted—"

"Look at this!" Henry interrupted, as he ran to the window. "This is going to melt tomorrow," he said, looking at the backyard. "I'm gonna have to go in."

The little one turned. "Huh?"

"School."

"Oh. Ugh."

"I know," the boy said, shaking his head.

Jack said, "The sky isn't pink. Some reason, when it's pink you know you're going to get a ton of snow. You know you'll be home."

The boy looked at him, changing the subject. "You never answered my question, Jack." The angel turned to face him. "What if you didn't get there on time?"

"You mean your friends?"

"I mean, what if they got hit? What if Joey and Patty…" He thought with a shiver. "What if they got killed? What would have happened?"

Jack didn't move. His words were true.

"We would have taken them home with us."

"Have you done that before?"

"More times than you can possibly imagine," he said with a faint smile and glassy eyes.

The boy said, "When I was little, in kindergarten, we'd go out for recess on this grassy hill by the water. And we'd see these seaplanes take off. The engines would start up, and they'd get really loud and they'd race across the water. The sun was so bright you couldn't see where they were going. They'd take off, and never come back again. We always wondered where they went and nobody ever knew. I used to think they went to heaven." Fred looked over at Jack. "Is that where they go, Jack?" the boy asked. "Do they go to heaven?"

"Henry!" a voice suddenly called from the hallway.

Henry bounded out of bed.

"That's my mom! You guys want to meet my parents?" he asked excitedly.

Jack turned pale. Fred did not. Jack went, "Oh, shoot. If you can see us and you're awake, then maybe your folks can too. Rats!"

"Isn't that allowed?"

"Uh," Jack stammered. "We kinda need permission to appear to people and…oh, Fred?!"

"Hurry!" the little one waved.

"Henry, this, this is all amazing. It's been a blast! We'll be back. We promise. Come on, little wing!"

Jack darted across the room, towing Fred behind him.

"Bye, Hen!" he waved with a grin that overtook his whole self.

The angels spun around, putting their hands on their hips, and with rather muscular, intimidating faces they said "we'll be back" with a deep Austrian intonation.

{ Chapter 12 }

Trapped!

"Where're you going?" Henry asked as Jack fiddled with the window's lock.

"We're skidooin'!" Fred said.

"But why? I'm sure the guys upstairs wouldn't be too mad."

"Don't be too sure, Hen," the little one said, looking a little more worried than he should have been.

"Wait, you guys. Why go back? I don't get it."

Jack continued to wrestle with the lock, trying to heft open the window, but it didn't open. "What's goin' on with this stupid thing?" he muttered under his breath. "Because if your, *eerrrgghh*, parents see us…let's just say there's going to be a bit too much explaining to do. Since, um, Fred, you want to field this one?"

"No," he said crossing his arms.

"Fred! Well, kid…" Jack began, trying to power-lift the window from its immovable place. "We're kinda not supposed to appear to people…heh, heh…*eerrgggghh*…without permission from the guys upstairs. This is still *not* opening!"

The boy frowned. "It sticks."

"*Henry?*" the voice called, even louder this time.

"Shoot!" Fred snapped.

The boy seemed concerned. "Jack, you guys aren't gonna get in like major trouble are you?"

Jack looked up in thought, struggling as sweat poured down his brow.

"Uh, heck no! Shoot, why would you even ask such a thing?" Jack bit his lip and turned to Fred with the most spine-chilling glare you ever did see.

The little one urged, "Here Jack, door!"

Jack tackled his partner. "No, not that way, dopey! They're coming that way! C'mon!" the taller angel yelled, pulling him.

Henry just watched.

Jack ran to one end of the room, Fred the other, furiously looking for an escape. Not looking where they were going in such a rush, the two splashed right into one another.

"Ooof!" they went, falling in a crunch and springing up again.

Fred bellowed, "There's no escape for the angels this time!"

"Here!" Henry yelled. "Go ahead, float through the wall!"

Fred shook his head. "We don't do walls. Well, Jack can we do that?"

Jack gave him that look which Jack does so well. The little one shrugged. "Oh well."

He yanked Fred by the arm, noticing the shadows of Henry's parents as they approached from the hall. "Oh man, we're dead!"

Fred turned around franticly. "Closet!"

Jack spun around. "This is *not* a *Laverne and Shirley* episode!"

Fred smiled. "Say, there's another great double act, Jack."

Jack ran round in circles. "Um, um, um...under the bed!"

The angels dove headfirst under the bed and slammed into something, tons of somethings.

"Ow!" they went, rolling back out.

Fred popped up by Henry, rubbing his head. "Man! Look at all the crap you've got under here!"

"Sorry."

Jack grabbed the little one's arms. "C'mon!"

Fred kept rubbing his bruised noggin. "You could kill somebody with all this stuff!"

Henry shrugged, agreeing.

Jack was tearing the hair out of his head looking for somewhere to go in this confined space. "What is this, Houdini's House of Magic?!" And after seconds of running around frantically, he just threw his arms up. "That's it. We're toast!" he yelled.

The little one sighed. "Bet you George Bailey and Clarence never had these kinds of problems."

"It's over. If they can see us, let them see us, Fred. I'm—"

The little one stared up at the ceiling. "This ain't gonna help…"

And there they were. The boy's parents came through the door. If it wasn't for the boy's harrowing adventure the day before, they probably would've just yelled "stop making noise and go back to sleep!" as they often did. But all kidding aside, the boy did nearly give them both a heart attack with his little trip. So here they were.

Henry's mom looked at the boy. "We heard noises a few seconds ago. Are you alright?" The boy was shocked, confused, and amazed all at the same time.

"Um, yeah Ma. I was having this strange dream. I was trapped in this… room, and I…couldn't get out, and these big people were…coming, um… yeah," the boy said, running out of story to conjure. He looked upward, smiling at the two trapped heavenly spirits sticking themselves flush against the ceiling above him, looking like pancakes whose spatula went crazy. "But I, uh, I'm fine now. I woke up. I'm here. Hi!" the boy waved. "How are you?"

Dad looked at him strangely and turned to the boy's mom. "Uh-huh. That's a good thing. Why don't you try to lay back down and rest, Hen. You had one helluva day yesterday," Dad said, as he made his way to the window. "Aren't you hot in here? It's hot in here. Do you think it's hot in here?"

Henry's mother looked at the boy for a moment. The boy's dad was always overheated; he had some sort of thing for the cold. He was notorious for that. We don't know what it was exactly. His friends at worked dubbed him Mr. Freeze for obvious reasons. He was a riot on vacation. The first thing he would do when he entered the hotel room was lower the air conditioning with a certain wild enthusiasm. "If you're cold, go get a sweater for Pete's sake!" he would say. But for once, Dad's insatiable need for coolness came in handy.

"Yeah, Dad!" Henry blurted out. "My God it *is* hot in here. Oh, man.

Heat. Woo!" The parents both looked at the boy. The angels did as well. "We're, I mean, *I'm* choking to death. (hack, hack) It's a regular reptile house in here!"

Dad grabbed the window. "Alright, Hen. I'll open…the window," he said, looking at the boy strangely.

Mom knew something was up; she just didn't figure it was the angels.

"What?" she asked, with a look that could force a convict to spill his guts.

"What, *what?*" the boy echoed. It wasn't so much that Henry was a lousy liar. The problem was that Mom was just too good at…doing what she did. *Momming* I guess you could call it. His parents looked at him. This was it! This was their shot! The escape hatch was open. *Go for it boys!*

Jack elbowed Fred. "Now!" The angels bolted for the open window. Escape at last!

But as they took off, the boy's father froze mid-step. And the angels stopped mid-flap. Mom turned around.

Dad wondered. "Is that too much? Too drafty?" he asked, feeling the breeze sent down by the angels' wings. He turned back to close the window.

Jack & Fred leapt back up to the ceiling, crashing again. *Bang!*

"Ouch!" Fred blurted out loudly, Jack's hand clapping over his mouth.

"Ouch!" Henry mimicked, trying to cover. Mom watched him. The boy started hopping up and down like he was having some kind of fit. She looked at him funny.

"Henry, what're you doing? What're you cracking up?"

"I stubbed my toe. Ow. Oh. Ah. Oh. Crap!"

"Henry!" she went, hands on her hips.

Dad grimaced. "You want the window closed or—"

"No! It's fine, Dad. Don't touch it!" the boy shouted.

"Alright, alright. Calm down. What's wrong with you?" he asked, looking at Mom. Their backs were turned.

"Go!" Jack screeched.

The angels made for the window again but his folks turned suddenly. *Again!*

Jack went, "Here we go. Oh damn!"

Get back, quick!

Jack & Fred shot back up to the ceiling, this time with the presence of mind to hit the air-brakes before smashing into it, their feet skidding on the wind currents.

Skreeeeeeeeeeeeeee!

Almost busted. Mom walked toward the window, closing it slightly.

"Jack," the little one whispered. "Jack. Jack?"

"What?!" Jack barked, stifling the sound. "What, Fred?" he whispered.

"I feel air sick."

"What?"

"Too much…(burp) ziti."

"Oh no. Fred, how many times have I told you…Ooh, ooh, wait!"

The parents turned back to the boy.

Jack whispered. "Alright. Dad is over there. Mom is turning. Go for it!"

Henry spotted them dart for the open window. "Go, man! Go, go!" he urged in silence as he got back to his bed, pounding it with his fist, urging them on to freedom!

Jack & Fred dashed for the window once more. It was looking good this time…and…*Oh, geez, she's straightening the room up. Every angel for himself! Ahh!* Mom turned left, Jack floated upward, just out of reach. Dad turned back around and Fred tumbled away. Mom moved again. Fred's wing almost brushed her arm! *Ahh!* The angels were doing aerial acrobatics.

They looked like super balls as they bounced off the walls and corners of the cramped confines of the boy's blue room. Henry looked at them out of the corner of his eye, trying his best not to fall apart laughing. But this was serious! They could get into trouble for visiting him. Right?

Mom was backing up! Above her, just out of reach, Fred twisted as her feet shuffled across the floor. He floated in her direction with his wing pulled over his arm like a drape. As she approached he pulled his wing away.

Like an angelic matador, the little one shouted, *"olay"* as she moved past.

"Okay!" the boy yelled, covering for the angel.

Jack had to bite down on one of his clenched fists. The little one was almost sitting on Mom's head. Fred tried choking back his laughter, covering his mouth with both hands and feet, until he fell backwards into the wall. *Bang!*

The little one bit his lip. "Mmmm."

"Henry," Mom started to say.

Dad looked around. "What the hell was that banging?"

"Angry squirrels?" the boy suggested in haste.

Dad was still in that comatose wash of sleep. "That's the second time I heard it in the last couple of minutes."

Mom suggested, "It's probably the roof latch, gotten loose again."

"I'll check it later," he said. "Look kid, get back to sleep. I have to get up soon, and so do you."

The boy jumped back into bed and they tucked him in. He felt so good he could've stayed snuggled under the covers and slept right there forever.

"Y'know Dad, it could be rats or possum or—"

"Henry!" Mom started to reprimand. She hated rats and mice, didn't want to hear anything about them, but she was so tired she started laughing. "Just get back to bed, *please*. Come on. Sleep."

The boy glanced upward. The angels were all squashed and pretzeled up there. They were out of space and developing fast-urging cramps in their arms and wings. At this rate, someone was gonna blurt something out, and Henry couldn't cover for it again. And if they made for the window, they'd probably get caught.

Jack shook his head. "Oh yeah, this is great."

Henry saw the desperation of their situation.

"So," the boy leapt out of bed. "The other night I had this dream this big wolf was chasing me…in the dream I mean, and he was chasing me around the bed…which is weird because my bed is pushed right up against the wall, right? So, all of a sudden…" The boy grabbed his blanket and threw it up in the air, over his parents' heads. "They flew out the window, right now!"

And they did! Jack pulled Fred by the arm, rocketing toward the window.

Jack was so busy making sure the little one was with him and the parents were covered, that he smacked his head on the half-closed window. Fred spun around, tilted his head to the side, just looking at the boy. Jack rubbed his bruised head while he and the little one hovered there for a moment, looking at the child, smiling. This was no mistake. That *something wonderful* Fred had always talked about with Jack: It was here. It was Henry.

"Go ahead," the boy mouthed.

"Thanks," the little one mouthed back. And he dashed out, pulling Jack with him.

"Henry! Come on! Stop playing now!" Mom shouted, her patience definitely gone, as she pulled the expansive blue blanket away.

Dad scooped him up and buried the boy under a mound of covers. "We all have to get up soon. Love you. Goodnight."

"G'night," the boy said to them as Mom kissed him on the head.

"I love that kid, Jack," the little one said as they looked at the boy one last time through the glass.

"*Thank you*," Jack said without words, pushing Fred out of the way as he did so. The little one didn't want to leave. He floated there holding onto the window, resting his foot on the sill. Dad turned and unexpectedly shut the window behind him.

"It's too cold in here now."

"*Yaaoowww!*" the little one screeched as the window came down upon his foot.

Dad didn't realize. He was half-asleep. He was slamming the window down upon the little one's foot over and over, thinking it was jammed.

"*Ow! Stop!*" the boy said to himself, feeling the little one's agony with every smash.

Jack stifled Fred's agonized screams. The little one flailed helplessly, writhing in pain, eyes popping out of their sockets, with tears bubbling up from the throbbing agony. He couldn't help it. His foot was caught! The more Jack tried smothering his cries, the more the little one struggled. Fred started pounding on the window pane with his wings, which were flapping like mad. The angels were going alright, but they would do so literally kicking and screaming.

"Here, Daddy!"

Henry threw off his covers again and darted to the window, unable to stand seeing the little angel in such excruciating pain. He lifted it, pushed Fred's foot through, then shut it very quickly before the parents said anything.

"Thanks," Dad said.

"If you pound it into the sides, the window slides back down. It hurt too much the other way. Goodnight! See you tomorrow! I mean later!" Henry dove under the covers in one swift move.

The little one darted back to the glass once more to say thanks and Jack flew up behind, pulling him away by the wings. In human terms it was the equivalent of yanking someone back by the hair. *Ouch.*

Mom and Dad looked down for a moment.

"Goodnight, boy," they whispered, absolutely exhausted. And they went off to sleep. But on the way back to their room they couldn't shake the feeling that they had just witnessed some kind of goodness. But whatever it was, it was gone now. It had flown away.

Dad turned to Mom as they went back to their room. "Do you feel—"

"Like we missed something?"

"Yeah. I don't know, something. I don't know."

"Like it was something…pleasant."

"Yes," he agreed. Dad and Mom got back into bed. "And that stupid roof hatch banged again. I'll check it later."

"Which means next year?" she said with a smile, giving her husband a kiss.

"And what was that *yaaoowww* sound? Sounded like someone got their foot caught in the door."

"Or the window?"

"What?"

"Oh nothing."

"No wonder where Henry gets it from," he said.

"He gets it from his *father*. You're as a much a storyteller as he is."

"Well, what do you want? It's 4:30 in the morning."

"Love you."

"Love you too. Night."

Mom and Dad chuckled and went back to sleep.

Henry laid in bed, upset. Would they come back? They said they would, but when?

"*Jack & Fred...*" he whispered.

{ Chapter 13 }

Before Dawn

George's spirit was still up on the rooftop, resting, when the angels flew back up to retrieve him. They scooped him up, and with their robust wings, Jack & Fred soared high into the remainder of the night sky. The earliest of birds soon awoke and began to sing their morning songs like prayers as the angels flew toward the clouds.

They were juggling George and the little one wouldn't stop making a fuss.

"Ow! Ow! Ow! What's wrong with you?" he shrieked, rubbing his sore wings. "Do it again and I'm gonna box your ears in, pal!"

"What did you want me to do? We're out, and you pull that window stunt?" Jack cried. "They almost saw us. If the boy can see us, his parents probably can too!"

Fred's anger was overwhelmed by the extreme joy he felt at what they had just experienced.

"He *can* see us. Oh Jack, do you think he'll be the one? Do you think he'll ask us to be his guardian angels, Jack? Do you, Jack? Huh, Jack? Huh?"

Jack made these big slashing movements with his hands, nearly bobbling George.

"Fred. Fred. Fred! Be quiet, calm down, relax, take a pill, will ya? This is probably just a one-time visit. He's gonna forget about us. He'll be sleeping peacefully and quietly from now on. And he's not going to need us."

"Oh but he will. He has so many more adventures to go on."

"Fred!"

The little one was silent for a moment, but only a moment. Then he started bouncing up and down, flying all over the place, jostling George to pieces, dancing to tunes heaven seemed to be spilling from its warm skies above.

"You take a pill! He can see us! Hee-hee! Woo-hoo!" The little one stopped a moment and thought of something. "Say, what if he *does* need us again, Jack? We do need like an excuse to come back. Kinda like, oh…I dunno. Maybe the kid has bad dreams or something, huh?"

"We're always nearby. Come on," Jack flew on. "They forget about us. People always do. Just look at Wallace. You know that," he said disparagingly.

"You don't mean that! This one's not like Wallace or anyone else we've ever met before. *He* saw us! You know that Jack," Fred insisted. "How did we do that anyway?"

"I don't know," Jack admitted. "That's the problem."

"What's the problem?"

"That is. Appearing to the kid. Just out of nowhere. He sees us? We must have—I don't know—set something off that made us appear to him in real life. How could he see us?"

"Set what off?" Fred wondered.

"Do I know?" Jack appeared to be completely confused. "I *don't* know. I thought only Archangels, or guardian angels, or any of the other big guys could do that kind of stuff."

Fred thrust his chest out, putting his hands on his hips.

"Jack & Fred. Spirits with powers and abilities far above those of normal angelic beings."

"I guess we *can* do it. I mean, apparently we *did* do it."

"Wow. I always knew we had it in us, Jack," the little one said with his proud chin stuck out.

"No, Fred. This is no good at all. This is serious. What we were saying to the kid was true. We could be in a lot of trouble."

"Trouble? After all these years, does it matter at this point, Jack? I mean seriously. Come on. Trouble. If we didn't get into trouble, we'd never get anything done. You know us."

"Yeah, but this isn't like stopping for lunch when we're not supposed to, Fred. This is really serious stuff. You have to get special permission from the guys upstairs to appear to people. That's big time. There could be some serious ramifications to this whole—"

"Ramifications huh? Look at you with the five-dollar word. Just call him Mr. Theeee-saurus. Geez!"

"Will you shut up and listen? This is not something we're supposed to be doing on our own. They have rules for this. People don't know about us angels flying around out here. I mean, a person can get really freaked out!"

"Does he look freaked out to you?"

"Fred. He just saw angels; something everyone down here says you're not supposed to be able to see. How's this gonna work out? 'Oh, hi Mom, Dad, I was talking to invisible people while you were tucking me in.'"

"Okay."

"Or, 'Hey guys at school, I'm exhausted because I've been talking to angels instead of sleeping last night.'"

"Alright."

"Or, 'Hey, Dr. Galackawitz, please load me up on Thorazine and toss me into this freaking rubber room because I talk to invisible people with a mad-on for midnight snacks of baked *freaking* ziti!'"

"ALRIGHT YOU IDIOT!!!!!" the little one burst out. George's spirit dislodged from their grip as they both stared each other down with fiery eyes. He fell back down to Earth. "Um…" Fred nodded.

"Damn!" Jack went.

They grabbed George neatly by the arms and soared back up to their previous location.

Fred shrugged. "What do you want me to say? Huh, Jack?" Jack shook his head. "What's the story? What do you want from me?"

"I don't want anything from you. I don't know what the hell to do, okay? Oh my God. I can't believe this."

"This is not a horrible thing. This is a blessing!"

"For us. For us, Fred. Yes. But what about the kid? 'Hey kid we really care about you! Let's hope you don't have a psychotic episode now!'"

"Ye of little faith my friend." The little one nodded downward. "You know, if you were one of them, you'd have an ulcer by now."

"I already have an ulcer, and I'm *not* one of them! Ughhh...what're we gonna do here?"

"I don't know, Jack. We need to go to Sidney."

"I know that. I mean, what're we gonna do about the boy?"

"You like him, don't you? Just like me. You see it, don't you? There's something different about him. There's something so special."

The little one's head hurt.

"Fred, people don't believe in anything anymore. I see them every single day. You do too. We do this, we're gonna screw up that kid. We're going to scare him."

"Jack...he saw *us*. He's our boy."

"Whoa. What do you mean *our* boy?" Jack asked. "We've helped many a kid, Fred. Just because this one saw us doesn't mean…"

Fred looked solemnly at his partner.

"But, Jack...he *did* see us. Whether it was a mistake on our part or not, he still saw us. And why can't he be the one? Why is it every time I ask you, 'Do you think this one can be the one?' you always say, 'Probably not. It's just a one-time visit?'" Fred asked in a gruff, imitating voice that wasn't at all Jack's. "It happened. Can't you just let it go at that and believe in it?" he asked adamantly.

"Because, Fred. Because not many people believe in angels. Especially ones like us. You remember the *last time*."

Fred brushed away the thought.

"Yeah. I remember," he said sadly.

"I just don't want you to—"

Fred snapped. "Don't want me to what?! Huh? You don't want me to hope for anything ever again because Raphael didn't believe in us? You thought he did. I know I did! So what? Huh? So what. He didn't believe in us. He was a jackass with a great talent. Nothing we could do. Why do you insist on giving up hope?"

Jack held onto George, raising his hands up beneath George's form as if he meant no harm, not making eye contact with his dearest friend.

"Nothing," he replied.

"Jack...what? What is it, Jack? Just say it for Pete's sake."

Fred tossed George into his partner's arms, flying off without him. Jack closed his eyes. His whole expression had changed, and he looked up at his best friend sailing away.

The taller angel sighed. "I just didn't want you to get all excited, only to have your heart broken again if this doesn't work out. Okay? Moron!"

"Huh?" George moaned, jostling in his grip. Fred turned around. The pals looked at one another, forcing a smile.

"Jack. What do you want to do?"

"Let's just find Sidney."

"Alright."

"I mean now."

"Now now?"

"Yes. The barrister will figure this out," Jack said, exasperated. "He always does."

"But George..." Fred's eyes bulged when he realized what Jack intended. Jack stared at him with that face of impending doom. "You have gone *right* off the reservation, Jack!"

"Fred—"

"We're playing hooky with a detached spirit now!"

"Oh, he's not any more detached now than he was in life. C'mon. We'll bring him to heaven...eventually. We're just gonna go on a little Sunday drive here."

"It's not Sunday, Jack. And it's almost twenty-four hours since he's passed on. You're talking about permanent damage! What about this guy?"

"C'mon," Jack urged. "This'll be fun for the whole family."

"Oh my God." Fred rubbed his forehead, almost dropping George again. "Oh my God, oh my God." He opened his eyes and looked at Jack, who was still staring at him. *"Oh my God."* The little one sighed audibly. "You're right, Jack, they *are* going to kill us for this one. This is a lotta wings, even for us."

"Well…"

The little one shook his head. Jack raised an eyebrow.

"Aw, why not. What're they gonna do? Yank us back upstairs? Separate us?"

Jack ruffled the spirit's hair. "You're gonna fix us, George! Fix us but good. You know that?"

George smiled but didn't make a sound.

Fred leaned in close.

"Jack. They're going to come looking for him. He's overdue."

The little one's partner stared into his eyes.

"I know."

The angels flew on with one real destination in mind, Sidney the barrister. Their minds were swimming; they were too filled with worry to make decisions now. All they knew was that they were tired and…

"Hungry," Jack said to himself.

The little one stopped, rubbing his tired wings. He turned around reluctantly and said, "Look, you're gonna be a real buster anyway, so I'll just say it outright. I'm starving."

"Me too."

Fred smacked his hip, eyes dashing upward. "Oh sure, it's alright when he's hungry!" he shouted to himself. "I'm dying for Chinese."

"Alright. We'll get two quarts of wonton soup, three egg rolls. Do you want a pupu platter or something else?" Jack asked unenthusiastically.

"I don't know. Problem is I'm *staaarrving*. We have that and we're gonna be hungry in a half hour."

Jack grimaced as he rubbed his belly. "Grease'll kill me today. I was burpin' up flames last time we downed the pupu."

"Shrimp toast did *me* in," Fred said.

"Yeah," Jack agreed, equally upset at the thought.

"Well what then? Pizza?" Fred asked.

[My Guardian Angels Jack & Fred]

"We had that last time. Hamburgers, no. I don't know. We're running out of choices here," Jack said, all disgruntled. "And time."

"We should have stayed and let Henry's mom cook for us. We could've had breakfast. I bet she would've made the blueberry waffles."

"Kid's mom did make good ziti."

"Stop calling him kid, Jack. He has a name!"

"Fred! Ugh. Why must we do this every day? It's only food. Why do we have to make a big, stinkin' production over eating? It's not like it would hurt us to miss a meal."

"It's a production when I'm hungry. When you're hungry it's alright. Go ahead, *you* go miss a meal!"

"Ugh. Fine. We'll get Chinese. I'll have agita on top of—"

"On top of what? Stop complaining for Pete's sake! That's all you do lately. Shut up!" Silence sat for a second, but just that. "Why? Do you think we're in *that much* trouble?"

"Yes." Jack threw his hands up, managing to balance George. It became a skill. "Alright? Yes! You gonna ask me that again today?"

"Then, like we said, we'll just go to Sidney and clear it up, that's all." Fred washed his hands of the whole thing. He couldn't be bothered worrying. That's what Jack was for. Worrying wasn't his thing. When he did worry, it upset him to the point where he couldn't even fly straight. Jack though, he could handle anything. At least that's what Fred thought. "Where is old Sidney? London?"

"London? Where the hell did you get London? Would we even be flying in this direction if he was in London? God!" Jack thundered.

"I thought he—"

"He's over here! London. That's the old office. I told you I got the info from the courier earlier. Where've you been?"

"Stuck with you," Fred barked.

"Well, you're not stuck, my friend."

"Yeah, well the door swings both ways, pal!"

"Fine. Take the moron on your own. See how fast you get lost! London. Sheesh. What is…hey!"

An angelic courier dipped out of the skies and she delivered a note card, deliberately handing it to Fred.

The little one was taken off guard. "Thanks," he said. The courier was a slight, little blonde thing, looking like a ballerina with big brown eyes. She winked at Fred, deliberately blowing a kiss as she flew off.

Jack chuckled to himself.

The little one frowned. "What?"

"Nothing, nothing."

"Go ahead."

"You're as bad as I am…with the girls. I'm just more obvious."

"You're just an idiot. What is this?" He looked at the card. "There's more news."

"Sidney?"

"No. Something else. Same place though. The campus. Oh crap!"

"What?"

"Guess who else is there?"

{ Chapter 14 }
On Their Way

Gears were scratching and grinding, and he could feel the vibration of the table upon which his hand was laid. Sidney's eye peeled open as the teletype spat out another message. He blinked away the blurriness and found what he was looking for as his eyes scanned the words across the page.

"Finally," he whispered, taking a deep breath and holding it. He sat up, letting the blanket, which Madison placed upon his shoulders, fall to the ground as he exhaled a stomach full of worry and looked about the office. She went home as he had instructed.

"Maddie!" he called anyway, but he could sense she had gone. Sidney sat for a moment, and another message suddenly came through, surprising him more than he would have liked. It was from Madison's identical twin, who was St. Peter's personal aide.

Elsewhere in heaven…

"There you are!" St. Peter announced as he scribbled in his giant book. His angelic associate flew over, a perfect duplicate of Sidney's own executive assistant, Madison. Peter glanced at her through his half-rim reading glasses and smiled.

"Gabrielle. Just the person I wanted to see."

"What's up?" she asked, handing him a mug of coffee, warming it against her hands.

"You're always cold," the saint said offhandedly. She and Madison looked identical except for Gab's black glasses. She was a lot less formal and hated work; all work in fact.

Peter shoved papers at her. "Take this one over to Tracy. Tell her I need the *whole* list, not this piecemeal nonsense." He handed her a pile of documents, sipping his coffee. "Lee's in London. I want all these faxed over to him. And Gab, get someone to corral that pet pick-up area. I can't have ten million cats, dogs, and *God only knows* what else, jumping at the new arrivals, looking for their past owners. And yeah, I know the line is long today. I had some trouble checking in a few of the newbies. Just shift it over. It's a disaster. Everything is going haywire today. That's what I get for leaving for a few hours. By the way, good coffee."

The girl raised her eyebrows. She was just as beautiful as her sister, but that's where the similarities ended. Gab was absolutely useless when it came to organization. She was totally carefree and worried more about the latest fashions than paperwork.

"What?" St. Peter asked.

"Nothing. Just…that's a lotta stuff that's all. Anything else, sir?"

"You know, if Madison came upstairs here, I would have no mess to contend with. If Madison happened to drift over from time to time, I'd be able to drink this coffee and take five. If Madison fixed this disaster…"

"Then Gabby would be out shopping!" the assistant screeched, pounding on Peter's podium, giving the old saint a run for his money. "I hate secretarial work, but it was the job I was assigned to. Okay? Deal with it!"

Peter slammed his book shut. "You'd rather be downstairs, shopping?" he asked with his hands on his hips. "That can be arranged!"

Gabby stepped up. And you had to give it to her. Nobody stepped up to St. Peter and got away with all their limbs intact.

"I'd rather be working in halos and gowns."

"What?"

"You heard me," she said with a sigh. "I have great fashion sense. So you're right, St. Peter. Madison would be better here. I'll file those for you."

She almost looked sad. Gab was a master of that face.

"What's that scent?" Peter asked.

"What scent?" she wondered. "Oh, that's jasmine. My perfume."

"I've smelled that before."

"I…wear it a lot. It's my favorite."

"No foolin' the old proboscis," Peter said, pointing to his face. "Even now."

She batted her eyelashes. "Do you…like it at least?"

"No, I hate jasmine." Peter was old-school. He had been around the block, a long time ago. He didn't play to pity parties. "But at least you make good coffee."

Gab looked like she was going to spit fire with the look she gave him.

"And get rid of those glasses!" he told her, pointing at the black rims resting on her nose. "You're a pretty girl and those things make you look ridiculous. They cover up your whole face."

Gabrielle put her hands on her hips.

"Yeah well, I guess the whole glasses-looking-good thing, takes priority over seeing, God!"

"Okay, okay," Peter conceded, going back to the book. "Look at this. We have an overdue."

"Um…yeah. I know."

"You know and you didn't mention it?"

"That was my next problem for you before we got into eyewear fashion. I'm not my sister and that's—"

"We've got a missing moron."

"Ex…excuse me?"

"George Moron. He's missing."

Gabby peered over his shoulder.

"Uh, sir. I think the listing says *Morano*. Maybe *you* need new glasses?"

"What?"

"Here," she nudged Peter, pointing in the book. "His name is George. George Morano."

"Yeah so. What'd I say?"

"Not um…that, sir."

"Funny. His file is all screwed up. Did you see this? Almost looks like it's been, I don't know…futzed with or, something."

"*Futzed*, huh?"

Peter glared up at her through his half-rims.

"What are you saying?" Gabby shrugged.

"It says he's due for arrival. Says that he's also overdue now."

"So?"

"So, if you go to this sub-index in the back of the book, part of it reads like he was already checked in, *ages* ago. That's not right." Gabrielle stared at him. "Whatever. Anyway, find out why he's overdue. These things are important dammit!" Peter slammed his fist on the podium. "Sorry."

"Maybe I should've gotten you the decaf."

"Is he theirs?"

"Huh?"

"Jack & Fred. Is this their guy they're supposed to be returning? Oh I swear I'm going to kill them! You don't make people wait once they've passed on. This is unacceptable even for them! They're off the map, aren't they?"

"That's the thing, sir. I don't know *exactly* where Jack & Fred went to. I can't keep track of all these angels. Um, so I wouldn't know if they were off the map. They may have just gotten stacked over Kennedy airport or—"

"They *are* off the map, my dear. I've been doing this job since before you had a pulse! I don't care *what* they're up to. I want them checked in immediately with that moron guy. Immediately!"

"Okay, okay. Speak into the good ear. You killed the other one. Sheesh!"

Peter leaned closer.

"Gabrielle…"

"Alright, alright! Sorry. I'm the assistant."

Peter whispered so the higher authorities couldn't hear him. "You people don't understand priorities. You can't have a detached spirit just floating around! I mean, do I honestly have to teach you guys this? And find out why this book has inconsistencies in it. I leave for a few hours and someone messes with my listings. You think it's my first day on the job?"

"I have no idea…"

"Gabby, just get it done please!"

"Yeah sure, I got it. I got it. St. Grouch-A-Lot."

"What was that?!" Peter threw down his glasses.

"Bad cough. *ERGHHM.*"

"And make sure the barrister gets word. Speaking of which, any idea when the Boss…"

"Nobody called yet, sir."

"Nothing?"

"No sir."

"Damn. Okay. Thanks, Gabs. Scoot."

St. Peter looked at the never-ending line before him. He called out to the new arrivals. "Welcome, my friends, to the day that never ends. Next!"

Gabrielle went over to the upstairs teletype to contact Sidney without St. Peter's knowledge, looking quickly at a note card she had tucked away in her pocket. Her cool facade dropped off and her nerves rumbled as excitedly as popping seltzer bubbles. It was not something to be taken lightly when someone with St. Peter's status said words like: *Off the map. Detached spirit. Overdue.*

She was doing a favor for the barrister. Peter was already doing his part to stall the higher authorities for the angels. But Gabrielle had to add to the mix. It was all for Sidney. Gabby had to stall for Jack & Fred while they got done what they needed to do. Gabby never lied though. She didn't know *exactly* where the angels were at this very moment. But she had a vague idea they were headed to a certain campus…

{ Chapter 15 }

Sunshine on Your Mind

It was about 7 A.M. and the boy's father had long since gone to work. Just as Henry began getting comfortable after his short night, the white alarm clock on the bureau began ringing away. In a time before snooze alarms, the boy got up and slammed the off button and jumped back into bed. The alarm clock never seemed to do the trick, but Mom was always able to wake her boy with little difficulty. Moms apparently know a little more than alarm clock companies when it comes to waking people up. Henry dragged his little self to the kitchen, where a warm bowl of oatmeal with cinnamon and brown sugar sat freshly made. He rubbed the sleep from his crusty eyelids and breathed in the air.

Usually it was all the same. The day, the hour, the morning, the walls and the floors, the light on the ceiling that hummed for eternity's sake. It was always the same since…forever. Except for today. Today was *not* the same. It was different and exceedingly so. It was as if you'd won a trip to someplace you'd never been before and you had to hurry and prepare. Because of that, going through monotony of the usual routine became something completely different and new. Everything was special now, even those most mundane things like getting dressed and brushing your teeth.

"So, how's the merry wanderer feeling this morning?" his mother asked.

"Fine."

"Fine," Mom repeated. "You sure?"

"Mmm-hmm," the boy grumbled, munching on the chunks of brown sugar that didn't quite settle at the bottom of the oatmeal. "That wolf was chasing me again."

"Same one, huh?" Mom asked, as she poured herself some coffee.

"Yep. Chased me all around the bed. He had shorts and a green hat," he said.

"Hmm," Mom murmured, drinking her coffee. "You've been dreaming about him for weeks now, haven't you? Ever since you were sick with pneumonia a few weeks back, you've been dreaming of him."

"He's scary. But you have to hand it to Furry, though. He might be spooky, but he's darn stylish."

Mom spat coffee out like a geyser. Henry pulled back to avoid the wet blast.

"Stylish?" she repeated, wiping her mouth and then the table with the dish towel.

"Yes. Very," the boy remarked.

"Where'd you hear that from?" Mom asked.

The boy sat in silence for a moment.

"That's what they said when I told them."

"Who?" she asked absently. "The kids at school?"

"No. Jack & Fred. The angels." Mom looked at him. "You know they came back last night?"

There was a sparkle in her eye. "Jack & Fred. Two of them?"

The boy stopped eating for a moment.

"Oh yeah. Jack & Fred. They're a team. A double act. Like Hope and Crosby. Bert and Ernie, you know."

"Did they tell you that?"

"Yes. We talked about a lot. They love your food."

Mom nodded, entranced by the boy's words.

"Really. Sooo…Is that where the ziti went? I saw the empty tray. Hen, you don't need to dirty three dishes."

"Of course I did. I told you, they came back."

"Well. Come on lil' doggie, move it along."

"Yeah, alright. I'm going to get dressed," he said as if he were preparing himself for a prison sentence. He dragged himself away from the table.

"Christmas Eve is on Saturday, Henry. It's not that bad!" she called, reading his mind about school. The boy sprung back around the corner of the kitchen.

"Oh, and Ma…Dad said he was gonna check the roof hatch. Don't make him lock it. Tell him to keep it open. They had a heck of a time trying to get out through the window last night, with you people in the room. You coulda gotten them in trouble, you know?"

"How is that, Henry?"

"I don't think they're allowed to appear to people. I scared the heck out of them, when they realized I saw them. So imagine *you*. I mean, they're busy enough. They don't need detention too, or whatever it is they get when they screw up."

"Oookay."

"Okay."

"Is that…is that why you threw the blanket over my head?"

"Of course!" he said brightly. "What'd you think I was doing? I'm not crazy!"

"Go ahead. Get dressed. You're gonna be late."

"When we were eating they also told me to tell you, not to work so hard. They said they know how exhausting it is for you nurses and you guys don't get appreciated like you should, but still, you need to slow down a little. But they said it's cool how you help people, just like they do. You make their jobs easier by being caregivers. That's what they said."

She smiled, warmly. Mom's eyes followed him as he walked down the hall. She opened her mouth to say something that wouldn't spill out. When the woman realized that she didn't know what she was saying, or what she was going to say…or something, it was already time for them to get going.

"And don't go back to sleep!" she called.

"I'm not!"

"No resting your eyelids either."

"Alright!" he shouted, mumbling something under his breath.
"What was that?"
"Nothing!"

Actually, sleep was the furthest thing from his mind. He stared at his reflection in the mirror. Henry felt so much older, like he knew so much more. And whatever he was the day before yesterday, it would never come back, and he was cool with that.

He dunked his toothbrush under the water pouring out of the bathroom tap, which was seemingly frigid next to the kitchen's. He stared absently at his parents' red and blue toothbrushes sitting in their holders. He bit down on his own, holding it between his teeth, and placed the other two closer to one another. He pointed to the red one, then the blue one and said, "This is Jack and this is Fred." Then he finished brushing his teeth.

"Come on, Henry. We're going to be late!" Mom called.

Mom's perfume was wafting in the air; she was in her nursing uniform with floral scrub top, helping the boy into his coat. The boy's head was elsewhere. He couldn't stop thinking about them. He wondered how old they were, how long had they been flying around, why he had never seen them before, and most importantly, where they were at the very moment he was putting his winter clothes on.

Henry pulled up his right mitten and said "Jack," and then he put his left mitten on and said "Fred." That's what it was all about really. Just as simple and as wonderful as that. After all, how could you be sad about going to school with sunshine on your mind?

{ Chapter 16 }
Big Red

The boy and his mother raced downstairs and into the backyard, where their red station wagon slept, still waiting to be turned over. But before you could get into the car, you had to pass the gauntlet. Yes, I said "the gauntlet," or in layman's terms, the telephone wire that stretched across the length of the interconnected backyards—where atop this near infinite cabling sat, neatly flocked, several hundred genuine New York City pigeons that were bored from hanging out on the elevated subway station pillars. They had one certain lust for life, and that was the insatiable need to dive-bomb any moving object that passed beneath them—cars, people, small animals, whatever got them cooin' at the moment. Need I say more? No, but I will.

Yes, mere mortals had passed the gauntlet with regularity, but there were casualties. Henry's woolen ski hat was among the count of the dearly departed. And there was Dad's winter coat and…well, you get the idea.

It was absolutely arctic out. You could hang beef out there. Henry hated cold days like this. Vinyl upholstery, though auspicious in some departments, has the unfortunate ability to conduct whatever temperature bears prominence, a flaw to be sure. The point was, you froze your sweet rump off in the old Chevy station wagon. So the boy, a man of ingenuity even in his single-digit years, always conveniently grabbed the green army blanket that his parents stowed away in the backseat, using it as a *sits-upon* while he and his mother rode to school.

Ah, a fresh new day! Then Henry's joy hit one stark realization: It was school. Rats. No matter what, it was *still* school. He had to go. Again. It was funny. No matter how they candy-coated it—what auditorium events they were having, class outings, guest speakers, or whatever—Henry never, ever, cared for school very much—at all! Sometimes the teachers thought the children were so simple that merely rearranging the seats in the classroom would, perhaps, make the class more interesting. But it didn't. It never did. And they weren't fooling anyone, most of all the children. It was all presentation; presentation and *attitude*. Kids understood that; nobody else did. But still…it was different today. Besides, how could he go back in the same frame of mind after what happened yesterday? How could he sit there, when all he wanted to do was fly…*like them!*

The car turned over with its usual noisiness, belching, growling, and coughing. It struggled to turn itself on, but it couldn't make it. Big Red was a monster of an automobile; a vehicle whose only intended goal was lying dormant in the backyard—not a lofty goal, mind you, but you had to admire its zeal. And it was very proficient at just that, too. Even if you could bribe it with food, it wouldn't move. *Ah, how about a lovely decanter of Penzoil, vintage '82. Mmm. Let it breathe a moment.* Perhaps. Probably would have been easier than this. But Mom was relentless. She wasn't gonna be stopped. She stomped on the pedal and coaxed the giant, bloated candy-apple carriage to cave in and start up. Henry, meanwhile, kept flinging the tire pressure gage Dad kept in the glove compartment. He wound his wrist up and fired away. And the white measuring line popped out of the thin metal cylinder.

"Will you stop playing with that silly thing? Put it back, before it breaks," Mom said with more than a fair hint of aggravation in her voice.

"And the temperature is…" the boy stated with a carnival barker's vocal strength. "Seventy-five. And what a warm seventy-five it is, too! Yeah, I wish!"

"Henry!"

"Can we move to Florida, Ma?" the boy asked, putting the silver tube back in its place.

"Sure. Why not," his mom, the nurse, said with a sigh.

Henry's mother was a quick driver. Not reckless, just quick. It was only a ten-minute ride, but for her it took five. And before you knew it, arrival. Oh, *the horror*. The pale morning sunshine blinded the boy as he exited the car. To him, the school was not all that dissimilar from its Siberian prison counterpart, complete with the pack hounds, rusted metal gates, clanging doors, and wailing claxons calling to order.

"*Ugh,*" he groaned with a shiver. It was just a lonely winter day whose last remnants of snow from the night before, sat upon the skeleton of leafage that was the hedge around the perimeter of the school. It was so cold out. Other than that, you really couldn't tell that it was Christmas time at all.

"Hey Ma…"

"I know, Hen. You want to stay home. And I'd keep you home, too, but Christmas Eve is soon. Better to get all of this out of the way. And I have a meeting with your principal later today. We're going to take about fieldtrips!" she said raising an eyebrow.

Henry shrunk back. "Oh Lordy."

"Uh-huh!" she said.

The one time you actually felt bad for the principal.

"You know…they *did* come back, Ma. The angels. The ones that found me. The ones that you said made sure I got home alright. I'm not making that up, even though you think I am."

"I know. You said. That's why the ziti tray and the dirty dishes were left in the sink. Henry, I'm not the maid. Clean up your mess. Do I need to tell you this by now?"

"No but—"

"And what're you doing up *that* late? I cut you some slack on the weekends but not on a school night. Especially after yesterday. And you finished a whole tray of ziti. You can't—"

"Ma, you're not listening. They came back last night. I had to give them something. They didn't eat dinner."

"Henry…"

"Ma, I'm not lying to you. They're real."

She looked at him out of the corner of her eye.

"Well, if they come back, make them help you clean up the mess before your father and I get up."

"Yeah."

"Henry? Be careful today."

The boy smiled. "Hey, it's me!"

Mom rolled her eyes.

"I'll pick you up at the usual time," Mom said with a smile and a sparkle in her eye. And you couldn't help but feel better. Mom made everything work out just perfectly. Even when you felt like crap on school mornings, you'd hug her and feel better, hopeful for the day even. She wasn't all that dissimilar from the boy's friends that snuck into the roof hatch last night, and as a nurse, her job was not all that different either. *They* were right. The difference was she could not fly, but that was also debatable given her driving.

"I'll be here waiting, at the usual time," the boy said, forcing an enthusiastic smile. He kissed her and started on his way. Then he stopped and ran back to the window, knocking on it for her to open.

"What'd you forget?" she asked.

"Tomorrow, can you make blueberry waffles?"

She smiled, uncontrollably.

"In case they come back Ma. I know they're angels, but they have to eat."

"See you later, baby. Love you."

"Love you too. Even though you drive me to jail."

"Henry. Go!" she nodded.

"This stinks," he mumbled to himself, heading for the stairs that lead to the cafeteria. The funny thing was, despite his complaints, the kid did well in school. He walked down into the darkness below. He was sure the kids who awoke to those San Diego mornings, were *slightly* more on the chipper side and remember school for the carefree joy that it was, but that certainly was not here in this place, and it most certainly wasn't now. And that's all that really mattered, didn't it? The boy thought that sometimes, in this place, he just felt lost.

Some distance away…over a strange wooded area without roads…

The little one said, "Brother, I think we're lost."

Fred looked around, holding George under the arms to keep him aloft, giving Jack a much needed break so that he could rant in peace.

"Where in the *hell* are we?" Jack screamed, throwing his arms over his head.

Fred shrugged and Jack went on a tirade.

"Outstanding. Prince Henry the Navigator over here. You're killlin' me, Fred! You're killin' me!"

George awoke. "I think we passed a Shell station a mile back. Why don't you guys ask for direc—"

"Shut up, George!"

{ Chapter 17 }

Wingdings, Where Else?

George slept soundly as the two cherubs flew him out of the woods to the top of a grassy hill, where a majestic garden lay beneath the trees, with pink, yellow, white, and red flowers somehow in bloom, despite the winter weather. A statue of the Blessed Mother stood watch over the lush green knoll. Jack & Fred bowed respectfully as they passed by.

"Hi, Mom!" Fred waved.

The angels circled around the cottage that was supposed to contain their wayward barrister. The small wooden structure was quaint if not beaten to ruin. Fred held on to the recently-deceased man as Jack scouted around the corner, trying to look through the grime-encrusted windows. The little one used George like a human squeegee to rub the grunge from the glass frame so he could get a better look inside. The lights were out.

Jack bolted around the corner. "There's nobody here, Fred!"

"What? You sure?"

Jack glared at him.

"Why the rush then, Jack? Why'd he want us here so fast? This is his place, right?"

"So the note said. Maybe he's at lunch, kid."

"This early?"

"Maybe!" George pointed with a expository finger. "Maybe he's—"

Jack lost his patience. "Where? Ya flakey pastry! Where?"

George shrugged. "Well, if you're gonna bite my head off, I'm not tellin' ya diddle-squat with a snowplow!"

Fred looked over at Jack with big eyes, shocked at the moron's audacity. The taller angel was purely disgusted.

"Silly man! Should use you as a doorstop in your next life, George. C'mon, Fred."

"What do we do, boss?" Fred asked.

Jack was upset. No Sidney. No resolution to this. Agita all afternoon.

He grumbled. "Food. I'm starving."

"Let's do it!" The little pressed to keep up as Jack lead the way.

A piercing wave of static buzzed in their ears, forcing the angels to hunker down and cringe. Suddenly, Artie's voice came over the air and spoke directly into their ears. He was one of the millions of angelic air traffic controllers, but his job in life was that of a New York cab dispatcher, and he had yet to make the distinction.

"Where are you going, please?"

The little one whispered, "George. George. George!" smacking him on the head.

George was startled awake. "The answer is four," he said, thinking of something else.

"Whatever you do," the little one said with a threatening finger, "just be quiet."

"I thought I like…was!"

"Shh!" Fred went.

Jack frowned at the little one.

"Where are you going, please?"

Jack replied. "Wingdings."

"That you, Jack?"

"Artie? Artie, that you?"

"Yup. Sure is."

"Say, Artery? Been a long time man. How are you?"

"I'm cooped up in this ratty, pigeon-infested clock tower directing traffic for you flyin' freakin' lunatics. How do you think I am, genius?"

"We'll bring you some breadcrumbs."

[My Guardian Angels Jack & Fred]

"Go soak your wings! That'll be four and a quarter."

Jack shook his head.

Fred looked over at him. "Well, what do you want? You asked for it!"

George woke up again. "Can I talk now?"

"No," Jack said.

George's arms flailed in Jack & Fred's grip. "That was rude. You should like go kick his butt. Come on. I'll help. Let's go get him!"

"George," the little one explained. "In a moment I'm gonna kick *your* butt."

Jack's eyes grew big. "Wait. I see it!"

Fred was beaming. "There it is! Roof ho! Wingdings!" He pointed to the large cross in the distance.

"Well, it's about time! I'm beat," Jack said.

The angels passed over the heart of the campus. They were finally where they needed to be. The cross led the way. There are literally dozens of angelic rest stops like Wingdings throughout the city—atop churches, houses, buildings, everywhere throughout the entire *world* in fact. But none of them had quite the charm—or if you wanted to be fancy about it, the *panache*— that Wingdings had. Well, that's what the rumors were anyway. But like all rumors, the boys just had to see it for themselves.

Atop one of the roof pinnacles of Wingdings, a thin angel sat softly at his post. He balanced his guitar on his leg while his fingers ran across the strings, his ears adjusting to the chords' sweet sound, his fingers tuning it as they did so. The angel readjusted his round-rimmed glasses over his distinctive nose. He set his guitar down, and went over to the other side of the roof, signaling the others who were hiding.

Jack & Fred glided down to the rooftop of the school's expansive business department, gently touching down on their tiptoes, wings folding back into position as neatly as breathing. They stood George upright, though his dead weight was dragging him to the tiles, despite the fact he was nothing more than a floating spirit.

For the administration, the business school was a veritable throwback to the hallowed days of yore, when academia's desire to flaunt their grand architecture was surpassed only by their insatiable thirst to impress the world with their self-admitted, limitless knowledge base. Some of the tenured professors on campus deemed it to be one of the last sterling examples of egoism at its finest. The angels however, were not so full of themselves, and just thought that a place with such a big rooftop would be awesome to house a giant restaurant everyone could fly to with ease.

As Jack, Fred, and George looked around, they could see that the rooftop was immense. This was the biggest building on the campus, measuring a full seven stories plus four inches above ground. The spacious rooftop was pitched with ornate, if not aged, tiles, and two grand pinnacles on either end. In the center, above it all, was a large green dome adorned with a golden cross, the guidepost that they had been following, which stood watch over the campus grounds. And just below was a giant white clock tower which chimed like Big Ben and housed, they supposed, Artie and his air traffic control unit. To the human passerby, it was just the ordinary school of business building—nothing more, nothing less. But if one could see as an angel could, you would notice that the pitched rooftop was actually a large café and rest stop for angels who were exhausted from their airborne journeys. However…the chairs were stacked upon the tables. The entire place seemed abandoned.

The boys looked for some sign of…anybody. But there was just no one to be had. Jack slapped his head.

"There is no one here, Fred."

"Why do you always have to be such a *crab* Jack? ALWAYS. Will you just hang out…?"

"I'm gonna hang *you* Fred, you know…"

"…Probably on the other side of the roof…"

"…Not on the other side. I can see the other side…"

"…Wait a few seconds and…"

"…And there's no one *here*…"

"…Bent out of shape…"

"…What? No, I'm not gonna wait a few seconds…"

"…Be a real creep sometimes Jack…"

"…Bent out of shape. Yes, I am Fred. And I'm not a creep, I'm…"

"Guys," George said quietly, though no one paid any attention to him.

"Closed!" Jack screamed, shaking his head in disgust at the little one.

"Okay? Are you satisfied, Mr. Investigator? We came in for closer look, looked around, and there's *still* nobody here! This place is shut down for the winter. Man alive! I can't believe we flew all morning carrying Captain Brilliance here, only to have this place be closed."

Fred reached out to stop him. "Well, hold on. Maybe there's someplace…"

Jack swooped around and began heading in the opposite direction. He'd had it. He was tired, disgusted, and had other things on his mind. He shut his eyes beneath the beat of the headache that was threatening to make his head explode.

Fred became disenchanted with the whole thing and said to himself in a harsh grumble, *"Where is everybody?"* cracking his knuckles angrily for annoyed emphasis, with George still in his grip. The man covered his ears in distress.

"OWWW! STOP! I hate that sound. I really hate that sound!" the drowsy spirit said.

"What? Oh you mean *this*?" Fred mocked, torturing the moron by popping the rest of his knuckles and snapping his toes as well.

"I told you," Jack moaned, somewhat repetitively. "Maybe it's closed for the—ooof!"

Flo tackled old Jack from behind, stuffing him in a gigantic ever-lovin' bear hug from which there was no release. Fred was laughing so hard that he shoved George, and the droopy spirit fell to the ground like a newborn wildebeest. When he saw that, the little one laughed that much harder, nearly choking himself to death. And as if Flo's appearance was the cue, everybody popped up, screaming at the tops of their lungs, *"Surprise!"* scaring Jack & Fred out of their skin.

The maître d' snapped his fingers, and a bright white light exploded and enveloped the entire roof in star shine. The glittery fallout sprinkled down, and everything set itself up automatically: the chairs slipped into place, the tables were covered in white linen, and rows of warm food appeared on banquet tables from nowhere, bedazzling the senses of all who were around. Talk about convenient! And it made cleanup easy as pie.

Thousands of heavenly angels rushed to surround the pair as if they were

Hollywood celebrities entering Mann's Chinese Theatre on the opening night of their hit film. Toby, the guitar-tuning angel, and his band, *the Ascents*, struck up The Fifth Dimension's, song, "Save the country," sending its melody dancing through the overhead sound system.

{ Chapter 18 }
First Cuts All the Way!

Jack & Fred were just *mobbed*. So many bright little faces, all gathered at once—angels as varied and as beautiful as the people they watched over. They all radiated a soul-warming goodness that was undeniably divine. They were *so* happy to see the boys again. It had been such a long time since Jack & Fred were with this many of their brothers and sisters in one place. It felt almost like they didn't belong. They figured that this, in some odd way, must've been what it felt like for Henry to meet them.

Jack & Fred, in a sense, didn't feel like they belonged with the others anymore; they considered themselves more human than angel at this point because of all the time they spent downstairs with the people they watched over, as strange as that was. Besides, realistically speaking, Jack & Fred were *older* than anybody there; they were globe-hopping when most of these angels were human beings.

Even though they'd regale the others with stories of their travels, the pair accepted long ago that they were not like the other angels at all. And to them, Jack & Fred were like the Lewis and Clark of humanity; explorers, seeing and doing so very much for so many people all over the place on Earth. (Or was that Lewis and Clark, the Sunshine Boys of angels. I forget.)

Nobody understood how many times the pair got their hearts broken for fighting for what they believed in or hanging on to the ones they loved too dearly. Some of the others said that the pair actually hurt themselves for wanting too much. But it was a different time now, for whether it was out of sympathy for their plight, respect for their resolute spirits, or the plain optimism that they carried along with them, the other angels cherished these two more than words or hugs or handshakes could ever say.

Poor George was inadvertently smacked awake by strange hands over and over. Jack & Fred looked at one another from across the crowded space of Wingdings, and for the life of them, they couldn't understand what it was they did to deserve all this praise. The boys never realized they were appreciated on this level. Many soft hands reached out to them, patting them on the back, wanting to *touch* them, just be near them at the very least. The little one looked over the faces to Jack. Jack looked back at him, with an unflinching stare. Fred shook his head, confused, his eyes glistening in the sunshine.

Jack shrugged, shaking his head like a lost child.

"I don't know Fred," was all he could mouth back to him.

The crowd throbbed, pushing them further away from one other. Both seemed so small among the rush of gowns and halos that were swallowing them up.

George was hefted up into the air and sent crowd-surfing across the rooftop. The moron freaked out when he was being moved by the angelic conveyer belt of hands.

"Ahhh! Ahhhh! Uh, help! Ahhhh! Hey this isn't so bad! Kinda! Whoa! I feel like a Muppet!"

The angels pushed the pair back together as they all rushed at once to say hello. The little one suddenly exclaimed to his partner, "Oh dear God, Jack!"

"What?"

"Oh no."

"Fred, what?"

"Is that…"

"Hey Fred, you know what that is?"

"*Sussudio?* Oh don't play that!"

"It's Phil Collins."

"I know it's Phil Collins, Jack."

"What's the problem? I love Phil Collins."

"So do I, but, that's got all these lunatics eighties dancing Jack."

"Oh, ugh. Ughhh! You're right Fred!"

"Stop that!" Fred yelled across the roof noise. "Have you angels no decency? What in the hell is a *Sussudio* anyway? Jack?"

Then the warm heart and smile of an old friend spread apart the rush of attention and celebrity that Jack & Fred were being so overly swallowed up in.

"Oh, it's the little fuzzies!" Flo declared, her dark hair flowing in the rooftop breezes. "I've missed you, little ones!" She all but tackled poor Jack again keeping him for her own, squeezing him till his eyes bulged.

"Fff…fff…Ffredd, help…"

All of five and a half feet, Flo could take down linebackers like dominoes if she wanted. She was the picture of elegance, intelligence, and cuteness wrapped up in one warm, pink-gowned package. She and her sister Ida ran Wingdings; it was their place, and a classy one it was, too. No half-hearted attempts here gang; the food, the view, the decor, the ambience, and especially the company were first cuts all the way! That's just the way they lived.

Flo squeezed Jack harder, causing him to gasp and expel his air supply.

"*Ughhh.*"

Fred was beside himself.

"My little babies, where have you been?" those warm brown eyes asked. "Ida and I have been waiting an eternity for you to come back and visit our new little café."

"Café?!" the little one exclaimed over the roar of the crowd. "Look at this place, Flo. It's humongous!" he declared, looking at the gigantic surroundings spread out before them.

"Oh, stop," she went.

"And look at you," Fred schmoozed. "What'd you do? Look at Little Miss Petite here! You've lost significant poundage. You're like wafer girl!"

"Oh yeah," Flo said rolling her eyes, subconsciously putting her free hand on her hip. "I'll call you when that happens."

"No really, you're…*devastating*," Fred said with an appraising eye.

"Even if you are giving me a line…" she said on the side, still tightly gripping Jack in a headlock. "It's the best darn one I've heard in a while."

"If I wasn't so angelic, I'd be talking *dirty*," Fred winked.

"Oh, get out!" she exclaimed with a gulp. "That warrants kisses anyway, though. Give me kisses."

Angelic Don Juan obliged.

Jack's hand reached upward for help.

"Fading…Fredd…Fff…red…heeelllp, breathe, can't (cough) air, wings squashed…"

Flo pinched the little one's cheek, remembering suddenly the other sweet flyer in her grip.

"Oh honey, how much we've missed you two," she smothered Jack, squeezing his cheek with her free hand, shaking him like a rag doll.

"*Flo? Flo!*" one of the attendees called.

Jack's eyes were shut. He was on the verge of dropping. The proprietress turned her attention away. Fred grabbed Jack's waning arm and lifted it. It fell, lifeless. Flo jawed impatiently with an angel named John, who managed to corner her amidst the mass of angels at the Dings. Fred tried again to wake Jack…still nothing.

Flo pulled herself away from the unwanted conversation, releasing part of her grip on Fred's partner but still dragging the angel along with her.

"Two months now, and the darn kitchen still isn't right," she said, visibly ticked. Fred nodded, his attention still on Jack.

Jack's window of opportunity was closing rapidly, so he drew in as much air as he could, on the way to collapsing, and reached out in vain for help. Fred chuckled, trying not to divert his eyes or attention from Flo's lovely face. The sight of her holding Jack like a floating, purpling, spare tire, stirred up a rolling laughter that couldn't be quenched, no matter how much the little one looked away.

Flo thought aloud, saying, "I mean the last time I saw you guys, I was in Orlando, Florida, and you were helping these parents and their boy find a new house and—"

"Hey! C'mon." Fred brushed away. "How long ago was that?"

"A long time ago. I was telling the Ida-girl about how…"

Jack was going out. "Flo…oh…oh please," he begged futilely.

Fred couldn't help himself. He lifted Jack's rubbery arm…*one more time!* The arm went rigid. Life sprang back into Jack. He was still breathing, but just barely.

"Oh my God, ladies and gentlemen, it's pandemonium!!!" Fred announced. "He's hulking up, folks!"

"Oh! Geez," Flo realized almost too late. "I didn't even notice. I'm sorry, Jack!" she said, biting her lip, embarrassed.

Jack gasped for air, wheezing heavily. Fred helped him stand again while Flo mothered him, rubbing his back rather harshly, petting his head.

"Are you alright Jackie? Hmm? I'm sorry sweetie. Sometimes I forget my own strength there, big guy."

Jack looked at her coyly. "You like the rough stuff, don't you?"

"Mmm-hmmmm," she grinned at him with raised eyebrows and delight in her smile.

The little one looked at them both through squinted eyes, a wrinkle in his brow, and an upturned lip.

{ Chapter 19 }

The Whole Enchilada

There was a blessed celebration on the rooftop that day. And the students and teachers inside the building all felt that warm, elated sensation (that the angels brought with them) in the depths of their hearts. It seemed like a world away, when it was only upstairs from them—not far at all. And it wasn't just this day. It was there all the time; you just had to believe to see it unfold…

Flo stood there with her hands on her hips. "So, where've you guys been? I was expecting you hours ago."

Jack shook his thumb at his partner. "Blame the navigator over here."

"Uh! Here we go!" Fred groaned.

"Two hours, Flo. He had us going in circles for two hours! I'm absolutely exhausted!"

"Me? You told me to go left!" Fred protested.

"Again. Right! I told you to go right! Right! Good God, man, don't you even know your left from your right?"

Flo pursed her lips together, trying to stay downwind of one of the infamous Jack & Fred squabbles.

"It's been so long since they were this happy," Flo thought to herself, smiling. She was really the only angel to notice what was unapparent to everyone else—that, when the boys scrambled eggs with one another, it meant that they were happiest, and closest.

"Needless to say," Jack continued. "We wound up in Secaucus. Ugh, the smell!"

Fred's face scrunched up. "Like beer and eggs. Woof!"

"Man alive, you think it's bad down here? You should see what it's like fourteen thousand feet up. It's like flying through molasses," Jack said.

"Yeah, Jack," Fred egged on. "What about them Jersey angels?"

Flo got a little taken aback. "Watch it. I come from Jersey."

The little one stuck his tongue out, then winked at her. Flo pretended to be shocked at his face and winked back.

"Well, you know," Jack said, "Your Jersey angels are just like your Jersey drivers. The drivers don't signal when they're turning, and the angels don't either."

"That's because they drive a lot in malls and parking lots," Fred suggested.

"I never understood that. What does that mean?" Jack asked.

Flo just stood with her hands on her hips, stamping her foot.

Fred bit his tongue. "It means they don't drive with normal people. They're all crazy."

"Errrrmmmm!" Flo cleared her throat and cracked her knuckles.

Jack grinned. "Let's not even get into their sports teams!" he chuckled, elbowing Fred. (Oh, they were busters, the both of them!)

"What sports teams?" Fred eked out. "Don't they have to import them from one state over or—"

"ANYWAY!" Flo yelled. Jack & Fred both leapt back, but not far enough out of arm's reach. "Let's get you two settled, shall we?" she prompted, grasping them harshly and yanking them off by the forearms.

"Ow! Slow down, honey," Fred protested.

"Where would you like to sit, *darling?* Hmm…"

"She's not happy," Jack said to Fred.

Flo thought to herself aloud. "How about…" She dragged them over to the roof's edge. For a moment, they thought she was going to toss them over. Well, maybe for more that just a moment.

"Here you go! My bestest of views. Someplace where you can watch all the little college kiddies pass by. Christmas Eve's on the way, so they're all getting crazy trying to finish before winter break."

"This is perfect," the little one said.

Jack turned to Flo. "Gee, how'd ya know?" he asked sarcastically.

Flo stepped up. "I've known you both long enough to know *exactly* what you like, and what you don't, *my dear*." It was nothin' personal, but you didn't even play with Flo.

Fred looked at the crowd around them; they were all sneaking peeks at he and Jack, "the celebrities" of Wingdings. The angelic diners whispered excitedly to one other when they caught a glance or straight eye contact with the boys.

The little one turned about. "Say Flo, where are the twins? Terry and Bethany? I don't see them."

"Not here yet. They've got a new charge now so they may pop by later, but I doubt it."

"They're guardian angels?" the little one asked, looking at Jack frightfully amazed and somewhat disappointed all at once.

"Yeah, why hon?"

The little one was taken aback. "God…I trained them when they were kids. Even *they* find someone to watch over. Huh."

Jack caught Flo's fleeting look, and turned away.

The little one's eyes opened wide. "SO…Flo, what is this today, a Shriner's convention?"

"It's college. It's busy."

Jack shook his head. "So this is college, huh? I'm waiting."

"Waiting for what?" Flo asked.

"I'm waiting for someone to notify me…you know, *when* exactly I'm supposed to be impressed," Jack replied with a grin.

Flo fell into the same argument she'd been having with these two angels for years now. "What is it with you two and school? It's not that bad!"

Jack looked upward, counting to himself. There were just so many things. Naming one of them was too dizzying. "It's…uh, I don't know. Too…"

"Confining, boring, unenlightening, unsatisfactory!" Fred shouted. "Well, maybe just the ones we've seen. Not all of them. These kids are too darn important to be treated so half-heartedly. We've witnessed it…too many times, Flo."

Flo rolled her eyes. "Did you two want the table? I think we have a vacant soapbox somewhere if that would suit you better."

Fred shook his head in disgust. "The boy doesn't like his school either," he said distractedly.

"Who?" Flo asked with a totally lost face.

Jack looked at Fred with daggers.

She frowned at the little one. "Who? Wait a sec…Where is he? We need chairs." Flo turned her attention away. Jack glared at Fred, ready to kill him.

"Van? Van Fleet!" she beckoned. "The louse…where is…oh, look who it is!"

Flo's baby sister, Ida, materialized out of nowhere. The proprietress couldn't be bothered with her slightly scatterbrained sibling and put her fingers to her mouth, whistling for the maître d', nearly deafening everyone with the piercing sound.

"Oooh!" Ida bubbled over in a high-pitch squeal, trotting across the rooftop with her tiny feet and that darling little walk of hers.

"It's Jack & Fred! Oh, c'mere my little cutie-wooties…*ooohh*."

The tall, thin cupie doll towered over her older sister. She had a flawless profile with long, brown hair and even longer model-esque legs. She could eat twice the amount of food as anyone when the sisters were people many years ago, and never gain a pound. Flo and every other female angel who was a person at one time, hated her for that. The two of them contrasted with one another in the looks department most times; everyone assumed they were the furthest thing from sisters, the resemblance was that indistinct.

Ida scampered over in her baby blue flowing gown, which matched her eyes, falling upon the pair of angels, blubbering and squeezing the boys' faces like crazy. Fred's puss was turning orange.

"What? Is there something in the water here? I have no feeling left in my cheeks!"

Ida was just squeaking away. Jack could never understand how such a beautiful body had a head attached, containing nothing but air.

"*Van Fleet!*" Flo bellowed.

The maître d' appeared from the opposite direction Flo had called him from. The handsome, perfectly coiffed, though exasperated angel stood tall before his boss. He was clad in a finely-pressed tuxedo holding his mop, trying to conceal its untidy presence behind his tall back.

"Heh, heh…(gulp) heh. Yes, sorry, Madame. There's…" He leaned down to Flo's ear, out of breath. "There's *trouble* in the kitchen," he said in his on-the-QT, hushed British voice.

"Not again," Flo moaned.

Jack frowned. "Rats?"

"At this altitude, nah," she dismissed.

"Actually," Van said. "It was behrds (birds), sir."

"Behrds?" Fred grimaced.

"Oh, for crying out loud!" Flo exclaimed.

"The problem…(gulp) is being remedied as we speak, Madame," the maître d' swallowed, feeling not so tall as he was.

Ida put her head on his chest. "Hiya, Van!" she gushed, chewing her gum with big puppy-dog eyes.

Van smiled faintly, all business, but he was hip to the flirting, and he let it slide when Flo wasn't watching.

"Madame Ida," he winked.

Ida sighed loudly, blinking her eyes rather vigorously, exceedingly less subtle than her would-be beau, Van. She ran her hand with its super-long press-on nails across Van's chest, dizzying him.

"Van Fleet!" Flo hollered.

Van snapped back to attention. Ida huffed and inspected her nails.

In the background, Wingdings' other angelic guests started forming a conga line amid the dancin' and merriment that coincided with the boys' arrival.

Flo put her arms around the guests of honor.

"Van, these are two very good friends of ours, Jack & Fred."

He bowed. "It is a distinct pleasure to meet you gentlemen. I've heard so much about you. Stories of your adventures are legendary. Forgive my informality, but I feel like I've known you forever. How may I be of service to you?"

"Get a load of this," Fred remarked to Jack. "Someone with manners."

Flo stood on tiptoes trying to put her arm around her star employee. Ida jealously nudged at her and the elder sister kicked her in the shin. The beauty hobbled away, mouth drawn open in pain.

"Van's aces in the politeness department boys. He's our maître d', the perfect host."

"As always, it's my pleasure to serve, Madame."

She grabbed him by the arm. "Van, I want them right over here, the edge seat, front row. I need chairs. Alright?" She turned to Jack & Fred. "That's my best. It's *the* perfect view of the football field, the campus, the kids, the whole enchilada."

"At once, Madame."

Van Fleet found himself a victim of some small bit of idol worship, uncommonly neglecting his duty to retrieve the chairs. He, instead, chose to stay and listen in to the renowned duo a little more, though far enough out of the way not to be noticed.

Fred scanned the rooftop, looking over at the buffet, the place settings, the hundreds of steaming food selections, the salad bar, and the dessert racks—gourmet food fit for kings, princes, angels, you name it.

"This is some spread you got here, Flo," Fred remarked.

Flo grabbed Fred's arm excitedly, as the conga line went drifting by with arms and wings a wavin'.

"You've got to try my Aunt Amelia's vinegar eggplant."

"Aunt Amelia was here! Whoa! Jack, remember she made the antipasto with—"

Jack sighed, subconsciously licking his lips.

"Oh, man was that delicious," he said, turning to Flo. "Few months ago, we were on our way upstairs, and we happened by her place, and she went bananas. She was so happy. She gave us stuffed peppers, the antipasto—"

"The vinegar eggplant," Fred added.

"The vinegar eggplant," Jack repeated. "A cake, a big box of biscotti…"

"Roasted peppers."

"Didn't I say that?"

"You said stuffed peppers Jack."

"Oh. Um…them too, and ah! We also had a tray of stuffed shells with meatballs, and a bottle of wine for our trip back to heaven. Just to be nice. It wasn't a special occasion or anything, we just came over to say hello to her. That's all. Fred and I had like, what?"

"Fifty?"

"More!"

"Like fifty."

"Well," Jack conceded.

"At least!" the little one said.

Jack turned back to Flo. "Anyway, mounds and mounds of Tupperware containers under the wall upstairs. We still have most of 'em!" Jack & Fred both laughed. "You should see. One wrong move and it turns into an Indiana Jones trap."

"We *still* have some jars of the vinegar eggplant," the little one said. "Saving them for a rainy day. God I hope it rains soon!"

Flo smiled from cheek to cheek. "That's my Aunt Amelia. Isn't she the sweetest thing? She'd give you half a wing if you needed it," she beamed.

"She's wonderful," Jack & Fred said together.

"Is she coming around today?" Fred asked.

"No, she's busy. But I'll give her a buzz. Tell me when you're coming back, okay?"

"Yeah," the little one said, slightly disappointed.

"Alright kids. Let me go take care of the restaurant stuff. Enjoy. I'm sure you'll find *something* you like here," Flo said, winking at Fred. "Everyone always does. Where are those chairs? VAN…oh!" She turned and found him not too far behind them, listening. "What're you doing here?"

The angels looked at one another.

Flo pulled the tall Van Fleet down by the arm and nodded at her wild hair-mussed sister, who was huffing louder and louder with every hobbling step she took on her way back over to scold Flo for her inelegant leg smash.

Flo whispered, "Get something to calm down the Bride of Frankenstein over here, so we don't have a massive scene when she decides to go postal in the next five minutes. She's got that rabid look Van. She's scarin' people. I don't have time to deal with that today, huh? Cool?"

"Three degrees below artic ma'am. I'm on the case."

"Heyyyy, Flo, sweetie…ohhh," the younger sister sighed, forgetting she was angry as Van Fleet blocked her way. He ran a hand through his floppy hair. Ida swayed on her heels, speaking in a sing-songy, carefree rhythm. "Good gosh golly Miss Molly! Aren't you the most handsome thing like…*ever!* And…what was I…oh! I remember. Am I supposed to be mad at youuu Flo? Huh, sis? You sweet honey-bunches of…youuu!!!" Ida was purely hypnotized by the tall man.

Flo whispered to her maître d', "You're good, *hunktacular*."

Van shrugged. "Ehh!"

Both Jack & Fred frowned at one another. They hated 'dopeyness.'

Ida twirled her hair round her finger, staring at the tuxedo-clad angel, as she spoke to Flo. "Well, anyway hon. I kinda forgot. Earlier, I kinda let in a couple of those cute birdies into the kitchen, and…"

Flo stomped off, snatching Ida up by the arm and towing her away. "C'mon Einstein."

"Flo, ow-wa!" Ida looked at the boys. "Bye," she said softly with a wave. She then turned her seductive gaze back to Van, like a cat on the prowl.

"See you later, Vanzy," she said with a voice of deep velvet.

Van's eyes sparkled.

The angels turned slowly to Van Fleet. The maître d' looked down at them cautiously, tugging at his collar.

Jack shook his head. "Vanzy, huh? Damn boy. Look at you. You dog."

"Um…this way if you would, sirs?"

"You hound!"

Fred was surprised. "We rate a 'sirs' huh?"

Jack raised an eyebrow. "That's a first."

Van zipped off, acquiring chairs from someplace before the angels could blink. He set them down and Jack & Fred sat across from one another just as quickly. Van Fleet then took the table between them and shoved it further toward the roof's edge, leaving the angels behind. Jack & Fred watched the table disappear before them. They looked at one another for a moment, as if someone had taken their lollipop, and then nonchalantly hopped over in their seats to catch up with Van's new location. The maître d' set their places, not batting an eyelash at their silent efficiency in getting acquainted with their new spot, for it made his job that much easier. Things here all worked so smoothly. Worries were as infrequent as raindrops in the desert, and apprehension was whisked away on the next passing breeze.

"There we go. Sirs, if there is anything you need, anything at all, merely snap your fingers and I'll be right here," Van said with open arms.

Jack nodded. "Thank you, Van Fleet. Say, you're a request angel like us, aren't you?"

It was as if Van Fleet had been graced with an honor he could not equate himself to. "A request angel? Why, yes sir! But not like you. My bosses, Madame's Flo and Ida, told me of your legendary exploits. I hardly consider myself in your category, sirs."

"C'mon, will ya?" Fred disagreed. "What're you kidding? You're polite, neat, you have women drooling over you, and you got your whole restaurant together here. You're terrific. Us, we do everything ass-backwards. Jack, am I wrong?"

Jack shook his head vigorously, not making eye contact, slightly embarrassed by Fred's out-of-turn comment in front of Van Fleet, the stranger.

"He ain't wrong. Besides…" Jack said, straightening himself, "Your bosses exaggerate just a little, Van."

"Be that as it may," Van blushed, "The other angels all convey similar tales. I still find your words overly generous and far too kind for one such as myself, sirs," he grinned like a kid on Christmas morning. "But I thank you for them anyway," Van said, bowing his head in a humbled (and a bit shy) acknowledgment. "I serve other angels, that's true. But, you," he looked up into their eyes, "you get to tend to the people. Real people. As much as I love my job, I'd surely give it up tomorrow for only a moment to serve a human patron sometime."

"I don't want to burst your bubble guy, but," Fred admitted, "it's really not all it's cracked up to be. Honestly, Van."

"They don't even acknowledge that we exist most of the time," Jack said, making light of the sincerity of the fact. "At least you have other angels who talk to you, say hello once in a while, acknowledge you exist, *anything*," he chuckled, dismissing the whole thing.

"You'd be surprised," Van said, looking away longingly. "Perhaps. I mean no disrespect, but you *have* witnessed it though, many times, taking care of people. Me, I would just like to see it, *once*. That's all. Just…just once," he shrugged.

The angels nodded in agreement.

Fred enlightened, "What you do for us is no different than what we do for them."

"I know. But to be needed by…" Then he caught himself. It was if someone had broken through the barrier, looked into that special part of his soul, and had seen all of the things dear Van Fleet longed, wished, hoped, and dreamed for—things no one else but he knew of. And he didn't mind that they could see it. But he kept it to himself. Van was all dignified and all proper you know, except when he saw the angels' faces. He just felt at ease, even for being an angel himself. It was a talent. It's what made Jack & Fred special. They just had the kinds of faces you knew you could entrust your soul to and never fear for it being kept or let go.

"Anyway, sirs," he clapped his hands, "I thank you for your time. Please make yourselves at home. Again, if there's anything you need at all, just snap. If you'll excuse me, I must tend to Madame Ida. Not to speak out of turn," he said leaning closer to them, "But she seems to be…rahnting (ranting) again. Madame Flo is getting chest pains. And guess who gets the grief?"

Jack & Fred laughed.

"See you later, sirs!" Van nodded and zipped off.

"Bye," Fred called, simply.

"You know, Fred," Jack thought aloud, "Maybe we are lucky, watching people, even though they don't ordinarily see us."

Both angels looked at one other for a fraction of a second and shook their heads vigorously.

"Nah!" they said together. Then there was a tinkling sound, almost so insignificant that no one but Jack bothered to listen for it a second time.

The pair looked around. They knew a good ninety percent of the people there. It was like old-home week. Jack was drawn to the sound; he heard it yet again.

{ Chapter 20 }
That Touch of Velvet

The little one turned back around, not knowing what to do first. They couldn't remember the last time they had a sit-down meal before last night at Henry's. They were always flying all over the place. Fred reached over to unfold the ornately folded napkins, and Jack instinctively grabbed his hand.

"Ow," Fred went.

"Can't you just leave them? They look nice that way!"

"Oooh, look! They're little wingies!" Fred snatched his napkin away and made it fly. "Flap! Flap, flap, flap, flap, flaaap…flaaaaap!"

There it was again. That tiny sound….

"Stop that!" Jack smacked the table. "Do you hear bells tinkling?"

"Maybe it's chow time."

"Huh?" Jack came back.

"Chow time. You know?"

Jack was in another world.

"See now," he scolded. "Look what you did. Now you ruined them," he said, tossing aside the napkin.

"Well, they aren't much good if they're folded, Jack."

"Give me that." He pulled the napkin away. "Great, now I can't fix it again," Jack fooled with his folding.

"So, what's your point? Hmm," Fred thought to himself, admiring the dovetail linen. "Better looking than the Chinese food place, that's for sure."

"Yeah, Fred. But…I, I…"

Bong! The Big Ben chimes clanged. Fred looked up.

"That's some chow."

Jack raised his eyes.

"Oh, my."

Everything just stopped. It was as if the rose petals marked her entrance to his nose just before her beauty crossed before his eyes. She and Jack were fixated upon one another. She was a *knockout*. He realized it must've been her that he sensed earlier after the car chase, and the time after that as well. It was the rose petal perfume. She must be the little girl's angel. Kristie, the one Henry had fallen for. No wonder. *"Look at her!"* Jack said to himself.

The angel was absolutely breathtaking. She eyed Jack delicately as she passed by. Stopping just a moment, she pushed the hair from her eyes, as if in slow motion, so that she could see him better. Then her slight form sashayed past the boys' table with deliberate elegance, winking at her Romeo.

Fred tried bringing Jack back from the paradise he was enveloped in.

"Jack. Jack? Jaaaackk?" Then the little one smashed down on Jack's hand with his fist. "Jack!"

"Ow!" Jack shook away the stinging pain. "What?!"

"What are you doing? Did I miss something here? Huh?"

Jack smiled from ear to ear. "Oh yes! Something indeed. I'm uh," he pointed, "going to swing on down to the football field and check out the um…uh, artificial turf and stuff."

"Stuff? What stuff? Jack? Jack, I think something in that melon of yours has finally snapped. First you're beat, then—"

"I'm getting my second wind. God, she's beautiful," Jack breathed involuntarily.

"Come on, Jack. You know *you*," Fred dismissed. "You think every new pair of wings that flies by is beautiful."

"Yeah okay."

Jack turned back around to the little one who was shaking his head.

"I mean it Jack."

"Whatever."

"This is me you're talking to. Me, Jack."

"So…"

"So *playah*, do we need to go down the list? There was: Amy, Tracy, Daniela, Celeste, Lisa, Maddie, Francesca, Cecily, Antonia, Christina…"

"But they weren't like this."

"Sure they were, in their own way."

The red velvet vision sauntered on to the other end of the roof, waving to several groups who were seated in the back rows, plates filled with a number of assorted delicacies. Jimmy, one of the seated occupants, got up, looped around his table, and began following the tantalizing, heavenly impression. His girlfriend dragged him back to his seat by the sleeve, more than a little annoyed that he was drifting so easily and paying someone else her attentions. But he couldn't help it. Nobody could. There was just something magical about Belle, something she exuded in each breathtaking stride she took. Above the roof, onstage, Toby stopped his set, and the rest of the band, *the Ascents*, brought their instruments to a dead halt. And without a care to their abruptness, the Beatles started flowing through their heavenly instruments, as smooth as the touch of velvet moving slowly across bare skin…woo…

"I give her all my love. That's all I do…" they sang.

Fred looked over at the moony band members, frowning at their sudden choice of Fab Four songs. *Look at everybody.* This was turning into a spectacle!

Jack just picked up and left the table without so much as an 'excuse me.'

"Jack, are you gonna…He's gone. Fine. Great. Good. I'll eat by myself. Or I'll talk to *you* people. I don't care."

"…and I love her," the band played on.

Fred smacked his hands down on the table. In a huff, the little one picked up Jack's neatly placed napkin, unfolded it again, and threw it off the roof.

"See? You like that, Jack?! They're wings. They're supposed to fly!"

Fred ran over to the other tables, nabbing napkins off angels' laps left and right, launching them.

"Hey!"

"*Do you mind?!*"
"*Watch it!*"
"*Pest!*"
"*Oooh!*"

The little one dashed about like a madman. "See, they can all fly! Free as bird, Jack!"

"*C'mon!*"
"*We're trying to eat!*"
"*Messing everything up!*"

"Oh, stow it, flighty!" the little one barked.

"And you!" he zipped over to the bandstand as Toby and *the Ascents* concluded the Beatles' "And I Love Her."

"Geez, Toby!" Fred screamed. "Why don't you play something a little more stinkin' mushy around here?!!!"

Toby turned round and looked at his band mates.

"Two…a one, two, three, four!"

"*Can't buy me loooovvveee…*"

"You see?" the little one raised his eyebrows. "Nuts. They're all a bunch of royal nut jobs."

George appeared from nowhere, tripping and falling on top of the little one, knocking him to the ground.

"What the hell…George!"

"Sorry, little flying person. Oh hey! It's you!"

"Yes it's me. Get offa me. These things on my back, they aren't decoration, they're part of me, like this!" Fred slugged George across the meaty part of the upper arm.

"Ow!" the spirit frowned, rubbing his arm.

"See? It hurts!"

"Hey Fred, where's like…your buddy, the other guy?"

"I have no idea."

"I saw him take off after some hot-lookin' broad on the other of the roof."

Fred shook his head. "Figures."

"Is this like…heaven?"

"No, it's Iowa."

"We're in Iowa?"

"No. It's a line from a…movie…George. Forget about it."

"Well, there's tons of food, women, cool music. That's where we are though, right? Heaven?"

Fred looked disgusted.

"No, George (sigh). This isn't heaven. We still haven't gotten you up there yet. I'm sorry. Really."

"It's all good, brother. This is like the next best thing!"

Fred's eyes lit up.

"Yeah. Yeah I guess it is."

"By the way, this girl—"

"Angel."

"This girl angel is looking for you."

The little one frowned. "Who?"

"About yo big, Asian girl, dark-rimmed glasses. *Very* hot."

"Madison?" Fred's eyes lit up. That meant Sidney was nearby. "Where'd she—"

"She's right behind you!" a voice called out. "But I'm not Madison."

Fred's eyes nearly popped out of his head.

"Aww crap."

"Try Gabby."

"That was my second choice."

"Clever angel. This is Mr. Morano, correct?"

"Damn. Where is Jack?"

"He's an overdue, Fred. You're in a lot of trouble. So's your partner. Where is Jack anyway?"

"He uh…" Fred stammered. Her sister Madison and Jack once had a…a *something!*

"He's with the hot broad in the velvet dress!" George blurted.

Fred used Flo's technique, and kicked him square in the shins, making the moron scream and hop away.

Gabby crossed her arms. "*The hot broad in the velvet dress,* no less. Yeah. That's Jack. Flies you all over the world, buys you dinner, and that's it. A girl, like my twin sis, becomes one of his ports-of-call."

"Gab, it's not like that."

"Don't even attempt to cover for him!" she grabbed Fred by the neck.

"I'm…uh…not. Bad Jack. Very bad."

"It doesn't matter. Peter is going to ream you two a new one. You're off the map, off the charts. I cover for you two because—because I'm nice. And that's what I get."

"You're not nice Gab. What's your point?"

"My point? You keep Peter on his toes, and I like that."

The little one's face had disbelief written all over it.

"Uh-huh."

"It's true. Only reason I'm ticked at you two is for what Jack did to my sis. Dumping her like that."

"He didn't dump her, he…"

She held out her hand. "Just…stop. I don't like people messing with my family. You know what that's like. But still, I like that you guys don't play by the rules. You're fun. You know how to have a good time. I've been doing paperwork like my sister for so long I've forgotten what that's like. I'm becoming just like her. It's true. I can't even tell us apart anymore."

George popped back over. "Well, you guys are twins right?" he asked. "It's okay hon, you just need to get…"

The little one hit George again. The spirit hobbled backward.

"Sheez Fred," he moaned. "What is up with you? I'm not your own personal piñata ya know?!"

"Gabrielle. Have you met the Mor…er…Mr. *Morano*," Fred wrapped his arm around the wounded spirit.

"No, and I don't want to. I'm supposed to escort him and you guys back up to heaven."

"Well Gab, we just got here. We came down to visit your sister and Sidney. They're here—"

"Yeah, they're here. But you know she can't stand you and *him*. You know I covered for you two. If I let Peter know you were here with this guy…"

"Thanks, I owe ya."

"Yeah, you owe me. I contacted Sidney for you too."

"Where is he?"

"Doing his barrister stuff, I guess. I have no idea! Just do me a favor. You and Peter and everyone else, need to STOP comparing me to Maddie, 'cause I'm not her and…"

Fred lurched backward with his hands out, surrendering. "Yeah well, tell you what. Why don't I rustle up Jack…"

She fumed even more at the mere mention of the name.

"I mean…uh…*him,* and *you* take Mr. Morano here on a tour!"

Gabby was shaking her head. "No, no, no. I can't."

"Gabrielle, c'mere," Fred put his arm around her with the moron under his other arm. "You hate office work. If you take George and us back up with you now, what're you gonna do? Hmm?"

"I suppose file papers all day. Especially with an overdue!"

"Exactly, exactly. We all know how long the flight is down here, *especially* if you live upstairs. So…why don't you stay. Take a load off, have somethin' to nosh."

"I only eat organic food. I go to this little health food store down in the Village…"

"They…*eww.* Jack was right. People in health food stores always look gray for a reason."

"Same with bookstores too," George added.

"Ya know," the little one mused. "Ya have a point there George I…ahem. Stop…just stop looking at me with them eyes Gab. You got them bug-eyed, creepy-ass glasses and…well anyway, I'm sure they have organic-like food here. Somewhere. I think!" She shook her head at the little one, who continued with his convincing sales pitch. "And besides. Look at you. Gorgeous face, hot figure. And George, um, well he looks good. Got that tall, Matt Dillon, lanky-yet-dopey vibe about him."

She pulled away from the little one and stared at George, then looked back at Fred.

"Why not! He's a good-lookin' *angel.*"

She looked him over, a grin creeping across his face.

George smiled.

"Uh…Gab. You remember, he's not an angel. He's just…dead."

"Oh yeah. Ehh, so. I've dated worse. C'mere Copernicus, lemme show you the buffet."

Gabby grabbed George by the arm and swept him away.

The little one shook his head.

"Dopey as hell, and he gets more dead, than most people do alive. Unbelievable. Note to self: In next life be tall, skinny and stupid. You'll rule the world."

Fred drifted to a part of the roof where no other occupants were. He heard someone call his name, then Jack's. He thought for a second someone upstairs was calling them back, but it wasn't upstairs. He began to lift off the rooftop, ready to fly, but stopped.

He opened his mouth as if to say something aloud to anyone within earshot, like the scant crew of diners near to him. They looked up at Fred as he hovered there oddly. The little one looked down at them and they grinned back, just as politely, saying something about what he was doing under their breath. Then Fred realized what it was.

No, it wasn't heaven calling; that was certain. It was the next best thing, though. The little one glowed and nobody knew why. And they weren't going to know. This was *his* thin slice of heaven. Why let everyone else take a bite (at least right now.) Fred was beaming. No, the voice wasn't heavenly. It was Henry. And he was in school. And he had written a story about them. And he was telling it to the class, proudly. Fred closed his eyes and listened, and it made him smile.

Back in school…

Henry was standing in front of Mrs. Brady's writing class, captivating the imagination of all who were within earshot. It was an on-the-spot assignment. "Write about your best friend." Normally the boy would write about his two classmates, Joey and Patty, but today—today the boy had two others in mind, and he wasn't afraid to tell everyone about them either.

Joey sat about, tapping his foot, humming to himself, which was quite unusual, even for somebody like him. Patty turned around and looked at him funny.

"*I don't care too...{Smack!} much for money. Money can't buy me love... Can't buy me loooovvveee...*"

Patty and Mrs. Brady looked at one another. Then they turned back to the boy confused and weirded out all at once.

"Oh," Joey finished, he himself wondering what he was doing and how he knew the lyrics to a song well before his time.

"*So,*" Henry continued, slowly. He watched his old pal cautiously, as the entire class turned around to stare at the lunatic.

Joey slid down into his chair, covering his face with his hand. Patty held her head up high thinking of how wonderful it was going to be to smack him later.

Mrs. Brady finally blinked and nodded for Henry to continue.

"I," the boy annunciated loudly enough to bring back the class's attention (and he had it alright). They were all fascinated. "I pushed Fred's foot out of the window and shut it. They had to leave. But I know, every night for now on, they'll always be here, watching over me. And I know they care. The end. At least until they come back anyway."

Mrs. Brady led the class in applause; they were all too happy to bestow praise upon their peer. Say what they wanted about him, no one denied Henry his writing; he could write alright! The kids had to give it up for that. And give it up they did. Their eyes were wide with wondrousness that moment and for the rest of the morning thereafter. All they wanted was more.

The teacher smiled. "That's an absolutely wonderful essay, Henry! Very imaginative and very well written." And when she finished expounding on his virtues, Mrs. Brady nodded at the boy anyway. And with a wink, Henry knew that he had done well by his teacher, and by his angels.

Mrs. Brady sat down. "I'm very impressed, guys. I'm very proud of you. Excellent work. *Excellent.*" She accentuated the last one, her face in Henry's direction. The boy sat a foot taller in his seat that day. He couldn't help it, even at that age, he knew that writing was what he was meant to do.

"Let's start where we left off yesterday," she clapped. "Page ten. Daniel, how about *you* give it a shot today."

It was Daniel, the "no one ever picks on me to read aloud" boy, who was chosen. Everybody was shocked, including him. They turned their attention to Dan, who was sitting as always, unnoticeably, in the darkened corner of the room where the fluorescent light blinked in spasms for the many long years of the worn bulb's life. *Pick him? Dan?* Goodness, the vibe that day was just too strange! They were all taken aback, so much so, that Dan had hardly a clue as to what page they were on. But nevertheless…

"Ten, Daniel," the missus called.
"Oh." *Flip. Flip, flip, flip, flip…flip, fliiiip.* "Uh-huh. Here we are."
"Let's go," she gently prodded with a scant grin.
Henry and the gang sat and listened, sat and listened, sat…and…listened. Whew! Daniel was a droner. Plant decomposition was more entertaining. They all understood why he wasn't picked for these tasks. All you heard was a faint, dull sound that barely resembled page ten and crickets chirping in the corners of the classroom. In his coma-like state, Henry felt the bead of those hazel eyes upon him a few seats away. Kristie's eyes turned to Dan and they rolled as she stuck her tongue out. The boy knew that expression as the undeniable face of mutual boredom and the feeling of being held prisoner, a sensation awash over all. Something was different though.
Henry smiled back at her. She had changed since she first met him. Suddenly, tiny pincers for fingers squeezed the fleshy part of the boy's arm, startling him with undeniable pain and near rage. Patty, Miss Hands, the boxer's daughter, leaned over with an amazed look on her face and whispered in the boy's ear.
"Geez, what?" Hen squawked.
"Do they really have wings, and fly and stuff?" she asked so delicately, as if nothing were amiss.
Henry tilted his head to the side, keeping a bead on Mrs. Brady to see if she was watching.
"Yeah of course they fly," the boy said, annoyed.
Joey pulled himself across his desk from the other side; Henry was flanked by the both of them.
"But, you can *see* them Hen?"

Patty looked over. Joey's eyes flashed to her, then back at the boy.

"I mean," Joey continued. "They're really...*there* and everything, right?"

"Yeah Joe, I can see them, and yes they can fly all over the place. Okay?"

Joey took a deep breath and resettled into his seat, eyebrows raising ever so slightly as he thought of his "walk" with Patty.

As if by a twin's psychic bond, she instinctively looked over at him, knowingly, taking a deep breath herself, flipping the pages of her book, in which she was already a good three pages behind. Her eyes expanded in realization of yesterday—that it was not just your average day of days. Yesterday was the start of something *miraculous*—something she just couldn't understand. It was something that made her elated, for it simply was joy. It was also something that she could not comprehend—or see, or touch, and it frightened her beyond words to think that there was actually something out there she could not physically grasp, even if it was as beautiful as angels. It upset her and Joey to no end.

Nothing like that had ever happened before. They had never even heard of anything *that* impossible, and at least if they did, they never remembered it happening to people like them, city kids. Those kinds of things happened out in Kalamazoo someplace, and they only took up sound bites at the end of the newscast, but it wasn't really *real*. Now they didn't know what to think about it. Especially the invisible aspect of it, and the quite literal laying on of hands.

Patty did not know whether to cry, or scream for joy, or fall to pieces all at once. Joey sat across the way, feeling no better. He swallowed hard. *He* felt it too. And there was little old Henry with his story, so simple but so powerful. And he just wasn't afraid. To Joey and Patty, he seemed to understand them—the angels—perfectly. But even if he didn't, he just set the two kids at ease somehow. It didn't matter for Joey and Patty, because there was nothing either one could do—neither in their thoughts nor in their words or glances—to make one another feel any more relaxed or accepting of what had happened to them yesterday. It was too much. And so they pretended that it didn't happen, for what else could they do?

And for every worry line and wrinkle in their little faces, Henry would sigh anxiously, so feverishly enthusiastic about when he would see the angels again, 'cause he knew he would. He just had to! It was funny; they seemed so far away, and yet just talking about them brought them right back. Maybe it was because they made a home within his heart when they touched it with God's love and theirs. Every time he heard them laugh, he heard himself beat with life.

"Yeah, they fly," Henry beamed. "They fly all *over* the place. Around my room, up to the ceiling, out the window. Kind of like Peter Pan."

"But do they have a nana?" Joey asked.

"A what?!" Henry and Patty blurted out.

The eyes. The teacher's eyes rose. Everyone looked down, frantic for that spot on page ten where she would ask them to read if they got caught. Rats! Maybe it was page eleven already. No one knew. You couldn't be sure. Good grief! How could you pay attention to that lifeless child! Blast it, Dan! Rats, again. Or would that be more rats? It didn't matter. Panic, panic, panic. Panic! Ah. Safe. The teacher's eyes returned to their sleepy-socketed positioning.

Henry sighed. The lost place heart-stopper, a finely-honed educational tool passed down through the centuries. The penalty: death by detention.

"Say there, Christopher Robin…" Daniel droned.

Dear God, he makes Eeyore sound like a party animal. What kind of human being reads like this? The class was in the early stages of becoming vegetation on stalks.

It was amazing how the children found ways to amuse themselves throughout the absurdity and boredom of their day. Joey reached across his desk, gripping the front tautly so that he could swing himself back around to proper desk stance positioning if Mrs. Brady's spotlights hit them again.

"Nana!" he said in one hushed blow.

"His grandma?" Patty asked, all a bother.

"No, you idiot. The big fuzzy dog. You know…"

Patty's face became a smooshed-up beanbag.

"Shut up, Joey."

Joey persisted. "Hey Hen, did they really fly or were you just making that up?"

"I-didn't-make-that-up," Henry replied like an automaton, as if he had been through this line of questioning for days now.

Patty belly-flopped across the desk. "He didn't make it up, stupid!"

"Oh you shut up!" the angry little snit-puss that was Joseph Cinnamo belched.

"Shh. She'll catch us," Henry mediated, in his U.N. desk placement. The two world powers to his sides straightened up in their seats and looked forward. That could only mean…blast! Teacher eyes! Why wasn't he alerted before?! Ah! *Traitorous vermin!*

Mrs. Brady interrupted. "Fine Daniel. So why do you think Pooh and Christopher Robin play Pooh Sticks?"

"They didn't have a football handy," Daniel ventured.

The children turned around slowly, looking at their less-than-exciting classmate with ridiculous eyes. Mrs. Brady smiled sheepishly.

"Sure, why not," she said to herself, rising from her desk in lost anticipation of something more. She tossed pages loudly. Oh yeah, she was thrilled.

"Is that what you do when *you're* bored Daniel?" she asked.

"Huh? Me? No. I just play some jacks."

"Jacks."

"Yeah. Or Yahtzee if I have the cup shaker. My brother always loses it."

For a moment, we thought Mrs. Brady had snapped.

"D'ya think Pooh and Christopher Robin would like playing Yahtzee?"

Dan the Man took a deep breath and flexed his fingers.

"Well, since they're in the thousand acre wood—"

"Hundred," she corrected. "There have been no real estate acquisitions in Mr. Milne's world over the last fifty years."

"Hundred aching…*whatever*. I would have to say no. 'Cause," he said with a convincing finger, "if they roll the dice in there, they'd like end up under a log or somethin.'"

How's that for reasoning?

"You weren't dropped as a child, were you, Dan?" she asked.

"Huh?"

"Fine. Never mind. Peter please go on. Page twelve."

"Oh," Dan huffed. "I get it. Um, no...*well*..."

"Peter!"

Wow. That woman was just too smooth. She got Peter and bumped old Dan like a day-old burrito. They think we don't notice these things, those teachers do. They hate dull readers as much as the next kid. So in mid-scrimmage, she tossed in Peter to dump Dan. Wow. The strategy was flawless, and well executed I might add. Wow overflow.

Joey slowly turned around. Patty leaned over. Henry was clued in.

"Yeah Joe. They fly, and the little one, Fred, he likes baked ziti."

"Baked ziti?" the persnickety one echoed.

"Yeah, baked ziti," the boy said again. "They wanted to stay for breakfast but—"

Here comes the mouth.

"Why don't you keep quiet!" the grating little creature bellowed.

It was Danielle Benedetto, but everyone in Henry's class, including Mrs. Brady, called her Big-Mouth Benedetto for simply one reason: She just was.

Patty turned over. "What's your problem *now*, Big Mouth?"

"You!" the pale, redheaded menace pointed, crooked fingers and all. "Why don't you turn around before I box your ears in, Patty!"

"Go box this!" Patty said, sticking her tongue out.

"What till lunch *Miss Wilson*," the Mouth sneered. "And you, Henry. I'm not finished with you yet."

"Oh, great," Henry mumbled.

"You stink and your whole story stinks. There is no such thing as flying people who can jump around and fly out windows and everything. And even if there were, they wouldn't like baked ziti!"

Patty leaned on her fist, staring at her book, trying to figure out where they were this time.

"How would you know, Big Mouth?" she asked.

Joey jumped in with an angry, waving fist. "Yeah Big Mouth, why can't flying people like baked ziti?"

"Why don't you two shut up and mind your own business? I," she said with an uppity face, "was talking to Henry. And don't call me Big Mouth! I hate that name, you little jerk!"

Joey lost his composure, and his whisper. "You ugly—"

Mrs. Brady had heard the talking for five minutes now, but she was waiting for the most obvious offender before she pounced (like her own private teacher's sting operation—too cool, but not if you were the stingee). There she goes, zeroing in on the sound producer.

Target Acquired…Arming! Joey twisted in his seat, which felt like a potential bear trap, and all but screamed, *"Snagged, sucker!"*

"Mr. Cinnamo!" The palm of her hand struck the flat of the textbook. Oh yeah, he was screwed! "Mr. Milne spent a great deal of time and effort giving his characters life and purpose, thereby making them as real as you or I. With that in mind, perhaps you'd like to spend a quiet moment right now, reconsidering the importance of your conversation with Miss Benedetto. Good. Now will you be joining me at three o'clock for a repeat performance of this reading lesson, or are you clear and focused?"

"I'm clear and focused *now*," Joey said, still annoyed at the pasty, redheaded menace.

"Very well, then we'll continue."

Big Mouth wore a smug look. Kristie shook her head in silent indignation, quietly looking on the entire time.

"Don't look so smug, Miss Benedetto," the teacher's voice reappeared.

"You didn't earn the name *Big Mouth* by being an innocent bystander, did you now?"

"BWA-HA-HA-HA-HA…HA!" the class went on for seconds.

Kristie didn't smile though.

"Carry on with your work Danielle. Let's continue with *The House at Pooh Corner*. Lisa, you read this time."

Henry turned back to Kris again, who sat quietly in the corner. She stared at him, looking as if the color had been drained from her features.

However, the Big Mouth was hardly shut. She was angry now. And she started up…again.

"Your story is *lousy*, Henry!" Onslaught of Ridicule, take two {Snap!}

began. "Why do you always have to use big words in your essays? You said that they 'maneuvered' around the room. Why couldn't you just say 'moved' instead?" the grating, annoyingly nasal voice clamored. She was relentless. "What do you think you are, the teacher's pet? Using fancy words, and making up flying people for best friends because you don't have any *real* friends. You don't have anybody."

From a distance Kristie grimaced; she could no longer pay attention to her textbook while Henry was berated this way. She was but a heartbeat away from getting up and hitting her.

"At least I have a best friend, Amy. You don't have *anybody*. Nobody likes you."

"Jack & Fred like me," the little boy said.

Big Mouth drew closer. "Oh yeah, well they're not even real. You made them up. The only people who can fly are angels? You can't see angels. No one can! People like you pretend to see them when they're *only children* and don't have any brothers or sisters or any real friends!"

Henry lost it. "Oh shut up, Big Mouth!"

"Huh!" Kris squeaked in surprise, covering her mouth.

"*Ooooooh!*" the class sounded, turning around.

Patty shielded her face. She didn't want to be implicated in this (but somehow she always was) 'cause her parents would kill her if she got written up again.

"Miss Benedetto!" Mrs. Brady screamed. "Perhaps you'd like to talk a little louder. Sister Amelia's seventh grade class down the hall didn't quite hear you!"

"But Mrs. Brady, he keeps bothering me," Big Mouth whined.

Joey looked flabbergasted. He just couldn't believe what he was hearing.

"All he keeps talking about is what's-their-names, Jack and Ralph!" she ranted.

"Fred," Henry corrected her.

"Who cares!" she screeched, throwing up her arms. "And then he called me Big Mouth!"

Mrs. Brady slammed the book shut. "Well he's right Danielle, you are a big mouth."

The class had a good old laugh for themselves…again.

"BWA-HA-HA-HA-HA…HA!"

The boy mused to himself: *Who in God's name laughed that extra "ha" after everyone else? Huh? Probably the same kid who grew up to be the single-applause person. You know, the one who claps last after everyone finishes? Or the guy in the professional wrestling audience that counts to twelve when the wrestler only bashes his adversary ten times. You see, it starts at early childhood and carries on for the rest of one's known life! Good grief, Chuck!*

"Now stop bothering Henry and everyone else in this room for heaven's sake."

Joey sat smugly, pointing a scolding, "you take that" finger at Big Mouth as Mrs. Brady spoke.

"And Henry, if *rude* people try to distract you by making their obnoxious comments, just ignore them and turn around. Don't give them the satisfaction of answering back."

Joey nodded at Henry, without invitation, punctuating Mrs. Brady's points with his gestures. This time it was a "yeah, that's right" nod.

"That goes for you too, Miss Wilson."

Patty shook her head. She knew she'd get involved somehow.

"Yes ma'am," she moaned properly.

She straightened her books out in front of her and grabbed for a pencil.

Joey nodded at her with a face of empathetic agreement, giving her a thumbs-up.

"And *you*, Mr. Cinnamo."

He turned, agitated.

"What'd *I* do now?" Joey thumbed at himself.

"Mr. Cinnamo—"

"Sorry, for whatever it was." Joey turned around and around to all of his classmates, hands held high in the air, like he was complaining or having a hissy fit, or both. "Sorry, sorry, sorry. Sorry! I'm so sorry, I don't even know what it's for anymore."

"Mr. Cinnamo—"

Joey spun back, irritated.

"Oh, what!" he barked at his teacher.
"Three o'clock," Mrs. Brady smiled.
"Sorry?"
"So am I, Joey. So am I."
Mrs. Brady gave Henry a quick grin and continued with her lesson. In the scheme of things, what did it all mean anyway?

"Now. How is Pooh similar to the book we read last week, *Padington*?"

Henry shined. He picked up his pencil, not before turning back to see Kristie in the corner. She waved to Henry and with a finger told him to wait a moment. In short order, she pulled from the pocket of her blue coveralls a small beanbag froggy. She held him, squeezing his belly to make him lean forward like he was bowing and saying hello over and over.

Big Mouth noticed this. Henry adjusted himself in his seat, glaring at the little wildebeest with an upturned lip. The Mouth then set her sights on Kris, who simply stuck her tongue out at Danielle, putting her thumb to her nose, making a funny waving gesture with her soft little fingers.

"That's from Jack & Fred!" she mouthed with an air of pride.

"*Humph!*" Big Mouth Benedetto scowled, and looked at her book reluctantly, perhaps for the first time all morning.

They couldn't help it. They were all restless. The children were all unsettled, like wild animals stirring just before an earthquake set off. Kristie caught Henry in her sights, winked, and smiled. The boy smiled back. It was like seeing heaven in his eyes. He wasn't lying about the angels. He did see them. Kristie wondered why she could not.

Joey glanced over at Patty, almost as if he wanted to apologize for getting her into trouble and for the fact that he was still so unsettled about their near-accident. There was no one else in the world who could help him, but her. Patty stared at him sympathetically. For once, the girl, older by only two months, could do nothing to make her beloved friend be at ease when she herself was a mass of twisted emotions.

{ Chapter 21 }

The Proposal

Back at the Dings…

Fred found himself at the other end of Wingdings, where a group of angels had gathered in a huddle. They were cheering on one of their own in the center. Little Julie the angel yelled inspirational things into one of the windows of the school of business.

"What's going on here?" Fred asked one of them, with authority in his voice.

Carol turned to him. "She's giving the kids answers."

"Answers?"

"Yeah, this teacher gave the college kids this impossible economics test, just to be a chop-buster. So Julie there is giving them the answers!" Carol said excitedly.

Little Julie, puffing her tiny chest out, screamed cheerfully, "Marginal utility. Supply and Demand. Vanishing Return. Four Bananas!"

From out of nowhere, Flo came bounding across the thoroughfare, yanking the little spirit off the roof tiles by the scruff of her tiny little neck, sending her reeling into the onlookers, which the matronly one carved into two neat halves. The boss lady grew threatening. Fred had seen this before, many times in many tunes, and opted to keep well out of her sights and clear of the demolition.

"If I told you once, I told you a million times!" Flo roared. "No inspiring the humans on tests!"

"Yeah, but that thing's impossible," Carol protested.

"I don't care!" she threw back.

Fred was cool, keeping himself down-wing of the action, as it were.

Flo drew herself all the way up into Carol's puss.

"Let them do something on their own. *They'll* work it out!"

"And what if *they* don't work it out," skinny little Carol said, steadying her hands on her finely-shaped hips.

"If they don't, we pay the teacher a visit in his sleep tonight," Flo assured.

The angels nodded to one another, relishing the idea.

"Besides," the proprietress continued, "if you do everything for them, what's the point in them learning anything? They'll just sit and wilt."

They all looked at her, unconvinced. But Flo merely glared at them, raising her eyebrows half a heartbeat.

"Hmm?" Flo sounded.

Heads were bobbing up and down in frightened agreement.

"Go on, little angels. Get lost. Show's over. Besides, they're opening up the buffet on the west wing."

Angelic eyeballs became wide and gleeful, mouths all salivating with Thanksgiving table fantasies.

"Oooh, buffet," they rumbled in unison, charging across the roof like starved pack animals.

"Ahh!" Jimmy the angel yelled, two seconds too late for the mighty angelic steamroller.

"Ouch," Fred remarked, watching Jimmy disappear in a dust cloud from the rush of a hundred feet, legs, and wings storming by.

When the cloud cleared, a cross-eyed angel with tweeting birds a'singin' around his head, popped up from the roof tiles.

"Oooh look. They can all fly," he said dizzily. "Flap, flap, flap, flap flaaap…" Bonk! And he went out just as fast.

Flo couldn't help herself. "Amazing, even angels go bananas over buffet."

She shook away the observation, grinning to herself, while slapping a sign on the wall near the open window. It read: *"Please, do not inspire the humans. And enjoy your stay at Wingdings. -From the management."*

The matronly one turned back to Fred, as if she were oblivious to her own actions.

"Personally I can't see it. The buffet I mean. I don't want to work for my food. Ah," she clapped her hands together, pacing, looking up at the sky, and putting her arm around the little one. "You see, hon?" They walked together. "They make me sound like the ogre. I'm not the ogre."

"You're the ogress," Fred said.

Flo ignored it.

"Even I throw the kids an answer or two, once in a while."

Flo jumped down on her hands and knees, leaning over the edge of the pitched roof, looking around suspiciously, and then yelling inside the closest window, *"Eleven!"*

Fred's eyes brightened. "I like you."

"Of course you do. I'm me. I know you can't help it. But so help me, Fuzzy, if I ever catch you telling anyone, I'll give you the old iron hand."

She waved it at him.

Fred smirked. "The hand that never tarnishes. You got it kid."

Flo's stern face melted like butter when she looked at the little one head on. "God you're cute!"

He held out his hand and Flo took it. She drew herself up and they walked some more.

"So where's your bodyguard?"

Fred crossed his arms. "On a non-stop journey to mush land."

"He found a girl already? Hmm. How about that! Man. Yeah, but it *is* Jack."

"I know."

"He *does* get around."

"I know!"

"Kid's a player."

"He's never *played* with you," Fred said kicking a piece of stray roof tile.

"He can't handle me," Flo said with a wink. "Besides, I'm high maintenance."

"I never thought so."

"Yeah, well, you never stayed around to find out."

The little one was taken aback. She balanced along the line of tiles, trying not to step on the cracks.

"Would that have made a difference?" he asked.

"Maybe. There's nothing wrong with you finding a home."

"Which means?"

"Which means, Jack likes being Jack. He always finds someone to fly to. But you, if you and him aren't flying together, you get all miserable. You'd rather be alone."

"So…"

"So, I've known you a long time, Fred. All I'm saying is…the two of you can't fly down here indefinitely. At some point they will—"

"Flo," Fred interrupted, pulling her back by the arm. "You know how long we've been down here. C'mon. You think they're gonna yank us back upstairs after all these years? Please."

"All I'm saying Fred is…you have somewhere to go if things change."

"Things have already changed."

She caressed his face.

"Who's the guy with Gabby, the one you brought along?"

"George."

"Is George a detached spirit?"

Fred walked along the edge of the tiles in silence.

"Oh my God. Hon, do you have any—"

"It's alright. We're going to see Sidney."

Worry was spread out all over her face.

"Flo, you know Sidney. The barrister's the man. He's been handling our little incidents and accidents for years now. He'll fix it." Flo looked at him cautiously. "When Jack gets back here, at some point, we'll just take care of it." Fred caressed her cheek, brushing her hair aside, running his palm along the contour of Flo's face. She closed her eyes, smiling. "We'll take care of it gorgeous. Promise."

"How do you do that?"

"What?"

"Make everyone feel better, all the time. My Superman."

Fred gave her a dismissing wave.

"I don't do tights," he said, grabbing two handfuls of belly.

"Really. You know, when Lois Lane falls, and she always does, Superman catches her. He never misses. But what about him?"

"What *about* him?"

"Who catches him, when he falls?"

"Superman never falls, you know that," the little one smiled and balanced himself along the roof's edge nearly falling over. Flo reached out and grabbed him, reeling him in.

"Then forget Superman. What about *you*, Fred? Who catches you if you fall?"

"I've always got Jack."

"Just remember something, little one. You always have *me*."

She kissed his mouth softly.

"Yeah," he sighed, not expecting it. Flo held his face in her hands for just a moment.

"So..." she changed the subject. "Didn't you two like the table? I gave ya the best in the house!"

"Blame him!"

"Aw, he's just found something that caught his eye. Love at first sight and all that other romantic crap," she disregarded with a sweeping hand, pretending to be uninterested, just to make the little one happy. She'd do anything for him.

Fred smiled. He could always count on her when the chips were down, or when there were just no chips to be had to begin with.

"*I don't know,*" she shrugged. "But I gotta go, hon. Restaurant to run. It doesn't run itself."

She moved to kiss him on the cheek.

"Flo?"

"What, babe?"

"Why?"

She looked at him.

"Why what, sweetheart?"

"The others. Why do they look at us like…" Fred couldn't explain, but she knew exactly.

"Because they see in you a strength, a love that never burns out. No matter what happens."

"We're not special."

"You are. Because you don't know you have it, and you don't know that you give it to all of us."

Fred shook his head. "What?"

"*Hope*. We see these college kids every day; so many of them are so hurt and lost. They're *so* sad Fred. We look down, then we fly down. And we feel for them. We feel it right along with them, and it makes *us* sad. But you and Jack give us hope when it seems like there should be none. You remind us that there is, though, no matter what. You make people and angels smile."

"How?" he asked sheepishly, wondering why they couldn't do that for themselves when they needed it. But maybe they did after all, without noticing *how*.

"That's just what you do. The others look at you two, and they feel that the connection between people and angels isn't as distant as it sometimes seems. When you're not here, well, sometimes the distance feels greater. Especially in this place." She looked around. "But when you're here, we've never felt closer to the people downstairs. That and…"

Fred blinked.

"Look at you. You're just too darn cuuute." She took his face in her hands and planted one. *"Mmwaa."*

The lovely proprietress put her head on his shoulder, blinking her eyes rapidly and sighing like an exaggerated version of her baby sister Ida.

"Go away," he dismissed, a giant smile creeping across his face.

"Bye, sweetie!" she mimicked in a sing-songy voice, poppin' pretend gum, and rubbing the lipstick from his cheek. "I'll see you later!"

"Go on," Fred waved.

"Come see me if you have the time," she said with dearest hope.

"I *always* have the time, silly."

She blew him a kiss with both hands. *"Byyyee."* Her pink gown danced over her as she sped away.

"Bye…Flo," Fred said to himself, realizing that he was suddenly alone. He saw George down below with Gabby, floating about, looking around at the new world before him. He felt himself move, but at that moment there was no place he needed to be. He knew that and decided to sit and do nothing.

{ Chapter 22 }

The One and Only. Who else?

Jack flew down to the football field, searching excitedly for *her*. He looked under the bleachers, inside the announcer's booth, even round the outskirts of the campus' back-road entrance, but the vision was nowhere to be found. His search came up empty, and his spirits did also.

"I think I'm losing it," Jack muttered to himself, wondering if she was real or just a delightful hallucination from a very tired mind.

He was so lit up one moment and so let down the next, like with everything else in his life. And he sighed, taking a moment to reassure himself not to be disappointed about this one thing too. With that, Jack settled down upon the goal post, folding up his wings, creating a cushion for himself to sit on. A wind danced across his face, and at that moment the trees and shrubbery on the perimeter of the field rustled. *Was it?* Jack spun around like lightning, but found only two human maintenance men moseying past quietly with their tools and soft, silent mushy feet, speaking in some language that was as far removed from its origin as could be.

"Just...forget it. God!" he said to himself, turning away.

He picked through his feathers absently, like people biting their nails when they're stressed. And the grass rustled again, only the maintenance men were gone this time, but Jack didn't care to waste his moments looking away from his dull preoccupation in wistful hopes of something more. He sat there, like a cat on a rail, preening, never losing balance—not once.

To be honest, he was happy for the one free moment in the day when he could do this without any distractions. The saying goes, "If you want to get something done, give it to a busy man." But the busy *angel* needed a break every now and then, even for something so mundane as cleaning his feathers.

It was like taking the accumulated lint buildup out of a dryer filter, only thicker. It wasn't a terribly important thing to do, but dusty wings just made things uncomfortable, and very irritating, especially for Jack. He was *most* sensitive to it. With all the flying he and Fred had done, lots of little things had accumulated inside his wings: bits of dirt, lint, burrs, some bugs—stuff like that. There wasn't a time ever in their lives when they wore the often-depicted downy-snow wings of the angels in illustrations.

Inside one of the outermost deep, blue feathers, he found a small, hard leaf jammed in between. And it was *reaaally* stuck. Jack picked and picked but couldn't quite dislodge the green spearhead from its awkward position. He became enraged. "Ah, stop it!" he growled at himself. Much to his frustrated chagrin, Jack had to stop what he was doing altogether.

He sat there for a moment and felt the winter sun's tiny heat radiating against his cheeks, not even bothering to notice the soft shadow that was slowly coming down upon his form. The angel took in a deep breath, sprawled his hands out to his sides, and then released it. Maybe yoga was the way. The glorious impression above him smiled, and she had to cover her mouth to contain her joyous laughter.

He was going to try it. He and Fred watched over a yoga lady once upon a lifetime ago, Jack remembered. The little one thought that maybe he should give this a try, 'cause it worked for everyone else. Only it didn't work for Jack. It never worked for Jack. And it still didn't.

Jack clenched his fists, snarling audibly as the pair of majestically angelic eyes watched him with delightful curiosity.

His peaceful expression became downright fierce. He bit down on his back teeth and in a fury grabbed his left wing and clawed through it with both hands in grim determination of his goal and in disappointment of not being able to find *her,* on the field, even though she was right behind him the entire time. He could not get rid of this *blasted leaf!*

The angel shoved his whole face inside the wing, ripping and tearing at the foliage with his teeth, like an angry tiger. And as if on request, or not, a petite little finger reached out from behind and jabbed poor Jack in the chubs with the sharpest fingernail she could find.

"Yaaahooowwww!" Jack howled, involuntarily flinging himself through the goal post he was sitting on.

"It's good!" she exclaimed, raising her arms as if Jack had touchdowned.

The old boy sat on the ground, giving pause to the electricity that was still running up the length of his body, catching his breath, and trying to stop his heart from beating itself out. He took a calm breath and realized—*ahhh*—his wing was all better. He heard a soft giggle above him. And a hand reached down before his eyes with the leaf sitting lightly upon her palm.

He drew his eyes upward, nearly blinded by the sparkling aura about her. The majestic one floated down before him, radiance dancing like sunshine across rippling waters. A bright white halo of gold floated above her head. Her tiny wings flapped with a hummingbird's grace and a helicopter's gusting fury. Silky brown hair fell across her face, covering her ears and beautiful brown eyes. She was absolutely breathtaking. And she was here at last.

Belle gently handed Jack the jagged leaf.

"You were looking for this?" she asked debonairly.

"Ahhh," the angel sighed relief. "You got it. You wonderful thing you," he said, completely mystified, with a handful of feathers stuck in the corner of his mouth.

"Thanks," she said.

Jack realized how forward that was and blushed an exceedingly loud red. *I never do that.* Who was he, this blushing angel, he asked himself.

"You know, Jack," she explained as she sauntered across the grass, "You should remove all the feathers before eating the bird. They don't taste good on their own, especially without salt."

"You're, hhrrrm…right. They don't." Jack sat, terribly embarrassed, plucking each feather from his drawn mouth one by one by…one. "Hey," he stammered, jumping to his feet in stark realization. "Hey, it's *you*!"

"It's me," she said straightly with open arms. "The one and only. Who else did you expect? That's what you came down here for."

Jack was always calm and cool, suave even. He felt like it was his first time at the school dance, as awkward as if he had a third wing.

"I, I… I came down to inspect the artificial turf."

"You have a problem with real grass?"

"Real grass is…fine, I suppose," Jack said.

She paced with her head down, but her eyes rolled up to look at him. "Artificial turf is terribly unpredictable, you know?" she said, reaching out to him. He clasped her hand tightly in his own and lifted himself up.

"Really?"

"Yes. It causes bad hops."

"Did today," Jack replied.

They looked at one another as if ready to play en garde yet again. It was definitely her. His hand smelled like rose petals now.

"My partner and I were going to get something to eat, up there," he pointed to the Dings. "And we *saw* you."

"Did you now? But your partner's not down here, is he?"

"No, he's not."

Belle jumped and flew up to the goal post. Jack dashed right up behind her—nearly forgetting how it was he could fly.

"Not the first time I saw you, Jack."

"I know."

"*How* do you know?"

"Your perfume. Rose petals. That scent was downtown after the chase."

"Sure it was me? Lots of angels smell of rose petals. That's our scent."

"True. But none of them giggle like you."

"I *did* like that funky traffic cop thing you do."

"Did you now?"

"Oh yeah."

"I knew you were there," Jack said with a confident smile.

"Yeah, yeah, yeah. People often do ridiculous things when they *know* others are watching. Am I supposed to believe that?"

Jack watched her as she drew up onto her tiptoes, casually sauntering across the horizontal yellow post like a balance beam, taking one step for every breath Jack released.

Jack reclined backward on his arm, throwing his leg over the other, looking up at her causally. "Don't really care what you believe, sweetheart."

"Mmm," she murmured, balancing, spinning on one foot, and turning to walk in the other direction. "You've got to be careful. With feathers I mean."

"Why's that?"

"You take too big of a bite, and you can *choke*." She ventured a glance and grinned. "They can get caught up in your throat and everything. It can be a real bother. The feathers I mean. You know."

Jack nodded.

"You're too tense, Jack," she said, "Your feathers were all bound up. I just helped to open them a little," Belle enlightened as she jumped in place like a ballerina, landing on her toes again. She leaned over to balance on one leg while the other drew up behind her.

"Yeah, *thanks*," Jack said, rubbing his newly comforted wing, eyes very enthusiastic. "Thanks a heap!"

"You're welcome a heap," she replied, reaching the end of the post, spinning back around once more to look at him. "You know, you have an awful nice coat of feathers, Mr. Jack," she said. "Kind of like down. You'd make a lovely pillow, really."

"Is that so?"

"I wouldn't mind resting my head against you."

Jack leaned closer to her lips.

"So what's stopping you?" he said but a breath away from her.

They stared into one another's eyes for the longest of moments until she broke the silence.

"So how're things with the boy?" Belle inquired.

Jack was taken by the question. "How do you know about the boy?"

"Doesn't everybody?"

"Not to my knowledge," he said, almost defensive of his boy, miles away. "Where did you hear that?"

Belle closed her eyes, nodding to one side in concession.

"Well, it could just be me. Let's just say I know things. They call it networking now, don't they?"

"And what exactly *do* you know?" he asked with a sly though apprehensive look in his eyes.

"Oh, I know lots of things," she admitted.

"What do you know," Jack balanced toward her, "about me?"

Belle sat down in place, averting his eyes and neatening her dress beneath her. She crossed her legs ever so daintily, looking at her nails. Jack stood grinning with his hands on his hips, that debonair Cary Grant awash over his features.

"Not all that much," she said, preoccupying herself.

Jack didn't flinch this time.

"Mr. Jack, request angel, several centuries along now. Partner's name is Fred. Jack is the serious one, mostly. Fred is the funny one, but you're both scoundrels and cause an equal amount of mischief when you're together in one place. Always in good taste though, I might add."

"You might," he glowed, taking a seat beside her with a more casual posture.

"Though when you tried driving old Marty insane, well…"

"Marty, that former angelic air traffic controller? Artie's brother? Him? He was an absolutely *annoying* guy! Used to eat pistachios when he'd talk to you over the air, crunching in your ear. Besides, that was a lifetime ago. How would you know anything about that? You're just a kid."

Belle tilted her head, waiting for the rest of the excuse.

"He works at Arrivals now, upstairs. Anyway, go on," Jack sighed.

"How long since *you* worked up there?"

"I'm strictly downstairs. I don't work in heaven."

"What's the wall for?"

"Our wall? God, you are nosey little Miss Muffet."

"Thank you."

"Ever hear of this thing people have called a sensory deprivation tank?"

"Yes."

"Wall's the same thing, with a view."

"I see."

The sun was in Jack's eyes. Every now and again it would appear and warm the winter air. "I like your dress. Red velvet."

"Smooth to the touch."

"Looks it."

"Feels it too. It's new. I flew down with it."

"Good choice. You have a good flight down?"

"No," Belle shuddered.

Jack moved closer. "Winds?"

"No. Well yes, but there were voices, sounds…it was too loud and I lost my balance."

"Voices. What'd they say?"

"So I hear you give St. Peter a lot of grief." Jack didn't understand why she moved on, but he knew Belle heard something.

"Peter's old school. He can handle us. He's handled worse!"

"Annnd," she continued, stopping to give him her direct attention. "You were just assigned to help a little boy named Henry. Isn't that right?"

"I don't know about 'assigned.' But…I'm impressed. You do your homework."

She turned to him. "Only in subjects I'm interested in. Only now, you have a problem. Several actually."

Jack crossed his arms.

"Namely…"

"Namely, you're harboring a detached spirit named George Morano. The moron, right? This is the guy who you carried along for the ride because you went back to visit the boy for your own selfish reasons."

"Selfish? Hey, now you hold on just a second, lady. You haven't the slightest clue what you're talking about when it comes to—"

"It's called…off the map? Isn't that right? What're you going to do when Peter finds out? You know the penalty for—"

Jack took her roughly by the arms.

"You listen, before you continue. We got sidetracked with George. Yeah I'll admit that. It was only because we didn't want that kid and the others to get killed on the damn subway after being lost all day. I wasn't going to let them tough it out because I had to get a guy who was already dead, upstairs. He'll have an eternity in paradise, it's not like a few hours is going to make a difference!" Jack lightened his grip, running his hands smoothly down the sides of her shoulders, letting go as he slowly backed away. He turned his head, looking off into the distance. She stared at him wantonly, his back to her. "And I don't know what *off the map* means. It's ridiculous. I don't know where that came from. Love is never something you can give people too much of."

"It's love then. You love this boy."

Jack turned around slowly.

"Honestly…"

"Honestly," she repeated.

He looked at her. "What business is it of yours?" Jack's knees bent, and he started to springboard upward to leave. She held him by the wrist.

"What business is it of mine? I'll tell you. It's because you watched over my little girl, Kristie. That's why. You didn't have to, but you did. You're right. It's something you can never give too much of. Even if they don't love you back." She bit her lip, sighing. For the first time, Belle looked weary. "You watched over that boy as if he was your own. You're not his guardian angels, but there you were. I had to meet the angel whose stories regaled this group at the café for decades now. The one with the partner, who everyone always spoke about. You guys were always talked about as larger-than-life spirits, mythical heroes. And I never thought it was possible for even one of us angels to be so self-sacrificing that they'd risk their own station and the consequences of going against what we're supposed to do, to help a person below."

Jack shrugged, humbled many times over. "It's just our job. That's all. So," he said, letting out a deep breath, "how come you keep disappearing on me?"

Belle put one hand on his shoulder and ran her fingers through his hair with the other.

"It's a *human* game," she exhaled. "When they're children, they call it 'hide and go seek.' When they're adults, they call it 'hard to get.' Haven't you ever played?"

Jack smiled.

"Sure, I know 'hide and go seek,'" he said unabashedly. "I didn't grow up in a turnip patch, you know." Jack took her by the hands and he danced her backward along the goal post. They started their verbal swordplay yet again and it spiraled out of control too fast to catch; but it was only because they were having so much fun.

She asked. "Where did you grow up?"

"That's a long story."

"Where's your partner?"

"That's an even longer story."

She smiled, ruffling his hair.

"Is your wing gonna be alright now?"

"Are we going to continue with this verbal tit-for-tat all day?" Jack asked.

"Only if you want to."

"Yes."

"Fine."

"No, my wing."

"Is fine?"

"Yes."

"I'm happy."

"Yes."

"Very happy?"

Jack laughed.

"You're beautiful, you know that?"

Belle got slightly off track. "I…"

"*Gotcha*," Jack winked.

She held out her hands, crossed over. Belle decreed, "I've met my match this day in battle."

Jack smiled warmly. "Mmm-hmm."

Belle and Jack rose to their feet and bowed respectfully.

"My lady," he said with a sweep of the hand.

"Dear kind sir," she replied in Shakespearean chords. "No one's ever beaten me before," she enlightened.

"There's a first time for everything."

"Including us."

"Is this a rematch?"

"It is if you want one."

"Okay, okay, stop! You're making me dizzy."

Belle extended a hand. "Even?"

Jack shook the hand. "Even."

"But be warned, my dearest," she beckoned. "I play a wicked game of checkers."

"Touché," he conceded.

Belle eyed him from behind, up *and* down.

"Yes it is."

Jack's wings instinctively covered his, um…posterior.

"Yes…well," Jack shrugged, feeling a bit awkward. "That's because I'm Jack," he winked.

Belle stretched out, looking over the length of the campus.

"Isn't it a glorious day to be out," she said so innocently.

"It is now," Jack said, eyeing her and the buildings, which didn't look so bland and claustrophobic when she spoke about the world. Belle leaped into the air, flying to the evergreens. Jack was right across from her, making a perfect pair.

She closed her eyes and seemed even more beautiful. Maybe it was the lofty setting and the greenery around her, or maybe it was her gentle beauty, a sweet sensation to Jack's every sense.

She sighed. "Wish I was one of these trees, with the wind blowing through them, swaying back and forth, on days like these," she said.

"No thanks. I'd rather be a guardian angel," Jack said unabashedly, looking off. "Like you. That to me is far more beautiful."

She looked at him.

Jack shrugged. "I don't even know your name."

Belle pulled out a small bell and started shaking it in front of Jack's eyes.

"I, um...I have *no* idea what you're doing. I was never any good at charades. What..."

Little Julie came leaping and bounding out of the woodwork (literally). She was flying out from the trees, screaming.

"Wings! I got my wings! I've been waiting for years, and now I've finally gotten my wings!" she spun around showing Jack and Belle her new additions. Jack raised his eyebrows, as they hovered above her by the trees.

"Oh thank you, Belle!" Little Julie propped up on her tiptoes and kissed Belle's cheek. "Get it? Bell! Ringing! Wings! Ha-ha! This is an absolute dream come true!" She jumped for joy, twirling and twirling, dancing like a mad ballerina. "I can fly! I can fly! I can fly! Wait!" The small one puffed her chest out. "This, is a job...for Julie!"

The little angel ripped away her smock, revealing a makeshift brown paper bag *J*. Jack and Belle looked at one another, absolutely bowled over.

Julie went running across the nearby field, leaping high into the sky for Wingdings.

"Up, up, and away!"

"*Incoming!*" someone screamed, as the patrons all ducked for cover. Van Fleet looked about furiously for the source of the whistling, and when he found it coming from above, he simply closed his eyes and covered his ears.

Belle and Jack cringed as Little Julie went careening into the Ding's kitchen. Pots and pans and silverware smashed and crashed all over the place. One lone lid cover twirled on its edge for what seemed like an eternity and then fell into silence.

A voice went out over the angelic band.

"Central? Yeah, this is Artie. Send in the truck. We got a real doozey here. Over."

The patrons slowly got up, sitting on edge, waiting for the small one to pop back up for air again. Little Julie crawled out, her head spinning.

"*Oy,*" she groaned, passing out.

Flo appeared before the disaster zone.

"Vaaaaaaaannnnnnn Fleeeeeeeeeeeetttt!!!"

"Coming, Madame!"

Belle and Jack looked at one another.

"Personally," she remarked. "I was always more of a Spider-man fan myself."

"Me too."

"Uh-huh."

"So, *Belle* huh?"

"Short for Anabelle. But…yeah."

"You're unbelievable, *Belle*."

"I know," she said flashing her pearly whites. "C'mon," she grabbed him. "I'll show you the rest of the campus."

And they were off.

Fred looked out across the horizon and saw two black dots moving further and further away, and he shook his head, wandering off to no place in particular.

She and Jack passed a number of angels by a nearby church bell tower.

"Hey, Belle!" they swooned in unison.

"Hello, boys!" she waved dramatically.

"You're a regular Meryl Streep around here," Jack said, enjoying her company thoroughly, much to the envy of everyone around him.

"Meryl ain't got nothin' on me," she winked.

"Touché," Jack winked.

And Belle flaunted it, too.

"I think I'm gonna like college," Jack said to himself.

Fred found himself on the opposite end of the roof, which overlooked the campus' vertical parking garage and the woods. The angels there, a scant crew of unfamiliar faces, counted the cars coming out of the two-story garage—ten blues, three red, two green, a yellow, and a periwinkle. And he watched them rush down every two to three breaths, preventing accidents from happening, as the kids zipped out of the concrete and steel structure with girls and boys and radios and dates and homework, and *home* on their minds. The commuter kids were all going home.

"I don't have a home," Fred said to himself aloud. None of the others heard him; some turned around with awkward looks, wondering why he was standing there by himself, though. He turned back and looked over at the field again, and Jack wasn't there. He was gone…with her, not him. And a hundred thousand angels ate and dined and danced and moved through the enormous café as if it were life as usual for them. And it appeared that no one was even slightly interested whatsoever in the little one, his problems, or his apparent lack of company. With all the waiters that worked for Van Fleet, and Flo and Ida moving about, and couples sitting at tables enjoying each other's company, no one noticed him anymore. And for that moment, without Jack, Flo, or the boy, he felt so alone.

"Fred?"

What was Flo talking about? Something wasn't…right.

"Fred?!"

{ Chapter 23 }
A Feather's Touch

Henry's older friend Anthony approached him in the schoolyard and the two shook hands like adults and greeted each other. They struck up a conversation by the unused front portion of the schoolyard away from the busy-bodies and other pain-in-the-necks.

Without warning, Big Mouth and Patty went flying by, grappling with one another. It was a clash of titans that would end in the utter trouncing of one or the other of them. Their hands grasped around each other's throats with white-knuckle torque, heads bobbing back and forth on their very sockets as they tried to choke the life from one another. But it was Patty, the boxer's daughter, who pressed the advantage that day, pushing the larger girl back upon her heels as they sailed past. It seemed as if the fair-haired Miss Wilson would win the day over her large-mouthed classmate. And not a soul, other than the boy and his upperclassman pal, noticed or appreciated it.

"I'll knock you into next week you little beast!" Patty screeched with a crimson, puffed face.

"Ahhhh!" the Mouth shrieked.

Anthony spoke with his hands. Both boys became so involved in their words that it almost seemed like the cacophony of sight and sound around them was nonexistent and inconsequential.

The monotonous hum of the yard drowned out Kristie's thoughts. She walked slowly, parting from some group of girls that paid her no mind in the first place. She stood there. People screaming, fighting, and running; all of it went past her. She looked up at the loud, crackling airplane roaring over in the winter-blue sky, engines sounding as if it were dropping altitude and falling. She looked around at this place. She was just getting used to it. How would she ever tell him?

Miss Kris tried to comprehend it all but couldn't. When she first arrived to this new school some weeks back, she decided that if she couldn't beat it, she'd just have to join in with this place. The schoolyard sounded like living inside the guts of garbage can that got smacked quite frequently with a large metal spoon. Kristie thought back all those weeks ago; she thought about the day he met her. She held her head at the thought, and when she peeked upward, in her mind's eye she saw him, her Henry. And across the yard, there he was…

Kristie saw the boy and knew it would be all right. So, she gathered up enough guff to walk over there to the fence where he was leaning, imagining a worst-case scenario of him yelling "get lost." But she knew he would never do that. He was her best friend. Perhaps she wanted to say it to herself; so often it was the face in the mirror that she couldn't stand. But the boy was something else. Henry looked so different when she was watching him from afar and he wasn't looking back. He almost seemed too lonely, even with the older boy speaking to him.

Anthony turned back to Henry, and from behind she gently gripped his shoulder, not startling him in the least. He was expecting her. That's just how they were…

"That was some story you wrote," the girl with hazel eyes said.

"Thanks," the boy replied warmly. He felt as though he could spill his guts to her at will, completely content in the vibration that they were just meant to be…friends, or more than that. It just was. And so goes the tale.

She pretended in front of his friend. "We didn't exactly meet yet. I'm Kristie."

"I'm Henry."

"I'm invisible," Anthony moaned, turning away.

Henry stood, hypnotized by her precious face. They were laughing hysterically but Anthony didn't quite get that they were playing with his mind, having met weeks earlier. They did these things because it amused them; they didn't care about anyone else.

"Oh, sorry there, ol' pal. Kris, this is my friend Anthony," he said, quietly pulling him over. "He's old. He's in sixth grade."

"Hi. Wow, you are old!"

Anthony, the proud elder, smiled deliberately.

"Yeah. Well, I'll just be leaving you two alone. I have some uh…" He looked at Henry and winked, elbowing him in the gut, quite obvious and obtrusively so. "I've got *business* to take care of. Later, Hen," he grinned slyly. "Miss," he bowed chivalrously. Kris bowed back.

Big Mouth and Patty went sailing by again, strangling each other with a somewhat more exhausted force. The Mouth maintained a slight advantage on this run, pushing Patty back on *her* heels, though they went mostly unnoticed by the three.

"Take care, Ant," Henry said, shaking his pal's hand.

Anthony winked. "Yeah, you too, kid."

After so many winks, however, it began to look more like a facial tick than an encoded signal for "enjoy the female accompaniment, kid." As Anthony moved on, he frowned, noticing the two girls trying to kill each other. He wanted to see punches, not strangles. So he settled himself down for a game of catch with Joey Cinnamo and his lonely football, also in the schoolyard, going relatively unnoticed.

"Boy, wouldn't it be nice if we were older," Kristie said. "When you're *that* old, you have *business* to take care of," the little girl pointed out.

She and the boy were intrigued by this fact.

"But, what kind of business?" Henry wondered.

"I don't know," she shrugged. "Those sixth graders begin learning the secrets of the world at their age. They're practically adults! I can't wait till we get to sixth grade." She stopped and bit her tongue. Henry pretended not to, but he noticed. "I wonder what else they tell them, that they don't tell us third graders?"

"All I know is, Kris, that they get science and social studies, and like tons more homework than us."

Kristie looked at Henry suspiciously.

"I think I can wait."

"So can I," the boy agreed heartily.

They looked at one another—a gentle though polite awkward silence sat for a moment. And both grinned unendingly because they both recognized it.

Henry raised a finger, playing again. "We've met before, haven't we?"

"We did." Kristie's eyes got bigger in remembrance of the thought, nodding her head.

"Cafeteria!" The boy bit his lip so he wouldn't burst out laughing. "That was the day—"

"Halloween."

"You were the doll in the pink dress."

"You were Luke Skywalker in the orange outfit."

"We were in…"

"The Haunted Locker Room!" they said together, laughing, thinking of the room no one ventured to, beneath the gymnasium. It was another one of their little adventures.

"After all those weeks, it took us *that* long to finally meet each other!" the boy said.

"Yeah, it stinks doesn't it? Wish we met when we were kids. Wish I had moved here back then. Or just lived next door. All that time we could've been having fun," she said.

"That *does* stink," the boy frowned.

"It *sure* does," she said putting on her best brave face.

"But you're here now, and you're not going anywhere."

Joey and Anthony built a nice head of steam and were passing and catching the pigskin with regularity. At one point, they charged one another, and looked like a pair of Brahma bulls in a soon-to-be head-on collision.

Kristie looked down. "Alright. Let's talk about it."

"What?"

"Yesterday."

"What about it?"

"Something happened to you, Henry." The little girl's expression changed dramatically; she looked so sad. "Do you really believe in all the things you wrote about the angels?" she asked.

"Yes. Of course I do," the boy said fearlessly. "You don't think I made it up. Do you...Kris?"

"I don't know what to believe. What *did* you see yesterday, Henry? Truth."

"I saw them."

"Saw who?"

"Jack & Fred."

"No you didn't."

"I—"

"It's a story. You write stories. You make stories up about everything—the pencil, the eraser, the desks. You wrote a story about the haunted locker room. We had that 'if you had all the money in the world' essay to do, and you read the story aloud, and changed it while reading it. I know 'cause you let me read it before the rest of the class. You made up that you wanted some anti-gravity room so you could invite everyone over for some space party. That's you!"

"So..."

"So, if you can make stuff up like that, why should anyone believe your angel story?"

"Because, they're *real*."

"They're not real. You know, my father once told me that when people are scared or hurt or lonely, they make things up. They even pretend to see things. I see you do it all day. You look like you're thinking about something else and you stare. You stare at things. And I always wonder what you're thinking about. I always think you're making stories up for whatever you're looking at. Like yesterday. You ran away."

"I didn't run away. I was following them."

"The angels?"

"Yes."

"I think you were scared because Joey and Patty almost got killed."

"They didn't."

"They almost did. And you were afraid it was going to be *your* fault. They're your best friends. You've known them since you were real little, even before you knew me. You almost lost them."

"I saw them fly down." Tears welled up in the boy's eyes.

"You didn't. The car swerved out of the way. And it broke down and stopped. There weren't angels there. Joey and Patty were just lucky."

"I don't believe you, Kris. *You* don't believe you, either. I'm sorry. And I don't want to hear anything more about this."

He started walking away from her. She put her arm through his to catch him.

The little girl sighed. "My mom used to tell me stories about them when I was a kid. The angels…"

"Mine too," he said surprised.

"When I was real little, I used to think my guardian angel lived in my laundry room. I wrote her and everything," she said, sweet reminiscence in her cheeks. "I even used to set an extra place at dinner for her."

"What's her name?"

"Belle. It was Belle. My parents and I were going to church, and I felt like she was just right there with us, just then. And all of a sudden, the church bells started ringing. So that's what I called her: Belle."

The thought made the boy feel happy all over.

"Belle. I like that."

"I was the middle child, so my sisters forgot about me. Everyone did. But Belle didn't. She always kept me company. That's what I believed. But I know I made her up. She wasn't real. My sisters told me that and I cried so hard, but they were right."

"Why do you say that?"

"When the doctor told us my mom had cancer, I prayed that Belle would ask God to save her. I prayed over and over again, all the time. And all that happened was my mother got sicker and sicker. She used to look so beautiful, and she was so sick and so skinny before she died, that she could barely breathe. And Belle never answered. No one did. I was outside with my sister, playing in the yard, and it happened. She was gone, and it was quiet and so strange…and we both knew."

"You told me this—"

"I never tell anyone this. I realized I didn't have a guardian angel. If I did she wouldn't have let me get so hurt. Angels are supposed to protect you from hurt. They're not supposed to let God take your mom away from you. They're supposed to fight for you. And she didn't. And I knew she wasn't real. I made her up. Someday you'll believe me. I just hope nothing bad ever happens to you. It hurts when you find out no one's listening."

"But…they got us home."

"No, Henry. *You* got us home."

"Maybe it doesn't work that way. Maybe they're not allowed to stop things like that. Maybe they just can't."

"Maybe. Maybe they're just not real."

She walked alone, crying in silence. Her head was throbbing. She felt like a giant hammer had dropped on it. She was overwhelmed by the sensation and started to stagger. Henry ran up and grabbed her.

"C'mere!" He lead her over to the far side of the fence. "Sit down. I never lied to you before. I make stories up but not about important things."

"So what!" she said, pouting. She put her head down, holding it with both hands, trying to blot out the noise of the world.

The boy's heart pounded out of his chest. He was shaking uncontrollably, angry and hurt and betrayed, and feeling horribly bad for her all at once.

"So…you think I'm making all of this up. What do you call this?"

He reached into his pocket, pulling out a long eagle-like feather. He brushed it against her hand, and she couldn't help but look up.

"They left this in my room last night. I found it under the bureau because they were trying like crazy to get out and not get caught by my parents. Where would I get this? This isn't from some pigeon you'd find under the el. And there aren't any eagles flying over the Bronx last time I looked. Here's your proof! I'm sorry for what happened to your mom, and I'm sorry you don't believe in them. But I do. And nothing anyone says—even you—is going to make me think different. I love you, Kris. But I love Jack & Fred too. I believe in them."

And the boy went off to be by himself.

She squeezed the feather and pulled it through her clenched hand. It was light and soft, and very real. Kristie brushed the feather against her face, and she closed her eyes, thinking of her mother. She took one shuddering breath and let it go. And for just the gentlest of moments, she forced herself to consider the boy's words, just a little—no matter how much it hurt. Maybe she wasn't really alone after all.

Over the campus, Belle stopped and clutched her heart, tears streaming down her face. "Oh my."

"What is it?" Jack asked, taking her gently by the arm.

"I haven't felt that in such a long time," she whispered.

"What?"

Belle smiled warmly.

"*Love.*"

{ Chapter 24 }

God's Gym

The shadow of a giant, hulking figure loomed over Fred from behind.

The little one stood there, shaking his head, happily oblivious to it at the time. He was thinking of everything Flo had said. He was thinking of the boy. He was thinking about Jack and the angel he flew off in search of. He was thinking *too* much. He stared off, his eyes wandering across the breadth of the Dings. It astonished him how everything worked with simple perfection, and how it was unlike any human equivalent.

"It's all so easy," the little one said, shaking his head. "Amazing. Absolutely amazing. Oof!" Before he could complete the thought, the humongous football-player-sized angel named Paul wrapped his arms around the little angel from behind, lifting him high off the ground.

"HEYYY!!!" he bellowed.

"God in heaven."

"How ya doin', Fuzzy?" the monster asked with a chuckle, his mile-wide dimples awash with bliss.

Poor Fred struggled like an animated Raggedy Andy in the giant's grip, swatting at the concrete blocks that were wrapped around his chest. It looked silly really. Fred was smacking at the colossus overhead like a wind-up fish-tank diver toy.

"Are you people crazy? Is that your problem? Tackling people when they're not looking!"

"It's more fun that way!" the giant said.

Fred relaxed in futility, his arms drooping down. "Ughhh, I need a vacation. Freaking old-home week!"

"I missed you," the giant said, pulling him in, hugging the stuffing out of poor Fred.

"Huuuhhhh!" Fred choked, his air supply being Heimliched out of him.

The mammoth put his face next to the little one's head.

"Isn't he the cutest little thing!" he exclaimed.

"Get a dog, will ya?" Fred struggled.

"I looovee you, Ralphie," Paul said cozily.

"Then why the hell are you squashing me to death? Oh, God. *Okay.* I'm sure the feeling's…ughh, mutual, Pauly. Geez, you don't give up, do ya? Whew! Alright! Let me down…please!"

"Oh, oh, sure," the giant obliged. He was all excited. "Oooh you're here, and it's Christmas time, Ralphie, and all the houses have their Christmas lights on at nighttime!"

Fred tried to realign his jaw.

"And would you please stop calling me, Ralphie?" he said a little more audaciously, outside of the titan's grip.

"But I like calling you Ralphie."

"But my name is Fred. It's like 'red' with a big *F* in front of it!"

Paul got quiet, unconsciously towering over the little cherub.

The little one looked up. *Ouch.* Paul was like, huge. For some reason, Fred had just suddenly realized this again. He always felt like a kid around him, but Fred was actually more than a few hundred years his senior! Give or take…

"I *like* calling you Ralphie," he said with features that screamed would-be pain was coming. "It reminds me of when you used to take care of that artist, Raphael."

"That's exactly why I *don't* like it Paul. I…" Fred stammered, looking at the giant's huge mitts, which he was rubbing together. "I can see that. It's a nice name. Ralph. Yeah. I'll buy that!" Fred shrugged at the indisputable behemoth. "You can call me Langostino if you really want to."

Paul looked at him in silence, then fell apart at the seams.

"You're silly, Ralphie," the big one said, poking him in the belly.

Paul was a giant animated character, he was. He looked like a curious grizzly bear of such immense proportions; he'd either love you to death or squash ya in a heartbeat. And when he laughed, he sounded like a four-year-old with toys.

"Yeah. Sure. No sweat, Pauly. That's me, bruised and silly," the little one said, not having too much of a choice—short of getting squashed again. "What is that?"

"Mrow! Mrow! Mrow!" it went.

"Paul? Paul!"

"Yes?"

"You hear that?"

"The cow cat noise?"

"Yes!"

"No. I didn't hear that."

The giant flexed his expansive chest, which had a "God's Gym" shirt over it. He looked about in wonder. "Say, little one, where's Jackie?" he asked.

"I don't know." Fred readjusted himself, looking at the curious behemoth.

"He's probably with another…girl! Hee-hee-hee!" he rumbled. "He's with lots of girls!"

"Yeah that's right, Paul. Lots of girls. Ha-ha," Fred mocked.

"Ralphie, Ralphie c'mere. Look."

Paul nearly turned his head 180 degrees in the opposite direction with a sickeningly loud crack.

"Whaaattt…God!"

"C'mere!"

He grabbed the little one by the neck, hoisting him up for a better parade view.

"I'm not making it out of here in one piece, am I?" Fred said to himself more than anybody else.

"See?!"

"What am I looking at, Paul?" Fred asked in his compromising position within the gargantuan's grip, high off the rooftop.

"I'll show you," the goliath said, with great big sparkling eyes, dragging Fred away from Wingdings like a tote bag in the breeze. The little one thought that this was his comeuppance for dragging George around the same way all day.

Fred gave himself up eyes. *"See, Fred. Spit up in the air, it comes back in your face.* Lord! Put me down Paul, you ham hock. What do you think you're doing?!"

"I want to show you something," the giant said.

"I really don't—"

"It wasn't a request, Ralphie."

"Gotcha."

"Here we go!"

"Anyone have a raw steak?" Fred pleaded to the diners as he was dragged behind the tremendous tow truck zipping off into the sky. He had *no* clue as to what was going on.

"Wheeeeeeeeee!" Paul screeched.

Fred crossed his arms and shook his head. "Yeah…okay."

Paul dragged him over to a grassy knoll at the beginning of the campus, near to where the angels passed originally.

"See them?" Paul put his arm around Fred. "They put it up every year. Takes them two days at least," he said.

They watched as the same two campus maintenance men Jack had seen earlier, unloaded the manger and the person-sized statues for the lawn nativity. The men worked studiously, carrying the statues and electrical equipment from their brown maintenance pickup. Fred pushed himself behind Paul's wings, worried that they would see him, given that the boy could. The little one didn't know to what extent he and Jack used their…for lack of a better word, "powers." And besides, Paul was good cover.

"That's beautiful," Fred admitted, peeking out. "It's truly beautiful, Paul. Thank you for showing me this. Really."

The giant grinned from ear to ear with wide dimples. He roughly mussed the little one's hair.

"I knew you'd like it."

"Why—"

"Why'd I take you here Ralphie? Because, you and Jack fly around so much sometimes you forget to look around. Christmas is coming you know!"

The little one smiled and patted him on the arm.

"Come on, little Ralphie. I'll take you back."

The men sensed goodness in the air, and they instinctively looked up to the sky, saying something in their own language, happily.

"Mrow! Mrow! Mrow!" the cow cat went as it passed by.

{ Chapter 25 }

Mallomars

Jack shook his head. "Swore I heard that thing again."

"What?" Belle asked, munching.

"A cow…uh…it's this yellow-eyed mutant cat."

"Wha…?"

"Nothing. Go on. Sorry."

Jack and Belle were sitting downfield, eating a box of Mallomars together.

Belle laughed. "Yep. She's the cutest little thing. My own little angel. Once upon a time, I was real in her heart. My Kristie."

Jack put his hand on hers. "And someday you will be again."

She sighed.

Jack munched on the chocolate treats. "I never put them in the freezer."

"Mallomars? Why not?"

"I like them at room temperature."

"You like these, don't you? If not, give 'em to me, buddy," she said as they leveled the whole left side of the box. She bit into another one, savoring the marshmallow insides, letting them melt in her mouth. "Isn't this great? We can eat all we want and not gain a pound."

"Says you," Jack said with a cocked eyebrow.

"Says me! Why do you, um…"

Jack had another and smiled. "Why do we gain pounds, Fred and I?"

"Mmm-hmm," she mumbled incoherently, gobbling too much at once.

"Milk, milk. Here, drink! Don't eat the glass."

"Ahhhh!" Belle sounded as she gulped down the frosty glass, smacking her lips and belching.

Jack winked, giving her the thumbs-up. "Class, honey. Real class."

She yanked away the box and they started tug-of-warring it, until the insatiable need for those maddeningly delicious treats struck him again and he decided to cheat and poke her in the ribs, wrestling them away.

"And Belle, to answer your question, Sidney told us we spend so much time down here that we become like them," Jack munched.

"Like people?"

"Mmm-hmm." He had one more before his belly exploded. "If..." Jack chewed like a cow. "If we stayed upstairs for any great amount of time, I guess we could go hog wild too."

"Lucky."

"What makes you say that?"

"Because...to understand and empathize with people so much that you become like them...you're blessed."

"Blessed." Jack looked away, taking a deep breath. "They call us angelic gypsies. And we are, too."

"Oh please. Get over yourself. Last one? Want?" she said, shaking the box.

"That's all you. I'm done."

She popped the last one in her mouth, holding it in her teeth for a moment, winking before gnashing down on it.

"God those are good. But next time, Jack, remember...freezer."

"Cool," he said with a nod.

She got up to brush the crumbs off her dress, smoothing out the creases with long hand presses.

"Besides, you talk about gypsies. I used to live in my girl's laundry room."

"Oh come on!" Jack shouted, tipping over.

The angels nearly tumbled off the post with laughter. Belle sounded like a seal. She and Jack laughed even harder at that.

"I'm sorry. Heh-heh. She wrote stories about me in her diary and said I lived in the laundry within the clothes. Funny thing was, she was right!"

"God," Jack said catching his breath. "That is too funny...*Anabelle*!"

"Don't call me that, please! You're so bad! I was new down here! I didn't know where you're supposed to watch people from. So, I hung out in the laundry with the clean clothes. Big deal! How was I supposed to know?"

"Could have been worse," Jack enunciated. "Could have been the attic."

"Yeah, or the basement."

Belle brushed the short wisps of hair from her great brown eyes.

Jack sighed.

"What is it?" she asked shyly.

"Lord...you really are *beautiful*."

"And I'm supposed to get all flushed and lightheaded with that compliment?"

Jack stared. "Yes."

"Darn straight."

"What's wrong with *Anabelle*, anyway?"

"I like *Belle*. That's what my Kristie called me the first time she believed."

"Oh."

Belle moved within kissing distance of Jack, who flinched not a millimeter. He raised his hand over his head and snapped his fingers. Music began flowing out of that great big jukebox in the sky.

"Where's that coming from?" she asked, all amused.

"Sometimes it's better not to ask," Jack said, with debonair flair.

The trumpet began singing.

"Is that you? Are you doing that?" Belle asked, amazed and curious and overwhelmed all at once.

"Louis Armstrong's doing that. 'Love Vie En Rose.' You like?" Jack asked, moving closer.

"I love," she replied, coming nose to nose with him. They looked at one another. (Makes you all gushy, don't it? No, me neither. Ahem.)

"Dance?" Jack said, holding her hand in his.

"Love to," she replied. They stood up in unison, embraced, and danced slowly the length of the goal post. "So tell me, hot stuff," Belle inquired. "How is it that you can make love songs materialize from nowhere?"

"You've been down here as long as Fred and I, and you pick up a few things."

"Like how to overwhelm a girl with absolute charm."

"Something along those lines."

"Mmm."

They twirled around on the chord change.

"'Sides," Jack smiled. "What makes you think this is a recording? Me and Louie are old friends."

"You're very continental," Belle complimented.

"I've got myself a heart full of love, and a mouth full of compliments, and not a living soul to share them with."

"Looks like your luck just changed."

"Looks that way."

"Hold me close and hold me fast. The magic spells you cast, this is love vie en rose," Louis sang.

Jack raised an eyebrow. "I wish we were someplace a little more romantic. Like Venice or Paris…"

Belle put her head on his shoulder.

"Forget Paris," she said in a sigh. "There's no other place, I'd rather be."

"Me neither," Jack said, closing his eyes, holding her slight form in his hands as if to never let her go. The warmth between them could light up Detroit.

The voice continued to sing. *"And when you speak, angels, sing from above…"* They danced as if they'd never stop.

And as the trumpet blared…they kissed.

Paul was swooning. "Oh Ralphie, look how adorable they are," the giant said as he towed Fred by the arm. "Aren't they precious?! Aren't they so cute?! Don't they make you—"

"Wanna puke my guts out? Yes, Paul. Absolutely!" the little one said, smacking him on the arm.

The giant frowned. Any time a giant frowns, it's not a good thing.

"Here!" Paul said, pulling two cold glass bottles of soda out from behind his back.

"Where'd you get those?" Fred asked, a little worried.

"Take one Ralphie!"

The little one looked at the bottle, curiously. "I don't know where this bottle's been Paul. You don't exactly have an Igloo cooler back there, do you?"

"RALPHIE!"

"Okay, okay. Geez. What is this…OH! Manhattan Special?!" The giant chuckled as the little one read the label. "'Pure Espresso Coffee Soda.' I haven't had one of these in ages. I love these things! Thanks Paul!"

Paul sipped his drink, winking at the little one. The little one popped the top and wondered aloud.

"Say, Paul? When we finish, can we go toss the bottles at Jack and Miss America over there? Ten points if you hit her…"

"THAT'S IT!" the behemoth yelled, crushing the bottle to glass bits in his swollen hand. "I'm taking you back! You have no passion, Ralphie, and that's all I'm going to say."

"Outstanding! Paul…" Fred suddenly realized his entire arm was going numb. "You're squeezing too hard, Paul. Oh crap, there goes my Manhattan. Paul? Paul! OW!"

"No, no. I can't hear you! I have no room for negative vibes."

"PAUL!"

"Be gone negative vibes!" he dismissed with his giant meat hook.

Fred bit down on his back teeth. "When we play football next time, you are *so* dead!"

"*Hee-hee-hee!*" the giant rumbled yet again.

Jack's shoulders slumped beneath him. They stopped dancing.

"What's the matter, Belle?"

"I didn't think she cared anymore. It wasn't my *fault*. If she only knew, when she hurts, I hurt. They don't know. People I mean. They don't know we're in the same boat as they are! We can't change what happens. We can only be with them when it does! Don't they know that? Don't they understand?!"

"Shh. Calm down."

"Jack…"

"You love her?"

"Yes," Belle said simply.

"She loves you."

"She used to…*yes*."

"Then," Jack said, rubbing her shoulders. "The rest will sort itself out…in time. That's all we have…*time*."

Belle sniffled. Jack handed her a handkerchief. She looked at him funny. "Where'd that come from?"

"Bat utility belt."

"Oh. You know, that boy of yours makes her happy. I know it. Ever since she moved." Belle thought a moment. "What're you going to do?"

"About him? About him seeing us?"

"Yes."

"Sidney. He'll take care of it."

"Jack, what if he—"

"I said he'll take care of it! Sorry," he said holding his hands out. Jack's ears perked up. "I hear the train," he said as the commuter rail train's horn moaned in the distance. *"What is it with that sound?"*

She looked at him for a moment. "Jack. How do you do it without going crazy?"

Jack pointed upward. "The Big Man. He's got our backs. And I have the little one down here to lean on. That's really all we need." Belle leaned forward and kissed his lips. "But I could use that, too!" Jack said with bright eyes.

"You're not the only one, Buster Brown."

Jack's eye peered upward as the horn bellowed again on its way through the station.

He felt someone tapping his shoulder. It was Sidney's assistant Madison, of all angels. Belle looked at her pleasantly, amused by the upturned nose and scornful glare she gave the both of them. Belle never worried about competition, but she did find it strange that Fred was standing behind the barrister's assistant, looking as if a giant had flung him around like a stuffed toy all day. The little one's arms were crossed over his chest, and he was visibly annoyed to no end.

Belle laughed though, in spite of herself. "Sorry, hon," she said, shaking the empty box at Madison. "We're all outta Mallomars. How about a banana?"

Jack fell apart.

Madison sighed. "Sidney needs to speak to both of them. *Right away*."

The little one shot Jack a glance, and instantly, the taller angel knew something was seriously wrong.

Jack looked at Belle and his wings moved instinctively, brushing the crumbs from his mouth and patting his forehead dry.

Somewhere in the distance the train horn sounded mournfully as it entered the station on its way back from wherever it had been.

Inside the ramshackle house that the barrister and Madison called home, Sidney paced back and forth looking uncharacteristically unkempt and noticeably unnerved by *something*.

He ambled through the cramped, stale-smelling office. He was admiring them as they sat side by side with one another though miles apart.

"You two were busy? I'm sorry. I'm sorry I interrupted you, I know that I did. Didn't I?"

"No!" Fred barked.

"Yes!" Jack shouted.

The pair looked at one another.

"No offense, Sids," the little one said, tossing his hands up. "But we hurry over to see you, and you're not in your office. We're over at Wingdings, chillin,' and zip-a-dee-doo-dah, we get dragged here by the snippet on wheels!"

Madison slammed something loudly from the other room.

Sidney rubbed his tired face. "I'm sorry to be so abrupt."

Jack reclined back in his seat, folding one leg over the other in an overly casual posture.

"No offense, barrister. This one over here is obnoxious," Jack sneered at the little one. "We all know that. But he *is* right. You know we like you to pieces, but seriously. What the hell?"

"I'm sorry, Jack. I said I was sorry. But I'm not going to apologize for trying to help. If it's that much of a problem you people can take off and go eat until you pass out, or whatever the hell it is you do!" Sidney slammed the desk, which was out of character for the normally diplomatic angel.

Jack & Fred looked at one another.

"Hey guy," Jack said, rising out of his seat. "I don't know who you are or where you're hiding our buddy Sidney, but we're gonna take off and look for him."

"God," Sidney sighed, rubbing his temples.

The little one got up to leave with his partner. "No, Jack's right. *Humph.* And for years people on Earth said the only good lawyer was a dead one, and here you are—dead and grouchy as hell. What are ya doin' man? Here we thought we could reform you from your wayward life. (Sigh)," the little one joked. "We're sorry Sids, but we're done! We tried to help you," Fred snickered. "But there's just too much maintenance required. You my friend, are a lost cause!"

Sidney stopped pacing and broke apart laughing. Jack & Fred did as well.

Jack ushered the barrister into the old lawyer's favorite comfy leather chair which Sidney took with him everyplace, despite how good or bad his surroundings were.

"You two…you two are characters. *Ughhh.* God. The only ones who can laugh at a time like this."

"Sidney," Jack said, solemnly. "What's up, kid?"

"*They* aren't happy."

Fred snapped. "So, who is?!"

"No, you're not getting me. They are *not* happy. Someone upstairs is damn ticked. Fred knows what I mean. They already sent down an envoy. What, this rings no bells? You don't get it? Peter's assistant, Gabrielle, twin sister of that one in there. Fred spotted her while you were busy playing 'score one for the home team' Jack! Why are you two staring at me like that? What's so…Do I have to spell it out?! THEY'RE LOOKING FOR THE MORON, YOU WHACKOS!"

Jack sat back down, covering his face with his wings. Fred turned away as he plopped back into the seat across from the barrister.

"You two are just amazing! You don't do your disasters in ones. Where do I start? Let me start with first things first. FIRST: You don't bring the guy home?!"

Jack started. "Sidney—"

"People have a right to go directly to heaven when they pass on. Do not pass *GO*. Do not collect two hundred dollars. That's rule one of your job, fellas. C'mon. WHY am I even telling you this? To do anything else is blatant bull...(sigh). You are dealing with a man who had an unfortunate accident."

The little one was pulling at the feathers in his coat that were dried out or dirtied. It reminded Jack of picking scabs; it drove him up the wall when the little one did that. He gave Fred a look that would peel paint.

"Does this not interest you, Fred?" Sidney asked, leaning over the desk.

"First of all, Sidney, the man was hit by an *ice-cream truck*. HELLO!"

"Fred, we're not here to debate whether his death 'scene' had enough punch. Are you kidding?"

"No. What I'm saying is that it was an everyday accident. It wasn't cosmically important—"

"Excuse me? It's his life and death we're dealing with! It *is* important, to HIM!"

Jack became slightly nervous, even for him, when the little one began to rise up off the edge of his seat, wings cocked back as if he was going to leap at the barrister. He was worried, because he knew, if in Sidney's panicked state he said something ill of the boy, Fred would snap just that fast and kill him...again!

Fred took a breath. "I understand how you feel on this, barrister. You were human and passed on at one time, just like George. And now Sidney, you're an angel. We can appreciate the fact that you made the transition. But there was a boy's life at stake. And to be very honest, you haven't done *our* job, ever. No offense, but you wouldn't understand what we go through. Or why. We had to help that boy."

"A boy that you were *not* assigned to help."

"A boy that came across our paths during our helping of others. Let me put it to you in human terms, because it seems like that's something you're more likely to understand today. It's like someone getting shot in the chest and a doctor happens to be driving by, and instead of helping he goes to the damn driving range to work on his swing! You're a lawyer, so I'm sure that concept isn't totally foreign to you, is it?!" Fred slammed the desk with both hands.

Jack leaped up, holding the little one back. "Easy there rock 'em, sock 'em!"

"Let him go, Jack."

"Sidney...."

"Let-him-go."

And Jack backed off.

Sidney went nose to nose with the little one like a marine drill instructor, speaking in a voice so soft and eloquent it conjured up far more fear than a raging lunatic. What the angels always admired most about Sidney was the way that gentle rage was focused inside the beating heart of their intellectual friend, though now it was uncommonly directed at them.

"Fred, at this moment in time, I'm the 'bestest' friend you have," he told the little one, who was not having any of it. "There are no boundaries I will not cross. No lengths that I will not go for you and Jack. Do not snap at me like I'm some dog, because whether we're good friends or not, little one, I will not tolerate it. Not from Jack. Not from you. Not from *anybody*. I care about you two more than you'll ever know, but I will not let you hurt *me*. Do you understand what I'm saying to you?"

Sidney reached under his desk mat pulling out a note card. He handed it to Jack, who squinted to make out the writing. When the words became clear, he fell back into the chair and handed the card to the little one as if he had been punched in the stomach. Distractedly, Fred reached for the message; the words themselves seemed to drain the color from his features.

"This," he started to say, "can't be right."

"Now," Sidney explained, "before we continue, I need to know that what I've told you has been made abundantly clear. So I'll ask again: Do you understand what I'm saying to you today?"

"Yes," Fred said, backing down, as did his partner.

"Good." Sidney sat down, shuffling papers for no other reason than not wanting to look in their eyes with the worries he had in his own. "I get this kind of abuse from everyone else. But I don't expect it from you two. I expect better. Where do you think I was earlier today? Playing tiddlywinks? I was upstairs trying to convince them not to drop the sun, moon and stars on you for what you've done!"

"What do you call this?" the little one said, setting the card back down on the desk. Jack retrieved it, swallowing hard. Sidney was no longer looking at them. This had gone too far, too fast.

Jack shrugged. "You were talking to them upstairs. So, how'd you do?"

"NOT TOO DAMN WELL, JACK! Not well at all. As you can see."

The angels sat quietly. They were looking down when Sidney said, "I need you to go back to the boy. As soon as possible."

Fred was taken aback. "But you just said—"

"I said you weren't assigned to Henry. But you met him already…P.S. the damage is done."

Jack shook his head. "That's not the way we look at it. That boy's a blessing, not a—"

"Jack. Listen," Sidney looked right at him, making Jack grip the chair arms. "You need to go back *immediately*."

"But…"

"Didn't you read the card? This is effective at midnight, on Christmas. Make time for your new girlfriend later."

Fred bit down on his back teeth. Even he wasn't going to be *that* snappy about Jack's new friend.

"The boy is important. Haven't you guys realized that by now? It isn't an accident. It isn't a mistake he can see you as angels."

The little one shook his head in disbelief. "But, I thought we did something that made him see us."

The barrister was angry. "Oh please. You 'did something.' C'mon now. Give the kid a little credit here."

The angels couldn't believe it; he really could see them just as they were.

"How?" Jack asked the old lawyer.

"Does it matter?" he replied.

The little one shook his head. "I guess not."

"Sidney," Jack wondered, "why aren't you telling us everything?"

"You know me. I'm thorough. I let you know the lowdown when I have all the pieces to the puzzle. And this time, I don't. Something's wrong, Jack. I was going to call you here with the intention of solely talking to you about the message on that note card. Maddie's sis dropped me a line on the Q.T. saying Peter was sending the heavies down to get you two. It's because of the moron being late!"

Jack slapped his head. "Oh crap."

"Yeah Jack!" the barrister squawked. "Oh crap indeed!"

For a moment, Fred thought about Paul. He was once a part of the 'heavies' Sidney spoke of. They were larger heavenly cousins sent to expedite angelic situations as it were, and they were not to be trifled with.

The barrister explained, "Instead of sending those big guys to track you down, Gabby came down herself, to see if she could smooth this over. Jack, you're lucky your ex, Madison, has a good rapport with her sis, or they would've gotten those big fellas to scoop you two up and carry you back whether you wanted to go or not."

Jack crossed his arms. "Sidney...ain't *nobody* gonna lay a hand on us."

"Unless," the little one added, "they're goin' in for some serious hospital time."

"I heard that!" Jack agreed, as they smacked each other five.

The barrister was still very upset. "Oh yeah, look. Here they are. I know. Mr. Tough Guy. And his sidekick, Little Wing."

Fred was insulted. "I'm nobody's sidekick!"

Sidney was unraveling. "And now Gabby disappeared!"

Fred interrupted. "Well she..."

"Yeah, I know Fred!" Sidney barked. "She went to play hide the halo with that Moron. I still don't understand that one!"

The angels seemed to be in shock. It was total disbelief. They were rambling and Sidney didn't know what to do. They didn't believe the card. How could they believe it, after all this time...

"You two aren't listening to me. YOU DON'T HAVE TIME!!!" Sidney's dark features blistered with a reddening glow. It wasn't so much anger as fear behind those once-gentle eyes. "Please. Jack," he pleaded, "Fred....I need you to do one thing for me. Go to the boy immediately. Drop everything. Are you hearing me? Do you understand what I'm saying?"

Jack's chest filled out. *"Yes."*

"Now," Sidney directed with his glaring eyes.

"What about the moron?" Fred asked.

"I'll take care of that. I'll get it smoothed over Fred. Now…go!"

Despite his pointed words, Sidney's heart reached out for them. He was very worried. Jack & Fred instinctively turned around as one, heading for the window. In his heart, Sidney always felt he owed them a debt of gratitude he could not repay. The angels once saved what was most precious to him in the entire world. He always reminded himself of this. Not a second of the day went by when he didn't.

"Boys," Sidney called as the angels turned in his direction. "There is a wave on the horizon. It's coming fast. You have a choice. You can duck beneath it and let it pass over you. Or, you can stand up and ride it all the way to the end. But make no mistake. It will not stop for *anyone*. It's important to me that you understand this."

"Come on, Fred," Jack said with a tap. He flew out through the window. Fred flashed the barrister a peace sign with a nod and flew right after.

Sidney walked into the adjoining room, seeing Madison appraise herself in the mirror, sucking in her gut, measuring the size of her hips with her hands. She seemed preoccupied with everything other than office business. Strange. The assistant turned and squinted, hard.

"Concerned?" Sidney asked.

"About my outfit? No, it'll do for…"

"No, I mean about those two."

"Jack & Fred? Oh, no. You'll fix it, I'm sure."

"Yeah, well. Don't get too worried Maddie, you'll hurt yourself."

"Oh, Sidney. Sorry. Just taking a moment for myself. Just being a girl."

"Hmm," he rumbled. Sidney looked at her strangely. It was as if she wasn't herself at all. "I...um...do me a favor Mads. Go get...I need to make a phone call."

"Sure," she said walking away.

There was a scent in the air, something familiar, but not familiar to the barrister's office.

"Any update from your sister?"

Madison turned around, looking at him, somewhat distracted.

"Sorry?"

"Gabrielle. Anything?"

Madison stared a moment.

"No. Nothing."

Sidney stared transfixed on something beyond.

"Alright..."

There was another piece of the puzzle which Sidney was missing. Everything was unraveling and it would only be a short time now. He stared out the window at the open sky.

"Godspeed! Please get there as fast as you can guys!" the barrister whispered, popping antacid tabs like they were LifeSavers, knowing full well you couldn't heal a frantic spirit with medicine.

He grabbed the picture on his desk, looking at it longingly. It was a picture of his sister.

"Sylvia, what do I do? I was trying to buy them more time...they don't have more time. It's gonna be my fault. I didn't protect them from this. What do I do now?"

{ Chapter 26 }

What, No Ziti?

The angels weaved in between the metal, erector-set track beds of the elevated subway as they raced pass the rail yards. Trains yawned and creaked and screeched as they were pulled to their sleeping places for the evening. The old yard hounds were released, yelping and carrying on as they surveyed their lands on guard detail. Beneath them, the buses crawled along the city streets with their starting and stopping engines, which revved and moaned like wounded animals onward through the city.

The air was thick with scents from everyplace. As the angels flew on they could smell Chinese food, pizza, Pepsi-cola, ribs, French fries, and hamburgers cooking, not to mention the ever-present bus exhaust and the creosote that lined the railway ties. But the angels associated these strange odors with their city and with their boy, Henry. So, nothing had ever smelled sweeter to them.

And there it was again! They saw the cow cat on the hunt. As they came up to the house with the yellow awning, they saw the creature delightfully shaking its rump as it made its way through the adjoining backyards.

Jack looked at Fred.

"Ready kid?"

"Yeah, let's go!"

They rushed to the boy's window. They slapped themselves up against the glass, breathless with the anticipation of seeing their boy. But the angels were more than a little disappointed to see Henry resting peacefully with a smile. They opened the window and floated into the room.

The boy's covers had been dumped off the bed during his sleep. The angels gently hefted the bunch of them back and drew them up to the boy's neck. They sat, dangling their feet off his shelves, waiting for him to awaken. But he didn't. They waited and waited. Many minutes rolled by; excitement rushed to their throats when the child rolled over in his sleep and they thought he'd awaken. But he didn't, not once. They were *very* disappointed. *What, no ziti?*

It was probably the most restful sleep Henry had in a long time. They floated over. Fred sat down on the bed. Jack sat perched atop the bedpost. And they did everything to wake him from his slumber: from fluttering their wings to clearing their throats loudly, to actually shaking the bed, but it was no use. He was out like a light.

They admired the room under the soft glow spilling in from the outside—they looked at the toys and all the marvelous little things, even the fish in the luminescent blue tank across the hall. And so, in a mix of delightful and disappointed emotions, they decided it was time to leave. And they would do just that. So they kissed him on the forehead, petted his head, and shrugged. There was not much else they could do that night.

On their way back to the window, they noticed a story that Henry had written for school. The title was "All About My Friends, Jack & Fred," and it was laying on the nightstand. The boy had taken it with him to bed so that he could show them when they came back, but for some reason he didn't make it past eight.

Across the top of the paper by the *A+*, and Henry's name, was written, "Extremely Creative, Very Well Written, and A Lot of Fun. You have something wonderful. Never let it go!" And his teacher's initials were in red ink.

They stood in the soft orange light flooding in from the street lamps outside, and the little one turned to Jack.

"Maybe that's why we were sent here," he said softly.

Jack grinned, agreeing happily. They went back one more time to see

Henry, but he was still out cold. There was something going on with the boy now; he looked pale. His color was off. He was tossing and turning. And he was sweating more than he should have been. He almost didn't look like the kid they met or had late dinner with. Something wasn't right. So the angels decided to stay; it wasn't a difficult decision to make. They flew back up to the rooftop and settled in for the night.

Fred said with an excited rush. "Man, Sidney was pissed!"

"You didn't help any!"

"Well—"

"Well nothin'," Jack said taking a breath. "You know he had our backs all those years. Think about all the stuff he did—*is doing*—for us."

"We're in trouble, Jack."

"Yeah, I know, Fred."

"Seriously."

"Seriously," Jack repeated. "Sid's a cool customer. He doesn't get ticked like that. Only time he does is if something's up he can't fix."

"Damn."

"Yeah. You were a little snappy, little wing, even for you."

Fred waved a dismissing hand. "Ah. I don't like anyone…"

"I know. No argument."

"…messing with the kid. With *Henry*. Not our fault. But we did right."

"I believe we did. You don't let someone that young go home alone."

"Well, whatever. What about you?"

"What about me, Fred?"

"Jack, you still ticked at me?"

"I wasn't ticked."

"Yeah you were."

"Okay, yeah I was. What the hell were you doing? You show up with that Madison and…"

"She *dragged* me there! I didn't even want to be there!"

"…and then I introduce you to Belle before we leave and you snub her like—"

"Jack, Sid's right! We have bigger things going on than you finding a new girlfriend."

"What's wrong with you people?! She's *not* my new girlfriend!"

"Whatever you want to call her."

"No, it's not that. Don't you get it? Her kid is Kristie. The little girl the boy is in love with."

"In love? Jack, he's not in love with anyone. He's nine."

"Well, call it what you want, but he loves her."

"So…"

"So. If she's important to him, it's important to us."

"No. You mean important to *you* because you dig her angel."

"Whatever, Fred. You don't understand. Forget it."

"No, I'm a moron like George. I don't understand *anything*."

The two sat in silence for the longest time.

"Here," Fred offered, giving Jack a Manhattan Special.

"Where'd this come from?"

"Don't ask. Just drink."

"I wonder," Jack said, taking a swig of the coffee soda. "What do you think they did with George?"

"I'm sure Flo took care of it for Sidney."

"You think so?"

"I…I have no idea right now, man. I'm exhausted. Give us a break for ten minutes. That George guy was a blessed spirit, but he was still luggage we should not have been assigned to in the first place."

"Not his fault. Sid's right. It's *our* fault."

"Whatever. Like we said. Worry about it later Jack."

"Yeah."

But the little one could not let it go so easily. Neither could Jack. It bothered them *that* much. They finished their drinks and set the empty bottles aside.

The little one thought about it. "You think it *does* have to do with us dragging him around? That Sidney scene?"

Jack took a deep breath. "Probably. He's an overdue. Peter had to have sent someone to retrieve him by now."

"He did. We went over this. Gabrielle."

"Maddie's twin?"

"Gabby's flakey. The other one is just snippy."

"Strange Fred. I never met Gabrielle. Madison and I—"

"Old news, Jack."

"Yeah. She's nice, other than bein' ultra-organized. But it's weird."

"What's weird? Why're we turning this into an Oliver Stone movie?"

"Well…you and I are partners right?"

"Yes, Jack…(sigh). Like Starsky and Hutch."

"I introduce you to everyone I know."

"Which is usually everyone I know, myself."

"True. Point is though…we're not brothers."

"Thankfully."

"Yet, we still keep tabs on each other."

The little one shook his head.

"You're losing us."

"My point is…don't you think she'd kinda mention a twin, especially an identical twin, if she had one?"

"Maybe they don't get along."

"Maybe. But still…just so people wouldn't confuse them Fred. Wouldn't you say, 'oh yes, you must've seen my identical twin doing yadda-yadda-yadda,' right?"

"I guess so."

"Well, yes or no?"

"You're the boss Jack."

"Yeah, that's funny."

"I mean whatever, you know? Told you Madison was a head-case to begin with. You always hook up with the whack-a-doos."

Jack shrugged. "Some of them are fun…"

"Uh-huh. Keep telling yourself that. Anyway, I had the twin, Gabby, give George a tour of Wingdings."

"Oh that's cute. What happened?"

"Somebody said somethin' about them makin' out on the west side of the roof behind a food cart."

Jack laughed. "Stinkin' guy. Geez."

"I know!"

"Puts *me* to shame."

"Brother, I was sayin' the same thing to myself. *Here's this dead guy...*"

Jack shook his head. They laughed for the first time in a while. Fred sat up on his arm, looking at the sky, which seemed lifeless.

"Hey Jack. Sidney didn't even offer us coffee. No cookies. Nothin'! That's not our Sidney."

"Yup, somethin's up."

"Sorry about…Belle. About being rude."

Fred stuck a fist out. Jack bumped it with his own.

"Wonder twin powers activate! It's alright little one. I've been short with you lately, too. I'm sorry."

"Really. It's alright"

"No. It's *not* alright. We're falling apart here. You're the bestest friend I ever had, Fred—ever *will* have. I…I have no reason to yell at you. I was wrong. I got a lot of things on my mind these days—a lot of things. I want you to know we're cool, God forbid anything ever happens."

"I knew that anyway." Fred nodded at him. "You have that…note card with you?"

"Yeah, I have it Fred."

"It's a mistake. It has to be. There would be no reason for what they're asking."

"It doesn't look like a mistake."

"It's got to be Jack. It's got to."

"You know what that means Fred…"

"I know what it means. It means the kid is our last shot."

"Yeah."

"What are we going to do, Jack?"

"I don't know."

The two angels tried to make themselves comfortable on the roof, but there was no possible way to accomplish that.

Jack turned his face away from the little one, because he didn't want his partner to see the worry in his features.

Fred looked at him and asked, "Do you like her?"

"Belle? Yes."

"A lot?"

"An awful lot."

"Oh."

"She...I don't know. She kind of showed me how stupid I've been acting. All wound up. Yelling at you, yelling at George. I can't do that anymore," he said, turning round to face the little one. "I'm giving the both of us agita. We're arguing *too* much. It's not like it used to be: simple. We've been waiting, praying for someone like Henry to come along, and now that he has I don't know what to do. I don't understand Sidney. How are we gonna...I don't know."

"A wise lady once told me don't be afraid of being successful. Embrace it."

"She was right."

"I guess that's why she was *wise*."

Jack shook his head. The little one smiled.

Jack did also. He sat up. "I mean, you don't see what's-their-names...I don't...." He snapped his fingers, trying to remember. "Any of those teams, the ones you mentioned to Henry, act like this. I mean after all these years..."

"Jack, you know who Abbott and Costello are, right?" Fred interrupted, closing his eyes.

"Sure," Jack said.

"Did you know that, when they weren't making pictures—I mean, off stage in real life—that the little guy, Costello, was actually the more aggressive, more antagonistic...P.S. he was the bigger pain in the ass." They both started laughing at Fred being Fred. "You know that?"

"No," Jack recoiled. "You're kidding me, right?"

"Nope," Fred grinned. "Everyone always thought Bud was the grouch, 'cause he was taller and he was always pushing the little guy around, telling him what to do and how to do it. It was really the other way around though. Bud was actually a very kind, very sweet person when no one was looking. A regular teddy bear. Nobody ever knew that, when they saw them on TV or at those public events all the time. But inside, they both knew. It was just between them...*the team*. You know?" Fred raised an eyebrow.

Jack smiled, closing his eyes. "Yes. I know."

"Oh. Just wanted to make sure. Say, what do we got planned for tomorrow?"

"I don't know. When tomorrow comes we'll worry about it."

"Are we going back to 'thee' campus, Jack?"

"If you want to go back to 'thee' campus, Fred."

"Such a stupid name."

"What do you want, Fred? They're college people. What do they know?"

"Not too damn much."

"You got that right. *Anyway*. Sure, if you want to go back to Wingdings, that's cool with me."

"Yeah. I mean we just, like...left!"

"I know."

"No goodbyes. Nothing. I'd like to see Flo again."

"About time you two finally did something about it. Been on-again-off-again for years."

"Uh-huh. Well. I'm going to sleep, bud."

"Mmm, yeah. It's late." Jack rolled over, resting across the way on the rooftop of the house with the yellow awning.

Fred opened his eyes.

"If sleep isn't like a necessity for us angels, why am I so darn tired tonight?"

Jack shrugged. "That, my friend, is the sixty-four-thousand-dollar question."

The little one shut his eyes. Jack stirred.

"Fred, did you hear..."

"What?"

"Wings."

"Yes."

"Good," Jack said. "At least I know I'm not going crazy."

"What makes you think I've got all my marbles, though?"

"Good point."
"Goodnight, Jack."
"Goodnight, Fred."

{ Chapter 27 }

Jack & Fred Everywhere...

It was the last day before Christmas Eve and Jack & Fred had become something of a phenomenon in Henry's class and throughout the entire school after word of the boy's story had gotten out. It was still a strange sight for Joey and Patty to see, to be sure. Kristie had never seen anything like this *anywhere*. A story did all this? And it all started with one little boy, her friend. *Impossible*.

Hope was a commodity in short order because of (or in spite of) the time of year. It was true. Henry's story became real for the school children; they were the pure of heart. They didn't need a lot of proof. The angels touched a chord with what had been long missing in their hearts, because it was something that everyone could relate to somehow. It was all about *hope*, and people understood that quite well when they had none, or when they had just enough to keep them alive. And the world was filled with a lot of *that* recently, especially this time of year, as people like Mr. Wallace could attest to.

The school children understood the true meaning of the boy's story, even though the parents didn't quite catch on to it. They just assumed it was the latest fad to hit them all. The kids saw it for what it was though: something good and honest and true. It wasn't that difficult. You didn't have to go beyond that to justify the meaning of such things. Angels and their message were just that simple, and that beautiful.

Kristie was on the phone with her grandma, telling her the whole story.

"It used to be, when I left the classroom door open for a breath of fresh air, and the wind accidentally blew the door shut, everybody would yell, 'Look out! The ghosts are coming in!' But after Henry's story, they all started saying, 'Hey! Jack & Fred are flying in!' or 'Look! The angels are hungry!'

At recess, the girls play hopscotch and jump-rope, counting off, 'One, two, three, four. Jack & Fred are at the door. Five six, seven, eight. The angels live near heaven's gate!'" She demonstrated to herself, dancing across the floor on her toes, to the accompaniment of laughter on the other side of the phone.

"The children played a game like tag today, where one person would be an angel and you had to catch him or her before they flew away. Another one they started playing is like Duck, Duck, Goose. But they changed things around a little, and called it Jack, Jack, Fred."

The old woman laughed, entranced, listening to the young one go on.

"Everyone sits in a circle and one person goes around tapping everyone on the head saying, Jack, Jack, Jack, Jack…and then they yell, Fred! And you have to chase the person around and around, and try to catch them before they go back home."

She took a breath, unable to keep herself still.

"Even when it was raining this afternoon and recess was held inside, all of us kids would get our coats, flop down on top of the desks with our arms and legs hanging off the sides, and flap our arms like we're flying with angels' wings. Sometimes a bunch of us put our desks together and pretend that we're a squadron of angels."

The old lady said with a chuckle, "The angels, it seems, are getting better public relations than Superman!" Kristie's grandma sighed. "I haven't heard you this happy in ages. Your friend is very special to you, Kristie. Don't let him go without knowing that."

"I won't, grandma. I even wrote a story about Belle. Grandma? Are you alright?" the girl asked, hearing sniffling.

"I'm fine, sweetheart. I can't wait to see you."

"Love you, grandma. I'm gonna give the phone back to Daddy."

{ Chapter 28 }

Invisible Eyes, Always Watching

In the winter months it got dark very early, but Henry's father could see clearly the blue, green, yellow, and pink twinkles of the tree wreaths on the second-floor windows of his home. They burned brightly as he walked home from the subway, weary from a hard day's work at the telephone company. He climbed the steps of his home in regulated and relieved strides, happy to be there at last.

The boy's ears perked up as he heard the heavy wooden door groan from its snug position, and he went bounding down the stairwell to meet his father.

"Daddy's home!" the boy yelled, nearly burning his hand on the banister as he raced down to meet him.

"Hello, my boy!" his father said, giving his son a big hug and carrying him the rest of the way up the stairs. The outside air was cool and brisk, but the house was very warm and smelled delicious. Henry's mother was making pork chops with cinnamon apples, and the smell alone could drive a person crazy.

"How was your day today?" his father asked, setting the boy and his bag down at the top of the stairwell.

"Oh, fine, Daddy. Mrs. Brady gave us another assignment for class. This time it was about where you would like to go over Christmas vacation. So I wrote about going on a trip to the beach with my two best friends, Jack

& Fred. And then tonight, I wrote a *sequel*," he smiled. "And I got an A+. Everybody loved it, too."

"That's wonderful, sport."

"Yeah. Everybody except Big Mouth liked it, but nobody pays attention to her anyway."

Dad smiled. That was his boy, and he was proud of him. And God bless the man, he always let him know it, too.

Henry ran off to watch the rest of his shows on television as the evening unfolded.

"Keep writin', kid! Hello!" his father said, as he stepped inside the kitchen and kissed his wife's cheek. Mom was putting the finishing touches on the cinnamon apples in the metal mixing bowl.

"What happened?" she asked, shaking the last of the cinnamon on the apple slices in the bowl. "You got out late?"

"No, I got out *early*. We got stuck at the Hunts Point station because of track work. The train was stopped there for a half hour. It was packed. Freezing out there. Feels like another storm's coming."

"It was raining all day. The news said it's going to freeze-over tonight."

"Lot sooner than that."

"I can imagine. You really needed that trouble on your way home."

"That just topped off the whole day," Dad sighed. Mom grabbed the towel and opened the oven. The heat warmed the house, making it very cozy. She put the cinnamon apples in the oven next to the baked macaroni that made pops and fizzles as it cooked through. She tossed the towel over her shoulder, where it stayed for later use.

"He looks extra happy," Dad said, nodding toward Henry as he hung up his coat. "Is it because you're making his favorite meal tonight?"

"No," his mother said quietly as she looked at her son sitting on the floor beside the couch, busy at something. "He got an A+ on his new story."

"Yeah, he told me that he wrote about his best friends, Jack & Fred. Who are Jack *&* Fred? The names sound familiar, but I just can't place the faces."

"The names do sound familiar, but I can't remember them either. Didn't he mention them recently?" Mom asked. "Maybe they just transferred to his school. Whatever the case, they seem to make him happy. I guess that's all that really matters."

"I guess you're right. He's looking better lately. Not as pale as he was," Dad said.

"That pneumonia really took the starch out of him last month. But since he's been getting some rest, instead of waking up every night, he's looking better. He kept having those dreams about that wolf. Anyway, I made a good meal for him tonight," she smiled.

"I know. I could smell it outside the door."

"Come on. We're almost ready."

Dad went inside.

Dinner was absolutely delicious! Dessert was pretty fantastic, too. Mom had made a batch of chocolate brownies topped with vanilla ice cream and caramel sauce. It was nice when she was home. What a meal on this cold winter's night! *What a meal!* It was good to be home.

{ Chapter 29 }

This Is Jack and This Is Fred

One by one, Henry spread out every toy on the floor until they were all surrounding him in a circle. Then he began pairing up characters, whether they belonged in a set or not. It was unity and fraternity for all!

Upon the heads of each figure in a pair, Henry would christen them: "This is Jack, and this is Fred!"

If two toys were in a pair—whether it was a boy or girl, horse, dog, elephant or bear, (whatever) with a touch and a sparkle in his eye, he'd give them the honorary title of "Jack" or "Fred." He would pick two up at a time and make them fly around his room and come in for a landing atop the comforter on his made-up bed. And the toys all talked; they had personalities all their own and a story behind each of them. And they were all *friends*.

The boy made his way to the living room. The Christmas tree danced with rainbow sparkles across garland-highlighted branches, twinkling with soft shadows drifting across the wall. And faces of all the varied decorations gave the semblance of a soul and beauty all its holiday own. The tree skirt beneath was empty, clamoring for more toys (not clothes!) in a few days' time. But in its precious emptiness, the anticipation made it beautiful. The small one laid beneath the tree, looking up at the infinite branch tangles above his eyes, holding the toy figures in his hands, making them soar around his face into the blinding multitude of colors above him.

"*Jack & Fred,*" he said to himself softly. "*Where did you go?*"

With passing glances and occasional eavesdrops from the kitchen, the boy's parents heard the names on more than one occasion and wondered to themselves if there was something more to the glorious feeling that was tugging at the back of their minds and the inside of their hearts.

They were both helping one another with the dishes at the sink.

Dad shook his head. "He was mentioning the Big Mouth girl again. He doesn't like her. What, she picks on him?"

"She picks on everyone, like the mother. She's a real gossip. He read the story to the class, and obviously the girl had some...*issue* with it."

"Why doesn't she mind her own business?"

"Old saying is right: Don't smack the kid; smack the mother!" Henry's mom said. "So school lets out today, and I'm waiting for him, and the girl gets up in his face and says something. And he just *screams* at her in front of the whole crowd of kids and parents. I was mortified," Mom said.

"Maybe he just had a bad day," Dad suggested.

"Bad day?"

"It's not like what everybody thinks it is. I've waited out there before," Dad said. "Listen...those kids can be really vicious to each other. They smell blood in the water and they charge!"

"So you're saying he's right?"

"No," Dad replied. "I'm not saying he's right. He shouldn't have screamed at her, but he's not a doormat either. And you can't go crazy about it."

"It's not that..."

"He's a good kid. I don't think it was a hangin' offense, this time lady."

"*This time.*"

"(Sigh) Why? What exactly did he say? Did he curse at her?"

"No. He just screamed at her 'What do you know about them?!' and something like 'You never even spoke to them. How could you say they're not real?!' or something like that," Mom tried remembering.

"Okay," Dad went.

"I made him apologize to her. The mother wouldn't shut up though. She kept going on, *and on*...."

"Oh, please. Let's not get beyond ourselves here."

"Well, she *was* right. He was rude."

"Did he apologize? Yeah. So, what else is there? They don't do public floggings anymore. We're a few years too late for that. Besides, she needs to put a tight rein on her own kid."

She smiled facetiously. "You're just like him, you know that?"

"And…*we don't have to share with anybody*. That's the *only child's* motto. Go ahead say it."

"Mmm-hmm. You two, both only children. You keep it up. He'll grow up like that, too. Then people all over the place will hear him repeat that and go, 'Who raised that child?'"

"With those people, it doesn't really matter." Dad turned with a grin, watching the boy play in the next room. He asked her, "Why does he call all of them 'Jack' or 'Fred'? I don't mean just one or two of them. He calls *all of them* Jack & Fred."

"I don't know," Mom said brightly. "They're his friends, you know that."

"Yeah, I know that. But—"

"What're you getting at?"

Dad moved over and leaned against the sink. "I don't know. I feel, something is, here, in this house." Mom stopped what she was doing. "That's… I don't know how to describe it. I walk home from work, every night, from the same job for eighteen years now, after taking the subway for an hour. Sometimes I get stuck, sometimes not. It's always crowded, and I work hard, all day. But I don't come home as tired as usual lately—or annoyed from the crowds, or upset, or beat like I used to. And I can't remember when, but it all started when I heard those names cross his lips. Jack & Fred." Dad pounded down on the table in delightful recognition of all he knew to be true. "I'm *glad* to be home!"

"You feel it then, too?" Mom asked, wearing the look of validation, proving to herself that she was not losing her mind.

"Yes."

"Then I'm not crazy either," she said.

"That, or we both are," he replied.

"Yeah, I guess so."

"I don't know."

"I don't know either," she said, turning the water off for a moment. "Is that so bad? I feel like I lost ten pounds and became ten years younger. I feel wonderful, all the time. Even when I go back to work, I carry it with me. And the day doesn't seem so long as it is. When it's over, though, I find myself racing home—and I'm not tired or anything. I just want to be—*here*—in this house, with you guys. It feels different, like a great weight has been lifted. Like something…has gone through the whole house and scrubbed it clean, and there's this fresh scent left afterward. You're right. We're both losing it."

"That's okay," he smiled. "We'll both have company in the asylum."

They laughed.

Meanwhile, in the living room, the boy sat surrounded by the toys, imagining them having the very conversation that was on the hearts and minds of his parents.

Mom looked over at him, and she couldn't put her finger on it. "Why… why can't I…remember, what he told me?"

"Who?" Dad asked.

"Henry. He told me all about Jack & Fred—who they were, *what* they were—"

Dad recoiled. "*What* they were?"

"Yes," Mom said simply. "What they liked to eat and how they talked to him."

Dad sat down. "Um. Who are they? *What* are they? What do they like to eat, and how did they help him? C'mon, inquiring minds want to know!" Dad laughed, but Mom was actually unsettled by the whole thing.

She stared through him, astonished, her eyes becoming glassy. "I don't know…any of it," she said somberly.

"What's wrong with you?" he asked, noticing the tears.

"Nothing."

"What's wrong?" he asked, confused.

"Nothing. I can't describe…" she waved it away, "*anything*. It's like fog over my brain, when I talk about it. I get…this way because I feel happy and confused all at once. He told me about them. And I listened, but when you ask me now who they are, I can't tell you. I draw a complete blank. All I know is that they're good."

"Well, I would hope so."

"No. You don't have to. They are. I just know that. *You* know that. You feel it, too. They're...oh, God." She shook her head, humorously.

"Sit."

"I just can't describe it. Can't. It's all I can do just to remember their names. What're—"

"Jack & Fred."

"God!" she shrieked.

"I think that may be it, *exactly*," Dad said. "We might know more than we think."

"I don't know anything right now," she laughed, rubbing her sore head.

"Look, do you want me to go ask him?" Dad suggested.

"Yes," she said immediately.

"I'll go ask him."

"Go ahead," Mom said. "But I don't think you'll get anything from him. That sounds horrible. He could be in some kind of dire trouble, but I know he's just not. I've never been so sure of anything in all my life." But then Mom thought of the way she saved patients, by following that internal sense she had, and remembered that this wasn't the first time she had felt this way.

Dad turned and looked at her.

"It sounds stupid, but...it could be that we're just not meant to know about this now," Dad said. "This is *his*. It's Henry's, whatever it is." They watched the boy flying the two action figures in his hands. "All I know is someone was watching out for him the other day, downtown."

"I know," she said with as sigh.

Henry's Dad went inside.

"So whatcha doin'?" he asked, crumpling his legs up in a ball beneath him, listening to them involuntarily creak with some disappointment. But Dad knew how to sit on the floor, and he knew how to set up toys. Dad was the man; he knew how to *play*. And playing was important. He was one of the very few Dads who knew that, for he himself had a great imagination. And he knew how to have fun, no matter what. If you listened to him when he relayed adventures and moments with the toys or about real life, you realized that this intelligent man was a master storyteller. That was wonderful. It was something you only hoped you could aspire to. And he loved his boy, and his boy loved him. That's what playing was all about. Chances are, if you did it right, you learned something about life, too, in small little parts that built up over time. I finally understand all of that now. You were smart, Dad. You were smart…and *fun*.

"I'm playin'!" Henry said. His father looked at the red cherry-picker fire engine full of tiny firefighters that Henry was rolling back and forth on the carpet.

Dad asked, "Henry?" and he pointed to each figure, one after the other. "Who's this?"

"That's Jack."

"And this guy. Who's he?" his father asked.

"That's Fred!" the boy said, sounding as if the answer to his father's question was already obvious.

Mom watched from the kitchen, unaware.

Pointing to the other toys on the floor, his father asked, one by one, "How about this horse?"

"Jack."

"And the cowboy with him?"

"That's Fred."

"What about the lady and the dog?"

"That's Fred and Jack."

"Is the dog's name Jack or Fred?"

"Daaaad! That's Jack!" little Henry exclaimed as Mom walked over.

Both Mom and Dad had to burst out laughing after biting their tongues for untold minutes.

Henry and his parents smiled as if forever captured in a photograph for him to remember. They found this to be absolutely adorable. They were learning about the angels. It was all unfolding before them for the very first time, as it had once happened to Henry. And the boy was glad that it happened this way, too. Henry kept right on playing with the red cherry-picker and its toy men.

But they had to ask themselves, *why*? It was right there in front of their noses; he had told them, and they *had* listened. But they just didn't make the leap like he did. They couldn't, though not for lack of trying or faith. They just weren't expecting the answer. They seriously wondered where these names came from, for Henry knew not a person alive by the name of Jack or Fred; there was not a relative, friend, animal, person on television, or character in a story that might have been called these names, *together*. The only thing they could assume, was that the names were just average names that fit almost anybody or that they were indeed new, cherished friends. That *must* be why every toy was called that. It was a celebration. It was fun. It kept the names alive every hour of the day.

It was just that simple. Mom and Dad suddenly stopped. Their investigation was over. They felt and saw the happiness in the household and on the face of the boy. They already believed, so they just resigned themselves to learning the true answer in time. All three of them were happy together, and that's how it's supposed to be. It didn't mean they weren't delightfully curious, though.

The situation for Henry was not as plain, for he knew what the names really meant. Where did they go? He thought they didn't keep their promise. And that hurt. He had to live with that knowledge—that his angels were out there *someplace* that he could not reach.

Did they get in trouble for visiting him? Maybe that's why they didn't come back. Maybe they didn't want to…

"No!" the boy insisted. "*That wasn't the reason.*" He wondered how long it would be till they came back: days, weeks, months, maybe years? It wasn't his imagination, that much was certain. Now was not the time to let doubt creep in, like it had with his little friend. He didn't know how things were going to be with Kristie, when she seemed so distant from his heart now, or how he would ever find a moment's peace until the angels came back. But life would move on, without waiting for him. That much was certain.

What was that? Something made him run to his room and look outside.

The boy threw open the window and looked down at the backyard; it was glistening! Somewhere in the distance he could hear the cow cat 'mooing' as it always did. The boy's eyes lit up. Suddenly, as if someone read his mind, the phone rang. He knew who it was.

{ Chapter 30 }
To the End of Love

"Come on," the boy urged, grabbing her hand as soon as she stepped out of her father's car.

The little girl giggled uncontrollably. "What, what, what?"

"Look…"

The entire alleyway of the boy's home had become a sheet of pure white ice leading down toward the backyard on a slant.

Kristie's cheeks lit up. "How did you do this?"

"Wasn't me," the boy smiled. "Come inside."

The boy's mother held the door open and the kids rushed through in a whirlwind. Ice skates were slung over his shoulder; the blades were smacking his arm with each bounce, all the way down the stairwell to the basement.

He held her hand, and without thought, she interlaced her fingers with his, so you could not tell where one ended and the other began. They were together no matter what.

"Come on," the boy urged her as they descended into the darkness with delight in their eyes. The basement was a dimly-lit museum filled with a staggering collection of oddities from the past. To the family, it was a veritable below-street-level time capsule with everything from World's Fair memorabilia to glass beer Steins to bicycles from years past, and everything in between. Once there, he and Kristie rummaged through an old closet, finding a treasure-trove of goodies. A second pair of skates was a lightweight request to be asked of this amazing collection of artifacts. And there they were! It was time to get suited up. They had to stuff Kristie's skates—or rather his mom's old ones—with cloth diapers and padded socks, but they fit!

Her cheeks were pink and she could not stop giggling as he hurried her down the length of the corridor to the back door. They fell over each other like two drunken New Year's partygoers, trying to balance on the skate blades as they clopped along tile floors.

The boy unlocked the great big latches of the metal door, its age showing with each creak it made. It took two tries but the boy forced it apart from the frozen metal door frame and flicked the backyard floodlight on. Then they saw it.

"Oh my!" Kristie covered her mouth in awe.

The yard was one perfectly smooth sheet of ice; it was as if a Zamboni had brushed across the rink before a hockey game began. The boy took her hand as a saxophone echoed in the air above them.

"What are you doing? Henry, I can't skate!" she said, holding onto the door frame nervously.

The boy turned around, bowing as if he were at a regal ball, extending his hand out for hers. She took a breath—just one—and reached out. He stared deeply into her eyes, which were glistening in the faint light of the yard. He skated backwards, taking her along, and she never looked down—not once. He held her close in his arms. They twirled and moved around the crystalline wonderland as snowflakes fell gently across their faces. And there in the yard, they danced as if captured forever in a painting; they danced to the end of love.

Above on the rooftop, Jack and Belle twirled their fingers in circles, making the tiny humans below mimic their movements and pirouette like gliding music-box figurines. Belle's wing lazily brushed the snow off the roof's ledge, letting it fall upon them like powdered sugar from above. Jack scooped her up in his arms and danced above the rooftop; their feet never touched the ground.

The little one was on the other side of the roof, shaking his head. All the romantic nonsense disgusted him to no end. He lobbed a snowball off the roof and someone tossed it right back, smacking him plumb in the middle of the face.

"What the—"

Flo glided up and melted the snow from his cheeks with a kiss. She pulled him away from it all.

"The only people who hate dancing, Fred, are the ones without partners."

The little one smiled as a thousand other angels appeared over Henry's rooftop in a rush of wind and snow, dancing the night away. They illuminated the sky like pinpoints of brilliant light, shining above a small area of the Bronx. Just like the small people below, the angels twirled in circles, dancing on air currents, to the accompaniment of Toby and his angelic band of musicians, *the Ascents*.

Kristie and Henry rushed to the top of the alleyway; they nodded to one another in recognition and went speeding down the length of the ice spread, holding hands, screaming for joy all the way down.

Inside the house with the yellow awning, Henry's father looked over at his mother and winked as they sipped their coffee, looking up at the ceiling. They didn't know what it was. They just knew something glorious was above them.

Belle put her head on Jack's chest; he felt the tears streaming down her face.

"Belle...what is—"

"Just don't stop," she whispered.

And he didn't. The house was aglow as the entire gathering of angels danced with one another. They were all there. Henry and Kristie danced joyously upon the ice, and as he spun her around, her skate caught the ice and it fractured.

"Oh!" she staggered.

Belle gripped Jack harder.

Henry grabbed his girl and twisted them away from the jagged broken line in the ice. Skating backwards on his heels, he twirled her, and the ice again fractured and broke. The boy's foot crushed through the hole, scraping the cold unforgiving concrete beneath. The little girl held onto him as he pulled himself out.

Belle was shuddering uncontrollably. She was sobbing so hard that her wings failed her, and Jack had to squeeze her tightly against him just to keep them both aloft.

Henry and Kristie righted themselves, managing to stay up, and then the ice split apart and opened up beneath them. They went tumbling backwards, away from one another, falling into the icy ruins which scattered into smithereens as their bodies and the world fell down upon them…

Above them, the little one was sitting with Flo on the far end of the roof. She had Van Fleet bring out hot chocolate and cookies for everyone. Despite Fred's sincerest protests, Henry's rooftop was fast becoming Wingdings 2. The little one feared that hordes of hungry, excited angels would never give the child a peaceful night's rest again, with all their constant partying upstairs. Flo was fairly happy, though. She never thought the Dings was going to be a chain. The little one, on the other hand, couldn't help but feel bad for his partner, despite all this mushy nonsense. He stood there with Belle across the way, who was wiping the tears from her eyes. The only thing Fred wondered was how much Jack—how much they—could handle before all this tore them apart. They needed to talk to the boy again!

{ Chapter 31 }

A Happy Ending Next Time

The boy ripped at his boot laces as he sat among the crumbles, tossing aside his skates one by one. He saw drops of red splashed across the ice slivers. He held out his palms and watched them bleed softly.

"Just a scratch," he assured, rubbing his hands against his pants as he stepped over the frozen shards to reach her.

"Don't!" she urged.

She worried about the sharp ice pieces beneath his socks, but he didn't care; he scooped her off the ground and carried her to the bench against the house. Henry placed her down softly and helped her pull off the ice skates. Kristie seemed as though she was ready to crumble beneath the weight of a burden, which she had been forced to carry on her shoulders, these many long days. The light dulled, the snow stopped falling, and the music silenced itself. In the distance, within the elevated station, a train slid into its stop with a loud grinding noise that pierced the eardrums with its grating disharmony.

He looked at her, remembering all those times he'd turn a corner in school and she'd find him instantly. She always did. There was always something that connected them. Many times they'd turn corners and find one another out of the blue, or simply pick up the phone before dialing and the other was there. That's how things were for them. He couldn't help it; he just smiled when he saw her. She knew it too. There was something about Henry that brought back to life some joyous part of herself, which she had buried once upon a memory ago; it was in a time before the grief, when she could float away and fly. When she touched him, she felt it run through her like wildfire. When she looked into his brown eyes, she believed he could set her free. When she danced with him, for just a small moment in life, she *was* free. They both felt the same thing. Their expressions gave it away, like a great voice whispering to the world what love was all about.

"Hi," she said, pursing her lips together.

"Hi," he replied, taken aback by her sad expression.

"Boy, look at you!"

"What's wrong?"

"You look like the world just fell down."

He sighed. "It did. I look that bad?" the boy asked.

"Terrible!" she kidded. "Like you're getting sick. No 'fense Mister."

"None taken, lady," he said, making for the basement door. "I'm going home. *Goodbye*," he joked, as they always did.

"Me too." She took a deep breath and held it for what seemed like forever before letting it go.

"What's wrong with you?" he asked simply.

"Kids in class are gonna be real mad. They'll only wish they got to see this. Too bad for them. I don't care anymore Hen. I just don't." Kristie kept wringing her hands over and over, looking around as if a ghost was going to snatch her up. "Imagine Joey? Oh, he's gonna be *so* upset. 'You guys get all the luck.' That's not what he says…no. He says, 'lucky dog!' That's…that's right. That's what he says. And the others, they're never going to believe this, Henry. When you tell them someday, they won't ever believe—"

"So what," he smiled. "What's wrong you, Kris?" he asked, reaching out to grab her hand. But she would not offer it.

"Why—"

"You don't look like Sister Mary Sunshine yourself either tonight. No 'fense."

She smiled uneasily. "None taken."

"Didn't you like this?" Henry held his arms out about him. "Wasn't this wonderful?"

The boy leaned forward, pushing his face out, as if he wanted to be as close to her as he could, to save her from whatever it was. She got up and started to pace.

"What's up Miss K?"

Her expression became grim. She moved close, kneeling down in front of him. "Henry, didn't your parents...didn't they tell you? Didn't *someone* at least mention it to you?"

"No...what?"

"Maybe he didn't tell your folks till tonight. Maybe...he probably didn't."

"What—who are you talking about?"

"My dad. I tried calling you last night but you never called back."

"I fell asleep early. Felt awful. We never were much good at phone tag, Miss Kris. You were just supposed to be on the other side like...usual."

She took his hands in her small mittened fingers.

"They're all cut up."

"I told you they're fine. Now, tell me."

"Today. Today's the last day, I...oh, Henry."

She broke down in tears, falling forward, hugging her friend with all her soul.

"What happened?" he asked, pressed against her soft little face that was still chilled from the outside cold.

"Tomorrow, Christmas Eve, I'm leaving. I'm going to stay with my grandmother in Connecticut until our new house is built. It's not going to be ready for a couple a weeks."

The boy took her by the wrists, shaking her gently.

"New house? What're you talking about? You never mentioned..."

The words melted away like popsicles in the sun.

The little girl shuddered. "When the house is built, we're staying in Connecticut. *I'm not coming back.*"

"No!" he blurted out.

She fell into the boy's arms, sobbing. And the only thing he could feel, was his breath being swept from his lungs and a surge of unquenchable grief, burning in deep seething pools within the pit of his stomach. He held her in his arms, his mouth wide open in disbelief.

"Why…why didn't you tell me?" he whispered. "I thought you were my best friend." She pulled back from him, scared. "Why didn't you tell me, Kristie?" he asked again, sad and angry and hurt all at once. "It's not much, but you can tell someone you care about you're leaving him forever!"

"I didn't know till a few days ago."

"Oh please. Come on!"

"No. Henry, believe me. That's why I was so sad that day downtown. I knew it was going to be one of the last times we'd be together. My dad didn't tell me until he had everything ready. He wanted to surprise me."

"I guess he did a good job!" the boy said, sighing deeply and rubbing his head, which was now throbbing with heat and pain.

"Please listen," she pleaded. "He got a better job there. When I found out, I told him I didn't want to go. He said he'd give us a new life. A chance to start over after my mom. Don't be mad. Please…I don't want to leave you."

She began getting all worked up again.

"Shh. I know. I know. I don't want you to leave me either."

Kristie couldn't let the boy go; she held on to his sturdy little frame.

A car horn sounded.

"Kristie, your dad's out front," the boy's mom called from the second-floor window.

Kristie shut her tear-soaked eyes. The lashes pasted to her gentle face. The car sounded again.

"I have to go," was all her mouth could force out, though she never made a sound. Only her precious lips spoke the words her heart could not speak.

"C'mon munchkin. You're gonna slide all the way up the alley on those," Henry said, looking at her tiny socks. They both laughed. It was the only thing they could do. He took her inside and she put her shoes back on, lacing them up all wrong. The boy took her back out to her dad's car, standing there with her. Henry thought that there was nothing quite so horrible, as escorting the one you care about to the very thing that will drive her away forever.

"Did you always know?" Jack asked Belle.

"They told me, but I wasn't sure it was going to go through. Once the kids met and Henry made my little girl so happy, I didn't…I tried to pretend it wasn't going to happen. I'm sorry, Jack."

He smiled. "Have faith, little angel. It'll all work out in the end."

Belle kissed Jack on the forehead slowly, and he touched her face, one last time.

"Don't let go of him, Jack," Belle said, nodding down toward the street. "Don't let go of that boy. He believes in you, more than you know."

Jack nodded. Neither could handle anymore, so she abruptly flew off toward the dark horizon, bells tinkling in the distance.

"Good luck, handsome!" Her whisper touched the inside of his ear. Jack closed his eyes, taking in the perfumed aroma of rose petals still on his lips and in the air about him.

He watched Belle with a great big lump in his stomach as she ascended high into the winter sky.

"Ahh…damn," he said to himself.

He sailed back down to the rooftop, eyes still watching, but she was already a vanishing blip in the atmosphere. He drifted back farther, and farther, and farther, until a gigantic catcher's mitt caught him in mid-flight.

"Hey!" Jack uttered, as the wind got taken out of his sails. "Freddd!"

"You okay?"

"No."

"Good," he threw his arm over his partner's shoulders. "We got cocoa and animal crackers on the other side of the roof."

"The Barnum's?"

"No, the cheap ones in the two-ton bag."

"I like the Barnum's."

"You don't know jack, Jack!" The taller angel sighed at the little one. "Oh c'mon. You *know* you like that one. That one makes you laugh Jack. That one—"

"Fred?"

"Yeah, Jack."

"Shut up."

Belle watched him from someplace up above, and went to pieces the moment Jack disappeared from her sight.

"You're the best thing that's ever happened to me, girl," she heard him say in a whisper only her heart could hear.

Down below, the boy stood outside the Buick that would drive the little girl away from him. Henry shrugged. "Well…Merry Christmas."

She sighed. "Let me go, Henry."

"Doesn't look like I have much choice."

"No, it doesn't."

"Do something for me?"

The boy looked at her.

"Anything."

She wiped her tears away and put on a stern face.

"Write about me. Write one of those stories about me, so no matter what, you can always remember that we were friends…and we were happy, and we were together. Not like this. Next time, make sure we're never apart. When you write our story someday, make sure you give us a happy ending. Okay?"

"Alright."

"And don't you ever stop, Henry. You write and write, until you have whole big libraries just filled with stories. You go and be famous, and somehow, no matter what, we'll always be together inside one of those stories. It'll be just the two of us. Alone. Promise me?"

"We'll meet again…"

"*Promise me*, Henry."

"I promise you," he said solemnly.

She looked away. "You're the bestest friend I'll ever have."

Henry put on a brave face for the both of them and smiled a smile that washed away the finality of the young girl's words.

"We *will* see each other again Kris. I'm sure we will."

"You think so? You make it sound like…like it's just supposed to be that way."

The boy rubbed the tears from the young girl's eyes, holding her precious little face in his hands.

"It is. I know it is. Believe me. We'll always be together. Besides, Belle is going to be there to watch over you."

The little girl took a deep, shuddering breath and smiled.

"I guess she is," she said with a sigh. "And Jack & Fred will take care of you, right?"

A lump caught in his throat, thinking of how the angels had seemingly left and gone away too. "Uh-huh."

"As long as we have the angels, I guess everything's going to be alright then. You know…I guess it's not their fault. You know? Henry?"

"Yeah, Kris."

"I love you."

"I love you too."

Kristie ran over to Henry with his arms open wide. They embraced, one last time.

"I'm sorry I didn't believe," she whispered. She reached into her pocket and pressed the angel feather between his hands before he could speak. She expelled every last ounce of joy in that final hug, as if letting the air out of a great big balloon whose helium was love. And then it fizzled and flattened…and died.

A chill ran down the length of the boy's spine.

"Oh, God, I've lost her." He thought about the angels, who he had not seen since their first appearance in his room. *"I've lost them all."*

What did it all mean? So the kids all liked his story. They all liked Jack & Fred. It was selfish, but he couldn't help but think of himself. He lost the one thing he loved dearly in that dark place that was school; she was the one constant that kept him smiling…*his Kristie.*

It was happening, just as he always thought, always feared it would. They were all leaving. Everyone he loved. A draft ran a mile down his back, and he swallowed a whole belly full of grief that had been resting in his throat since the time his love turned a pale face to his eyes. Henry looked at the slender feather, gently holding it in the palms of his hands.

"Goodbye Kristie," he said to it. And the car drove her home.

{ Chapter 32 }

At Long Last, Home

It had been some hours since the boy's father and mother had laid him down to sleep and his dad bid him sweet dreams. He waited and waited, but still, they did not come. Until finally, when he had given up all hope for the night, a sound! And the boy leapt up instantly as the window unlocked and was hefted open. He needed to sit. The day was all too much for him. Though he had imagined it since their first meeting, now it was actually happening. They were coming back! The boy found it strange to be in the place he was in, for it didn't seem real. But it was, and part of him was exhilarated, but that part burned out hours before, and he was uncertain what to feel.

"There you are," he said. "I've been looking all over for you!" Henry exclaimed, jumping off the bed in spite of himself.

The angels piled in with smiles, which soon disappeared when they saw the sad look on the boy's face. They knew what that face meant. In another time that was them, and it wasn't like that now, but the memory of it still brought up feelings that they nervously swallowed back down.

"You can still see us, Henry?" Fred asked curiously, keeping his distance.

"Sure I can!" the boy exclaimed happily. "I thought you left for good. I've been *waiting* for you. I didn't think you were coming back. I missed you guys."

He ran over and embraced the angels, and their hearts were at ease.

"Thank, God!" the little one yelled excitedly. "We were worried."

"About what?" the boy asked.

"That you might not see us again. That it was a fluke. That maybe you'd forget," the little one shrugged.

"How could I forget you?" he asked, looking back and forth at Fred and Jack. "I *never* forgot. I can see you! No one believes me, but I still see you. I don't care what they think. Even if they do call me crazy."

Jack laughed. "We're all a little bit crazy."

The little one drew closer. "They call you that? Crazy?"

"Sure they do. All of them. They like the story I wrote about you, but… they all think I'm nuts because I believe it. I know you're real," the boy said with conviction. "So, what does it matter? They miss out, it's their loss. I know what I have, and what I saw."

"We're sorry kid," Jack said.

"Why should you be sorry, huh? Because they're stupid…because they don't believe in *anything* but what they see in front of them? Doesn't matter to them. Nothing does. That's why they act that way."

"We know it's not easy," Jack tried explaining, "to hang on to a belief, even as strong as what you have, when the whole world is downing you. We understand how hard it is for you, down here, to believe in us. Especially when we're invisible to people. *We understand.* So don't think it's one-sided, kid, alright? That's just the way it is, with the whole upstairs and downstairs stuff. You know? If we could…" Jack started, unable to finish his thought.

The little one said, "What, you don't think we'd stay for breakfast? Eat breakfast all the time with your mom and dad, and you…in person, in the flesh. Let me tell you something. If it was possible, if we *could* do it, we would. Believe me, we would!"

"Believe him," Jack said, subconsciously rubbing his belly while thinking of blueberry waffles.

"We just can't," the little one said.

"I understand," said the boy. "I told Kristie that too. With Belle, and her mom and everything."

"I know," Jack replied. "I just wish having us here, wouldn't…I wish things would be easier sometimes, so we could enjoy them more."

"Yeah, but, Jack. Think about it," the boy said. "When you talk your head off in school all the time it gets boring, right? But when you're in silent reading time, and you're *supposed* to be reading, and you sneak over and talk to someone without getting caught, that's where the real fun is. The *not getting caught* part. Right?"

Jack shook his head, like he was the kid. "Right."

"Besides, look at them. Except for a few people, look what I go to school with. You guys think this started just now, with you? No. They've been like this forever. They're not going to like or hate me, any more than they already do."

Fred explained, "That's because you're different. Anytime someone challenges the everyday crap people see and comes up with something different, they give them a hard time for it."

"Guys, tell me, what happened to you? Did you get in trouble?" he asked sadly. The two angels looked at one another. "You do like being here, right?"

"No kid. We *love* being here," Jack said. "We love *you*, Henry. But we were always here."

"Where, Jack? I never saw you," the boy insisted, hoping to God he didn't miss them by accident.

"Henry," Fred began as he floated down to the boy, "You won't always see us like this. An angel can only truly help you if you believe in them, even when you can't see us."

"I did. I do. We *know* this. But I see you, now. And I didn't see you come back."

Jack insisted, "We were always here, Henry. Tonight is no different than the last. We still checked in on you," he said.

"Why didn't you say hello? You coulda woke me!"

Fred looked at Jack.

"You see, you weren't looking for us right, Hen," Jack said.

"I don't understand," the boy replied.

Jack took in a deep breath and started to explain. "Henry, when you started naming everything 'Jack & Fred,' we were there with you, *all the time*. And in your heart, you knew that too. You *knew* we were there. Deep down, that's why you'd always name things, just to let us know that you were aware. We heard you. And you heard us. You knew this in your heart because you were looking right. You *weren't* looking with this," Jack pointed to Henry's head, "like other people. You were looking with this!" the angel said as he signed a cross over Henry's heart. "That's what kept us alive. Your belief in us."

Fred turned to the boy, "Angels like us, we're everywhere. All the time! When the happy things come, and the not so happy things. We're always around. It's hard, but no matter what, you just have to believe."

"Henry," Jack continued, "What we do and where we go is because of God. He loves everyone here on Earth, an *awful* lot. So He created us to show you guys that, no matter what, you are never alone, and that He is always with you. *We* are always with you. Angels aren't about seeing divine images, or ghosts, or miracles happening all the time. An angel can be as simple as a tap on the shoulder, or a present to someone, or just a pleasant feeling—a reminder of God's love. You can hear us when people laugh hysterically, when they're having fun, or when someone's in agony and is screaming out in pain. We're always here. If you look for the little things—if you listen—you will find us. But if you are looking for magic tricks, you'll only find disappointment. That's why God created the Harry Houdini's of this world."

Fred spoke, "Your friends in school liked us, but they never truly believed. They've completely forgotten about us already, I'm sure," the little one said.

Henry looked at Fred and Jack and shook his head sadly.

The little one said, "One hit wonder. It's just a fad with them. It was something to distract them from the usual homework and crap of their day so Christmas would come faster, and it did. You've always believed though, Henry. Through it all. We know how much you had to put up with. We know they called you crazy. We know how they tried to break you into pieces. *We know*. That's why, when you were getting beat down, we wouldn't let you fall to the floor. We wouldn't let you go down. Your belief, as true and as wonderful as it was, and is, wouldn't let you fall. If it did, we would have never met in the first place."

Jack said, "It's easier for people not to believe. Because then they can live however they want and not have to think of the repercussions of who they hurt, even themselves. Someday, a long time from now, people will want to believe again, because you can't live with nothing to believe in."

The little one looked at the child. "You understand what we're saying, Henry. You understand, because it worries you too. Why are you afraid, Henry?"

"I'm not."

"You're afraid when you let your imagination run wild at night. That's why you don't like to sleep. That wolf…"

"How do you know…?"

"You're afraid they'll torture you in school for us, like they always do about everything else."

"Stop."

Fred put his hands on the boy's shoulders. "And you're afraid what'll happen if you go so far with your stories and they don't understand you. You're afraid they'll hate you and leave you alone. Always. No matter how much you deny it, you're afraid of being left alone, Henry. Like with Kristie."

"And guess what, Fred? I already am. They all *did* leave. Every last person in school, one by one. Even you. And I had *nobody* all these months, until she came along. I have two wonderful parents who I don't see most of the day. What happens when this all comes to an end? What happens after you leave tonight? You *won't* come back again. And then they'll be nobody. The only friend I had in this world moved away. And the rest of them—the rest have their own little things to do, which *do not* include me. Joey and Patty, are Joey and Patty. I'm the odd man out with them. I'm always the odd man out. My friend Anthony tries his best, but he still needs to be with kids his own age. And Kristie's gone. Poof. Just like that. Gone. So that's it. There isn't anybody anymore.

"So big deal. I won't have anybody in school to curse at me, or make fun of me, or worry about my stories, and then I won't even have you. They'll be nobody Fred, *nobody*." The boy swallowed. "Then it doesn't really matter, does it? You know what I'm afraid of, Fred, really afraid of? Jack?"

The angels shook their heads.

The boy whispered, "You know what I'm afraid of? I'll tell you. It's not so much being alone that I'm afraid of. I'm an only child. It doesn't bother me like it does other people when their brothers and sisters aren't around them for any amount of time." The boy pulled the angels closer. "What I'm afraid of, Fred, is being alone, and *liking* it. I'm afraid that I won't care anymore, about anybody or anything, because I'll *like* being alone. I'm sick of these games in school, Fred. I can't stand it anymore. Every day shouldn't be like slow torture. Every damn day shouldn't be a fight to just *be*…everyday. And no one notices. Nobody realizes, except me. And everything happy should not have to leave so fast either. A happy hermit who hates the world, whose best and only company is *himself*. That's what I'm afraid of, Fred. *That's* what I'm afraid of. It was me you know. I took us on the fieldtrip. I told Joey about Sesame Street. I know it's not real, but I hoped. I wanted there to be some kind of great adventure outside of that boring old school we go to. When you have nothin' you can always hope that maybe that *world* was real. I told Joey. And Joey led us all the way. And I wanted to tell everybody I nearly got us all killed. Especially them. But seeing you made me forget. It made it all go away until now."

Fred insisted, "But tonight you're not alone. And you *never* were alone. And you never will be alone, Henry. Yeah, sometimes life *is* slow torture."

The boy's eyes were wet with tears.

"You want the truth. I'll be honest with you," the little one said. "We shouldn't say this." He saw Jack out of the corner of his eye. "But yeah, that's what it's gonna be like, for a long time. For many years to come, you'll face it in one way or the other, the same kind of rejection by the mass of people that surround you. And you'll feel alone, and maybe because of them you *will* grow to like it. But you got to remember…"

The little boy was crying.

"You *have* to remember what it is that makes you special in the first place. You are *not* like the others. You are *different*. *That* is what makes you so special. But through it all, you have to remember who loves you most. And if you can't find a friend that you can lay that claim to, remember the Lord is always there. From the beginning to the end. And *that's* why you have us. Always. Remember, kid, people forget or don't know, or don't realize, God pushes most the ones He loves best. Jack and I, and you, are proof of that, if there was ever proof to be pointed to. You take your pain and you use it as your strength, and never back down to the world around you.

"The Big Mouth Benedettos of this world can only speak so many words before they realize how sad and empty those words really are. Even Kristie…as dear to you as she is. They're sad people, because *you* show them that you have something they can never take away from you: your faith in all that you know is true and right. Faith in another day, faith in yourself, and faith in the God you love. That's what being special is all about, kid. You're gonna have it for a *long* time. So get used to it," Fred said with a happy face. "We have. And who knows. Someday *something wonderful* might happen along your way."

"I think it already did," the boy smiled. "I just think it somehow got lost."

Jack gripped the boy's shoulder. "It'll never be lost. Just believe."

"Come with us," the little one held out his hand. "Come with us and we'll show you how great it can truly be," Fred told the boy.

"What?" the boy asked.

"Life," the little one replied. "You have a gift to use. Someday you will."

"What am I going to do with this gift? Huh, guys?" he asked, both sorry and grateful all at once.

Jack said, "We don't know yet, Hen. You have to find that out on your own. But if you believe in us—if you truly believe—we can help show you the way there."

"You know I do. *You know it.* No matter what. Even when I get this way."

The angels looked at him.

"You know I believe in you, Jack & Fred."

"Then," Jack said, shutting his own eyes, "lay down. Close your eyes. And fall asleep, Henry."

"But you—"

"We'll be here. We're not leaving," Fred whispered. "Remember, just believe. We'll be right here."

The boy took a deep breath and let it go. His eyes peeled open, slowly.

"Wait! Whoa, guys! Where are we going? Whoa, geez!"

Jack & Fred lifted him off the bed and dashed up to the ceiling, holding the boy firmly by the arms as if to never let him go. Henry gasped as he looked down upon his room, which looked like a dollhouse cubicle from that height.

"Oh my God, I'm—"

"Floating?" Fred suggested.

"Yeah."

Jack smiled. "Ain't it cool?"

"Oh my God!"

He looked down on his room, feeling funny at how it appeared from the nook and cranny vantage point of the ceiling.

"We're going on a little journey," Jack enlightened. "A journey into that imagination of yours, and we're going to show you something really quite beautiful, because it's all you. Once you have the courage to face up to it, you can conquer any nightmare and anybody who tries to hurt you along the way. You're free to do anything—anything your heart desires. Come on, it's nearer than you think!"

Henry leaned over to Fred.

"Boy, Fred, that Jack's a smart cookie isn't he?" Henry whispered.

"Yep," Fred sighed. "That's why his name comes first in the title."

Jack winked at the boy.

Henry stammered, "Yeah but—"

"Let's go!" Jack yelled.

And they were off! With a strong gust of wind and a little wing propulsion, Jack & Fred flew out the window and soared high into the broad, blue night sky with their boy, Henry.

The boy's stomach lurched, and his every sense was enlivened by the adrenaline inside him. Henry and the angels darted past the clothesline outside his house, and flew up into the large cedar tree that often made scary shadows across his bed and floor. It was funny; for the first time *ever*, his body had nothing to weigh it down. He was flying, free!

"I can't believe I'm dreaming all this!" Henry shouted to his angels. "It seems so real!"

The little one shrugged. "Who says you're dreaming?"

"It's as real as you want it to be, Henry!" Jack shouted back. "We're taking you on a ride, but *you're* the one that's gonna provide the place we go to. Hold on!"

The angels thought to themselves that, unlike George, this was a weight they didn't mind carrying.

Henry looked around at the wide-angled world about him, trying to convince himself of how real this actually was. He was flying high into the sweeping bands of the starry night sky with angels, but he felt safe and secure (and strangely warm) in just his pajamas as he was carried away in their arms.

Out there above him, celestial pinpoints were burning strong and perfect in their halos, glimmering delicately. And the moon lay above the whole, domed world, lighting it up like a night game in Yankee stadium. And there they were, with the rush of ascension running through their spirits and their hearts beating quickly.

The wind rustled the tree branches wildly, shaking the leaves like peanuts in a sack, but the boy and the angels flew straight through them like streams of water, without obstruction or bother. The rough, pitted, gnarled bark folds stood out in clear, dark detail, for what was once an object from the distance of a bedroom window was now an intricate sight to behold. Little knotholes ran up and down the wooden pole, and if he listened closely, Henry could hear the squirrels inside their homes, squabbling in clicks and pecks over their winter's supply of nuts and acorns. He took in a deep breath of crisp, sweet-scented air, to the point of near euphoria as the breeze ruffled his mane in tumbling falls. And the friends rose higher and higher over the gigantic tree out into the world.

For the briefest of moments, Fred pointed out the Big Dipper and the belt of the hunter, Orion, far ahead in the burgeoning stratosphere. Henry could see the streetlights below them twitching on and off with timers and accenting the street corners with a faint yellow-orange glow. At the end of the block, smoke billowed from a building's furnace, far into the atmosphere. And for some wild reason, Mrs. Kline's dog looked up at the trio in the sky, and began barking excitedly at them.

"Will you shut up!" Fred yelled. The dog silenced itself.

"Man," Henry thought. *"Jack & Fred must be special. Dream or whatever, nobody had ever gotten that mangy mutt to keep silent. Nobody."*

"Come on, kid! Flap your wings!" Jack told the boy. "*'You can fly! You can fly! You can fly!'*" he mocked.

"That sounded like Peter Pan," Hen said.

"Of course it does," Jack replied. "Where do you think *they* got it from?" he smiled.

"Wow." The boy bit his lip.

"Copyright infringement," Fred muttered in the child's ear. "You'll see, we'll get screwed over for that one too!"

"Fred!" Jack admonished.

The little one shook his head. "Never mess with the Big Man upstairs, or the Mouse. Ya don't win!"

Firmly holding the boy in hand, the angels climbed farther into the lofty heights with each passing breath.

"It's amazing."

That's all Henry could think. And when he looked down, it all seemed so little. The house with the yellow awning became a small box, upon a flat landscape on one giant, spacious, light-dotted map.

The angels suddenly began singing Sinatra.

"Fly me to the moon. Let me play among the stars…"

Henry cringed a bit, for as adept at other things as they were, Jack & Fred were certainly not choir boys.

"Guys! Guys! I think you're scaring the dog. Oh…look out!"

"What, Henry?" the angels asked together.

"Plane!" he ducked.

"Whoa!" the pair went.

"*Aaahhhhh!*" the trio screamed, barely missing a large passenger jet swooping down in front of them.

"I think that was a 747," Fred remarked.

"No way. Looked like a plain 727 to me, Fred," Jack discounted.

"You know planes?" the boy asked.

Fred opened his eyes wide, letting the air wash through his face.

"Yeah! We do 'I spy' on some of the longer trips down here," he said to the boy, almost forgetting to argue with his partner. "Please…727? You'd argue with Moses if you could, Jack."

"If Moses was as wrong as you are on a consistent basis, yes. I would argue with him too. But you're no Moses, Fred."

"If I were, I'd smack you with that staff and part you in two!"

The boys had that look in their eyes, and Henry was in between them, and there was falling involved here.

"Whoa! Hey, hey, hey! Stop!" Henry shouted, trying to referee the cherubs. "C'mon angels, no fighting. Pay attention to where we're going."

"Hey Jack, he sounds tough there," Fred quipped.

"I don't know, Fred. He looks like he could start smacking us around," Jack said with a wink and a nod.

"You bet your wings I could!" the boy threatened.

"*Ooooooooh!*" the angels went, laughing.

"Oh *no*, Jack. My arms…I think oooh, I'm gettin' them Charlie horses in mee arms, Jackie-boy!"

"Charlie horse? Really, Fred?" Jack asked with big eyes.

The boy's eyes bulged. "Oh, don't you even *think* about it, buddy."

Jack smiled. "*Ooh-oh.*"

Fred tried to contain himself.

"What is it, Jack? Are you okay?"

"Fred? Fred, my bursitis is acting up again. And my arms…they're suddenly…"

"Don't!" Henry gripped their arms tighter. "Jack!"

"Hee-hee!" the little one went.

"Fred, *guys*. Oh, I'm gonna smack you silly."

The angels lightened their grip.

"God! Don't do that! Don't drop me! What's wrong with you?" the boy chuckled. "No…No, now stop. Stop! Stop!!!"

"Alright, alright!" the little one said, like a mischievous little bug. "Ow!" he screeched as the boy pinched his chubby little arm. "Ow (snicker). That hurt. Stop that!"

"Even?" Hen asked.

"No, I'll getcha later."

"Oh, will you?!"

"Guys," Jack called. "Look over there."

Henry looked up, cool air splashing over his face.

"Hey, what is that big thing heading for us?" the boy asked.

Fred squinted for a moment. "Looks like a falling star to me."

Jack & Fred looked at one another and gave no answer.

"Okay," Henry mumbled to himself, a little surprised.

The wind tumbled against his face and he could see starlight reflecting against the puffy, cottontail clouds that just hung still, above them. The trio barrel-rolled and blasted through one of the clouds, and the angels began flapping faster, and faster, and faster, gaining speed.

Fred shouted, "Warp speed, Mr. Sulu!"

{ CHAPTER 33 }

OUT BEYOND THE BREAKERS

They gripped the boy's arms even more securely than they had initially and soon they were streaking toward the upper atmosphere in a blinding flash. Henry could feel the vibrations through his arms as the angels powered themselves upward. And when he could pull himself away from the frightening rush of weightlessness, he could see the angels at his sides carrying him all the way. Jack had determination in his features, his wings beating so intensely that they were a blur and could only be seen, incidentally, if your eyes had caught the right rhythms of the speed, like helicopter blades in the breeze.

They were so far from the place he called home and they plowed ahead so fast that Henry couldn't even turn back to face the sky behind him in the rush of these unending breezes. The little one's hand reached across Hen's face and pressed down lightly on the boy's eyelids to keep them shut in what should have been dizzying speeds. Without words or thought, he just trusted in them, and flew, all the way to the end of the line on their journey up.

The boy didn't quite know where they were going, but he knew that, as long as he was with Jack & Fred, everything would be alright. Even when he couldn't see them, he felt at ease—at peace. It was the safest, warmest, most wonderful feeling he had ever felt, softer than his blue blanket, warmer than his mother's hugs, and more fun than Dad playing with him on the living room floor. And it seemed almost impossible, for those things were so special, and yet it was true. It was a feeling that Henry didn't want to let go of. It was an angel's touch, and he never wanted to let that fade away. And so they passed through the world's skylight of white haze and escaped the confines of the small blue marble with ease…and were on their way.

Henry closed his eyes and grinned rather happily at the thought.

And then without bother, they said, *"We're here!"*

Their breath was tickling the insides of his ears and face as they whispered.

Henry opened his eyes to see Jack & Fred floating before him.

Jack smiled. "Do you like it?" he asked.

"I'd like *anywhere* that I was with you guys."

The angels looked at one another and smiled.

"But what is this? There's nothing here." The boy looked around at the plain light grayness around them. The whole area was shrouded in a thick fog—empty. Just waiting to be filled in. The child thought for a moment. "I'm not dead…am I?"

"Nooo," Jack dismissed. "Just…"

"…look," the little one finished.

And there they were, at an ocean, out beyond the breakers.

"This is wonderful!"

"Just a thin slice of heaven, kid!" Fred said loudly as he looked out upon the world around them.

It was like rubbing the sleep from your eyes. One moment everything was blurry, but as they sailed on, it all became sharp and in focus, and strikingly so. Below them, the ocean poured mightily from faucets, spreading out wide, a big blue-green swimming pool for giants to play in. The Earth looked like a puffy white cloud face with scrunched down eyes, lifted from an explorer's navigational chart of the ancient "flat" world, sitting deep in the sky.

The cartoon-like face took a long breath and blew out smoke streams in bellows blasts, streaking across the sky with long plumes of sky writer's lines. A great hand took a sugar sifter and shook it until there was a pure sand beach that stretched out to infinity, below. And a grand orange beach ball was smacked by an equally gigantic hand and went sailing across the sky, until it decided to hover above the world as the sun.

Jack led the trio of flyers onward, pausing only for a moment to point out a series of foamy white caps atop the rolling waves. It was a perfect replica of the indelible image of Ocean City, Maryland beset in the boy's mind. It was just as he'd always wished—to fly out over the water, out to a place in the ocean you could only imagine swimming to on your own. And he was there with them!

The sun was at their backs, and when Henry turned around, he was blinded by its golden rays. Its warmth radiated all over. Jack pointed to something that resembled large gray stones, which appeared behind the foamy white ruffling in the sea. As they swooped in lower, they could see that it was a school of fish being followed by a snappy group of dolphins.

Jack gave a gentle tug and led Fred and Henry down to the water's surface. Fred held him high over the water as Jack lowered himself down to the waves, hovering there for a moment, dangling his feet in the cool blue sea below. He extended his hand and a dolphin jumped up and rubbed its snout against it, and the angel smiled.

"Say hey to Henry," Jack told the creature, which made a happy gurgling sound.

Fred smiled. "Go ahead, boy. Go find the dynamite!"

Jack shook his head. "He's not Flipper."

"Yeah well, he looks like him."

From the East came flocks of seagulls, flying low, skimming along the water's surface and dunking their heads, retrieving their first catches of the day. They glided away on invisible air currents, sailing off to land nearby. As they flew on, they coasted by the boy and the angels, both of whom were having the time of their lives, jumping and speeding across the blue-green waters of the ocean beneath them. The flock dashed past the trio, excitedly dispersing in several directions, squawking all the way.

The little one ducked. "Ahhh! Look out! baygulls!" he shouted.

"Hey!" Jack yelled, swatting at them, giving chase after some of the more persistent of beaks sniped at the boy and Fred. "Flying rat scavengers! You want a piece of me? Oh don't even think about it! You guys dive-bomb me and it's on! IT IS ON!!!"

The boy laughed, his face glistened as the sun reflected in his eyes. Grief filled Fred like a helium spill, but he swallowed it back down. It was the same with his partner. Jack's heart pounded, but he flew straight on anyway. They couldn't escape the reality of it. It was the last time they'd ever see Henry like this. And it was the *best* time. Fred looked over at Jack and smiled without words. Jack knew it too. But they were going to savor every last moment of it anyway.

{ Chapter 34 }

The Coolest Feeling There Ever Was

Jack exclaimed, "Hurry, hurry! We don't have time. There it goes! Over there," he yelled, pointing to something in the distance. "Look over there! Quick!"

"Oh, Jack." Fred smacked himself in the puss. "Not again. Man!"

Jack shook the boy. "You see it, kid? Oh, baby."

"Gotta be a hundred footer at least," the little one said, eyeing it cautiously. "Dude, we're gonna get slammed!"

Jack was in his seventh heaven. "Forget slammed! If we weren't angels we'd probably get killed!"

"Uh, what about me?" the boy nervously asked. "You two guys aren't serious, are you?"

"It's just too cool. Oh! The wave's peakin'! Hurry!" Jack screamed.

The little one shouted, "That sucker's huge, Jack!"

Henry smiled wide. "We're really gonna do this, aren't we?"

Fred protested. "This is just too much! C'mon!"

Jack tugged them toward it.

Fred raced to catch up as always, and the horizon grew smaller and smaller, getting closer by the second. The wall of water was barreling toward them at unimaginably fast speeds. It was a pure vision of sheer raw power and indomitable strength, lumbering its sliding girth along a slow path toward the shore and *whoever* was in its way. It was coming…and there was nothing you could do about it.

Jack stopped and stared at the wall of water longingly for a moment.

"Oh, now this is just too sweet."

Fred moaned. "Come on, Jack, this is ridiculous! We're gonna get crushed!"

"Go man, go! Go! Go! Move it, Fred! Move it!" Jack screeched as they raced with the boy, whose heart was in his throat.

"Let's hang ten and four feathers!" Fred decreed.

"What does that mean?" Henry cried.

"I have no idea," the little one shrugged. "Feels more like Jan and Dean than Jack & Fred."

From out of nowhere, the angels came shooting down out of the sky with their boy, dashing beneath the shadow of the rolling behemoth.

"Let's jam!" Fred yelled, as he ripped the boy away and tossed him like a football to Jack, who was positioning himself for the perfect ride.

Jack snagged him—and in one windmill-like motion, flung the boy up in the air. Henry landed flat upon the angel's back as Jack shot through the water on his belly, dropping in on the wave as it reached new heights.

"Okay, Hen!" Jack called. "Get ready to paddle."

"I can't believe we're doing this. Jack! You're not a surf board! We're gonna get squashed by this thing!"

"Don't look at it!"

"What?!"

"C'mon kid, trust me!"

"God!"

"Exactly!"

Henry crouched low to the angel's back as the shadow behind eclipsed them both.

"Whoa…whoa, Jack!"

"Ready?"

"Jack…"

"Paddle! Paddle, paddle, c'mon. Here we go. Paddle!"

The boy and the angel paddled in tandem, kicking their feet like mad as the wave jacked up and began to haul them high into the sky.

"That's it!" Fred yelled from a distance. "Go!"

The wave sent them to the roof.

When they reached the top of the world, the boy stood up, balancing on Jack's back closing his eyes as the glorious sensation hit him. *He was free!*

Using his wings, Jack lifted the boy over his back and tossed him across the way, flush into the little one's arms.

Fred cradled him, absolutely blissful as they rode on together. *"Hey Hen! Here we gooooooooooooo!!!"*

"Whoooooooooooooohoooooooooooooooooooo!!!"

"Oh yeah!!" Jack shrieked, setting up his top turn, gliding on, then crossing one foot over the other.

"There he is!" Fred screamed to the boy as Jack went sailing past on the right. "See!" Fred danced; his feet were gliding across the water without a board, with the boy in his arms. *"See Jack over there? He stylin'! He stylin'! We stylin'! We stylin'!"* the little one said, shaking his booty like he just didn't care.

Jack cut back with a foam-bouncy recovery, going to the top of the wave, his wings spreading open, catching air off the peak, sending himself spiraling over and over and down—all the way down—into a quadruple somersault. He held the air he caught beneath his wings long into the moment! And, then he smacked down onto the face of the wave again feet-first.

"Woooo yeah!" he screeched.

"Baaaabbby!" Fred bellowed. The little one made his way through the top of his arc, carving lines in the water like a mad razorblade. Water shot through his toes in a delighted rush of foam. It was perfection. It was pure gold! And he and the boy both loved every single minute of it.

Jack dropped in, slamming down on his heels. He let his hand reach out to touch the cool wet surface, water flowing through his fingers in jet blasts.

The wave broke and a pocket started forming. And the tube reared its beautiful self.

Fred yelled over the thunderous rush of water, *"Hang on, kid. We're going in!"* The boy hung onto his neck for dear life, excited and scared to death all at once. The wave was beginning to slowly collapse. Fred couldn't help but think about *Star Wars*; it was the boy's favorite, and his as well. "Henry, at that speed, will we be able to pull out in time?"

Henry smacked the angel's shoulder. "It'll be just like Beggar's Canyon back home!"

Two loud thunder booms sounded as the boy and angel soared in. Fred watched the section falling and made a very gentle bottom turn, standing flatly on one foot, adjusting his trim, then folding himself back into the pocket, leaning forward. The little one tucked the boy in clear and away from the collapsing ceiling. They were in the tube, baby!

Time moved in Department of Motor Vehicle precision and pace. The world fell before them like dripping honey. Henry reached out, feeling the moving wall in between his fingers spraying up onto his face, and he looked up at Fred. The angel's hair, wet-mussed with seawater, stuck to his face, blocking his eyes. The boy reached up and brushed the little one's hair away so he could see. Fred looked down, winked, and smiled.

"Ain't this just the coolest feeling there ever was?" the little one screamed above the roar of the ocean.

The boy smiled. "Yes. Yes it is!"

Jack was thrashing over the falls, and for a moment, the boy and the little one were eclipsed by the falling sections, but for only a moment. Fred crouched low and the boy kept his head tucked under as the walls were closing down around them, and the tunnel of light before them grew smaller and smaller by the slip-sliding second. The massive expanse of water came tumbling down, and the tube collapsed onto itself. Fred kept his bead only on the small rays of sunshine that were touching his face through the contracting iris ahead, making way for their exit...

Jack peeled out and came around, watching for a moment, for a sign. And just as the tube squeezed out its insides, a blast of whitewater billowed forth, and Fred and Henry *rocketed* right after it on gusts of sea salt and foam, safe! Jack nodded. Fred smiled down on the boy and Henry smacked him five, congratulating the angel.

"Good one!" Jack yelled, relieved and more than a little fond of the maneuver.

"Good one, kid!" Fred called, wiping the water from his face.

"You too, little one," Henry called back, winking.

"Lateral!" Fred shouted, heading into the whitewater as he gently tossed the boy into Jack's waiting arms.

Jack cut back and he and the boy, climbed to the top of the remaining wave section, again. The angel did crossovers with his feet, dancing across the blue skin surface.

"How's that?" he asked.

"Dude!" Henry exclaimed.

They came up, riding along the breaking lip of another wave, somersaulting over the top—catching an innumerable amount of airtime going over the falls (courtesy of Dr. J's wings). They spun out and around, doing mid-air pinwheels and landing smack dab in the turbulent cauldron of swirling white beneath them—on Jack's feet.

"Wooooo! How about that?!" Jack called to the boy in his arms.

"Yeah, baby!" Fred yelled, from somewhere round the crest.

Jack peeled out, bringing the boy, who was on the angel's back, into the safe, flat shallows, which bubbled and fizzled over in their awakening calmness.

The kid smiled, mussing Jack's hair. The angel picked him up out of the water, balancing him on one finger by the flat of the boy's foot, spinning him.

"Ahhhhh! Stop it!" Henry went, laughing away. Jack was hysterical.

The sea touched the little boy's nostrils with its effervescent twinge, warm sunshine filling Jack and the boy's insides with joy.

"Gotcha!" Fred cannon-balled down into the water, right next to his partner.

"Ahhhhh!"

Jack popped his head out from under the sea, and Fred shoved him right back under. He grabbed the little one's leg and dragged him under the foam with him. The two wrestled beneath the sea, then pulled one another back to the surface, as they lost their air from horsing around and laughing so much.

"Where is he?" Fred asked.

"Uh…um. There he is, in the shallows," Jack pointed.

Fred squinted. "Okay, I see him."

"I could get used to this, Fred."

"Me too. We finally had the holiday we always hoped for."

"God! Yeah…" Jack's eyes bulged. "I'm *actually* out of breath, you know that?"

"(Huff) Yeah," he smiled.

"Where's Henry?"

"Over there."

"Fred, I—"

"Jack, Look out!"

The two cherubs were so preoccupied with the location of the boy that they forgot that these monster waves sometimes come in sets—twins, or in this case, triplets. And when you weren't ready… *Crunch!* The two spirits were flattened by the heavy-handed onslaught of the fresh wave's form. They were tossed upside down and inside out. The angels landed on their heads and arms and rumps, again and again and *again*. They were thrown in tumbles, like spinning in the insides of a great washing machine that someone had forgotten to turn off. The wave finished its demolition run, and the angels were dispatched into the calm sea again.

Henry looked on from a safe distance, as the dolphin found its way back to him.

"Do you think they're all right?" he asked as the dolphin popped over. "They must be, they are angels, for Pete's sake."

The creature made some sort of gargling agreement and bobbed its head up and down.

"Come on," Henry said worriedly. "Take us as close to them as you can. Let's see if they're all right."

The dolphin hefted the boy onto its back, but they found no trace of the spirits. Henry feared the worst. But the dolphin began bobbing its head up and down in the water and pointed with its snout to something in the white, foamy waters. Something moved beneath the fuzz and froth left over from the wave. A bunch of bubbles came to the top, then a little hand, and then Jack's head.

"There they are!" Henry exclaimed.

"Fred?" Jack called in an exasperated voice. "Fred? Ugh." Jack reached underwater and hauled up a saturated pair a wings and a coughing angel from beneath.

"Wipeout," Fred mumbled, as they began to make their way to shore with much effort amid the rolling waves and currents.

The little one coughed like mad, trying to get rid of all the salt water he had gulped down.

Jack patted him on the back, and the cherubs tried to regain their composure. Fred rubbed the sea salt from his eyes.

"Argh!" the little one growled in his best pirate voice. "We be payin' a visit to Davey Jones' armpit."

"Armpit huh?"

"Aye Cap'n Jack. And what be that song?"

"What—"

"That there song. What be that?"

"Oh. *That* be 'The Last Train to Sudzville,'" Captain Jack illuminated.

"Argh. Really?"

"Argh, little one. Them Sea Monkeys be right lyrical."

"Sounds about (snicker, ahem) right."

Fred began choking on his own laughter, coughing again. In the distance, Henry began rallying about something, motioning for them to turn. The dolphin fired off a blast of sound, dunking his head, leading with its snout. Something was on the rise.

Fred couldn't see them. He still had salt in his eyes.

"What is that?" the little one strained. "What on Earth are they saying?"

"Who?" Jack asked.

"*Who*...who else? The boy."

"I know it's the boy, Fred!"

"Well then, what are you...*what?*"

"What? What?" Jack asked exasperatedly.

"Henry and the fish—"

"Mammal."

"Whatever…how about crab, Jack! Look. They're…wha…*around?* What around? What…"

The little one spun around and there it was, another wave. Only it was much, much…*much,* bigger. It sat for a moment on the horizon and started falling toward them. Fred's big brown eyes grew to saucers. The first few were monsters, sure enough, but the last—that was just one *bad* mother!

Jack caught the little one's intensity. "What is it? You alright?"

Coughing was all Fred could spill out. He pointed frantically to something behind Jack.

"What is it, Fred? Henry? He's cool. He's over there, see? He's waving. Hello. Hello, Mr. Dolphin," Jack waved. "They didn't get smacked, Fred—neither one."

"No, no, no," Fred thought. But all he could do was cough and choke some more.

"What? What is it? Oh—the wave. Yeah, it was rough. We're in good shape now, though."

This was not helping. Fred kept pointing and shaking his finger at the wave, which was now obscuring the sky behind them.

"I am *not* doing charades with you now, okay? You know I'm not any good at—"

Finally, Fred blurted out, "Look out!"

Jack turned. It was practically on top of them. Fred dropped his arms, almost waiting for the water's pounding.

Jack merely stared, patiently. "Ah, shh…"

"Come on, Jack!" Fred scrambled, yanking his friend away by the arm, trying futilely to lift off. But they couldn't because wings don't work when they're *that* wet. The angels looked at Henry. Henry looked back, covering his head, bracing himself—as did the dolphin, who covered himself with his flippers as best he could, dunking his head. The aquatic friend gurgled at the boy. Henry could only wait.

"Ouch," he cringed, closing his eyes.

Jack just looked at the wave; he turned away, checking his wrist for the time. But he didn't have the time. He didn't wear a watch. So he looked up at the monster, then turned to Fred instead.

"You are a klutz. You know that, right?"

Fred took a breath and dunked underwater, pulling Jack down with him.

And the wave rolled on.

They bounced along the sea floor for innumerable seconds, like sea basketballs, until they were gently swept up onto the white, sandy beach.

The foamy waters fizzled.

They laid there, flat on their backs, bellies moving up and down, all huffing and puffing. The air smelled softly of coconut oil and Coppertone, washing across them in slow breezes.

"Land ho," Jack moaned.

"Jack…"

"Yeah, Fred…"

"Ouch."

"Yes, Fred. Ouch."

"You know something, Jack?"

"What's that, Fred?"

"Wings don't work when they're wet."

Silence.

"Let me guess. You're giving me up eyes again, aren't you, Jack?"

Angels cannot lie, so Jack didn't answer.

The dolphin dropped Henry off at the beach nearby, and he found himself sprinting over to the angels, who were all but finished catching their breath and shaking off the dampness.

"Goodbye!" he shouted, waving at the dolphin, who gargled back at him. Henry caught the last shot of sea spray from their wings as the angels dried themselves in the wind and stretched. It reminded Henry of Mrs. Kline's noisy, shaggy dog, when he got wet, and how he would shake off his moppy fur all over the front porch—and Mrs. Kline.

Jack flapped his wings and flew over to Henry.

"I'm sorry to say it kid, but it's time to go. Are you ready, Hen?"

"Are you guys all right, can I help?"

"It's *really* time to go, Henry," Fred murmured.

"This place is wonderful!"

"Just a thin slice of heaven, kid," Fred said to himself, pulling a fish from inside his wings and stuffing it into Jack's mouth.

Jack grinned and waved like he was just plain dopey.

"Guys?"

"Yeah kid," Jack said tossing the fish at the little one.

"What's beyond the beach?" he asked, looking at the white sands. The angels didn't answer. "What's over there?" Henry asked again.

They smiled but still didn't answer.

"You sure I'm not dead?"

"No," Jack whispered. "You're not dead." He looked over at the little one, who bit his lip. "Honest."

Henry pieced it together. "But this…this is…?"

Fred whispered in his ear. "Like I said, a thin slice."

Henry stared into the light and the beach before him. "Of…heaven."

The little one tapped the boy's shoulder. "Let's go."

The boy shut his eyes. And when he opened them again, he was home.

{ Chapter 35 }

Goodbye Henry

The angels realized that it took all those lonely, disappointing years to make them see how wonderful they had it now. And they savored every moment and breath of it as they settled the boy back into his bed, covers and all.

Fred smiled. "We're glad you came with us tonight."

"Me too. Can we do this again sometime?" the boy asked, the innocence of the question destroying Jack's train of thought.

"We can come here anytime you want, Henry," he said to the boy.

"Why are you guys so sad looking? Did I do something wrong? Did we stay too long? Do you have like a curfew or something, when it comes to visiting…" The angels' hearts were beating. "…people? Are you going to get in trouble for taking me here, by St. Peter or someone?"

Jack couldn't help but smile, wrinkling his mournful features. He took the boy by the shoulders and sat him down, gently, and Fred stood right by his side.

The angel looked into the boy's eyes.

"Henry…(sigh), this is probably the last time you'll get to see us like this—*really* see us."

"What do you mean, Jack?" Henry asked.

After everything they told him earlier, the angels still could not help but be sad anyway. Jack began to get choked up. He moved his hand distractedly across the plush surface of the bed comforter, his finger outlining the sewing seams. The boy looked down, suddenly realizing he was indeed back home.

Jack handed the boy a note card he had been keeping with him for some time now. It was the one Sidney gave them…the one they tried not to believe.

The boy read aloud:

"Dearest Angels: We regret to inform you that there will be a redefinition of your duties as of midnight tonight, Christmas morning. Forthwith, Jack is recalled to heaven by way of train. Please arrive promptly at the Pelham Bay Station for departure. Upon your return, reassignment to the training of angelic recruits and new fliers will begin immediately. To Fred, rendezvous at Wingdings. There you will meet with a liaison officer bearing further details of downstairs assignments. Be well. -The Management"

Tears welled up in the boy's eyes.

"No," he said shaking his head.

Jack grinned, faintly. "We'll always be in your heart, Henry."

Henry looked at him, then quickly at Fred.

"That's why you told me all that stuff about not seeing you. You knew. Oh God. Why?"

Jack looked down.

"Jack? Fred? Guys?" He looked back and forth at both of them frantically. And they put their heads down. "I knew it! I knew you wouldn't come back. What happened? *Why?* Don't you like me? Don't you want to see me again?"

The little one drew nearer. "Of course we do, Henry, but—"

"But why, Fred? You're angels. You're supposed to be able to do anything. Why did they do this to you?"

"We can't just do *anything*," the little one said. "You told Kristie that. You were right. We're just like people. We can't do whatever we want. There are rules."

"But why?! Why do you have to go? You said you'd always be here for me.

Always. Why're you leaving me now? You're the only thing I have left. And you're leaving. What am I supposed to do now? I'll be all alone."

Jack insisted, "You're *never* going to be alone."

"No, I'm going to be alone, Jack. All alone. And there's not a soul in the world left anymore. You're all leaving me."

The little one shook his head. "Why do you think that?"

The boy was furious. "Not you too. You don't leave me. I leave you, understand? I won't let you hurt me."

The boy walked toward the door. The angels just watched. He turned around, and ran toward them, crying his eyes out.

"I'm going to miss you," he said in their ears. *"You know that?"*

The angels fell to pieces.

"Why can't you just stay? Appear again…"

Jack insisted, "They're calling us back Henry. If you look for us with your heart you will always find us, no matter how old you get, or where you go. Just believe."

"I know," he sobbed. "But why can't I see you anymore, like now? Jack, so you're upstairs—sneak off, like I did on the fieldtrip! And Fred, if you're down here, you can visit any time. They won't know!"

Jack held the boy. "Henry, we're angels. We have been for a *long* time now. And in all the time that we've traveled across this Earth, helping people, we never met anyone who loved us as much as you do. Angels are sometimes allowed by the guys upstairs to appear to people on Earth. We weren't given permission to appear to you, but you saw us anyway, like we were real people. We're supposed to be invisible. But to you, we just weren't. It's because you believe. You saw us. At first we worried we did something wrong. But we didn't…and we never regretted it. We knew you loved us, the way we always loved you."

"Oh, no. You did this for me? You'd risk getting into trouble for me? Now you're going to go away. It's *my* fault."

"It's nothing you did, kid," Jack maintained, holding the boy. "It's just… time to go."

"But—"

"Let us go kid. They recall us after a while. Even Fred and I. They call it long-term parking. When you're down on Earth too long, eventually you gotta go back. It's all right. I promise you."

"I'm so sorry. Figures, we finally meet and now they take you away. We got hosed, Jack!"

The boy began sobbing again. Fred knelt down before him. Jack's heart was breaking as he was watched the two of them together. Then, the boy looked up. His eyes lit up with a manic fervor and the idea that danced along with it was equally mad.

"Fred, Jack, I have an idea. If you can't come back…" The angels looked at him. "…then, take me with you."

Fred eyes saw only blinding white.

"I'm not letting you go."

"We can't, it's not your time," the little one insisted.

"Make it time. Take me with you."

"You have a precious gift, Henry. You have a life; you have a family, parents that love you. We—"

"Then I'll come with you. And we can come back and visit them. We'll find Kristie…wherever she is in Connecticut, and I can meet Belle. And we can go to that place. Wingdings, right? And we'll bother St. Peter, and visit your friends, like Sidney. You mentioned him the night we talked, right? We'll fly *everywhere*. I know, three's a crowd but…I wouldn't be a third wheel. We could make it work, if you wanted. I'd be quiet and wouldn't bug you or…I wouldn't bother you."

"That's not the point—"

"Really. I'm not a scooch or nothin'."

The little one backed away.

"We can't—"

"Come on!"

"Just—"

"Please, Fred—"

"Henry—"

"Please guys. Take me home with you…Fred…please? Please Jack?"

"Henry we—"

"Come on, Jack, please?"

The little one held him, but the boy wouldn't let go.
Jack begged. "Henry, listen—"
"No…"

"Please, Hen," Fred pleaded.
"No, Fred, I'm not letting you go."
"Listen to me, Henry."
"No, Fred."
"Listen. Do you…" The boy finally stopped struggling. His whole body went limp. "Do you know how many people we've seen, Henry? Thousands. Maybe *millions* of people, from places and countries all across the globe. And only one person ever believed in us. Only one. A long time ago, Jack and I were painted by a man named Raphael. But once he finished that painting, we were little more than an afterthought to him. You, Henry—you are the only one that ever loved Jack and I for who we are. I don't care that we've lived a hundred lifetimes or have seen millions of people. All we want is *you*. When you called for us, we came for you, and now we will never ever leave you. And it's not your fault. It's just the way it must be. Rules are rules. And sometimes rules have to be broken to save someone you love, and we love you, Henry."

"But, Fred," the boy asked. "What are *you* going to do?"

The angels looked at one another, then back at their boy.

"Smile," the little one said. "We're going to carry on. And you're going to be happy again and go back to school."

Henry looked right through him. "No," he shook his head. "I'm finished. I am *never* going back. *Never.*"

The little one looked into his eyes.

"Because you're not wrong Henry. You're *not* wrong for believing in something that's too ridiculous for people to believe in. We're real. Don't let anyone else ever try to convince you otherwise what your heart already knows is true. Even when you're all alone in your belief, hang on. We believe in you. No matter what, keep us shining bright in their eyes."

"I'm never going to see you again, am I?"

The little one shrugged.

"Forever…?"

"Forever is a long time Henry, and forever doesn't always come."

The boy sighed.

Jack grabbed him, shaking him gently. "You keep us alive, Hen, because we *are* alive. You write, and we will be there in all your stories."

The little one stepped back, broken.

"And," Jack reiterated, moving forward. "He's right. Fred's dopey sometimes," he smiled, trying to light up the boy again. "But he's right with this. You *are* going to write about us. You understand? You're going to write about all the things we did, and all things we never got a chance to do."

"That's what Kristie said before she left. I don't have any more happy endings in me to write, Jack. There aren't any…not anymore. They're all just endings. I'm never going to have anything happy again."

Jack knelt down to the boy and held him by the arms.

"You're going to keep us alive in your heart…and you're going t—"

Fred bit down on his lip, swallowing the pain. He started shaking with every word Jack spoke.

"You're going to tell everybody about your crazy friends, the angels. And you're going to tell them that…th…that *Fred* usually starts the arguments and all the rest of the nonsense. And what a real buster he is, an…an…and all the other stuff. Hen, write them a summer reading book that isn't torture to do a report on two days before school starts, because you enjoyed the summer vacation they tried to take away from you! You do this for us, little guy, so that people believe, so that all the hurt, the heartbroken, and the lost have something to hold on to, something to believe in. You remind them of us. You remind them there are little fuzzy angels like us flying around when they're not looking, and if they put a foot out of step every once in awhile we'll be there to kick butt and take names. People are hoping someone believes in them, let them know that somebody does, because the Big Man upstairs always believed in you. You do that for us. Because people need to know that they're loved. Do that for us…and we'll treasure you forever."

Henry grabbed Jack and hugged his friend, as to never let him go. But he did.

[My Guardian Angels Jack & Fred]

"Jack?" Henry asked as he cleared his eyes of the tears that were flowing. "What happens now?"

"I have a train to catch!" he smiled. Fred looked away. "And as for the rest, we don't really know, Henry. We have to speak to our lawyer."

They laughed through their tears. "It's silly, I know. But old Sidney, our angelic lawyer we mentioned him in our talks—the barrister. We don't have like a whole legal firm, though Fred and I probably coulda used it over the years, but he's a good friend, and he'll help us."

"Will God punish you?" Henry asked.

The little one shook his head. "God doesn't punish, He only cares, Henry," Fred told the boy, sniffling as he did so. "He does, you know. He cares very much. He's the one who sent us to you. He told us to help you find your gift. You know, we've met many, many people, but we care for *you* most of all. You have a gift, Henry. You believe in us. So believe that we'll always be there. Just look with your heart, and you'll always find us. We'll be standing on both sides of you."

The angels tucked the boy in and floated over to the window, preparing to leave. "I love you Jack & Fred. And guys..."

The boy blinked.

"Will you be my guardian angels, Jack & Fred?"

He looked around frantically. He awoke. Was he dreaming? But they were gone.

"Goodbye, Henry."

"No! Oh no. They didn't hear me! Come back. Oh God, they're gone. No, guys, come back! Come back!"

He vaulted from his place of rest to the window.

"Guys!" He threw open the window and the cold ran through him. The sky was blue and gentle and still; the stars were far away, sitting in place, unmoving as the city churned its perpetual hum from nowhere but all around. The street lamps bounced on and off in designated intervals, and the long garland decorations hung across the avenue in the dark, laying quiet. He looked out at the length of the street to the elevated subway platform, and

nothing moved—nothing whatsoever, nothing at all, as if the world was as exhausted as he was, standing there with little exertion. It was all quiet.

A little voice yelled out into the night, but there was no echo. A soft face stood lost in the window of a million homes down below.

"Please come back, please? You didn't give me a chance. I just wanted to ask you one thing…"

{ Chapter 36 }

Shivers on Whispers, Across the Sky

The breezes sent shivers on whispers across the sky. There was a great sense of uneasiness and urgency, and it drove Sidney to sit down on the worn orange couch of his temporary living quarters. The barrister found himself transfixed by the carpeting in the corner of the room, admiring the intricacies and unimportant, tiny features of things no one ever seemed to notice, or had reason to. The dust on the ridges of the door frame, the cobwebs in the corner, the broken marble on the statues, the chips and scratches on the bookshelf, and the small, metal knight that stood ever-righteous and unmoving in his stature upon a pedestal, holding up half the bookshelf, as was his proud duty.

The Torchiere lamp's incandescent flare made the room seem sharp and in definite focus. And then the light flickered, but when the chimes twinkled for no reason at all outside—no reason whatsoever—it was of no question to him that something was indeed horribly wrong—something was amiss in all things he knew to be right in the world.

Everything seemed to radiate an unwanted alertness, a presence. It was *something*. The barrister's gut feelings were more akin to premonition, and though he knew Flo actually saw things happening before the day, his gut feelings would be just as accurate, only more imprecise and puzzling when they first hit. They stirred him to dizziness, until he admitted to himself that something was indeed wrong and the cause needed to be found out. He felt the same feeling ages ago with his sister, Sylvia, when she went missing. He rose from his seat and at that second the doorbell rang. Sidney immediately knew what it was.

A smaller angelic messenger stood slightly hunched over in the porch light. He was almost a counterpart of sorts to one of the previous little visitors who had come earlier in the day. He bowed to Sidney, saying nothing, handing him an oversized postcard—a message of some sort. The barrister looked down upon him, trying to find some clue of the message's weight in the gaze. The angel lowered his eyes to the ground, as if he had been humbled. Methodically, the sharp legal mind raised the card to his glance.

In the hallway, Madison was walking toward the study. She removed her blue apron, straightened her all-black turtleneck and pants, and swatted the lint from her clothes. She saw Sidney standing before the open door as he brushed his hair back with his hand. The executive assistant looked curiously at what unsaid business was occurring immediately outside.

"Sidney, what is it?" she called.

Uncommonly, the barrister did not turn around. Sidney walked toward her, now exceedingly curious. The messenger at the door bowed mournfully, and the lawyer put a hand on his shoulder as he moved away. The small one sprung off the pavement into the dark sky.

"Sidney. What is it? What's happened?" Madison demanded.

The barrister's tall features all but withered to dried paper and flaked to the ground. He rubbed the dark hair on his head and handed the card over to the young girl.

Madison, nervous, grabbed the card, her eyes sprinting across the note like a typewriter.

"*Oh, no.*"

{ Chapter 37 }
One Last Thing Before We Go

The two angels flew into heaven with George, who had been enjoying many of the specials Wingdings had to offer, not the least of which was Gabrielle, Peter's executive assistant, who was nowhere to be seen at the moment. Sidney did indeed smooth it over, or else this would've been loads worse. Flo kept George full-bellied and happy and locked in the clock tower until arrangements could be made. So it was time to set things right. Jack & Fred pushed George up to St. Peter's mammoth podium, just slidin' him along on his heels for the ride.

The saint adjusted his spectacles as he dipped his quill into ink for the new entry.

"Next," he said solemnly, looking down at his book, with the light reflecting off his readers. "He's an overdue. Several days now," the old saint said to them, not looking up once.

Jack sighed. "We're late. I apologize."

"Yes," the old one nodded, leafing through his book for George's entry. The discrepancy in the sub-index that he had noted earlier while researching George still bothered him. Peter made no mention of it to the pair though as they watched on. "You two can go."

The angels looked at one another.

The normal witty repartee with Peter was gone. They didn't do their job; they were wrong and they knew it, despite the extenuating circumstances.

Two other angels attended to George, whose spirit was in an advanced state of over-tired. Jack & Fred turned and started to set off to Earth to see Sidney before reporting to their new duties.

"You did a good job with the boy," the saint called. "Proud of you."

Fred's smile was a mile wide; he smacked Jack on the shoulder. The other two angelic attendants held George by the arms, taking him lightly inside his new home, paradise.

"Hey, guys," the sleepy-eyed moron said to them. "I never said thanks."

"For what, George?" Jack asked, slightly embarrassed. "We treated you terribly. We, we…tossed you around like a Raggedy Andy doll. You're late, you're…"

"The other angel guys at Wingdings told me about you two. That you're famous. That ya help a lotta people. Kinda cool that for a few days you were the ones takin' care of me. See ya around."

Jack grinned. "Take it easy, George. Enjoy."

He looked at Fred, who was frowning. They were both surprised. Before leaving, they took one last glance at their wall. It looked so empty without them.

"Come on Fred. Let's get the final arrangements with the barrister. Then we go to…whatever."

{ Chapter 38 }

End of the Line

"Jack. I'm glad we saw Sidney again. Felt lousy about our last meeting. He's always a gentleman."

"Always was. Yep."

"I still don't understand why we have to fly back down here. We were just in heaven. Why this?"

"I don't know little one. It's just protocol."

"You hear it?!" the little one shouted, very angry. "That noise! There! It's that damn cow cat again."

"Stupid-looking animal."

"C'mon! God! Stupid thing has been following us since downtown Jack. It stares at you with them eyes! He wants to fight too."

"Fred, he doesn't want to fight, Fred."

"He threatened me when you weren't looking."

"God."

"We went past him and he waved at me with the claws—"

"Paws."

"Whatever. He was like, 'c'mon bring it wingy!'"

"Yes, I'm sure he called you 'wingy'! Silly angel!"

The little one smiled. Jack shook his head and gave him up eyes. He was gonna miss that.

"Jack. I thought they'd give you more time to visit the rest of the downstairs gang, besides Sidney. To...say goodbye. You know."

"Me too, Fred."

"I'm supposed to see Mr. Wallace again for Christmas. Sidney told me he'd get special dispensation for that. I promised the man."

"I heard him. I'm sure they'll let you go."

"They better." The little one sighed as they touched down upon the elevated train station, the end of the line for people, as it apparently was for angels—for this team—as well.

Two subway trains sat neatly parallel to one another, waiting. The motorman, the same angel Jack had yelled at several days back, walked past, adjusting the glasses on his nose, smiling now at the angel.

"Good to see you again," he nodded.

Jack waved as Fred looked at him with the same disgusted face his partner wore the last time they were here.

"It's funny," Jack said. "The day we were on the train. I had this horribly bad feeling when I saw him." He nodded at the motorman. "And I snapped. I called him a damn vulture. I just knew—"

"I'm so sorry I was asleep."

Jack looked at the little one.

"You're gonna be all right, kid. You have to go see Mr. Wallace for Christmas, like you said. And Sidney tells me..."

Fred began shuddering uncontrollably, shaking his head.

"No!" Jack said shaking his head adamantly, pointing his finger at the little one. "Don't." He couldn't bear to see the little one cry now. He couldn't. He couldn't fall apart. He had to be strong, for both of them. And for the boy. "Can't...can't do it, Fred."

The little one bit his lip, pinching his eyes shut.

Jack continued on. "Sss...so, the barrister says you're going to live over at Windings with Flo and the gang. That's a great arrangement. She really loves you."

"You're not a crab. I always call you that. But you're not."

"Yeah I am, and you know it. That's mah job! Besides, you have Flo. Hey! That was a long time comin'. Hottie deluxe. Look at you, playah!"

{ My Guardian Angels Jack & Fred }

The little one blushed.

"You're gonna be very happy, Fred. You're going to have a good life."

"I *had* a good life."

"I asked Sidney if it'd be all right if you could check in on Henry again. The boys upstairs said yes. You're going to have the boy to watch!" He grabbed the little one by the shoulders. "So you won't get to watch over him constantly, because of your new job, but…you can still pop in every now and again. You're lucky! You get to watch him grow up. You get to see him when he's on his first dance, when he gets his driver's license, when he falls in love, gets married. You're going to get to see his kids!" Jack walked toward the edge of the platform with his arms tucked behind him. "Besides, that's too much work for me anyway. Three's a crowd. I got an important job to do! Something brand new. All the people that die and go to heaven. I'm gonna be their trainer. The people that want to help us angels? I get to train *them*. I get to train them to be angels, and…and, to help people…and us. The newbies! Training generations, because Peter tells me some rough things are going to happen in the years to come. So I'm going to be too busy anyway, so it's just as well. It's a great thing."

"What about our wall?"

"They're gonna turn it into an office."

"No, I mean. I still got some of the vinegar eggplant under the wall in jars. Don't let them take it. I want it mailed down here. It's mine!" the little one said with a sparkle in his glassy eyes.

"What do you mean yours?" Jack laughed. "Mr. Midnight Snack! You attacked my ziti the other day and you…hey you! I'm talking to you. Come on now." Jack jabbed at him, throwing air punches. "Come on, tough guy! C'mon!" Jack punched at his arm, and Fred leaped up and hugged him.

The little one repeated the boy's words in a whisper. "He was right. We got hosed, Jack. *We got hosed…*"

"Yeah Fred, we did."

The angels were crying so hard, they could barely breathe.

But like always, they weren't afforded the luxury of falling to pieces. So they went on, no matter how much it hurt.

Jack smiled, his face beating red. "Say hello to everyone for me."

"All aboard!" the conductor yelled.

"I will." The little angel swallowed hard as Jack stepped off the platform and moved inside the train coach. Jack stood in the doorway, his chest puffed out as always, strong, ready to take on the world.

"You take care. Jack...I..."

"Me too, Fred. Me too."

Fred held up his hand, waving. Jack waved back. And the doors slid shut, then suddenly stopped. Madison reeled her foot backward and dragged Jack back out of the car.

"What're you doing?" he asked.

Fred ran over.

"I think you boys need to come with me."

{ Chapter 39 }
All I Want Is You

"*You idiot!*" the boy cursed at himself. *"All you had to do was ask them! You had all the time in the world, surfing all night. All you had to do was ask!"* His heart was beating quickly. His mind was frantic. Thoughts were overloading his brain with the weight of a heart that was breaking inside.

Not a creature was stirring; *yes it was.* The creature was him. It would be Christmas soon. And his mind couldn't even focus on it or worry or hope to care. School was over for him. He would be home tomorrow, and the rest of the tomorrows for now on, he had told them all. He wasn't going back. And they were gone. He couldn't shake it. *They were gone.* And they weren't coming back. Just like her. The noise in his ears sounded like a flood of violin strings falling downward, in wailing discontent and complete sadness.

They were not coming back. Not now, not ever. And he couldn't just let that happen—not this way. Not *forever*. It wasn't right; it was unacceptable. He had to get them back somehow. He just had to. *It was your big mouth. Damn big mouth of yours. You talk to them about everything. You ask them everything except the one thing they needed to hear. So selfish!* They found him, saved him. Now he would go save them and bring them home, once for all. Oh, his mind was a flood of thought, and his heart was churning from the pain, but his resolute spirit wouldn't let them go.

The boy put together a sack of specially collected things from his toy trunk and climbed up the metal ladder, which was permanently affixed to the center of the hallway by the stairwell, where it had always been, since forever. The ladder lead to the rooftop; it was the same one the angels floated down on the first night they arrived.

Remember that night...

And the stuff in his bag jingled as he snatched up his slippers and climbed up the rungs: hand and foot, hand and foot, hand and foot, as his grandfather had instructed, once upon a midnight ago. He climbed like a monkey, and he was proud of it because it would lead him to where they were.

It was the last time. So he climbed all the way to the top.

He pushed with all his might against the heavy wooden roof hatch. He pushed and pushed, and the metal ladder shuddered enough to make him clutch the rung in dire fear. Beneath him was only the stairwell. He would fall fifteen steps all the way down to the front door. Faint moonlight crept in through the dirty offset skylight, illuminating the banister all the way down. If he fell from this height, there was no mistaking it. He would be dead.

It's bright tonight. They have to still be out there. He climbed one step farther up the ladder to where his little body could not fit, his head and back sandwiched against the roof hatch. And he pushed—with all his might. And whether it was anger or love, it worked! And the wood and tin hatch burped open, creaking all the way. The boy held onto the hatch, precariously teetering on the ladder with the rest of his body.

The hatch itself always made sounds. It was nothing his parents weren't already used to on those windy eves over the years. *They wouldn't wake up now.* He insisted. He stuck his little fingers through the opening between the partly open hatchway and the cover itself. Suddenly, he lost his grip and the hatch fell down upon his fingers cutting into the entire row. The pain was unbearable; the weight of the cover itself was breaking his fingers! He was in agony, and the only thing he thought of was Fred getting his foot stuck in the window. He imagined his mother would kill him if she saw him even attempt such a thing, hurting his fingers in such a stupid way.

All I want is you.

He took a breath remembering them, knowing he could not go back to bed now. His brain was awash with sights and sounds and memories of them. He was fixating now on the smallest detail, the most mundane of routines, for they were all steps in getting him to his angels once again. So he did everything by the numbers, shoving the hatch upward with all his weight, out of his way, resting it against the roof's backsplash, and there he was, on top of the world. He was so young. To do something like this would be absolutely ridiculous at any other time. It was so dangerous.

He climbed up the rest of the way, jumped over the rim of the hatchway and onto the roof, tossing down his pack. The boy, in his rush to get there, forgot about a coat. He set the hatch cover back down gently over the roof opening, wiping the wood splinters and tar grit from his palms, annoyed. *He was actually here.* His fingers on his left hand were already turning black and blue, and bleeding at the knuckles.

He took a deep breath. The air smelled so clean. The world around him was wide and ominous. The screeching car from across the avenues and down below scared him to all heaven, and he had to catch himself from falling backward. But with the high-tiered edges and the massively flat expanse, no one was going to fall off. *You couldn't unless you jumped off.* And best of all, no one knew he was up here. He'd made it. They hadn't heard him. Not the neighbors, not Mrs. Kline's mangy dog, not his sleeping parents. But the angels would know.

So he took his stuff and crept on tiptoes along the roof, now scolding himself like an adult to not step on the roof's air bubbles. Doing that causes leaks, Dad had said, and he settled down in the depressed center of the roof, where the drainage hole, with the grate on it, sat. He tossed down the sweatshirt. he lifted from the bureau, to act as a sits-upon. And he plopped down. It was all cozy beneath the side of the roof, in his own little warm alcove, just he and his lonesome, and he unpacked all his bagged items like St. Nicholas in a rush. It'd be Christmas in a few hours. He kept forgetting all about that.

Everything was there: the Fisher-Price blue and yellow kiddie telescope— which he could not see through, at any time before. But he was determined to, tonight. He had a canteen filled with chocolate milk. It wasn't cocoa, but the cold chocolate would have to sustain him in his mind. Snow gloves, heavy, perfect for the cold, if he could zip the zippers on the forehands. A View-Master, the delightful little orange-red, click-and-move thing with images from *Happy Days*, and *Mork and Mindy*, and others. It really was useless. Why did he bring this thing? He scolded himself with a grimace, tossing it down.

Beneath, Mom's eye opened. For a moment she heard a *sound*. Then the eye shut just as fast. Henry somehow knew it too.

He dug farther into the bag to find a scarf, a strip of wire, an ice skate tightener, a headset Dad had brought home, and a walkie-talkie. He pulled out a small flashlight. It worked. But it would run out, so he shut it. And though the world said that no matter how hard you wished, how hard you pleaded, how hard, in your own hopeless moments, even in your imagination, that your deepest wishes would not—could not—come true, Henry refused to believe that. He believed only in what everybody else said was impossible. He believed in *them*. And no one was going to tell him differently. Nope. And nobody was going to take them away. Nobody! And because he believed in them, he also believed that his ridiculous plan was going to work, along with all these worthless gadgets and toys. But that sinking feeling crept in—harshly. These things were empty and useless. Everything except the walkie-talkie. The anxiety streamed into his eyes, but *he wasn't going to cry*. He had to be like them. They didn't have time to be upset, nor did he. He had a job to do. If only he knew how to operate something electronic—make some kind of radio...*some*...some *something* that could call...

He turned back to his pack and pulled out the walkie-talkie. It would have to do. Dad would've known how to make something. He was so good with electronics. But he wasn't here. The walkie-talkie was all he had; they had to hear it. He turned it on and it made a loud staticy call. And so he got up and tiptoed. He had to move around. He'd done this thousands of times in the house.

He only had the one though. The other walkie-talkie had a busted antennae. He took out the batteries from the broken one and tried to make a go of the other. Henry knew that if he found a soft spot in the static that meant *he'd caught something*, a...a frequency, a *break*...someone. He spun around and around, the cold or the motion making him dizzy. And he felt out of breath and scared all at once. But he closed his eyes and swallowed. As he breathed, his chest ached. But he was not going to be stopped, even though it was cold—*very cold*. And the moon was out, and it was perfectly clear, but it was *freezing*. He shut the talkie down and grabbed the light sweatshirt which he was sitting on. He was shivering uncontrollably. He scolded himself for taking all these useless crappy things, but no coat.

Henry shuffled his things around and pulled out the last bits of his little survival pack. He found a set of battery-operated Christmas lights. He had yanked them from the living room display. They were battery-operated for small trees and hobby sets and store fronts and train setups. He could use these. *Right?* He threw them over the metal rods of the television antennae, fashioning the lights into a design. God, it was high up! Upon completion, he stepped back and smiled.

"They have to see that!" he said aloud. "You *have* to see that. There're no Christmas lights up this high. You have to see that. You have to see that!" He almost stomped his feet. He bit his lip. *"Just have to."*

He walked back to the pack. "Just have to."

He settled down in his little rooftop corner niche looking for something to cover himself, but there was nothing. And the thought had arisen that maybe he could go back and get a blanket—or, actually, *should have*. It was too late now. If he went back downstairs they might hear him.

"I'm upstairs now and I can't leave until they get back and that's all!" he said aloud, teeth chattering. The boy's thoughts rushed in a manic stream, uncontrollably now.

He looked down at the Morse code designations on the outside of the walkie-talkie. The full alphabet was there. He was actually *angry* that he was a kid. He wished he knew more than this.

"Even stupid E.T. knew more than this! He had no problems phoning home!" the boy thought. Is that where the thought to do this came from? Did it matter...? After years of television and movie bombardment, who knew what came from where any longer. He was reading the Morse code bar on the side of the device. *S.O.S. S.O.S. S.O.S.* Three short. Three long. Three short. He reached for that puny nothingness sack of goodies and put it over his legs. *S.O.S. HELP. S.O.S. HELP.*

"Wish I had brought the Speak and Spell with me. (Sigh). Calling Jack & Fred. Calling Jack & Fred. Come in, guys. It's Hen," he talked into the walkie-talkie. "It's Hen…and I want you back, back *home*." His throat burned in the temperatures. "Come on, guys, it's almost time for *breakfast*. Blueberry waffles. Promise. I just have to ask you something. You left too soon. Come back, guys. Come back…please guys. It's really cold out here, and I don't know how long I can stay up here, so hurry back."

He sat and thought for a moment, then continued on into the night. The only sound was the tweeting of the portable intercom in the frozen quiet. He kept tapping in the code over and over again, long into the night. S.O.S. S.O.S. S.O….S…S…. And it fell silent.

Hours passed.

The boy laid there—there in the rooftop silt, frozen chills enveloping his whole self. The cold wasn't even bothering him any longer. He looked up at the sky. It had turned pink in the hours he was up here. He smiled lightly.

"Jack…Jack it's going to snow. Remember what you told me? I…I remember. No school…no school ever again. Ever…"

His body became numb and then he fell away into the blackness of his own frightened thoughts. He could not awaken, for he knew not that he was dreaming.

{ Chapter 40 }

Absolutely Heartbroken

The barrister sat in his favorite leather chair off in a darkened corner of the study. An expression of sheer dread ran across his stern, unmoving face.

Jack & Fred glided in through the study's window with unspoken haste and stood before their mutual friend in silence. The room was quiet for what seemed like an eternity. Then Sidney's voice punctuated the eerie silence about him, spilling out the words that he had pleaded to heaven he would not have to say. Unflinching, he stared at them, directly in the eyes.

"At approximately 1:36 Christmas morning, the boy you know as…your Henry, will be admitted to city hospital, running a fever of 105. They don't expect him to last the night."

"Oh, God," Jack involuntarily exclaimed as he raised his hand to his mouth, trying to smother the outburst of sadness that his heart wanted to exclaim.

Fred's eyes grew wide. His mouth drew open and he exhaled what felt like his dying breath. The angel's heart had been utterly shattered, and only emptiness remained inside.

"But, we just left him!" the angels said to themselves.

Sidney leaned forward in his chair, tears welling up in his eyes, an ache in his very soul. He opened his mouth, and his throat burned, and his stomach turned over, but he could not do a thing to help the angels. In his mind, he failed them. As much as the child meant to the barrister and the other angels, for his unswerving belief in angels, it was nothing compared to what Henry meant to Jack & Fred. Sidney was more overwhelmed at the sight of the two, than he was at the news, which he was the unfortunate bearer of.

Weakly, Jack turned to Fred. "Come on."

The little one, totally despondent, continued to look down. Jack turned his head to Fred, not looking him in the eyes; he couldn't bear it. His sadness melted into fear and anger. Enraged, he grabbed Fred by the arm and shook him violently.

"COME ON!"

The little one snapped out of his stupor, breathing heavily—trying to choke back the tears. The two rushed headlong into the darkness, racing at incalculable speeds to their boy. The few patrons leftover at Wingdings watched Jack & Fred fly away and made the sign of the cross, sending a prayer to heaven for a seemingly hopeless cause.

Sidney watched their bright angelic trail as they charged up into the sky, and then vanished. He raised his hand to his mouth and shook his head, breathing in deeply through his congested nose. The barrister reclined in his chair, pushing his spectacles off his eyes, rubbing the tears from them. He took in a deep breath and let it go, trying to draw some measure of strength from a reserve he had long since tapped.

Sidney tried to focus. He started tidying up his desk and in doing so, knocked over the picture frame showcasing his sister Sylvia. He popped the back off, and pulled out the dog-eared crinkle of a photograph from where it had been placed. The barrister stared at his sister Sylvia, then pressed the photo against his heart.

Jack & Fred answered his prayers once upon a time when he was human. They had found the girl when she went missing. There was some kind of argument in Sidney's family over money, at the time, and she ran away from home, never to be found. Sidney was a hardened, ruthless lawyer, who was as brilliant as he was merciless in and out of court. But the loss of his sister, the one person in life he loved unendingly, broke him. He threw away his career and had spent years, utilizing all legal and non-legal means to locate her. An otherwise non-religious man, Sidney closed his eyes one day, and when he opened them, he found himself in church, praying. And Jack & Fred listened that day. They found her…

The strain on the barrister's heart over the years had been too great. And it was not long after Sylvia was located, that Sidney's heart had given way. And they were separated yet again. And so, for many long years, Sidney waited to see his dearest again. It was the reason Sidney the barrister dedicated all his time to Jack & Fred after he passed on. It was, in small measure to him, the only way he could thank the pair for locating what was most precious to his heart. And when they needed him to take care of things most, he couldn't do it…Sidney felt like he clipped the very wings from their bodies.

Why couldn't I fix this one?

"Oh God, I just killed them."

The barrister closed his eyes and held the photo of his sister against his heart, tapping it with every beat. Madison peeled her face from the door upon which she had been listening. The cold reverberated through her spirit as it always had…

{ Chapter 41 }

Baby, It's You

As he rolled down the hall upon a small sit-down vehicle called the Big Truck, from when he was a kid, laughter echoed in the boy's ears. All around him shadows played across the wall; crooked, contorted, twisted forms that reached and grabbed and danced. Some shadows resembled a line of small men in top hats who moved with the rhythm of the swaying of the outside trees caught in the streetlights. The wind was blowing through the house. There were strange sounds, like a choir moaning and wailing, and it wouldn't stop! Piano chords sounded as if they were being stomped on and smashed, voices humming loudly. He closed his eyes and opened them again. And it was all still there. Everything looked the same in the house with the yellow awning, but it all felt…uneasy, and not quite right. The boy heard what sounded like a tape recorder playing in reverse at high speed, skipping, and static, and the echoes of an orchestra playing backward. *This was home. Wasn't it?*

"*Ssshhhh,*" a voice sounded from down the hall. The boy's ears were piqued by it.

His mom and dad were entertaining company in the kitchen. He could smell coffee. That wind…it was getting colder. Why doesn't someone close the window? The wind wailed through the hall, and the boy kept hearing voices whispering but couldn't for the life of him make out what they were.

"Strange," he remarked to himself. The fish tank in the dining room. His mother never forgot to put that light on for him at night. It was so dark. What was he supposed to remember? Henry couldn't think of it. *What was it?* There was just too much noise. It sounded like a riot somewhere.

The boy had a hard time rolling the old truck down the hall. It kept getting stuck. Maybe it was his legs. He couldn't seem to move them right. Shivers ran up his back. He put his hand on the red-balled handle shifter of the toy truck, revving the plastic machine loudly to draw away the attention of his parents and their guests. He couldn't see the strangers' faces, but they were sitting there in the kitchen all the same. He became angry; why didn't they even turn and notice him?

His parents were laughing, laughing at him with their guests. Who were they? "Get out of my house!" the boy yelled. They screamed with laughter, even harder than before. He kept telling himself this wasn't right.

"No, it isn't, Hen," *a voice said gently*. "It's you."

"Me?" he asked aloud. "I'm not afraid of *anything*." The boy sat there on the toy truck growing angrier.

"This isn't just anything," a night watchman said, passing by in the hallway. He was in old clothes, with a cap on his head and an anorexic-looking dog. He swayed his lantern over the boy's head. "You went the wrong way. You should go back."

"How?"

"You know," the man said, tugging at his dog's collar, drawing him down the hall toward the boy's room. "C'mon Cholly!"

The laughter screeched. The boy rose off the Big Truck. He wanted to leave but he couldn't. The walls on either side of him seemed to stretch upward into infinity. There was a red fire alarm on the wall, with a glass covering and a handle underneath. There was an inscription on the glass that read: *In case of emergency, call Jack & Fred.*

Henry took a step back. He hadn't remembered the alarm being there before or what "Jack & Fred" meant, but for some reason he knew that a fire alarm was not supposed to be there. Not in the hallway!

"*Ssshhhh,*" a voice sounded from down the hall.

Henry looked down the hallway toward the front room of his house, which was always used for storage since his crib was moved out of there.

There was something about that room. It was always very dark in there at night. Henry had not dared go near it by himself. He spent many nights waiting till morning to go to the bathroom, afraid something would come running out of the front room and attack him. Though petrified, tonight, Henry was drawn to that room.

"I can't feel my hands," he said aloud, trying to flex them.

"Ssshhhh," a voice sounded from down the hall.

The child continued his journey closer to the front room, and once upon it became dread-stricken. There was a chattering noise. It wouldn't stop.

And then applause! It sounded like a thousand people clapping and cheering.

The laughter in the kitchen grew louder from behind him. When the boy turned and looked back, he couldn't make out anything; the space around him was all a blur. The orchestra playing backwards started up again.

"Ssshhhh," a voice sounded from down the hall.

He pressed forward again, toward the darkness. The doorway was unusually large and the room inside was devoid of all light. There was nothing...The darkness crept up around the edges of his vision; it was almost as if the child was gradually shutting his eyes as he moved forward. He felt cold; the shivering became worse. His body felt like it was having some kind of seizure; he couldn't still himself. But the laughter seemed to fade away.

"Ssshhhh," a voice sounded from down the hall.

The boy took a step through the dark room's entrance. A gruff snorting sound erupted from beyond. It sounded like an animal! He moved slightly into the room's blackness, just beyond the doorway, allowing it to swallow him up as he investigated. Even among the dark and shadow, the boy thought he saw something move. Maybe it was his eyes. He drew himself back. The noise began again. The sound. It was harsh breathing. Then it growled. He couldn't help himself, he had to see whatever it was. Henry leaned his head in closer, holding onto the doorframe feeling, deep down, that he was not going to make it out of this place alive.

Suddenly, a massive claw reached out from the darkness grabbing the boy by the throat, lifting him high into the air. It bellowed an ungodly howl that reverberated within his ears. He couldn't breathe. And a voice sang out, clear as day.

"*Baby, it's you! Tra-la-la-la-la-la-la...laa!*"

"*Ssshhhh,*" a voice sounded from down the hall.

LOOK OUT!!!

With its free paw, the creature drew itself up on two legs, crushing the doorframe with its bulk, making way for its girth and head to fit through. Tears of pure terror streamed down the boy's face. He felt electricity surge up his body from his feet to his neck, and his entire form became paralyzed. He couldn't scream or cry out; the beast held him, admiring his small human form, as it moved into the faint glow of the hall.

The gangly creature walked upright like a human being, wearing green shorts with suspenders and a top hat. It was the wolf who always stood beating at the door of his mind for many long weeks now, through sickness and good health. It was the darkness that plagued his dreams, though this was so real; he couldn't wake from this. The creature stood upright a good nine feet all, the size of a fully-grown polar bear. He couldn't move. The wolf looked almost comical, save for the rows of razor-sharp teeth that pleaded to bite into the boy's flesh without hesitation. He barked and bellowed unearthly animal cries. Its hot breath which smelled like wet dog food, whipped the boy's hair off his face. The creature delicately rubbed its snout along the contour of the boy's neck, salivating as it admired him hungrily. Henry closed his eyes, trying to calm himself enough to move his limbs again, which had been frozen these many minutes as his mind danced within its incapacitated form.

The wolf licked its lips favoring the boy's jugular, looking as though he would, in a heartbeat, rip his throat wide open and feast. Henry realized he would die if he didn't fight, and he wouldn't allow the creature the pleasure of claiming him for his meal so easily. He felt the feeling come back to his right arm, and he moved slowly but surely, hitting the beast. He struggled in its grip. He kicked and thrashed his arms about, but it didn't affect the wolf other than angering him further.

The beast fractured the railing over the stairwell into splinters with a solid blow, sending the wood chunks falling down below with a loud racket. The giant canine held the boy over the abyss. The boy found his voice, and screamed for his parents, but all he heard was that laughter again, and it was getting louder. The child kicked his legs back and forth in the air, trying to beat the enormous forearm of the massive black wolf to no avail.

Henry clawed and scratched at the beast, but it was only when he leaned forward and sunk his own teeth into the aberration's hairy mutated arm, that the creature sang out in pain and absolute horror. The boy dangled in its grip precariously. As he looked down, the stairs pulled away, stretching down forever to infinity.

The wolf dangled the boy by the scruff of his neck, and the clothes on his back began to tear. Henry threw his arms around the wolf's arm trying to climb back up, yelling, "Don't! You'll drop me! I'll fall down!"

The pointed, razor-sharp teeth smiled wide at him, and in a voice that rumbled from the back of its throat, the beast yelled, *"Then…fall!"*

The boy could hear the fabric shredding in his ears. "No!" Henry cried out.

At the very bottom of the stairs, a light blinked on in the vestibule. Church bells clanged in the distance. The entire stairwell was engulfed in a strange pale glow. The boy stared. A thin, spindly creature emerged like an animated shadow. It fidgeted and spread itself against the wall. The oily creature rubbed its two-dimensional face and leaned its wiry frame against the stairs; it peered upward and pointed at the child. Its black tar-like fingers curled and motioned for the boy to come down to him. The apparition began inching its way up the stairs on all fours in a contorted way, as if it were double-jointed; the limbs were reacquainting themselves with every movement forward. The wolf tossed the boy up in the air and caught him by the seat of his pants, with an even firmer grasp than before.

The black, slippery form below again invited the boy down to him with its slithering outline and serpentine fingers. He reached for the child's hand, and the boy pulled back. And electric guitar wailed uncontrollably outside. The shadow became disenchanted and faded into the walls, disappearing it seemed, for the moment.

The wolf reeled the boy in like a fish on a line, and with all its canine might, it tossed Henry down the hall like a sack of potatoes. The first thought that ran through the boy's mind as he slammed against the hard floor was that he'd be crippled forever. To his amazement, his body could move. Henry took off without hesitation, searching for a place to hide or escape. He wondered where the two dark creatures had gone to.

But he didn't have to wonder long; the wolf, moved deliberately on its haunches, demolishing the walls of the hallway around it. The plaster and dust created an uproar of smoke and outlined the wolf like a chalk outline at a crime scene. Henry, terrified, ran into the kitchen yelling. The creature being in his home seemed so ridiculous yet so frightening.

"Mom! Dad! Help me! There's a wolf in here!"

His parents sat there but didn't acknowledge him. All they did was laugh, looking at one another from across the table with their guests. Henry couldn't make out who the other people were; it was a man and a woman, but they just sat before the table with their backs to him. The boy turned to see where the wolf was, but the dust cloud obscured everything behind him. When the white cloud cleared away, the beast was gone. For just a moment, Henry thought that the creature had evaporated and left the ruins of the world he had fashioned. Without warning, furniture pieces went sailing across the living room and the commotion started up again. The wolf, just out of sight, was howling at the moon as it pulverized the entire living space.

The boy turned back around to his parents, hollering, "Mom, Dad, you have to…"

They were gone, as were the guests. He still heard their laughter, though. Through the kitchen door, the boy could see the wolf pass by in a flurry of motion, pounding everything to pulp without obstruction. The ceramic statues in their showcase were shaking from the vibrations, as were the doorframes. The whole area was bathed in a blood red light. Everything seemed vague, indistinct—as if you'd gotten Vaseline in your eyes. Plates, silver platters, and utensils were spinning softly in the crimson kitchen air. In the next room, the couch, ottomans, and chairs were floating around of their own accord, spinning about the room.

"Just look what's going on, *please*," he begged, but no one was there to hear him.

Then quiet again. He moved to the recliner, the only piece of furniture untouched by the wolf's tirade. The recliner opened, reached up, and swallowed the boy whole. He got out through the underside, crawling back into the kitchen, again.

"*Please look!*" he screamed.

But they didn't hear. They were gone—*all of them.*

A flood of indecipherable sounds all spoke to him— they were voices from not-too-distant memories; he could hear stories and ideas from weeks of contact with people. It was the sounds *of madness* blistering in his ears. He ripped his pajama top off, holding his head as the mad cacophony rushed into his eardrums and beat into his brain. The boy fell to his knees, his heart a flutter, not caring what was happening.

"Mom, Dad, I think I'm having a nervous breakdown."

"*Ssshhhh,*" a voice sounded from down the hall.

The insane laughter screamed over the incessantly painful hum of the world around him. He heard echoes of conversations, still hanging in the air.

"*Why, do you think I'm crazy too? Like the others?*"

"*I think he's just crazy,*" Big Mouth blurted, cackling like mad, on and on and on…

There was a sound, as if something had exploded below, and the entire house shook violently from the racket. It seemed like every ounce of goodness was being drained from the house with the yellow awning. Henry's eyes bulged and he shook away the confusion in his head. When he turned around, Joey and Patty, clad in school uniforms, were sitting in their desks where the kitchen table used to be. A handheld bell clanged as if a proclamation was about to be decreed. Joey and Patty ate graham crackers, dunking them in milk ever-so-delicately as the wolf howled into the night, nowhere to be seen.

Joey looked at Henry and raised a glass, smiling to no end.

"You almost killed us!" the child said to him. Hen took a step back. "How cool is that?"

Patty grinned a devious grin, never taking her eyes off the boy. She drank from her glass, waving with her few free fingers.

A man who resembled an undertaker came over to them with a towel over his arm and a pitcher of milk on a waiter's tray, filling Joey's glass until it spilled over the sides and onto the table.

"Why thank you, Edmund," Joey said to the man, his expression turning slightly sad as he continued to stare at Henry.

Henry took a step closer. "Joey…"

Joey sang, *"Can you tell me how to get…how to get to Sesame Streeeeeet!!!"* Patty laughed so hard milk went shooting out of her nose. The children screeched with glee. She wiped her face with a shirt sleeve and looked into Henry's eyes.

"Goodbye, Henry," Patty said mournfully, blowing him a kiss. Joey raised his glass and winked. The girl continued to eat her snack as a car crashed loudly into something outside. The boy kept feeling as though it was a person that got hit out there.

A woman screamed.

"Oh my God! The children! Somebody's hit the children!" a female voice yelled. Henry wheeled around and fell backward. Joey and Patty were gone. There were broken animal crackers with their heads off all over the desks.

He heard a sound like paper pages rustling, and books began dropping down upon his head from the bookcase that normally sat in the hall, but now was towering over him. The hardcover editions fell in a veritable hailstorm that would not cease. He peered up at the shelves as they emptied themselves by ghostly hands. A God-awfully loud screeching noise, like grinding metal, erupted, as Henry crawled back to the hall. *Where was the Big Truck he was riding?*

And then, the beast's fist smashed through the kitchen wall and clear through to the hallway. The wall shook from the creature's blow, and the empty bookcase came tumbling down in a flurry. Henry pulled back, covering himself.

There was nowhere left to go…

BOOM!!!

He was buried beneath tons of wreckage. The boy clawed up through the wire lath and plaster and wood, cutting his forearms on jagged edges everywhere. He looked up. *He was alive.* And that's all that really matter. The bookcase's wooden frame lodged itself into the wall behind him, shielding the boy like an umbrella. It was but an inch from his head. He felt wet droplets trickling down upon face. Then a sound, like an oil refinery exploding, and the other wall blew out as the hairy wolf's fist pushed through. The paw, which resembled a hairier twisted version of a human hand, pulled back, and vanished back into the wall. Henry had no time left to lose. He had to leave, now! A voice beckoned to him.

"Go now, kid! Run!"

Hot on his heels, the beast emerged, cutting a swath through the wreckage, annihilating wall after wall as the boy sought refuge back in his room. *It was his only hope.* He ran past the lady police officer who was directing traffic the day all of them escaped downtown.

Officer Burrows just shrugged, cackling as she directed.

"I haven't felt like this in years," she said loudly, smacking her hands together. "Woo…Let's go, people. Head 'em up and move 'em out little doggies! C'mon now…woo!"

The Big Red station wagon blocked the boy's passage, parked sideways across the hallway. *How could it fit inside?* The boy struggled with the front passenger door, forcing it with great haste, to burp open. He dove through the front seat pushing himself to the other side. *He had to reach his room. Had to…*

In the back seat Mr. Wallace sat, grinning faintly at the child, shaking his head in dismay as he tossed a liquor bottle away. Henry could see a thick dust cloud behind him outlining the oversized creature's form. It grinned its pearly fangs amidst its molasses-black fur; falling plaster chunks rained down on the beast. It savored the moment as its prey had nowhere left to go.

The beast raised its fist high into the air and Henry pushed himself backward out of the car, landing on the seat of his pants. The wolf jumped up and slammed down upon the ground causing a cavernous sinkhole to spread open the floorboards. Wind from the blow could be felt across the child's face. *It was so cold. So very cold…* The car teetered precariously then fell clear into the abyss, Mr. Wallace and all. The boy could see him wave as he fell down below. Henry wasted no time, and bounded through his room's doorway and flung the door shut behind him. It was the last place to go. No one was coming. He was alone.

The beast was coming closer. He could hear the wolf slowly but surely thumping toward his room. Henry tried to open his closet, but the sliding doors wouldn't budge. The wind howled through the screen window and the growling grew louder as the beast drew nearer. *There was nowhere left to go!* There was a noise like someone beating down on drums and tinny cymbals. Henry fell to the floor, crawling on his belly underneath his bed. He thought—*he hoped*—that maybe the beast wouldn't find him and would just keep going.

The boy laid there flat on his stomach, breathing hard. His heart beat so fast that his chest throbbed with pain. Almost forgetting himself, Henry reached out and pulled down the dust ruffle, futilely attempting to cover his presence below. The boy smothered his loud breathing and fear with his forearm, biting down on his own flesh to do so. He crossed his legs one on top of the other to keep them from trembling any more than they already were. His feet became cramped very quickly in the confining space under the bed, but that was the least of his worries. There was harsh snarling, nails scratching against the door, and then silence.

Henry stared through the quarter-inch space between the dust ruffle and the door, yet he saw nothing. It was a vain hope that the wolf had gone away, destroying all that it had to, or *wanted* too. But still…he prayed.

The boy let out a sigh of relief, and wondered for a second where his parents were, if they were all right. Preoccupied with the thought, the boy stared vacantly off into the distance, as wet droplets fell upon his hands and face again. He peered through the space in the dust ruffle. Something on his shelf caught his eye. Neatly placed and with almost-smiles on their faces, sat two stuffed animals, *friends*. One was a bear and the other was a dog, with an expression quite gruff. Henry frowned at them for a moment. These *friends* were never in his room before, but they were somehow familiar. *Were they from a story, once upon a time or…*

Somewhere. It was on the tip of his tongue. Henry's eyes grew wide and he took in an excitedly deep breath.

"*They. Where are they? Not my parents…them. The…I can't remember!*" He mumbled something and then cursed himself for his mind's muddle.

He heard Kristie giggling.

The feather that he had given her dropped to the ground. He reached out and grabbed it, feeling its silkiness, rubbing it against his cheek and closing his eyes in sweet remembrance of...*what were their names?*

He looked out across the room. There *she* was, dressed in blue overalls, in a child-size rocking-chair. Kristie pressed her feet into the ground rocking back and forth, faster and faster.

"Kris!" he unconsciously uttered, slapping his hand over his open mouth just as quick. She smiled, closing her eyes and shaking her head.

The beast came bursting through the door, crushing it into chunked, splintered pieces like so much driftwood. Then she was gone; chair and all. Fear had constricted his vocal chords and pinched the part of him that needed to breathe. So he laid still; all he had to do was lay perfectly still and the animal would bring the room down upon the boy's ears, and *leave*. He had to be silent. And then it would leave him be *forever*.

The wolf, almost curiously, slapped at the boy's bureau with the back of its massive canine paw. He peeled back the top of the wooden furniture as if he were ripping apart an orange with its fingers, exposing the inside nails that held the pieces together. With its gaping maw, it gathered up a handful of the boy's clothes spitting them out with a snort all over the place. That the beast was so easily amused by something so trivial as stray bits of laundry struck the boy as odd, almost whimsical. Throwing clothes about in heap; it was something a frustrated kid would do. But Henry remained frightfully still. The creature was still wearing its torn green shorts with suspenders, without the hat. Why?

"He's scary. But you have to hand it to Furry, though. He might be spooky, but he's darn stylish."

"That's my voice," the boy said to himself.

The wolf turned its attentions to tearing apart the sliding metal closet doors, ripping them from track and hinge. He sniffed about the space, looking for some trace of the child but found nothing and went back to pawing at the furniture.

"Thank God I didn't hide in there," Henry thought to himself, closing his

eyes as a rush of terror shot up from his belly and into his throat like a geyser. "*That would have been the first place he looked!*"

"*Sure would have!*" a detached voice said from nowhere, seemingly answering his thoughts.

The beast turned and proceeded to bash and flatten every single toy on the boy's shelves with a certain unbridled passion for decimating all that was gentle and precious in the boy's world. It wanted to destroy everything that brought Henry some sense of joy. But somehow, it just couldn't finish the job. You could see it on the creature's face; it was some sense of frustration. Somehow or the other, its ferocious blows missed the stuffed bear and the dog, which fell onto the floor, untouched by the beast's rampage; it was almost as if the twisted aberration couldn't harm them if he tried. Henry peeked through the dust ruffle at his fallen friends, his *only* friends in this frightful mess. The beast seemed to preoccupy itself bending and twisting the broken metal doors of the closet. Henry reached a hand out slowly and tugged at the bear and dog's legs, reeling them back under in a flurry of motion. He held them under his arms, as if he were taking them under his wings and into his protection. Just like…

All his toys—every single one—were smashed into smithereens. Henry couldn't believe it. It was that stinking beast!

That voice spoke to his thoughts again.

"*She's a real beast. One time, when I was like a kid, I mean younger than you…*"

Henry turned.

Anthony slid under the bed with him. The older boy propped himself up on his elbow, lying down on his side next to Henry. The boy looked at his old friend, completely aghast.

"Oh God, Anthony. What are you doing…here?"

"My sister Janey invited Big Mouth and that wolf over my house for some girl stuff, right? And Big Mouth and that damn thing got into my room—"

"Ant, how are we going to get out of here?"

"And can you believe the nerve of these two? They're into all my things. And Furry there winds up breaking *all* my toys. Everything! Just like…well, this! It was incredible! I was SO ticked Hen!" Henry's eyes bulged. "All my cool stuff. My G.I. Joe's, the Transformers, He-Mans and a few of the…the Star Wars stuff." An almost tear seemed to bubble up in Anthony's eye.

"Nooo!!!" Henry mocked, laughing uncontrollably. "Say it ain't so!"

"It's so, it's so!" Anthony pretended to sulk, speaking, it seemed, to himself as he rubbed his phantom tears. "Ah well. Such is life."

Henry took a breath.

"Please, Anthony. Listen to me. We have to get out of here. He's going to kill us…"

"Yeah. It sucks, doesn't it?"

The wolf lifted the toy shelves high into the air, kneading them into oversized tinfoil balls, tossing and kicking them around. The creature took one of the curled-up shelves and jumped up and down on it, flattening it even more with each leap of its enormous furry feet. It mangled things with its paws, ripping the light fixture down off the ceiling. The plaster pieces fell down like snowflakes, gently drifting under the bed; dust was blowing into the boy's eyes.

The wolf, proud of its symphony of destruction, licked its lips, sniffing the air around him and grunting loudly. When the boy turned back to his friend Anthony, he was wearing an outfit that made him resemble Han Solo.

"Anthony, please…"

"Say, what happened to your girl, Miss Kris? She's not dead is she?" Henry closed his eyes. The apparition that resembled his dear friend just rambled on.

"Anthony…"

"Sorry, kid. We have to get down to the cafeteria."

"Ant, is it hot in here? I'm burning up!"

The specter wiped its brow. "Hmm…maybe it's just you," he shrugged, sipping a soda that somehow materialized in his hand. "Care for a frosty beverage? Fresca anyone?" Someone was playing off-melody notes on a piano outside as the echo which resembled Anthony, spoke.

"Well," the phantom said, sipping its drink and tossing it away, letting the can roll past the boy, as soda ran out in gulps. "I better get over to our table

Hen. It's almost time to start class. I don't need to get killed this early in the morning Henry. Honestly. It's a real *brother...*"

"*Brother?* Did you just say..."

"Yeah, I did..." He mussed the boy's hair. "Anyway, I'll see you later at recess."

"Take care, Ant," the boy said rather hoarsely.

"You too, kid." He turned to leave, pulling out his sidearm. "Oh, and Hen. If anyone bothers you, like a bully or something, well..." he winked, "you know better than anyone, nothin' beats a good blaster by your side—"

He chucked the boy on the shoulder looking around for the beast.

"Help me, Anthony!" Henry shrieked, losing his patience. "HELP ME!!! FOR GOD'S SAKE, HELP ME!!!"

"Hey...Hen. May the Force be with you amigo." Anthony dove out from under the bed, ready to fight.

"*Noooooooo!!! Anthony! Come back! Don't go out there!*"

The wolf stretched its human-like arms out, flexing its paws, as sharp-edged, blade-like claws extended out from its digits. The boy's heart raced feverishly. He squeezed the stuffed animal friends beneath his arms tighter, waiting for some sign that Anthony was okay. He was...*talking* to the creature.

"Hey, Furry, what's shakin', other than you, baby?! What's this? You, you want a hug? Nah. Sorry there hairball, we can be friends, but we ain't gonna be picking out curtains together. Hold it. Wait. No, wait...stop. No! *Nooooo!*"

A sickening noise echoed throughout the room; it was like that of a celery stalk snapping in half, and then a hard thud. It sounded like someone dropped a bowling ball, letting it roll across the floor. It was moving closer; closer to the bed.

The boy wondered, "Oh God...is it his...?" Henry scrunched his eyes shut, taut with fear, as the heavy thing rolled toward him. Something warm and sopping wet pressed against his hand, lightly. *He had to see...* As he drew his eyes open, he found the small decapitated toy head of one of his Han Solo action figures.

"Anthony?"

The beast's gargantuan mutant toes pushed themselves beneath the dust ruffle, almost hitting the child in the ribs. In a panic, Henry slid back toward the other side of the bed, careful not to expose himself to the wolf's bloodshot eyes. He squeezed the stuffing out of the friends, staring unblinking at the fur covered feet, which looked not-at-all like any canine the boy had ever seen. He couldn't help but notice the shiny black, gnarled nails of the beast, and how mussed and ruffled its night-black fur was—all torn and covered in plaster chips, dust, and grit.

It's so hot in here! I'm burning up! That sound. WOOSH! A faint light flickered beyond the creature, and before long, tongues of orange flame were lapping up the length of the wall, catching the curtains ablaze. Everything was burning uncontrollably; it wouldn't be long now.

Without effort, the wolf gently (if not politely) lifted up the front end of the bed. It shoved its sweat-soaked, misshapen head beneath, almost nose to nose with the paralyzed boy. Its sickening, vomit-smelling breath fanned the child's hair backward with each heaving exhale, causing Henry to gag.

"*Heyyyy*," the wolf rumbled loudly. The creature's large eyebrow raised with an otherwise delightful expression.

Henry eyed the beast straight on, completely frozen, his eyes bulging from his skull. Behind the creature, the entire room was engulfed in flame. Everything around them was crackling and popping as it crumbled steadily. The smoky tang of scorched wood burnt the insides of the boy's nose and throat.

The boy whispered, "Oh God, guys, where are you?"

Suddenly, the wolf recoiled like a scared dog far smaller than he was. The beast threw the bed against the flame-enveloped walls out of pure disgust. With the blistering flames licking at his face, the boy rose up and dashed through the wolf's legs out into the hallway again. He knew what he had to do.

"I have to find you!" he yelled. "I've got to bring you back here. You belong here, with me! This is your home! This is where you two belong!" he called out to the angels. It was not so much his mind recalling their image, but rather the indelible impression which they left in his heart that would bring them back again.

Henry stopped in his tracks, breathless, looking around at the twisted world around him that was quickly falling to pieces. "Where are you?"

Outside in the real world…
"I love you Jack & Fred."

Oh, how that gentle voice reverberated throughout the twinkling of every star in every constellation—over and over again.

Fred shut his eyes.

Jack & Fred rocketed over the city at speeds no other being could maintain. They glided through rows of intersecting spotlights waving across the sky. The two angels passed over a Christmas tree vendor somewhere on the ground. The wind whipped through their hair. Their faces were illuminated by bright, moving shafts of light that detailed every feature. Fred looked down at the ground, trying, in an infinitesimal way, to distance himself from his grief. His eyes, sharp from the moisture of his own tears, focused on two small boys selecting a special little tree for their Christmas celebration.

"How closely they resemble us," both angels seemed to remark to themselves. Another column of light shone about the cherubs, and they glowed like two falling stars streaking across the lost night. The children below fawned over their tiny tree. It was so small, and bare, and tired, flaking to the ground—needing only a little love…so much like their boy.

"Then, take me with you."

Fred eyes saw only blinding white.

"We can't, it's not your time," *the little one insisted.*

"Make it time. Take me with you."

"You have a precious gift, Henry. You have a life; you have a family, parents that love you. We—"

"Then I'll come with you. And we can come back and visit them. We'll find Kristie…wherever she is in Connecticut, and I can meet Belle. And we can go to that place. Wingdings, right? And we'll bother St. Peter, and visit your friends, like Sidney. You mentioned him the night we talked, right? We'll fly everywhere. I

know, three's a crowd but…I wouldn't be a third wheel. We could make it work, if you wanted. I'd be quiet and wouldn't bug you or…I wouldn't bother you."

"That's not the point—"

"Really. I'm not a scooch or nothin'."

The little one backed away.

"We can't—"

"Come on!"

"Just—"

"Please, Fred—"

"Henry—"

"Please guys. Take me home with you…Fred…please? Please Jack?"

"Henry we—"

"Come on, Jack, please?"

The little one held him, but the boy wouldn't let go.

Jack begged. "Henry, listen—"

"No…"

"Please, Hen," Fred pleaded.

"No, Fred, I'm not letting you go."

Jack felt wet droplets splashing against his cheeks and forehead and eyes. He looked for the rain but it wasn't falling; it was Fred's tears. Jack flew closer to his partner and reached over to him. Never even looking over, the little one reached across and held onto Jack's arm. The two flew on, not to be separated—not now, not ever.

Within the nightmare from which Henry could not awaken, a courageous vigor replaced his fear and surged through the boy's veins. The boy looked around for them excitedly but found nothing. *They need time to get here. They will! I have to call them!*

Henry had to all but tie the stuffed animals to his hands to keep them from flying out. This world was crumbling; it was all gone: his house, his toys, his parents, everything. All he had left was his belief in *them*, and himself.

He stood there in the shambles that was his former life, looking for a sign. There had to be some way to break free. There *had* to be a way to get beyond this horror. To live again. He looked up…and there it was. The oddly-placed fire alarm on the wall he passed by earlier. It was still there, intact!

"*Bllowwrrarrghh!*" the beast bellowed, as something, probably the bed, crashed across the back room. The shiny red metal box gleamed down upon him. Henry jumped up to it but realized that the glass cover was stopping him from pulling the handle. The metal spoke that should've been there to smash away the glass enclosure was missing. He looked about the floor for something that would shatter the smooth reflective face. Below him, there were books; hundreds of them at his feet—all in colors without names, waiting it seemed, to be written. A breeze blew across the hall as Henry knelt down to them. Between the cracks of the rubble, one book laid on its spine, flush and open. The pages tossed themselves over and each page was blank—empty, just plain cream paper. The wind kicked up again and blew the volume shut.

Whump!

On the cover of the burgundy book was the infamous painting, *the Sistine Madonna*, with his angels Jack & Fred. He turned to a page at the very end of the book and read aloud: *So the angels were at their usual spot on Earth, a wall that separated the house with the yellow awning from everything else. They were looking up at the passing clouds, thinking about their boy.*

"That's it!" The etched letters shined: *In case of emergency, call Jack & Fred!* He had to break the glass.

Henry placed his two stuffed friends on the floor for a moment.

"You guys stay here, I'm calling the boys. This has got to end, now!" he instructed them. The stuffed animals just stared up with permanently-affixed smiles, twinkles of light dancing across their eyes. He looked down for the red book with the angels' picture on it, then hefted it up into his arms, nearly toppling over from the weight. He could see the doorway of his room, and most of the corridor, collapse in on itself.

"*It's all over now. It's all falling apart,*" the boy said to himself, shaking his head regrettably. The fire was spreading throughout the entire house.

"*Arrrrrrrrooooooorrraaaa!*" the creature bellowed.

There was no more time. His skin was burning from the heat around him. Henry lifted the red book up with both hands, and in a feat of pure strength and courage, he hurled it at the glass.

The beast was writhing in pain. *"Brrwwaaaarrrrh!"*

The glass shattered into a million pieces, falling down upon him like a harsh rain. With legs like springs, Henry leaped into the air, grabbing the alarm's handle with both hands. He hung onto it, but it would not budge.

"Rruurhhhh!" the beast went.

"C'mon, c'mon," he struggled. "Guys, I need you," he said, straining. The boy wrestled with the device, but it stayed strong to the box. He looked up, half wanting to give up. In place of the ceiling above him, he glimpsed the starry night sky sprawled out as far as the eye could see. *Infinity…*

"Don't get swept up in this dream again, PULL!!!" he urged himself. The boy swung his feet, using his weight to fall so he could pull down the alarm handle. He swayed back and forth like he was trying to go faster on a swing set. So great was his exertion, that his hands stung from the ripping strain. But, he hung there, and would not let go…

The ravenous creature now loomed over him, foaming at the mouth. And then, with a scream that was louder than the wolf's, Henry exclaimed, *"Jack & Fred!!! I believe in you…my guardian angels, Jack & Fred!!!"*

He planted his feet flush against the wall like Spider-man and pushed off—pulling down the alarm handle as he fell.

The boy fell backwards as if in slow motion, slamming his skull on the debris as the alarm wailed away. His limp body laid upon the jagged edges and pointed glass shards scattered about the floor. Henry's eyes peeled open, looking up at the blue sky spread out wide above him. A shooting star darted across, its light-streaked tail lingering long into the moment.

The beast recoiled.

"Gotcha furbag," he whispered smiling at the creature.

The soft touch of a silky kiss pressed against his cheek. Down the hall, he saw the outline of a small, silhouetted form amidst the parting drafts of plaster dust.

"Guys? Is that you?" Henry called to it.

Bubbles filled the air about his head, and a faint green light shone down upon the little figure of Kristie.

The boy was drawn and tired.

"Kristie," he said weakly. "You're not real baby. I know this…"

She stood there, dunking her plastic ring into the soapy pink bottle, blowing bubbles down the hallway.

"Goodbye, Henry, *forever*," she said.

The boy was unsettled.

"No," he stepped forward. "You're not who you pretend to be. This is not right. This is not what happened. Not at all! She's not dead! She's just in Connecticut!" In short order, she pulled from the pocket of her blue coveralls a small beanbag froggy. She held him, squeezing his belly to make him lean forward like he was bowing and saying hello over and over. She stood one blessed moment, and waved a soft farewell to him.

"This is ridiculous." He turned to the beast itself. "*You* are ridiculous."

Henry looked at her again. "Go back to wherever you came from. You're *not* her."

The apparition of his beloved stepped backward, looking at the boy sorrowfully, doing its best to foist a guilt trip upon his soul as it disappeared in a swell of bright green light around it.

Henry grabbed hold of his two friends on the floor, and the beast chuckled. It held its belly and pointed to the boy, laughing. The child was beyond fear. Henry was the nicest person you'd ever want to meet, but turned on his head; you didn't know what this one was capable of, no one did. He kicked the beast squarely in the shins. The wolf shrieked in pain as the boy ran through its legs again, urging it to follow him. The house's foundation was slowly giving way. Smoke filled the air and made it nearly impossible to see.

Henry found himself bouncing off the hallway walls like a pinball as he ran, and the structure shifted. His path was beset with holes, but he would not allow himself to fall into them. But it gave him an idea. He could see clearly to the basement through the abyss caused by the creature's thunderous jump earlier. The boy leaped over it and grabbed a blanket which was tossed aside by the wolf. He flung the small cover outward and it grew to many times its own size. The blanket spread wide over the abyss, obscuring it from sight; the boy was setting a man-trap for the hairy behemoth.

"Come and get me, you big hairy oaf!" he beckoned to the abomination, gathering up the stuffed animals in his arms. The wolf just leered at the boy and began swaggering down the hall—then jogging, then running in earth-pounding footfalls. Again, Henry couldn't help but notice that his house was not this big, normally. Meanwhile, the fire alarm continued to blare for help, but no one had appeared yet.

The wolf came thundering down the hall. Henry turned away and ran, diving into the dining room.

"C'mon, stupid, come and get me!" Henry yelled. The beast ran straight for him, oblivious; it fell right through to the bottom of the house, however far that was in this topsy-turvy dream world. There was not so much as a sound from its mouth, only the sound of splintering wood.

The smoke in the house was rising. The boy paced, waiting. He had been burnt before, for his haste. He knew this nightmare was not finished yet. The fire alarm rang and rang, and suddenly stopped. The crackling of burning wood was all you could hear in this shattered house. All of the fish in the aquarium within the dining room swam and Henry flicked the blue light on.

TINK! TINK! TINK! TINK! A noise in the backyard sounded.

He moved to the dining room window, waiting. Wind tousled his hair and screamed unmelodious tones about him, then died. A ray of sunshine shone through the window, along with a chubby little arm.

"Henry. Henry we're here!" the voice said.

Henry reached out with his arms and closed his eyes; the stuffed animals had disappeared from his charge.

"I'm right here," he said to the voice. "Take me home."

Another voice came through, *"Come with us. It's time to leave this awful place. It's time to go."*

The boy almost felt himself saying "I can't!" and wondered why.

TINK! TINK! TINK! TINK!

Henry felt the warmth surge across his face from the sunshine. The sound of seagulls and crashing waves could be heard in the distance, with a scent that was almost like citrus, though far more lovely.

"*Florida, Henry,*" the familiar voice said. "*That's where all the seaplanes go.*"

"I…" the boy tried to say.

The wolf reared up through the floorboards, covered in wood chips and dust.

TINK! TINK! TINK! TINK!

Henry looked outside the window for some—any—escape.

TINK! TINK! TINK! TINK!

Out there in the yard, in the darkness, there was…a shadow. It was the one from the stairwell, and it was doing something…hitting something.

TINK! TINK! TINK! TINK!

Henry moved closer to the window. The spindly wraith was more defined as the firelight from the burning house shone down upon it. It wore a black cloak now over its dark sinewy form, with its face covered in nylons and a dark hat. The shadow moved deliberately without obstruction.

TINK! TINK! TINK! TINK!

"*This is the end,*" a horrid voice rumbled in his ears.

A dark light shone on the man in the garden. He was hitting something with a hammer…*hitting*…

TINK! TINK! TINK! TINK!

The boy turned back around, almost as if instructed, and the man in the darkness was there before him in the room—the shadowy thing was smacking its hammer into something metal.

TINK! TINK! TINK! TINK!

A chisel. He was chiseling—no—*carving* letters into a gravestone.

TINK! TINK! TINK! TINK!

The aberration stepped aside.

H_{ENR}…the slab read. The man in the darkness held the chisel in his hand, almost threatening to continue. The boy's eyes were wide, and he kept perfectly still.

"*Goodbye, Henry!*"

Cathedral bells sang. Voices rang out. And the dark spindly man laughed, mockingly at the boy, preparing to strike the final blow.

The light outside was still there, but the peaceful voices weren't. Henry turned to see the wolf lifting the dining room table over his head. It smashed it into the ceiling and the light fixture, sending spears of glass down upon its furry hide—but the light in the room did not falter!

The beast held the table over its head and smiled again at the boy and said very plainly, *"Heyyyy!"*

And then the wolf and the shadow began to laugh. His parents and their company began to laugh hysterically again down the hall. With a firm thrust, the wolf kicked out the stand for the fish tank, and the aquarium came crashing to the floor with Henry's fish.

"My fish!" the boy yelled. All the lost fish scattered, trying desperately to breathe, choking to death. The boy looked up at the wolf again and the beast laughed harder. Its broad chest moved up and down in heaves, and its midsection quivered with enjoyment.

Against the window pane there came a knocking. Then a voice.

"Henry, wake up. Come on, Henry, get up. Snap out of it, boy. It's all just a dream!"

Henry turned hopefully toward the window, but he saw nothing. Almost forgetting the laughter in the house and the peaceful voice for a second, he looked down at the backyard outside his window. He saw two glowing figures waving frantically at him.

"C'mon! C'mon!" the voice called to him. *"Hurry up! You don't have time. Hurry boy!"*

"I can't," Henry yelled to the voice that sounded so much like himself.

"All you have to do is believe."

Henry turned around and the wolf stopped laughing. His expression became sour, and he grunted and snorted; his large nostrils flared as smoke billowed from the burning room's walls. His eyes bled tears, which rolled down its hairy face.

"Heeeeyyyy," it grunted through grit teeth admonishing the boy for listening to the voice. Henry looked at it. The beast was faltering. In a deep

garbled sound, the creature muttered to the glowing figures outside the window, *"Go away, both of you!"*

A gentle voice said, "If you look for love, you will find things like goodness, caring, faithfulness, courage, and loyalty. When you look for love, you will find love, and when you find love..."

The boy's heart quickened. "That's where all of us angels will be," he finished.

The beast's muscles flexed and he hurled the entire dining room table at the boy. Henry fell to the floor and covered his head. The table went reeling, like a battering ram, shattering the window pane and the wall behind him. Henry, in a clump on the floor, could hear the loud crash, and all the pieces falling to the ground in the backyard. The boy slowly took his hands away from his eyes and face, and looked up without fear. The laughter had stopped and the creature stood there with its paws on its hips, enraged.

"Rrrrrrr," it growled through its clenched jaw. Henry felt a cool breeze on the back of his neck. He turned and looked.

"Henry, it's you."

He and the beast looked out through the gaping hole in the side of his house. Down below, the glowing figures stood there among the debris on the ground. They stared up at the boy, motionless. Henry looked at the wolf. For a moment, all his fear left him, and he said very loudly to the beast, "I don't believe in you. I believe in my guardian angels, Jack & Fred!"

In his hands, the book with his angels on the cover materialized—

The beast crouched down low to the floor, then sprung high into the air, and landed with an earth-shattering quake. The impact rocked the entire house off its foundation.

The wolf charged at him. And Henry ran toward it.

Henry ran and ran—determined, courageous, fearless, tired of all the madness in his mind. He raised the book over his head and slammed it down upon the beast's skull, rendering the creature inconsequential and dead. The boy turned in one swift stride and slammed the shadowy creature holding the chisel with the book as well. The chisel and hammer were flung from its hands, as the child broke its back beneath the weight of his passion. He reached down, pulling the nylon mask from its face and found it stuffed with paper pages, story pages.

He pulled one of them out, looking at it. It read:

THE BOY TURNED IN ONE SWIFT STRIDE AND SLAMMED THE SPINDLY ABERRATION WITH THE BOOK. THE CHISEL AND HAMMER WERE FLUNG FROM ITS HANDS, AS THE CHILD BROKE ITS BACK BENEATH THE WEIGHT OF HIS PASSION. HE REACHED DOWN, PULLING THE NYLON MASK FROM ITS FACE AND FOUND IT STUFFED WITH PAPER PAGES, STORY PAGES…

The boy walked toward the fallen giant that was the wolf. It reawakened.

"Oh, dear," the beast said in a polite British tenor. "Right nice blow old chap, I must say. My head is simply *spinning*."

"You're dying," he told the beast that was his own dark self.

"Oh, I know that, young man."

The boy nodded in recognition.

"You have so many stories to tell. Do you want them? Sometimes in life you have to fight for what's really important to you. No matter how hopeless it seems. So I must ask again. Regarding your stories…do you want them? Do you? They were mine…"

"They were never *yours*."

"Quite right lad. Quite right," it conceded. "Here." The beast handed him loose pages from the floor. "Take them. Every last one of them; they're *all* yours."

The boy stared down at the pages. "There's nothing written here yet."

"Watch."

The wolf grabbed a section of floor, held it, and dropped it in the boy's arms. And before it could touch his fingertips, it flaked to paper.

"Life. It's all one grand story. All of it. We're all just characters you know. Someone right now is writing *our* story. Go ahead. Touch anything. And tell me, how badly do you want your stories to be told? How badly do you want to *live* tonight?" he asked with a grin, winking at the boy.

"*This bad!*"

Henry raised the book over his head, and slammed it down upon the beast's skull; one final blow. The creature broke apart into story pages and flew away in a heavy gust of wind.

"I'm not afraid of you anymore…and you have no power over me."

"Good show, lad! It's all just a dream, you know. We wolves are really quite civilized. Despite what people say! Cheerio!"

Henry walked into the hall. It was pristine. He moved on and a light shone down from the roof hatch. He was exhausted, but he moved on anyway. He touched the ladder rungs lightly. He reached, and pulled, and strained, and with one last burst of energy he was up into the light.

Then everything around the boy shattered in a million paper pieces…and flew away.

On the rooftop…

The cold breezes blew through again, stirring Henry awake. His body had gone numb from sleeping on the cold rooftop for so many hours. He lay there silently, his body weary from such a long night's dreamtime terror—but there was a sound, a buzz in his ears.

It was an incessant chirping. It sounded like the giant ants from the old drive-thru monster flick, *Them!* It startled him awake even more.

"Come on back," a voice said.

An unending, incessant sound. And his senses felt as though they had been sitting in a box these many long hours.

"Roger."

Then the voice itself opened his eyes wide.

"Where are you, please?"

He looked around, startled, then slumped back down as the sounds faded. The boy stretched out, trying to pull himself up, but he couldn't move.

"Oh, God! What…" Henry passed out just as fast.

In the twilight, the frozen child slept, breathing slowly, almost not at all. The walkie-talkie, on its last legs, battery fading, shrieked with a staticy call. The boy had barely woken up again; still he couldn't move. He reached for the black box slowly.

Deep voices…

"J and F…on approach."

He perked himself up, squinting his eyes, holding the little speaker-box just so. "C'mon," he muttered.

The box squealed and it paused for an eternity, then a tinny-sounding voice rang in...

"ON APPROACH TO JFK. THIS IS JOHN F. KENNEDY AIRPORT. DO YOU COPY?"

"COPY."

"Flight 11-9-75, you are clear all the way in."

"No!" the crippled boy shrieked, falling away. "Noo..." and he tossed away the squawk box, and it died where it fell.

They were here. They were coming. *Just hold out a little longer...*

{ Chapter 42 }

No...That's Home

"Oh God," Fred bit his lip. "Jack, what is that?! What is that?!" he screamed, frightened, for he knew what it was. The glowing lights flickered high over the horizon.

"It's..." Jack faltered.

"What is that?!" Fred called again.

"Oh, no. No. That's home," he said, making out the letters that were formed by the battery-operated Christmas lights on the antennae.

"No. That..." Fred paused. "Jack, it says *Henry*," the little one said in a tiny voice, looking at the still form on the roof. "That's our boy."

Part of them wanted to stop a moment, for if he couldn't wake up, they couldn't bare the sight.

The angels swallowed hard and screamed to get to the house with the yellow awning. They could not take their eyes off the roof for that moment. And their hearts sunk when they saw him. The boy was face down, lifeless as could be.

The sign flickered over and over, but they could barely look at it now; the backwards *N* was smiling loudest of all the letters.

Jack saw the little boy. He wasn't moving.

"Oh, Jesus," he cried, flying down.

"Henry!" the little one screamed.

Fred reached the boy first. Jack scooped him up in his arms like a rag doll. He wasn't moving.

"Henry," Jack directed loudly, but the child wasn't hearing. The lead angel looked at his partner. "He's freezing to death." Fred eyes darted back and forth. The words were there, but he couldn't comprehend them.

Jack cradled him. "Henry."

The little one shook his head. "No. Not you too. C'mon, Hen." Fred held the limp arms, putting the boy's head in his lap. "C'mon, get up. Get up. Get up. Get up."

"C'mon, Henry, wake up," Jack urged.

The boy was an icicle. He wasn't responding.

Fred never turned away his gaze, when Jack glanced toward him.

Jack put his head to the boy's chest.

"Come on, Henry, wake up. *Waaake* up. I can hear your heart. Wake up Henry, you're alive," he said, rocking the boy whose body was all but frozen.

"Henry...Henry wake up," Fred said, frightfully calm, closing his eyes, sending all his strength, his heart, all of his angelic warmth into the boy. The love radiated from the angels' bodies. Jack put his hands over the boy's heart.

Fred's gentle face looked upon him, his mouth quivering. *"Please..."*

Thump!

It had never stopped beating! It had just gotten *reaaally* quiet for a moment. No, it never stopped. Not once—not ever. It was still there. The little boy's heart never faltered.

Jack smiled, faintly, "That's it kid!"

Fred brushed the hair from the boy's face, holding his cheeks in his hands. The boy's eyes slowly rolled round like a doll's and they were all glassy, but they were there.

"That's it," Fred sniffled. "That's it, Henry. Come on. We can hear your heart. You're alive! Stay with us."

"Knew you'd come back," Henry whispered, tears in his eyes. The hastily-made electric sign behind them flickered out, all except the backwards *N*, which remained a moment longer.

"We're back, kid," Jack said, thinking—hoping—that it would just end like this, and everything was going to be fine. Fred couldn't speak.

"I beat him. The wolf…he's dead. I'm so tired."

"You didn't have to freeze yourself to death, Henry," Jack gulped with a grin, choking on his own tears. "You know?"

Henry nodded. "I'm sorry. I had to get you back."

"Sorry?" Jack wiped away the tears with his arm. "What've you got to be sorry for?"

"I let you down." The boy was so ashamed.

"You're the bestest thing that ever happened to us, kid," Jack said.

"Wasn't going to just let you go. Not without a fight." The little boy smiled. "Tried my best."

"You did good, kid. We're very proud of you…you know? Hen?"

The boy didn't answer.

"Hen?!"

"Yeah, Jack."

Jack started breathing again.

The angels held him.

"You can stay," the boy said, running the angel's feathers through his fingers. They felt like satin. "Right…right?"

"We can stay forever," Fred said.

Henry smiled. The boy took a slow, deep breath and released it.

"I don't feel right, guys." For a moment, it didn't look like he would ever feel right again—like he wasn't going to last. He was fading away.

"Henry!" Jack yelled.

"Yeah," Henry said.

"Jack," Fred nodded over with his swollen eyes. Jack threw open the roof hatch loud enough to wake up people ten blocks away.

"*Wake up!*" he screamed. Fred covered the boy's ears, holding the child in his arms.

"*Wake uppppp!*" he screamed again, in his angelic voice which human senses (not their ears) could hear. Jack flew down the hatch and physically jolted the parents' bed to wake them up. A frightened chill stirred them instantly.

In the moments Jack was gone, the boy looked up at the little one.
"Where'd Jack go?"
"He'll be right back. Just relax. I gotcha. You're not going anywhere."
"Get him. I have to ask you something."
"It can wait. Just lie still." Fred cradled the little boy. "I have you…and I'll never let you go. Just rest…just rest. Jack'll be right back."

The boy sighed. He could do nothing else. His little chest filled out.
"Hey!" Fred screamed. "Don't you go on me, you understand?! Hey!" Fred looked over toward the hatch. "He's going to wake your parents. They're going to get you help." The words meant nothing to the little boy or the angel. Not even twenty seconds had passed, and it had felt like a small lifetime.
"I don't want help, Fred. I'm fine, now that you're here."
"I don't care. C'mon, Jack!"
Henry reached for the little angel's hand, which he clasped forever more.
"My angels. Love you, Fred."
"I love you too, Henry," the little angel whispered.
"Can I come home with you now?" the boy asked, closing his eyes.
The angel closed his eyes.
"Jack!"
Jack arose through the hatch, a second before Fred called again.
"I'm here!" he repeated over and over and over. "I'm here. I'm here. I'm here. Give him to me Fred, quick."
Fred gave over the boy reluctantly. Jack held his head close to his chest and floated down the ladder and into the living room, the boy's spirit in his arms. The little one was not even a breath behind. The cold air pulled down by his wings was drawn into the house. His parents were right there, running frightfully down the hall.

{ My Guardian Angels Jack & Fred }

Jack set the boy down in the recliner, and the two spirits took position as guardians on either side of him. The boy fell asleep again.

A slow wind billowed over the rooftop, agitating the makeshift guidepost antenna; the backwards *N* slowly flickered away, until it too died like the rest of the letters.

{ Chapter 43 }

Grave Disturbances

Over Connecticut, Belle was hit by such utter grief that she simply fell to the ground behind Kristie's grandmother's house. It wasn't the first time in these many long months that she had fallen. It was all coming to pass. She heard the voices that assailed her senses on the flight down from heaven; they all made sense now. Belle gathered herself up, tears rolling down the cheeks of her precious angelic face. She reached into the torn pocket of her beautiful velvet dress and found her bell smashed to jagged porcelain pieces.

At Wingdings, most of the angels were suddenly called away. They lifted up into the skies like small white orbs streaking past the corners of your eyes. Hundreds, even more than that.

Van Fleet's entire tray of empty glasses slid off his left hand, crashing onto the rooftop; something James Van Fleet has never done, before or since. The crash permeated the air, and it seemed like angels everywhere heard its fearful sound, for they all looked up wherever they were. James turned to the few patrons of Wingdings, then to his bosses, trying to put words to his disbelief and horror. One glass rolled along the breadth of the pitched roof and fell softly, five stories down to the frozen pavement. It crashed, a million crystal slivers dancing on moonbeams. The sound caught the attention of a passing human security guard, who rubbed his cheek and marveled at the strange sensation of sadness he felt on his graveyard shift.

Van Fleet pulled his mop close to him, almost like a trusted walking stick, the only secure thing at his touch, and he held it for what seemed like an eternity, uneasy. Looking up from the roof's vantage, the sky suddenly appeared wide—bigger than it had been. Clouds rolled in and the world was changing color about him. He turned his gaze to the pink flowing gown that flapped loudly in the breeze, as the angel wearing it rushed across the café with extreme haste.

Flo appeared visibly frightened, searching frantically to find her sister.

"Ida! Ida! Id—"

Ida appeared, with her crochet work in hand, terribly nervous, holding her big sister by the hands. "Flo? Flo, what's the matter, honey?"

Flo was trembling with fear. The younger one took her sister's face in her hands and held her steady.

"What, what…tell me what's wrong! What's the matter?" Ida asked straight away.

"Oh, God, I was right. I dreamt about it. I was right!"

"Right? Right about what?"

"Their boy, their Henry. Oh, Lord Ida, it's terrible…it's terrible."

"What happened? Tell me."

Flo looked away, lost. "They'll be crushed. My little angels won't recover from this."

Ida's eyes widened. She raised a hand to her lip, looking in her sister's eyes as if she understood. Ida opened her mouth to speak an unspoken word—a word that just couldn't come out.

Flo nodded in recognition. "Go. Go get Sidney…and go get the rest of the gang. Bring them back, no matter where they are now."

Ida turned to leave, strength and determination on her face.

"Ida," Flo called. She spun around. "What if we can't help him?" she whispered.

The young angel looked into Flo's eyes.

"Then we'll take him home with us tonight," she said so innocently.

Flo sighed, "Please hurry. There isn't much time left." Ida looked at her for a moment, then dashed off.

The control tower was buzzing with angelic traffic. Artie's switchboard became silent…then started up in a flurry. It had done so several times these many long moments of the night. The board quieted itself again. The campus sat in silence despite the goings-on of those above.

He looked at one of the multiple lighted blips on his board. They had all gone out, except one.

He stared, perplexed. "Who is this?"

"Mr. Artie?" a deep, aged voice called from the controller's board.

"Yes, Mr. Foster?"

"Mr. Artie, I think we're in a lot of trouble," he said simply, with the resonance of Louis Armstrong's singing voice.

Artie rubbed his nose and looked down.

"I think you're right, Mr. Foster."

A ripple was sent throughout the angelic community like a stone falling into the waters; only instead of a gentle wake, the stone had caused a veritable tidal wave to brew, and it was only heartbeats away from crashing down upon everyone.

His duties spent, Van Fleet looked upward, for what exactly, he did not know. Maybe some sign of something. And a sign was indeed granted. The Archangel Raphael flew over. And Van felt himself swallowing his own heart, as if that were possible.

"Oh, boy," James went.

Inside the house with the yellow awning…

"What were you doing up there, Henry?" his mother asked, standing before him. Henry, exhausted, just shook his head.

He smiled. "I knew they'd come back."

His father bent down and hoisted the boy off the chair, walking down the hall and placing him atop the upside-down mess that was once his bed. His mother sat down beside him.

"Come here, Henry. Let me feel your head," she said sternly.

"I'm fine, Ma. I have to ask them…" Henry said quietly.

"Just come here," she repeated, wearing the face of caution.

She pressed her hand against him, then kissed his forehead as if she were double checking her suspicions.

"Ma, I have to…"

"You're roasting, Henry. Come to the bathroom, I want to take your temperature."

"What's wrong?" his father asked.

"Feel him. He's burning up!"

Dad's face became a worried mass of emotions.

Mom jumped off the bed and lifted her son up into her arms.

"Get the car. Get it quick."

A strange thought touched the boy.

"I'm never going to see Kristie again."

Mom turned to Dad, breathless. "Hurry. There's no time to lose."

{ Chapter 44 }

Green Lights

"Just say 'Jack & Fred,' and even if you don't see us, we'll be right by your side."

"No matter what?" Henry asked.

"No matter what," Jack reassured.

The car hit a bump in the road and kept moving. The boy's eyes opened slightly, and his mother looked down at him. He lay there in her lap as she petted his soft face. Mom had dressed him very quickly, as his father got the stubborn station wagon started. Henry felt very warm and lightheaded. He barely remembered getting into the car, except for feeling the wind, which was so cold and strong that night. But he was used to it by now. The snow was falling steadily. It seemed strange to get into the car so late at night. He was so used to going to school during the daylight hours.

The station wagon drove on, speeding through deserted streets, rolling over the snow-powdered, white avenues. Mom kept him wrapped in a blanket on their journey. Henry could only watch as shadows cast from the passing streetlights above played across the car's front seat. As they drove on, the same monotonous shape kept appearing. The shape always danced up across and over the seat back. It was always haunting, like the shadowy creature in the dream. But in light of that, the boy realized that the cast shadow was not that of a specter. It was his own...his own shadow. Henry grinned at the realization that he had nothing to fear anymore. It was all behind him. He shut his eyes and dozed off. The shadows of angel wings were cast alongside that of the boy's.

Above the red station wagon, Jack & Fred raced on. The flew ahead to make sure all of the traffic lights had changed over to green before they had reached them; they also made sure that the few scant cars driving around at the odd hour were well out of the way of the big red station wagon as well.

The angels arrived at the emergency room entrance of the hospital moments before Henry and his family. They came soaring in for a landing, majestically, as if gracing the world with their beauty for the first moment ever, eagle wings and all. One could scarcely say they appeared as small, cute cherubs. Hardly. They seemed as mighty and as far and away magnificent as their larger brethren—beyond anything that has ever passed before human eyes. They wore stern, brave faces with interminable resolve, steady in their eyes.

The revolving red emergency beacons from the incoming ambulances bathed the angels in flashing crimson light, and they looked as though they could turn the world upside down with their very thoughts. Patients were being rushed in on gurneys, and their guardian angels stuck closely to them on the way. For the first time, Jack & Fred knew what that was like. The little angels supported the limp necks of their beloved, standing by them, massaging their brows, whispering words of safety and comfort to them continuously. But they all looked up when Jack & Fred passed through.

The big red station wagon came to a grinding halt in front of the emergency room terminal. The angels all stared in anticipation as the boy's father carried his son into the hospital, with his mother running beside them. Every angel knew what the boy meant to Jack & Fred, and they felt saddened that the first time they got a chance to see him, the boy was crippled by fever and sickness. They nodded solemnly and made the sign of the cross, sending their prayers to heaven. They prayed that this special boy would live to tell his tale.

The boy was rushed inside. And when Jack & Fred turned the corner, they were astounded. Unseen to the parents and boy, an entire honor guard of angels stood like centurions, facing one another from across the corridor, lining the entire breadth of the hallway. The twins, Terry and Bethany, old friends of the pair, took time away from their human charge to be there for their former teachers. Fred nodded to them both. There were thousands of luminescent faces, all of which Jack & Fred knew by name. Friends, brothers, and sisters one and all. And they were here at their time of most need. That's what it all meant in the end: helping, caring, and loving one another.

"Paging Doctor Cipaletta to the emergency room, immediately."

{ Chapter 42 }

In the Hands of the Angels

Henry's parents stayed by the boy's side throughout the night.

Jack & Fred, though invisible to them, stayed beside him too. His temperature was still dangerously high, and the fever was getting worse. The angels remained with their boy, stroking his hair and face, making sure that the blankets covered him throughout the night.

The night nurse insisted that Henry's parents go home and get themselves something to eat, perhaps take a nap. But they didn't. His parents decided to stay; they would take shifts. One watched while the other rested. Henry's mom was a nurse, and it was professional courtesy that allowed them both to stay past visiting hours the length of the dark night. The hour was so terribly late. The nurse took a moment to fix the boy's bed and straightened up the room. Outside, the snow had all but eclipsed the window. She got a blanket for the boy's mother as well. The nurse looked down upon the small child and prayed to the Lord.

"A shame, such a terrible shame," the nurse said quietly to herself.

Heat radiated off the child's brow. And for the slightest of moments, he stirred. It caught Jack & Fred's attention. Then nothing.

The boy was still, breathing in slight, gentle rhythms; his stomach moving up and down softly. His little arm was tethered to an IV. Henry's mom and dad looked over their boy, just to the side of the angels.

A nurse spoke to the parents, though the little ones could not hear what she was saying. Their boy was sick. A doctor with a clipboard and thin black spectacles on her nose led the boy's parents outside. Mom lagged behind, kissing the boy gently on the forehead.

Fred moved closer to his Henry and rubbed the boy's face with the back of his hand softly—almost forever. He began sobbing uncontrollably but smothered himself with his own hand, covering his mouth, quivering through tear-soaked eyes.

"Oh God, Jack. He was so...*cold.*"

Jack took the boy's hand in his own and put the other on Fred's shoulder.

"He needs you," Jack whispered. Fred choked back his grief and clasped Jack's hand, blinking the tears from his eyes.

"He needs *us,*" the little one replied.

The nurse glided by again. She finished straightening the boy's room. She adjusted the small one's pillow, keeping him just so. Comfortable. At peace. The nurse looked thoughtfully at the boy, unaware of his angels. She reached into her pocket and took out a green scapula and kissed the icon.

"*Immaculate Heart of Mary, pray for us, now and at the hour of our death... Amen.*" Then placed it around the boy's head.

She ran her fingers through his hair.

"So little," she sighed and walked outside, closing the light on her way. Jack & Fred glowed in the darkness, keeping watch over the boy like a divine nightlight, never deviating their glance for a moment. And for *just* a moment, the boy stirred again. He rolled over and laid perfectly silent.

Henry saw himself floating head-over-feet in an empty, hazy pink place—like he was adrift in the fuzzy insides of a great octagonal room. He saw his body tumbling over and over. And for the first time, his body felt free—no sensation in his fingers or hands or feet, as if a great weight had been lifted from the whole of his self. He was free to go. *Free.* His mind was in a complete dizzying euphoria—a warm brightness in his senses—and all he did was tumble.

He was weightless; falling in slow motion like the snow outside the window pane.

"*Jack & Fred,*" he whispered as he turned around to his right and saw one of the angels falling along with him. Henry gently reached out to him as he drifted weightlessly in the air. A light shone down upon him and he was pulled toward it.

The little glowing person extended his arm—a small, chubby arm. When Henry got a hold of it, he felt at peace, he felt safe, and he would not let go. For some reason, he could not see the little one's face. He closed his eyes for a second and felt the warmth of the other angel; it ran across his face like a whisper. The boy looked down at the glowing arm and saw his hand, which shone in golden splendor. A small voice from one of the glowing people below called up to the boy and the other.

"*Do you have him?*" the voice from below called.

"*I have him,*" the little voice that was connected to his hand said, "*And I'll never let him go.*"

The glowing person's grip grew tighter, but it felt as gentle as snow.

Henry felt the warmth radiating from the little person and smiled. Henry opened his eyes and looked toward the light, and the light smiled back at him. The light outlined the face of a small cherub. It was Fred. And to his left, Jack had appeared by his side as well. The boy hugged his angels, and they carried him away. They floated upward…together.

{ Chapter 46 }

And That's What It's All About

And when the boy opened his eyes...his journey upward to the light, had stopped. He had to ask them:

"Will you be my guardian angels, Jack & Fred?"

Fred stood with a shocked expression on his face, his mouth agape, his eyes wide. He quickly looked at Jack, whose heart sunk with a gulp.

"You..." the little one started to ask Henry, but he could not find the words to speak. "Do you mean it, Henry? Your guardian angels?"

Jack moved closer and put his hand on Fred's shoulder, for he had a feeling in his heart that this was all truly happening.

"Yes, Fred. I want you and Jack to be my guardian angels. Even if they reassign you, you'll always have a place to fly to. You'll always have *me*."

Fred began shaking and he looked down at the floor, mumbling in a little voice, "I can't believe this, Jack. I can't. I just can't."

Jack's grip on Fred's shoulder tightened, holding his friend near.

"Fred," Jack whispered, "Fred, he means it. He really does. Henry, you asked us what no other person ever did."

The little one lifted his head and had tears in his eyes. "I know. He *does* mean it. After all this time...and all those faces that just looked through us when we helped them. Always invisible to them...but you found us. And you didn't care if we were small, either. You *always* believed."

The boy smiled. "And I always will, Fred. I couldn't let you go."

Fred smacked the boy against the leg.

"OW!!! What...what the heck? FRED!"

Jack chuckled, smacking the boy against the other leg.

"Yeah, Fred!" Jack mocked, winking at his partner, doing the exact same thing to the boy. "Don't (smack) hit the kid!"

The angels spent untold minutes whacking the kid across the puss with their wings doing the whole "whoops-we're-sorry" routine all the way.

"JACK, FRED!!! WHY ARE YOU HITTING ME?!!"

The little one put his hands on his hips. "You pull a stunt like that again, you get Jack and I that scared like that again kid, and we'll kill ya!"

"GEEZ, SORRY!!!"

Jack agreed. "Well you should be!"

Fred leaned closer to the boy. "Henry, are you sure you really want us? We are kinda small, right Jack? We're not Hercules unleashed here."

"Yeah, Fred you're right about that. We are kinda small," Jack said softly. Fred raised an eyebrow surprised at his easy agreement.

"I don't care," Henry said, as he reached for his angels. The cherubs lifted him high in the air and hugged him nearly popping the IV out. Henry whispered in their ears, *"I love you Jack & Fred."*

The angels wore smiles that shone all the way to heaven. They hugged their boy and would never let him go.

"Now what'll happen to you?" the boy asked.

A beam of sunlight poured through the night and snow-covered glass and pointed down at the angels in one simple beam, like a spotlight. It stayed there for a moment. Then the light spread out and enveloped the boy as well.

The light spoke to the angels.

"Yes sir," Jack said. "No. Alright. Yes...Yes sir, I am sure."

Jack looked at Fred, calm as can be.

The little one stepped up. "Yes sir, I'm here," Fred whispered. "He's the one we've waited for all these years." Fred looked at the boy. "Lord, he's the *something wonderful* that we've always dreamed of. Could we stay, please?"

"Yes sir," Jack replied to the light. "We would. Yes. We would give up everything for him. Yes. Really? Nice! Thank you...what? No sir, we're ready to go now. I know she needs the containers back."

"They're under our wall!" Fred yelled up at the light.

Henry tugged at Jack's wing. "Is he cool with you staying?"

"Hang out a sec. He does things in His own time. That includes conversations, Hen. He was just asking about Aunt Amelia," Jack whispered to Henry. "Old friend of ours, makes delicious dinners. Lovely woman. We hog all her containers. She's been bustin' the Big Man's chops about…Yes, sir, I am listening!" Jack swallowed as the little one elbowed him.

The boy snapped back to attention and shut up as well!

Fred urged his partner in a harsh whisper. "Jack, ask 'em! Make sure it's all right?!"

Jack pushed the little one, nearly shouting above their whispering conversation. "Okay, you pain in the…uh, SIR! Sorry! Sir, this is our boy here. If you'll grant us this blessing, we'd like to take up permanent residence at his home, or wherever it is his life takes him." The light blinked. "Yes, sir. Guardian angels. He asked us."

Jack & Fred smiled at the boy.

Jack continued. "And when it's time…well, then we'll take him home with us. But not today…"

The little one gave his two cents. "Yeah God, don't kill 'em. We don't want to turn this into one of those Hallmark 'I'm dying for the holidays' movies.' I can't stand those." The light blinked vigorously in agreement. "What? *I KNOW!!!* Right? Sheesh."

Fred peered over at Jack as the light thought for a moment, and then it spoke to them again. It asked them something about one of their little past "incidents."

They listened intently. Jack grabbed Fred by the shoulders and shoved him forward. "Tell him, quick!" he grumbled out of the side of his mouth.

Fred called out, somewhat audaciously even for him. "The air traffic controller. Marty. Yes, we remem…No sir. It was more of a facial tick sir, not a stammer." Fred bit his lip, swatting Jack, as the light got brighter. "Sir, if I could…uh-huh. Uh-huh. Well not really. Lemme tell ya why Lord…"

Jack fell into Henry's arms, clutching his chest.

"He's arguing with the Big Man, oh…Lord!" The light turned its attention to Jack. "No sir! I was talking (gulp) to the boy! Sorry!"

Fred debated, "I'll give you that, Lord. Yes…I, I…uh-huh. Okay. No…it's…it's a personal taste thing. Hey, you're the Boss. I'm just a little fellow. Uh-huh. Well, it's like this. For me, they taste different."

Jack turned to the boy and frowned. What were Fred and the Big Man talking about anyway?

The little one explained. "Yeah Lord, I do think they're better. Granted, you have the other one that has the string for carrying. I'll grant you, they get an A+ for portability. Yes? Oh, but of course, I like the animals. I saw it! YES! The Christmas one, right? Yes, it is green. They're making one with baby animals now; is that right? It *is* right. Interesting. Was that on your say so? Of course. You're right. That was a silly question. The ones you already have are first cuts. I'm just saying I like the other ones. Okay…um, Lord, I don't mean to hold you up, but one thing? The boy. Can we go back with him? Thank you, Lord. Thank you…with everything we have, with all that you've given us. *Thank you.* Yes. Love you too. We'll give Peter a call. And we'll return Aunt Amelia's containers. Will do. Sorry she bugged you. I *know* he's excited. Yeah, they all are. Yes. Yes sir. I do. We promise. Hmm? Yes sir? Oh, it's called *Quietly Chamomille*. Soothes the belly. You're welcome, sir. And sir, again…thank you. Merry Christmas!"

"Thank you, sir," Jack yelled, waving and blowing a kiss. "Yes we are blessed sir," the angel said looking at the boy. "It is! It is the bestest Christmas present *ever*…"

The light shone down on the boy and glowed brightly for a moment.

"Thank you, God. Thank you for choosing me. I'll make you proud," the boy said. The light smiled. "And thank you for my angels. I'll cherish them forever."

And the light zipped back into the sky, illuminating the clouds.

"Wow," the boy said.

"Whew!" Jack went, rubbing his brow.

"What on Earth was that all about?" Henry asked.

"Tell him," Jack said.

"What…what's what?" Fred pointed. "Oh. God disagrees with me."

"Oh brother," Henry went.

"No. He likes the Barnum's."

"Barnum's?"

"Animal crackers. Just like Jack."

Jack frowned.

"Heh…no wait," the little one corrected. "I just got that. No, no…I mean God likes the Barnum's like you Jack. You have good taste!"

Jack winked and smiled with an "I told ya so" kinda puss.

The boy blinked in disbelief.

"You argued with God over animal cookies?"

"No, no. I didn't argue at all," the little one said, pointing a finger of authority. "He's the Big Man. I'm only the little one. He likes Barnum's? Barnum's are the stuff. You think I'm going to argue with Him over… anything? Uh…no! *I'm fresh sometimes, but I ain't stupid!!!*"

The boy smacked the bed. "My Dad likes the Barnum's."

Jack added. "He's in good company."

"Can we go home now?" Fred asked.

"To heaven?" the boy wondered.

"No, silly. The house with the yellow awning. That's our home. We have a home now. Thanks to you Hen."

The boy said, "My gift was not only my imagination. It's also you. My imagination allowed me to believe."

"Nah," Jack replied. "That was your heart kid."

The boy smiled. "That's what I'll do. I'll write a story about you and me someday."

"We know," the angels said.

"And I'll tell everyone about what you look like, and where you've been, and how you argue."

"And how," the little one suggested, "he starts it all the time," he said smiling at Jack.

"Or how *he's* always hungry," Jack added, smiling back at the little one.

"And about this night," Henry said.

"We know," the cherubs said again.

"And how do you know all this?" Henry asked.

"Call it divine intuition," Fred winked. "A little bird told us. A dove, more like it."

"Still a buster, you are," Jack said, shaking his head.

"Guys! What if I go to sleep and forget all this when I wake up?" Henry asked.

"You won't forget Henry," Jack said. "You faced your fears and you've won. It's time to move on with your life."

"No, wait! Just tell me. How am I, you know...How am I going to know if what I write is okay? How am I going to know if it's all right with you guys?"

Fred put his hand on Henry's shoulder. "When the time comes, we'll just tap you on the shoulder and you'll know it's us, and you'll know it's all right. If you're ever in doubt, just follow your heart and it will find us."

"Will I ever see you like this again?" Henry asked.

"If you look, you'll find us, Henry," Jack said.

The boy sighed. "I *know*, Jack. But will I ever like, see you and Fred the way I see other people."

"Maybe, Henry. You do have that gift," Jack said.

"But if not," Fred told him, "Don't be discouraged. We'll always be in your dreams, in your heart, and especially in your stories."

The angels hugged the boy.

"Goodnight, Henry."

With that, Henry awoke and found himself in his hospital bed. It was odd, he thought that he was already wide awake. But there he was...and they were gone. He turned over on his side, closed his eyes, and rested peacefully. His fever was broken, and his sickness was dissipating with the nighttime skies above. *Fading away.* The nurse and the doctor stood watch over the boy, amazed. Then they left the room and let Henry's parents talk with the boy.

It was early morning. Mom and Dad had never left the boy's bedside since the night before. They were there as Henry woke.

"Hi," his mother whispered. "How do you feel?"

"Exhausted, but not hot like before."

"The doctor said your fever broke," his father said.

"Mmm-hmm," Henry said and faded back into sleep again. His mother and father looked upon their son and were grateful for the miracle that had occurred before their very eyes.

{ Chapter 47 }

And Then, the Twist

Jack & Fred were compelled to fly outside to the hospital rooftop. It was Christmas morning and a blizzard had fallen over the course of the night. The world was enveloped in snow dunes and glistening trees. For a moment, heaven seeped out of its portal and spread its beauty across the once gray and sullen land. And it was right there before their eyes. For once, everything was perfect.

St. Peter was waiting in a crisp white suit as a dome of light blocked off the few snowflakes that fell all around them.

"I know," Jack said. "We violated every rule in the book and you're still ticked at us, right?"

The little one stepped up with his partner, clapping him on the shoulder. The old saint just stood there with his arms crossed over his chest.

"We love this boy, Peter. And you *can't* separate us now. We didn't mean to go over your head…but the Big Man says it's cool! Plus…"

Jack & Fred reached for plastic wings, the type which used to be given to children as souvenirs on airplanes, and held them out for the saint to see.

Peter shook his head, amused. "So. You two. You're a riot, you are. Break all the rules. Cause everyone grief. And they make you guardian angels?"

Jack stared unflinching. "And…what's your point?"

St. Peter strode up to them. The angels were rattled beyond compare, but they would not budge an inch. Peter looked at them, frowning. The angels stood, ready for anything. He jumped toward the pair to ruffle them and for the slightest of moments they thought they'd catch a beating. Then, without incident, Peter smiled warmly and mussed the hair on their heads.

"I'm so proud of you two. I knew you'd make it."

The little one kicked at the snow, glowing red. "Aww Pete!" He flew up and ruffled the saint's hair...then suddenly stopped, realizing it wasn't funny or okay when you did that to Peter. Jack slowly reeled Fred in, as if the angel was sent out on the clothesline of no return.

Jack consoled, "Sssorry, there...um...Peter. SAINT Peter."

"ANYWAY," Peter continued, reaching into his suit's breast pocket for a comb, fixing his hair back the way it was. "I knew you two were gonna get here someday. I will admit that I put the good word in for you. I just didn't know all of it."

"Well," Jack said. "Thank you for always backing us up. We know that..."

"You're welcome," Peter interrupted. "But that's not what I mean."

"You mean Sidney? He's a heck of a guy and..."

"No, Jack. That's not what I'm talking about."

Jack rubbed his head.

"I'm not following here...uh...Peter."

The little one looked around suspiciously. "Wait a tic, Pete. What do you mean you didn't know 'all of it'?"

"Well, Fred...Jack... I found out something very interesting just recently. Unfortunately it was too late to tell you once the ball started rolling. They never told me ahead of time. I wouldn't have let them do this to you had I known. As unsettling as this adventure had become, for the most part, it was all pretty straightforward...and then, the twist!"

The crowd from Wingdings surrounded the rooftop converging on the pair.

Peter shook his head. "I didn't want you to find out like this."

The little one and Jack went back to back, subconsciously preparing to brawl with the mob of other angels encircling the pair. As the boy once said, the angels were from the Bronx afterall.

Jack pointed at Peter and the others with a threatening finger. "If you tell us we've been on Candid Camera this whole time, brother, are we gonna be pissed!"

Peter shook his head.

The angels had fists at the ready. The little one and Jack spread their wings open in a fighting stance.

"So," the little one asked. "Who's first?"

"That's not going to be necessary," a voice called.

"Hey Jack!" the little one said aloud eyeing the other angels cautiously. "I don't know whose gonna catch a beatin' first. But all I know is, we're statused, people. We're official now. SO, you can *all* take a walk!"

Jack nodded. His eyes were sprinting across the faces of the angels approaching them. "That's right little one. It nullifies the orders you sent us earlier. So we are NOT going back upstairs. ISN'T that right St. Peter?"

"Honestly," Peter said with a smile. "Don't listen to me. Listen to *him*."

Fred looked around. "God?"

"Not quite," the same voice echoed again.

Jack stepped back.

"George?" He looked over his shoulder at the little one, then back at Peter, who seemed a bit put off by the whole thing. George sauntered forward. "What the hell are you doing here? We brought you home!"

"Well," George said in a somewhat more articulate-sounding voice. "I'm back."

Jack frowned. "You don't sound right either! You sound—"

"Smart!" Fred shouted. "And not Fredo Corleone smart either!"

Jack raised an eyebrow. "Oooh, Godfather reference."

The little one whispered. "It's a big story. Had to fit in at least one!"

"Good call pal. SO GEORGE…what's the story morning glory?"

Flo, Ida, and the Wingdings gang, appeared among the other angels and they moved closer, looking at the moron even more strangely than they usually did. When the pair realized that the others were here for reasons other than them, Jack & Fred stood down.

"George," Jack faltered. "This is serious here. We have no time—"

"I know this is serious, Jack."

The little one snapped up. "Now you listen here. Our boy—"

"Is going to be fine," George said with a wink.

The little one had his hands on his hips. "Did they drop something heavy on you? I can't understand why—"

"That's what I'm here for: to drop something heavy on everyone!" George glided across the roof's promenade, removing his new-arrival gown, revealing an Armani suit beneath. "Jack. Fred. I have to say, you surprised even me. I thought you'd catch on to it. You two are pretty quick on the uptake."

Everyone looked at the man; as puzzled as they usually were with the moron, something was still very wrong here.

"C'mon boys!" George said with a dismissing hand. "Put the pieces together here! You're smarter than this."

Jack looked at Peter. "What is he…?" And Peter nodded. "Oh God. Oh God, Fred."

The little one caught on immediately.

"No! No, no, no…you?…"

"Yes, yes!" George said gleefully.

"Oh my God!" Fred covered his mouth and Jack had to grab him.

Flo stepped from the crowd with Ida and Van Fleet by her sides.

"What?" she asked. "What is everyone talking about?"

George winked at Jack and the little one.

"You two got it. Finally!"

Flo pushed the pair aside. "Okay, I'm stupid here. What is going on?"

"He's a plant!" Fred yelled.

Paul stepped up from the crowd. "Yeah, he's sounds like a vegetable all right."

Ida eeped aloud. And Flo put her hand to her own mouth. She grabbed her little sister and slapped her hand across her mouth as well.

Flo shook her head in utter disbelief. "Noooo…Jack? He can't be! C'mon."

Jack shrugged at her.

The other rooftop angels backed away from Flo when she turned three shades past crimson. "You made them get this crazy for nothin'?! How selfish are you?"

George reassured them. "Nooo. Let me explain. First, it wasn't selfish. Second, it wasn't for *nothin'* my dear angels. It was for the boy. That's what this was all about. To see how far you two would go to save him. I'm what's called an evaluator. I follow angels and see if they're ready to become someone's guardian angel."

Jack bit his lip. "Why the whole charade?"

"Yeah!" the little one chided. "You could have just asked us. You didn't have to put us through all that agita for nothing!"

"But as I said before, it wasn't for nothing. You two, of all angels, should know that the things we experience in life aren't for *nothing*. It was all a part of the Big Man's plan. Jeremiah 29:11 hello? It's because, as you guys said before, the boy's *a one in a million*. He's very special. You needed to meet him, because he *is* going to write about you, write about us, at a time when the world will be upside down and inside out and they'll need us most. The Big Man arranged all of this. As you said and as we all know, He works in mysterious ways. I'm one of them."

Ida waved her hands over and over several pages behind the rest of the group.

"Wait a sec! Ya mean?! Huh! He's *not* a moron!

George smiled. "Thank you."

Flo stomped her foot. "You weren't even human."

"Well," George said, "I was at one time, but not recently."

Belle drifted down in a whisper, putting her hands on Jack's shoulders. He turned and kissed her warmly. She pointed at George. "He's already an angel. Been one for years now!"

The former moron snapped his fingers. "Right on the nosey, good lookin'! You got it!"

The little one stepped forward. "How? You even registered as human! We checked you in with Peter upstairs!"

George performed a small tap-dance shuffle and threw out his arms.

"How? Why, acting, my good man!"

"But we saw you get killed on the street. Right, Jack? We saw him get killed," he said to the other angels. "We're not crazy here!"

George guffawed. "We all scream for ice cream! Hee-hee. You saw me get hit by an ice cream truck. In December no less? And you weren't a little skeptical? Mister Softee. Ever see how slow they drive? And in Manhattan? I thought it a little farfetched at the time, but your penchant for desserts and sweets led you otherwise."

Jack shook his head. "But your tags—"

"Were the same tags I was born with. My real name is George Montoya. We…*doctored* the tags a bit."

"You can do that?" Jack asked.

"Oh yes, Jack. *They* can do anything. When I died, I had a landlady and a cat. The cow cat you saw. The one that followed you all the way from Manhattan to the Bronx, then to Westchester when you were at Wingdings! *Hellooo*. Did the cat take the six train to the Bronx, Jack, Fred? I think not! He's one of us too!" The little one frowned at George. "He's my little lookout. Here he is! Hellooo Cowy! Give papa some kitty-puss! C'mere!"

George lifted up the fifty-pound cat with some effort, nearly dropping him; he went nose to nose, snuggling with the odd, wall-eyed, yellow-pupiled creature, who seemed to dislike even its master, and jumped away.

Fred had the willies. "Still don't like that damn thing."

Jack nodded. "I heard that."

Ida slapped her legs. "Well," she announced popping her gum, "he can't be *all* bad. He's an animal lover!"

George winked at her, then sauntered up to Belle, grabbing her arm, attempting to twirl her. Belle wouldn't have it and nearly snapped his arm clean off. Jack loved her!

"Well," George continued. "Everything was true up to a point. I died suddenly. It was years ago, but it happened. Know how? I slipped and fell on a patch of ice, smacking my head. Boom! Last thing I thought as I laid on the pavement was 'you moron.' Then I went out like a light. What a way to die! I wasn't sick a day in my life. I was going for the bus, heading out to Hollywood to be professional actor. I had an agent and everything. Did a whole bunch of off-Broadway stuff. Plays. Like this!" he shrugged. "When I came to, I was in heaven. And someone told me I had a job to do. I said okay. I mean people, the name 'Morano' was a dead give-away. Seriously. Could you think of a more perfect name for someone so daft?"

Flo pointed an angry finger at him. "But if you're an angel, no matter what tags you messed with, Jack & Fred would've seen the difference. They've got more experience than any of us. They can see people *disguised* as angels. They do it all the time."

"Yes, my dear, that was a tad challenging," the former-moron said, gathering Flo's hand in his own and kissing it, much to Fred's chagrin, and Flo's as well. He turned to Jack & Fred. "Think back my dear double-act. In all the excitement, no paramedics ever showed up, did they? They tended to Wallace. But I was killed, and nobody notices, even in Manhattan? No one makes a phone call? For crying out loud!" George said with knee-slapping fervor. "I was disguised…even the ice-cream truck wasn't even real!"

"How?" Jack asked.

"CGI, my little friends! Computer-generated images. It's all the rage years from now. Star Wars, George Lucas? Surely you know him. His special fx division, *Industrial Light & Magic*, they have very bright angels watching over them. Good stuff, huh?" George laughed. "They fooled you!"

Paul grunted, balling up his meaty hands into fists. "Youuuuuu bastard."

"Paul, Paul!" they yelled, holding back the behemoth by a thread.

George continued, "There were also little hints, nuances if you will…"

"On the train," Jack conceded. "You said you heard Henry's parents praying. New spirits can't do that."

George nodded.

Fred shook his head woefully.

Jack asked. "Who else was in on this?" He peered upward hoping no one would look back.

"Her!" Sidney yelled, dragging Madison along by the scruff of her neck.

"Very good, Sidney," George smiled. "How'd you know?"

"Little things. Maddie always came and went. The delay in messages, especially from Peter. St. Peter always keeps in touch. The time she was checking herself out in the mirror. You forgot these!" Sidney pulled out a pair of dark-rimmed glasses. "I found them in a drawer!"

Fred frowned. "Wait. Those are Gabrielle's ugly glasses."

"I actually forgot to slip in my contacts that day," the girl said.

The old saint stepped forward. "That's just it Fred. There is no *Gabrielle* either," Peter said raising an eyebrow, much to George's chagrin. "Sidney and I compared notes. Twins? No way. My Gabby also has cold hands all the time like Madison. She was warming them on a mug of coffee she gave me. It's a tick some angels have when they come over to the other side. They forget they're angels and still have human traits, like being cold all the time. People can have traits like that…but two of them having the same preoccupation with cold? Unlikely. They may be twins, but they're still individuals. And the other slip-up was the perfume."

Sidney surmised, "Maddie always wears *Obsession*. I'd know that malodorous aroma anywhere. It still hangs in the air over my office. Maddie was wearing jasmine that day in the mirror." The barrister looked at George as if he wanted to put his lights out.

"And," Peter added with a certain justifiable grin. "We both smelled jasmine in the Louvre."

George shrugged. "So, they are twin sisters. They like sharing perfumes. So what of it?"

"Thing of it is," Sidney explained. "It's as elementary as no one has ever seen the two of them together. Identical twins never like being so far apart if they can help it. And upstairs and downstairs is a good distance apart. Madison was a good executive assistant, sure. But if you think about it, other than cooking, I usually keep my office in pristine order, Jack & Fred can attest to that, they've been in there enough times." The boys looked at one another. "Sorry fellas," Sidney excused himself and the angels shook their heads at the old lawyer.

The barrister continued, "So, she wouldn't need to be good at office work. The perfume, the black rims, the preening, worrying about her clothes—those are all Gabby traits that slipped through the Madison facade. This girl doctored the communications, the messages, the note cards, and Peter's log book."

St. Peter moved forward. "George, you were originally an entry in my book, and then your name disappeared."

"Why?" George asked, knowing the answer full well.

"Because when you died, they put you right to work and carried you into heaven through the pet door. The one we use for all the animals of all the people that pass on."

George tugged at his collar.

"They logged you in differently. I found you as an overdue in my book, but you were *checked in* as part of an alternate sub-index so that none of us would know. I initially found that, by accident. Gabrielle, or whoever she is—"

George grinned. "Sandra. That's her real name."

"*Sandra* doctored the book, but she forget that lil' index. Never did like office work huh, honey?" St. Peter asked. "It was a moot point for Jack & Fred to carry you back into heaven George. Belle was right. You were made an angel long ago."

The barrister shook his head at the angels. "Clark Kent trick. Just add glasses," Sidney said, slapping the ugly dark rims on Sandra's nose. "Hiding in plain sight. That's what my old man always said. I should have caught it. Just too many other things happening at the time."

Sandra looked at her ex-boss. "Don't beat yourself up hon. Dual personalities. Like it? One ruse was I hated office work and wanted to go shopping all the time, and played the hottie-secretary Gabrielle, for you Petey. And then the other side, where I played that anal-retentive millie named..." she threw her hands out, "*Madison*. C'mon Sidney. It wasn't all bad. I did genuinely like you."

"What does that matter now?"

"C'mon barrister. You know we were always friends, throughout it all. My mission was bigger than you. Bigger than any one of us. But I always did take care of you."

The barrister looked at her with a nod. "Yes you did."

George continued. "You are right, Sidney. If you weren't so immersed in taking care of the angels, you would've made the connections. Sandra did things like watching Sidney and Peter in the Louvre. Another set of eyes were always watching. And, yes, there are angels here, there, and everywhere. That answers your other question you two," the man said to Jack and the little one. "Peter was not involved either. Neither was Sidney. Back in the Louvre, unbeknownst to you fellows, Sidney gave a note card to a courier which said only his location and why he needed you immediately. Sidney was going to tell you that you were going to be separated by midnight Christmas morning, regardless if you found anyone or not. Guardian angel-wise, I mean. Sandra exchanged the note card the very second the courier took off. Instead of going to the barrister right away, we rerouted you. You received it and it told you to chase down Mr. Wallace, which would eventually get you to the boy."

Jack nudged the little one. "See, I told you! Oliver Stone crap."

The little one was furious. "Did you get Mr. Wallace drunk, too?"

George recoiled. "How could you ask such a thing, little one?! We don't harm people to facilitate the process."

Jack tossed his arms up. "Well, hell, we don't know what's real or not anymore!"

George folded his arms up. "Why do you think you two went tear-winging after a car? A car chase? Come on. Angels with your credentials doing one of those? They give the first-years those kinds of assignments. It was as you thought. Mr. Wallace took you right to Henry. Meeting me around the corner just made you stay long enough for the boy to see you. You were trying to carry me, and you overheard the kids, and that's when Henry saw you."

Flo asked. "What about Belle? What about Kristie?"

George smiled. "Henry needed to meet Jack & Fred so his story would make Kristie believe in Belle again."

Belle stood there with her arms crossed before her, and George caught her actually smiling at the thought.

"And," Flo continued. "What about Kristie?"

"I don't know. Not my job. I just make the introductions. Someone else connects the dots."

Flo persisted. "After all your long-winded explanations, you've got nerve saying that. Ha! And what about Jack and Belle?"

"That was really, well…that was an unfortunate side effect."

Jack smiled and grabbed her hand; Belle was equally beaming. Fred was rolling his eyes.

"Given Jack's rep, though..." George scoffed. "It didn't come as a huge surprise."

Belle frowned at George *and* Jack, who was raising his hands as if he was innocent...of *everything.*

The little one stepped up insistent. "But Flo wasn't in on this!"

George shook his head. "It would've been easier if she was, but no, she wasn't. Her concern for you, Fred, was genuine. I knew if I approached she'd tell you immediately. Woman loves ya!" Fred blushed three shades past fire engine red, but he grabbed Flo's hand anyway. George said, "Her loyalty to you outweighed anything else. It was nice of you to set Gabby—I mean Sandra—up with me, Fred. We actually had a reasonable excuse to speak and exchange notes. Ha-ha."

The little one shook his head, looking at Flo. "Yeah. I guess the clues were always there. Gabby or Sandra or whoever, let it slip at Wingdings. When I made my intro to George, she said 'he's a good-lookin' *angel.*' Sorry bud," he said to Jack. "My bad."

Jack shot daggers at George, as did the rest of the group.

Jack & Fred looked at the faces of the other angels, then at Flo and the gang at *Wingdings.* They turned to the senior man in charge, and St. Peter nodded at them. The old saint was so shocked that even *he* was not let in on this little play. But his joy at what was to come, outweighed his regret at being bamboozled. He winked knowingly at Jack.

"Well, George," Jack said, cleaning the pretend dust and soot off his hands. "Ya got us. Right Fred?"

"Absolutely, Jack. All these years we're out here flying around like we're the stuff on wings, and we get completely and totaled bamboozled, by an actor no less."

"A great actor, Fred!" Jack pointed out as the two sauntered toward George.

"A *great* actor, my friend!"

"Worthy of Shakespeare."

The little one frowned. "I was always more of a Neil Simon fan myself."

"As am I, little one. But yes! Totally!"

George was shining in his own light so brightly that he suddenly realized the angels had brought with them the entirety of the heavenly host. And they were ticked!

"You really are a moron, though," Jack said.

George reached for Sandra, and they started shuffling backwards. "What…me? You mean the role of George the moron, right? I'm just a guy called…"

"No," Jack shook his head, cracking his knuckles. "I mean, Fred said it originally. You *really* are a moron."

"No, Jack," Fred added puffing out his wings and cracking his neck. "More like a jackass."

George gulped. "No one likes a sore loser, little one…heh-heh."

"*Moron*," the little one repeated. "Did you actually think we were going to let this slide? Hmm? Moron!"

There was a low rumble, and the rest of the heavenly host had their arms out, converging on George and Sandra. They all said "moron" over and over, looking like zombies on the loose.

"Why do you insist on calling me that?!" George barked.

Belle pushed George backward. "Because after your assignment was officially considered over, you failed to consider what *we* were gonna do to the guy who put these two through hell for three days. Comprende, Georgie?"

Jack winked at her. "That's my girl!"

"But," George stammered. "I was on assignment!"

"*We* were on assignment," Sandra corrected.

"We know," Belle said.

George insisted, "The Big Man—"

The lovely angel sauntered toward him. "Works in mysterious ways. Yes. You've said."

"But Anabelle…"

Belle moved closer as the pack of angels behind her did as well. "I like the name, BELLE."

"Sure…uh, that sounds great Ana…uh…Belle! BELLE!" George had his hands out before him. "It was a plan to get Jack & Fred and the boy together no matter what! What's so wrong about that? I did my job! You should be thanking me!"

"US!" Sandra corrected again.

"We," George stammered, "had a plan!"

Belle grinned widely, immersing herself in the sheer joy of having the angelic armada backing her up. "It was a brilliant plan, George. Just brilliant. Absolutely. Right, Flo?"

"That's right, honey. George, you *do* know when you mess with my little fuzzies though…"

Fred shook his head. "Don't call us that, *please!* There are other angels around. GEEZ!"

"But I like calling you that!" Flo insisted out of the side of her mouth.

"If this is going to work woman, I refuse to be known as one of the lil' fuzzies! God! I am *so* embarrassed."

"Wait'll you see what I got cookin' back at Wingdings tonight handsome. *Don't* be so embarrassed."

Fred beamed. Jack looked over at him, shaking his head happily. "You dog," he whispered.

Flo corrected herself. "As I was saying," she continued as the angels backed the two culprits into the wall on the furthermost side of the roof. "You mess with my lil' cuties here," she turned to Fred. "How's cuties? Does *cuties* work for ya?"

"(Sigh) Cuties is fine."

"You mess with them, you mess with all of us."

George held his hands out again. "Okay, calm people. Calm. You're right; you win. I'm a moron."

"You are!" Flo said. "And more to the point, we don't like you very much."

George was frightened now. "Really?"

Belle shook her head.

Paul plowed forward. "Really!"

George gulped. *"Crap."*

Flo insisted, "We don't like you. And we don't like your little helper either!" Sandra grabbed George and hid behind him, to no avail.

Ida strode up. "Yeah! You, you, dopies!"

Flo shook her head. "Yeah, like she said."

"And ya know what Flo?" Ida continued, "I think those ugly glasses on *Sybil* the whackjob over there, stink too! Right people?!"

"Yeah," the angels grumbled. St. Peter nodded his head in validation.

Ida grabbed her sister. "Heya, Flo. Dontcha think sneaks and informers and liars kinda spoil the overall 'ambi-ances' of our restaurant, even though this is like an…um…hospital. And hospital food is like eww…icky and…stuff."

"Uh-huh."

Ida giggled. "Vanzy, what d'ya think?"

The ever-astute maître d' stepped forward speaking in a proper British voice. "I say, string 'em up by their Buster Browns and play a game of piñata."

"Yeah!" the mob of angels cried.

Ida snuggled up to him. "Oooh Vanzy, you're so forceful. Mmmmm."

Jack looked over at Fred and mouthed. *"Vanzy?"* Fred shook his head and shrugged.

George held out his hands as the angels' breath touched his face, they were all so close. "People, people. Now listen. I'm an angel just like you."

"No," Fred corrected, "You're Mr. Evalulator."

George protested. "Well yes! I *am* an evaluator. Do you know what that means? I have a duty!"

"Jack," the little one called. "I never met an evaluator. Does that mean anything to you?"

"Not a damn thing little one. An *evaluator*. And that one. She's a, a…"

"Schizoid!" Fred added.

"Yeah!"

Sidney raised a cocked eyebrow, grabbing Jack and speaking under his breath, "Girl *did* know how to cook though."

Jack whispered back. "True that." And they bumped fists.

Belle frowned at them both.

Fred shouted, "You made one crucial mistake, George. One thing you failed to understand."

"And what, pray tell, is that?"

"Jack and I…like the kid said, we're from the Bronx, and brother we don't play…we don't take crap from *nobody*. Guys!"

The angels surged forward like mad villagers on the hunt for Frankenstein's monster—without the torches and farming implements.

Jack smiled. "It is Christmas after all, George! Angels! Trow 'im down the chimney!"

The angels hefted the spirits up, crowd surfing them over to hospital's exhaust port and stuffed both George and Sandra inside. And when they could fit no longer, Paul made a running charge and sat atop the chimney, stuffing them in with his rump for good measure.

"Aieeeeeeeeeeeeeeeeeeeeeeeeeeeeeeeee!" they wailed.

Fred cringed, looking at the giant angel as his muscular rump squashed down on the flailing hands of their former associates. "That's—"

"Wrong, Fred." Jack shook his head in agreement. "So wrong!"

Van Fleet raised a glass, kissing his sweetie Ida. "Twist ending *this*, my good man!"

Paul smacked his hands clean and shouted "hey!" to the crowd who bellowed back in response. It was just what Paul did…

The giant looked around and the now masterless cow cat was there staring at him with those eyes. Paul nodded at the creature, and it smiled and jumped into his arms.

"Look at you my little Oreo cookie!" he said to it stroking its ears.

"Jack," the little one recoiled. "That's—"

"I know."

"The damn thing has human eyes!"

"Fred?"

"Yeah bud."

"You are *good* my friend."

"Nah."

"Yes you are."

"Nah."

Jack smacked his arm. "Yes you are!" He hugged the little one and they both smacked the heck out of one another, play-fighting.

"Yes, you are!"

Fred spun around. Bethany was standing there with her hands folded up before her. "Hiya boss. Remember us?"

She and her fraternal fair-haired, blondie-headed twin Terry, stood there humbled.

Fred hugged them both, but especially the little girl who was always a favorite of his.

She smiled. "We did good Fred."

The little one looked at their halos and gowns, noting they were guardian angels. "I'm so proud of you."

"We just wanted to say…thank you." She kissed him on the cheek. "You know, we…"

Terry continued his sister's thought. "…we wouldn't have missed this for the world."

She smiled. "You take care Fred. You too Jack."

Terry shook their hands. The pair stood there watching the young ones; they were once teachers and students, but now they were all equals, and it made them happy.

St. Peter strode up. "Fellas."

"Peter," Fred whispered. "The boy, he actually asked us."

"I'm so proud of you. Very good job boys…now, get your butts moving. You're guardian angels now fellas!" The angels beamed. "Go get your boy well again."

"Our boy?" Fred asked still amazed by it all.

"Of course," Peter said with a wink.

"Thank God," Jack whispered.

The old saint smiled. "Exactly!"

Across the promenade the barrister smiled, walking away from the celebration on his own. The handsome dark-skinned angel nodded happily to himself as he went back to his office.

Jack & Fred leaped in front of him.

"What?" Jack asked. "You don't say adios muchacho?"

The barrister, with a stern expression on his face, flashed them a duplicate of the note card they had been given regarding the boy and the redefinition of their duties. The pair looked at him for a moment. Sidney suddenly smiled and ripped the communiqué in half. He grabbed them both by the shoulders, laughing.

"And our wall?" the little one asked.

The barrister shook his head in disbelief. "You two, worry about a wall? YEAH! They're moving it…to the house with the yellow awning. Satisfied? HA!"

The two of them looked at one another and bashed fists together.

As they excitedly set off, Jack turned around abruptly.

"We never said thank you, Sidney."

The barrister shook his head. "You never have to. You know that."

The little one grinned to himself as Jack said, "Let us owe you one then."

The two looked at one another.

"What…" the barrister asked slowly. The angels wheeled Sidney around, pointing him at Paul in the distance. They motioned for him and his cow cat to move over…and behind the giant, was Sidney's long lost sister Sylvia.

The barrister's jaw dropped. He stood there speechless.

The angels smiled.

Sylvia walked over to her brother, her smooth skin and chocolate eyes gleamed in the bright light that was all about them. Tears rolled down the barrister's face but he could not speak.

"I hear you're looking for a new assistant," Sylvia said. "I've been waiting a long time to see you again Sidney. Remember the last day? You promised me lunch when we'd meet up again. Time to pay up 'barrister!'"

Sidney threw his arms around her, knowing in his heart, that he would never lose her again.

"How…?" Sidney asked.

"How come I'm here? Heart disease runs in the family Sids. Like brother, like sister."

"I shouldn't be so happy you…died that way. But oh my God, you're here!" Sidney grabbed her and twirled Sylvia high over the roof. "I have so *much* I want to talk to you about!"

She smiled, touching the side of his face. "We have an eternity to catch up."

Jack & Fred were already in the air when he whispered a breathless *thank you* to them. They waved and nodded back.

Jack said off-handedly, "I would love to hear somebody play 'Let it Snow,' but the Vaughn Monroe version."

"The one at the end of 'Die Hard?'"

"That's the one."

"You have very particular tastes Jack."

"I do, yes."

"Uh-huh."

St. Peter was dancing with the gang below, and the little one called out to him as the two of them swung by.

"Hey St. Peter, can we try something we never could do before?"

Jack added. "We always wanted to…"

The old saint rolled his eyes. "Go ahead!"

"Thanks, chief!" Fred saluted.

Peter shook his head.

Flo and Belle flew up to them and kissed them goodbye for now as they went back to the boy.

Ida screeched. "Hit it boys!" And the angels started playing Phil Collins *"Sssudio"* again.

The little one zipped ahead of Jack, both soaring high into the sky. "I still hate 80s dancing Jack, but I can't stop doin' it!"

"Darn catchy crap, ain't it Fred? C'mon, keep up. We're gonna be late!"

The angels danced above the hospital, and Ida screamed over the loudspeaker. "Raise the roof, people. Look out now!"

{ Chapter 48 }
We Did It!

Mom and Dad went downstairs for a cup of coffee and soon returned to their son's floor. As the elevator doors wheezed open with un-oiled, metallic strain, they saw two small children emerging from their Henry's room. One was taller, the other a bit shorter. Both of them wore corduroy pants and bright, colorful, wool sweaters up to their necks—with suspenders to hold everything in place. Henry's mother and father walked toward them instinctively.

The little one's eyes brightened.

"Hello ma'am, sir," the taller boy said.

"Hello, Henry's parents," the little one waved with a smile.

"Hey fellas," Henry's father said, in his own majestic way.

Mom knelt down to their level.

"Hi. What are you doing up here, little one? It's so early," she asked happily, holding him by the shoulders.

"We're doing *visitings*," the little one said, looking at Mom brightly.

"We wanted to bring our pal something," the taller boy said to Dad.

Mom took the little one's hands in her own.

"You're so familiar to me." She looked over at the taller boy, then back at her little friend. "You'll forgive me for asking this," Mom said, "but I don't know your names."

The taller boy's eyes rolled to the side. The little one did not want to risk a look.

Mom looked at them. Jack peered over at Dad.

Jack clenched down on his teeth. "I'm...um, I'm...Jack," he swallowed nervously, waiting to be swatted or caught or both.

Mom and Dad looked at him.

"I'm Ralphie," the little one said, sticking his little hand out to shake Mom's. Jack did as well, with Dad.

"Pleasure to meet you," Dad said.

Mom asked the little one. "Why is it, I feel like I know you?"

His eyes lit up with pure joy. "Maybe you do."

Mom shook her head. "I don't know where, but I *do*."

"You'll remember later on."

Jack looked at them with anticipation.

Dad said to them, "Henry's lucky to have such good friends."

The little one dismissed his words with a wave.

"Oh, we're not just his friends, we're his guardian ang—"

The taller boy coughed loudly, elbowing the little one with little regard for conspicuousness.

Mom looked up at Dad.

"Sorry?" she asked, confused.

The taller boy smiled. "He means we're his pals."

"Ralphie" put on a convincing, though partly embarrassed, smile.

Jack stood solid as the little one clipped him with the edge of his foot.

The taller boy showed his pearly whites.

"You two are just adorable," Mom said, as she started looking around. "Where are your mothers? They don't allow children your age up here by themselves this early. I don't think they allow anyone up here this early. Do they, John?" Mom looked to Dad.

"You tell me, hon. You're the nurse."

Ralphie's eyes got bigger. "Um..."

Jack's face got all scrunched up, bearing a startling resemblance to Popeye.

"Don't worry," Dad assured. "You're with us. Nobody's going to bother you." Jack looked at Dad. He was so proud of him. *No wonder why the boy loved them both so much.*

"Someone's waiting for you?" Mom asked, concerned.

"Um." It took a moment, but the taller boy thought something up quickly, and it was the truth. "Someone upstairs is *always* waiting for us." Jack smiled and stuck out his hand. "It was nice to meet you guys. Really nice…uh, ma'am, sir. We have to be going now, right Fred?"

Ralphie. Ralphie. Rats!

Jack's breath was pulled out of him. He suddenly felt that sinking feeling. Oops. (Oops nothin'! Jack knew deep down, it was intentional…and happily so.)

"Goodbye," the little one said, hugging the boy's mother.

Mom laughed, feeling the light of a thousand answered prayers there in her arms.

"Bye-bye, little one," she said, almost happily crying. She looked at the little angel in her arms. "You'll come by and visit us soon, promise?"

Fred smiled, feeling the same thing. "I promise Ma. And don't work so hard. You wear yourself out. People at home need you too."

Mom shook her head without words.

Dad ruffled Jack's hair; the parents were just compelled to embrace the brightened ones.

Henry's dad waved. "Take care, you two. And…thank you for being so kind to my boy," he said, looking at Jack.

"You're very welcome, Dad!" Jack said.

Mom stood up, looking at her boy's angels.

"I'll bake you guys cookies next time when you come over, all right?"

"Cookies," the little one's eyes grew wide. "Or…maybe," he swayed back and forth, "blueberry waffles?"

"Oh, don't worry, I'm sure you'll be seeing a lot of us," Jack said. "You can count on it. Especially for breakfast."

The two "children" held hands and walked out into the hall rather quickly, keeping up with the delightful charade.

"Take care now," Dad called as the children walked down the hallway.

The little one looked up at his partner and whispered, "My God, she bakes too. Talk about a lost art."

"Ssshhh," Jack chuckled. "Not yet."

"She makes great ziti!"

"I know!" Jack elbowed his partner. "Hey Fred, she green-lit the blueberry waffles!"

"YEAH BOY!" they shouted, bursting into laughter, and high-fiving one another.

Sunshine filled the hallway from the windows in every room on the ward. The children looked as though they were walking into a sunrise. Mom and Dad watched the vision down the hall, making their way to the exit.

Dad just couldn't keep still. "I'll be right back. I'll walk them back upstairs."

The man trotted down the hall, but when he turned the corner, they were gone.

A tall, thin janitor in his blues, stood mopping the floor, and on his nametag—*Van Fleet*—could be seen clearly.

Dad looked about in stupefied amazement, breathless.

"Did you—" he started.

"Just missed them," the man in the blue work clothes said. His astute, British tone was an unmistakable sound.

"Where'd they go?" Dad asked.

"Home," he said with a smile and a glimmer in his eye. It was like light dancing off swimming pool waters, but the reflected glow came from his work basin instead.

Dad looked at the man oddly as he dunked his mop in the strainer bucket. He wrung the mop and looked up at the boy's father.

"You might still be able to catch them," the janitor said. As he released his grip, the handle shot back and the strainer barked open. Dad mouthed "where" and the janitor nodded toward the stairwell door. "But I wouldn't count it," Van Fleet said, grinning. The man in the blue overalls never deviated his eyes for a second. And he nodded again, squinting with a smile. "Have a good one, huh?"

He gathered his mop up into the bucket, wheeling away on squeaky wheels.

Dad turned to the elevator doors.

"Wh..." he spun back. The squeaky wheels sounded but no one was there.

"What in..." Dad ran up the stairs, but the only thing up there was the roof. He punched through the door. The hatch slowly pulled back, latching itself into place—the red lettered, AUTHORIZED PERSONNEL sign, flaring in the alcove flood lights above him.

Henry's father did a 360 degree spin up on the roof, running...stopping, moving, hands falling to his sides; then he looked up and understood. There was sunshine...and laughter, and the snow around him was all melted, despite the city looking like a winter wonderland with its collected frosty feet of blizzard fallout.

Dad stopped for a moment and closed his eyes. He could hear the ocean...

Then, he couldn't get his feet under him fast enough and tripped several times before reaching the stairs again. He looked back over his shoulder, just in case he didn't miss anything. Lord, how excited he was!

Mom watched the nurse, from the night before, straightening up Henry's room, maneuvering around him as he slept peacefully.

The nurse noticed the change in the boy's color, with a grin and a fluff of a pillow, which she placed gently beneath the boy's head.

"Are you feeling better today?" the nurse asked the boy's mother in a whisper, knowing the answer herself.

Mom shut her eyes and mouthed "much" with great emphasis.

"Good, good," the nurse said, moving to the doors so they wouldn't wake up the little boy. "He looks very peaceful. So do you."

"Please," Mom rolled her eyes. "When they're sick, you're sick with them," she said with her hand instinctively over her heart.

"Don't tell me," the nurse waved. "I have four babies. One gets sick, they all get sick. And they laugh, but meanwhile I'm choking to death!" she said, smacking her hip.

"I know, I know."

"I still can't get over this one, though. I've been an RN for twenty-three years now, and I ain't never seen a boy as far gone as he was come back...like, like it was nothing. His fever broke last night, but before that he was all tossing and turning. I knew he was getting worse, and I prayed. Lord, did I pray. Then, suddenly, without warning, he turned over and fell fast asleep. It was as if the weight of the world had been taken of his shoulders." One could see the passion in the gentle, though staunch eyes of the caretaker. "We were all worried," the nurse said. "We didn't think he was going to make it."

Mom's eyes became all bleary, and she looked off. "Neither did I."

Dad rushed in. The nurse spotted him half a second before Mom did, and she looked at the running man with a confused face.

"John, what's the matter?" Mom asked.

"The children Mary," Dad huffed. "They're gone."

"You missed them."

"No. They went upstairs."

"Upstairs?" the nurse interrupted, with loud commitment in her voice. Henry was stirred by the noise. She pulled the parents out into the hall, looking over at the boy, "The only thing upstairs on this hospital is the roof."

"Yes! The roof!" Dad echoed. "That's what I'm talking about." Then he noticed something on the table. "Who brought those?" he asked, moving into the room with determined strides.

Mom frowned. "They weren't just there!"

"I don't know," the nurse said, reading her thoughts.

Two stuffed animal friends sat on the table.

"Look what they left him! Aren't they the sweetest little things!" Mom declared.

"I'm sure they are," the nurse said, with a hand on her hip.

Dad appeared confused. "What do you mean? You were right here. The two kids just came in ten minutes ago."

"No one was here, sir, and I've been in here for the last fifteen-twenty minutes, tidying up. No one came in; no one went out. And there's no visitors allowed up here till eight o'clock anyway." The nurse looked at Henry's mom, as if she should know that because she was a nurse herself. "And they don't allow young children without a guardian or such."

"Then who—" Mom started to say.

"Come here, Mary," Dad insisted. Mom and the nurse went over.

Both stuffed animals had tags on their collars. Henry's mother scooped up the dog and Dad looked at the bear and he read what was written on both. The nurse peered over Mom's shoulder as she read aloud:

"Dear Henry, just a little souvenir of how much fun we had together. Remember, no matter where you go, or how old you get, we will be with you. Always!

Love,

Your guardian angels,

Jack & Fred."

The parents looked at one another, then turned to their boy who had a smile across his sleeping face.

"Jack & Fred," Mom said with a tear in her eye. "They're your angels."

"They said it," Dad said, unflinching. "Taller one's name was Jack. And the little one, called himself Ralphie."

Mom looked blissfully distant, fixated on nothing in particular.

"No," she corrected. "Fred. His name is Fred. Jack called him that by accident. Didn't you hear him?" Mom asked, astonished. "The ziti, remember? The hungry angels. *Breakfast?* Blueberry waffles. The ones in Henry's story. They are real. He knew it all the time."

Before Dad could say anything, he and Henry's mom heard cherubic laughter coming from down the hallway. They knew who it was, and they knew their prayers had been answered. Henry awoke as the laughter sounded throughout the hospital. Everyone heard the sound, for their hearts were listening. The angels would play a role in the nurse's life, too, from now on. This is this first time she'd ever thought about angels being real. From then on, she'd never forget.

His parents turned to the boy, as if they were waiting for his words.

"That's my guardian angels, Jack & Fred," he said with sleepy eyes and scratchy voice. *"Told you they were real.* They were here all along. You just have to know where to look. And when you look with this, Mommy and Daddy," Henry pointed to his heart, "not with this," he said, pointing to his head, "you'll always find them. *Always.*"

Questions were on the tips of their tongues, but sometimes keeping quiet and listening with your heart answers everything. Sometimes, one's faith is to be tested in mysterious things. That is how the angels come alive and sing.

Jack & Fred flew upward to heaven. They pulled their human clothes off, piece by piece, tossing them as they went, freeing their wings from their suspenders' holsters.

"Thank God, Jack! Stupid turtleneck things…with… Ha-ha! Jack? We can do it, Jack! We really can do it! They saw us! They actually saw us. We can really appear to people now, and they saw us!"

Jack laughed to himself. For a moment, he thought he was almost dreaming. He couldn't believe they were here. The little one looked over.

"Jack? Are you alright?"

"Fred. Fred we did it. Did you hear me? *WEEEEEEEE DIIIIIIIIIDDDDD ITTTTTTTTT! YAHOOOOOOOOOOOOOOOOOOO!!!!!*"

Jack dove at the little one. Both were yelling for joy, hugging the ever-living stuffing out of each other.

"We did it, Jack! We did it! *Wahhhhhoooooooooooo!*"

They flew in spirals and corkscrews and figure-eights, dancing, singing, and screaming like crazy. The sunshine was just pouring down.

"Oh, oh my God!" Jack gasped, out of breath. "Hey! Hey c'mere, Fred! Slip me some wing, ol' buddy! We did it. We really did."

"This is what it feels like?" the little one asked.

"Yes!" Jack smacked his hands together. "This is what it feels like!"

"Oh my. I think it almost feels better 'cause—"

"We waited so long?"

"Yeah, Jack. Yeah, I guess. Wow. It feels like the weight of the world is gone. I'm just happy…that's it!"

"And you know what? We have a whole lifetime to be happy. All the tomorrows, and tomorrow's tomorrows. We have all the time in the world.

And after all that, we don't just have someone to watch over. Our boy believes in us! That's something…that's *something wonderful*. And you little one, were right, from the very beginning." Jack smiled. So did Fred.

They were in absolute bliss. Every time they closed their eyes, they saw exactly what their boy was doing. Henry was resting. And they were all happy.

The little one stopped, with his hands on his hips.

"Oh…and, nice job there, man of a thousand disguises. You almost had us pegged for sure," Fred admonished.

"I flaked."

"You flaked?"

"Yeah."

"Oh, well," Fred shrugged and they flew on together. "Wait'll we tell the guys."

For a moment, Fred thought of something.

"Jack?"

"Yeah, kid?"

"I got me a thinkin'. If we can appear as human beings now, and people *can* see us—all *sorts* of people—maybe…"

Jack smiled.

Fred raised an eyebrow.

"Well?" the little one asked.

"I—" Jack started.

"Don't say no."

"I wasn't going to say no."

Jack's smile stretched from ear to ear. He shook his head.

"Okay, Jack?" Fred smiled back.

"Okay, Fred," Jack replied, flying on.

"But when?"

"(Sigh) Brother," Jack mumbled, giving the little one up eyes, and started flying away.

Fred raced after him.

"C'mon, Jack. Jack? Jack! Jack, when can we appear again? Huh? When can we do it?"

Jack threw his hands up over his shoulders. Fred tried to catch up. The orchestra struck up.
"Hey. Is that you, Jack?"
"No, that's Old Blue Eyes, Fred."
"Nice touch."
"Weather wise, it's such a lovvvely day…"
And the angels sang along.
"Come fly with me. Let's fly, let's fly…Pack up, let's fly away!"
"Hey Jack."
"Yeah Fred, now what?"
"How come we didn't sing the whole song?"
"Copyrights Fred."
"Oh well. Let's hum! Can't get us for that!"
Jack grumbled. "Stinkin' lawyers!"
"I heard that!" Sidney called from below.

Jack & Fred flew back home, to the house with the yellow awning. This time the trip was easy. They felt strong, for they were believed in and loved. There was nothing else in the world like it.

Just Imagine, the Final Chapter

Over time, Henry got older. He grew up to be a big, strong young man. His clothes didn't seem to fit anymore. His hair grew wild. The fish tank in the dining room was replaced by a desk with a computer on it, and the person he saw in the mirror every day looked quite different from what he was used to. The time had come for him to choose a college, and he decided upon a certain familiar campus. For some reason, that choice just popped out at him, like it was all right or something. Perhaps it was because Wingdings was on the campus, too. Everything was going great, but he always felt like something in his life was missing...

It almost came as no surprise to him when he learned his teacher was out with the flu; his class was cancelled that afternoon. He was going to his car, pushing open the heavy school door with that feeling he was escaping from prison, just as he did as a kid, always ready to leave and have fun outside of the academic walls of that place. And there she was...doing the exact same thing. Kristie. *His Kristie.*

They had lost touch for so many years, but there she was again. Just as before. Neither had to say it, they just knew. They ran into each other's arms and he twirled her madly. She kissed his lips, and held him in her arms.

"I'm not letting you go again," she whispered.

He held her precious face in his hands. "Told you I'd write us a happy ending next time."

A few weeks later, after a meal of pork chops with cinnamon apples and a dessert of brownies and vanilla ice cream, Henry's parents would tell the boy a story of when he was young, and how he would name everything "Jack" or "Fred." And they would ask him if he remembered the one morning, when he woke from that long night, to find the stuffed bear and the dog left in his room as presents. And he did. And it was only later on that they told him about the two visitors he had when he was fast asleep. I guess they could finally disguise themselves as human beings after all; they never thought they could, but I guess they can do it.

After talking so much about that one special night in the past, the boy would lay down to dream. He dreamt of *that* special night from long ago, a night when he played with a dolphin and went surfing down a mountain of water in that hazy place whose landscape he could not remember. It was a night when he played with his guardian angels, shortly before he saw them in person for the last time.

And one April morning, in his sophomore year at college, those very thoughts gave him an idea for a story, and he started jotting them down in the back of a notebook that he used to sketch pretend movie posters for the films he hoped to someday write. Later that night, he began tapping away at the computer keys. As he did so, he would keep remembering his adventure from that night and time long ago with Jack & Fred. When he would think about them, a wide, happy smile would form on the face of this young adult, even though it was a child's smile he was wearing. He remembered his two angels. Fred was the little one: always funny, a little rambunctious, a bit chubby, and he liked ziti and meals of all kinds. And Jack was only a little taller than Fred. Jack always tried to be a responsible leader, but he was just a loving soul who was as much a scoundrel as his partner.

I remember that night as though it was yesterday. Perhaps it was. This is Jack & Fred's story, but it is mine also. I would know it better than anyone, because my name is Henry.

I want you to know that it was my guardian angels, Jack & Fred, who were the inspiration for this story in the first place. They never abandoned me once throughout any trial or tribulation of my life. At one point when I was writing this, I looked at the screen full of words before me and wondered if what I had written was good enough; if it told the world in the clearest, plainest words what my angels were all about.

{ My Guardian Angels Jack & Fred }

I looked at the screen and wondered if my guardian angels would be proud of the story. As I sat there and wondered about the words and the future, I felt a touch on both of my shoulders, as if someone rested His hands on me for a moment. I turned around to see who was there, but there was only the cool night breeze pushing the clothes on the clothesline back and forth outside the dining room window.

I knew it was not the sleepiness I felt, nor the light reflecting off my glasses. I looked past my nightstand, with my hairbrush and my picture of Kristie, toward the bear and the dog on the shelf (with their tags and inscriptions still intact). They wore distinctive-looking expressions with a twinkle in each of their eyes, and I smiled. For I knew who it was. A tear came to my eye and two voices in my ear said, "We love you, Henry."

And I whispered back,
"I love you too, my guardian angels,
Jack & Fred!"

So the angels were at their usual spot on Earth, a wall that separated the house with the yellow awning from everything else, looking up at the passing clouds, thinking about their boy.

"Jack?"
"Yeah, Fred."
"Jack…What're you thinking about?"
"The boy."
"Me too."
"Goodnight, Jack."
"Goodnight, Fred."
"Goodnight, Henry."

THE END

…At least until they come back, anyway.

Jack smiled. "You ready to go home, now that this little adventure is coming to an end?"

Revived and smiling, Fred looked into his friend's eyes.

"An end? Jack I have a feeling this little adventure is just beginning."

Jack turned away, visibly annoyed. "Here we go again."

Printed in the USA
CPSIA information can be obtained
at www.ICGtesting.com
LVHW092140301123
765377LV00018B/91/J